JAMES A. HERRICK

SCIENTIFIC MYTHOLOGIES

How Science and Science Fiction
Forge New Religious Beliefs

11/6/08

IVP Academic

An imprint of InterVarsity Press
Downers Grove, Illinois

InterVarsity Press
P.O. Box 1400, Downers Grove, IL 60515-1426
World Wide Web: www.ivpress.com
E-mail: email@ivpress.com

InterVarsity Press® is the book-publishing division of InterVarsity Christian Fellowship/USA®, a student movement active on campus at hundreds of universities, colleges and schools of nursing in the United States of America, and a member movement of the International Fellowship of Evangelical Students. For information about local and regional activities, write Public Relations Dept., InterVarsity Christian Fellowship/USA, 6400 Schroeder Rd., P.O. Box 7895, Madison, WI 53707-7895, or visit the IVCF website at <www.intervarsity.org>.

Scripture quotations, unless otherwise noted, are from the New Revised Standard Version of the Bible, *copyright 1989 by the Division of Christian Education of the National Council of the Churches of Christ in the USA. Used by permission. All rights reserved.*

Images: Matthias Clamer/Getty Images

ISBN 978-0-8308-2588-2

Printed in the United States of America ∞)

Library of Congress Cataloging-in-Publication Data

Herrick, James A.
  Scientific mythologies: how science and science fiction forge new
religious beliefs / James A. Herrick.
    p. cm.
  Includes bibliographical references and index.
  ISBN 978-0-8308-2588-2 (pbk.: alk. paper)
  1. Religion and science. 2. Science fiction. I. Title.
BL240.3.H47 2007
201'.65—dc22

2007038407

P	19	18	17	16	15	14	13	12	11	10	9	8	7	6	5	4	3	2	1
Y	24	23	22	21	20	19	18	17	16	15	14	13	12	11	10	09	08		

CONTENTS

ACKNOWLEDGMENTS

A number of individuals and institutions have provided important support, information, inspiration and encouragement during the long process of writing this book. Michael MacIntosh and the members of Christ Church PCA in Grand Rapids, Michigan, on more than one occasion allowed me to present and refine my ideas as part of their adult education program. Similar opportunities were provided by Christ Memorial Church and New Life Fellowship in Holland, Michigan; Robert Herrick and Riverpark Bible Church of Fresno, California; Thomas Prichard and the Minnesota Worldview Leadership Project; the graduate student Christian fellowship at Princeton University; and the Veritas Fellowship at Butler University in Indianapolis, Indiana. I am also indebted to Peter Jones for his invitation to present an early version of the book's introduction as part of a public lecture at Westminster Seminary in Escondido, California; and to Logos Bible Software of Bellingham, Washington, for the opportunity to speak on the concept of science fiction's shaping of modern myths as part of the Logos Lecture series.

Thanks also to David Anderson for generously allowing me access to his extensive archive of science fiction films, and to the staff of the Eaton Collection of science fiction works at the University of California, Riverside. Linda Koetje of Hope College provided valuable assistance in preparing the manuscript, for which I am very grateful. I also received crucial research support through the Guy Vander Jagt endowment at Hope College.

Among the many authors who provided guidance through their publications, I am particularly indebted to Professor Mary Midgley for her groundbreaking work on the religious uses of scientific theories, to Steven J. Dick for his histories of the extraterrestrial life debate, and to Walter Sullivan for his early work on the same topic. I also discovered much useful historical information in science fiction reference works by John Clute and James Gunn, as well in David Darling's remarkably comprehensive *Internet Encyclopedia of Science*.

I have appreciated the support of Gary Deddo and Andy Le Peau at InterVarsity Press, both of whom were willing to entertain the unusual idea of a book on modern scientific myths. Finally, I want to thank my wife, Janet, and daughters Laura and Alicia for their patience, prayers and interest, not to mention their willingness to watch an apparently endless stream of old science fiction films. I would like to dedicate this book to my parents, Robert and Deloris Herrick of Madera, California, for their unflagging support.

1

INTRODUCTION

Movies and TV series create universes for us, in which a God
called by that name is nowhere to be found,
yet the ever-present suggestion is that there are
creators in the shape of aliens from other planets who have
created life on Earth, for either benign or evil purposes.

MASSIMO INTROVIGNE

The idea of a universe full of life . . . [is] more than just another
theory or hypothesis; it is rather a kind of worldview.

STEVEN J. DICK

Science is my territory, but science fiction is the
landscape of my dreams.

FREEMAN DYSON

Toward the end of his career in the early 1950s, the world-famous Swiss psychoanalyst Carl Gustav Jung became fascinated by the Unidentified Flying Object (UFO) phenomenon that was sweeping both the United States and Europe following a reported crash landing of a flying saucer near Roswell, New Mexico, in 1947. Though he was among the most respected intellectual figures of his day, Jung read widely on the fringe subject of UFOs in an effort to understand the phenomenon. Jung pored over books with titles such as *Flying Saucers from Outer Space*, *Flying Saucer Conspiracy* and *The Truth About Sau-*

cers. To his credit, Jung was among the first established intellectual leaders to recognize that the saucer craze was not to be lightly dismissed; something of major importance was afoot, or aloft, in Western culture.

Carl Jung was also deeply interested in religion, especially the modern revival of ancient Gnosticism, a revival he personally promoted. At a time when other scholars were rejecting or simply ignoring UFO reports, Jung came to a fascinating conclusion: the UFO phenomenon must be understood as the emergence of a powerful mythology in the post-Christian West. So important did he consider UFO accounts that Jung wrote his last book on this subject, a work published just three years before his death in 1961. In this book, titled simply *Flying Saucers*, Jung writes that "we are now nearing that great change we may expect" as the human race enters a post-Christian spiritual era. The great scholar went on to assert that he was willing to put his "hard-won reputation for truthfulness, trustworthiness, and scientific judgment in jeopardy" in claiming that UFOs were a deeply significant *spiritual* phenomenon.

Jung labeled UFOs "visionary rumors" that marked the dawning of a new age in the Western world. Flying saucers represented to the public nothing less than "new gods" that met "a new psychic need" created by the stress of a scientific age, an age without God. These new deities had invaded not our air space, but a collective cultural imagination "already toying with the idea of space-trips to the moon." Therefore, Americans and Europeans "had no hesitation in assuming that intelligent beings of a higher order had learnt how to counteract gravity . . . and to travel through space with the speed of light."[1] "One thing is certain," he added, UFOs "have become a living myth" with their "extraterrestrial 'heavenly' powers." Jung then drew this striking conclusion about the Western world's spiritual longing as we entered the so-called Space Age: "The present world situation is calculated as never before, to arouse expectations of a redeeming, supernatural event."[2]

Carl Sagan, scientist, author and tireless advocate of efforts to contact extraterrestrials, drew a similar conclusion about the human spiritual quest in the age of space exploration. In 1973 Sagan wrote that "there is today—in a time when old beliefs are withering—a kind of philosophical hunger, a need to know who we are and how we got here. There is an ongoing search, often unconscious, for a cosmic perspective for humanity."[3] Sagan, like Jung, points out the human need for meaning and a sense of direction, usually understood as spiritual needs, and ones thus traditionally addressed by religion. However, it was precisely the timeless religious answers to our deepest questions that Sagan and many in his audience rejected in their search for a new spiritual perspective suitable to a scientific age. Sounding the same theme, author, futurist and inventor Ray Kurzweil has recently written that in the dawning age of explosive technological change, "we need a new religion."[4]

My purpose in this book is to explore the various ways in which the Western world's present spiritual needs are being addressed by a new mythology, an emerging canon of transcendent stories that provides meaning to our lives and that organizes and directs our individual and social decisions. And as we shall see, today's myths often arise from rather unexpected sources. In particular, I will focus attention on the mythmaking work of two powerful engines of cultural influence—speculative science on the one hand, and the works of science fiction on the other. Along the way I will also contrast our modern scientific mythologies with the traditional Christian narrative in the hopes of revealing some striking parallels, but more important, the very real contrasts that indicate the presence of a wholly new mythic framework for the Western mind. Lurking in the background of this discussion will be the question of whether our largely unexamined new mythologies actually represent what their advocates claim for them—that they are a much-needed alternative to more traditional perspectives on God, people and the destiny of the human race, an alternative that will open a spiritual pathway into the increasingly technological future.

LOOKING TO THE SKIES

The popular 1951 movie *The Thing from Another World* closed with one character urgently uttering into a radio microphone words that became a famous warning: "Watch the Skies! Watch the Skies!" Legendary science-fiction editor and author John W. Campbell wrote the film's screenplay. Following the tremendous success of his blockbuster film *Close Encounters of the Third Kind* more than twenty-five years later, director Steven Spielberg told a 1978 *Rolling Stone* interviewer, "The movie will only be successful if, when [people] see it, they come out of the theater looking up at the sky." Perhaps the efforts of Campbell, Spielberg and many others to encourage us to look up at the sky have been far more effective than we might suppose. A few examples point out science fiction's great capacity to shape public opinion but also, and more surprisingly, scientific opinion.

In April of 2007 researchers Travis Taylor and Bob Boan presented a paper titled "An Introduction to Planetary Defense." The essay was described in the press as "a primer on how humanity can defend itself" if space aliens decide to invade. "The probability really is there that aliens exist and are old enough to have technology to enable them to come here," Taylor said. An astronomer and physicist who has worked for both the Defense Department and NASA, he dismisses the late Carl Sagan's suggestion "that any beings advanced enough to master star travel will have evolved beyond war." Taylor commented, "It's a wonderful idea that has no basis in reality." Thus, an alien invasion contingency plan "makes sense." The plan "tells us that if we were attacked by aliens, this is our best defense."[5]

Or we might ponder an outcome of the British census of 2000 that surprised everyone involved in collecting and assessing the data. In response to Question 10, which asked about religious affiliation and allowed respondents to write in unlisted religions, 390,000 people indicated their religion as Jedi. Nor was Great Britain alone in its embrace of what might now be called a new faith. More than 79,000 members of the adult public had the same response in Australia, 58,000 in New Zealand and 20,000 in Canada. Even factoring in an e-mail campaign that undoubtedly increased the numbers, a rather surprising international religious phenomenon was apparently developing around the George Lucas *Star Wars* film series. Indeed, at 390,000 adherents in Britain, the Jedi faith would be, according to the BBC, England's fourth largest religion after Christianity, Islam and Hinduism. Only 270,000 adherents in Britain listed their faith as Judaism, making it now fifth in size after Jedi.[6]

Americans can look closer to home to discover the social influence of vivid narratives about space and its alleged residents. For example, a 2002 Roper Poll commissioned by the Sci-Fi Channel reported that three-quarters of Americans are spiritually and psychologically "prepared for the discovery of extraterrestrial life." A surprising 82 percent of males polled indicated that they believed in extraterrestrial life. And those polled apparently were not expecting just simple microbial life to be discovered on a wandering asteroid. A separate poll questioned Americans about their expectations for the year 3000. Newspapers reported that "the poll found considerable interest in the central theme of most science-fiction movies and TV shows—the possibility

that humanity will meet extraterrestrial intelligence in the next millennium."
In fact, 56 percent of those responding to the survey said they believed that
"space aliens will be discovered," and most people in this group "also believe
the other-worldly creatures will be both superior to humans and friendly."

Hence, more than half of the adult population of the United States believes
that contact with "superior" and "friendly" space aliens is likely in the next
millennium. The poll's director, Michael G. Zey of Montclair State University
in New Jersey, author of the book *Seizing the Future*, had this to say about the
study's discoveries: "I'm not surprised by these findings," to which he was quick
to add, "although I don't believe they are caused by the popularity of science
fiction." If not science fiction's vast cultural influence, then what is the explanation of this widespread belief in benevolent and highly advanced aliens? "People
want to believe that there is superior life in the universe, and that these aliens
will be able to upgrade our own lives. This is a form of wish fulfillment."[7] This
belief in benevolent aliens therefore constitutes an active hope for a "superior"
or transcendent life in the universe; perhaps not God, just something better
than us. But labeling this hope a form of wish fulfillment—Sigmund Freud's
famous term for the origins of religious ideas—does not rule out science fiction as one source of that wish.[8]

The confidence of so many twenty-first-century American adults in extraterrestrial contact and the ensuing benefits approaches an essentially religious
faith in intelligent aliens. Whence this newfound faith? Is it plausible that this
widespread hope would have nothing to do with a centuries-long effort to introduce the public to virtually divine extraterrestrials in a vast array of cultural
artifacts? Among the most popular movies of 1951, *The Day the Earth Stood
Still*—based on the 1940 Harry Bates short story "Farewell to the Master"—
introduced audiences to a benevolent and highly intelligent extraterrestrial
named Klaatu, who brings Earth a message of peace. Scriptwriter Edmund H.
North openly acknowledged that Klaatu—who is killed by soldiers but revived
through advanced technology—was intended satirically as an alien Christ.
(During his sojourn on Earth, Klaatu takes on the suggestive earthly name of
Carpenter.) North acknowledged that he hoped the Christ analogy would be
subliminal. Twenty-six years later another enormously popular science-fiction
movie—Steven Spielberg's award-winning hit *Close Encounters of the Third
Kind* (1977)—would equate extraterrestrials with angels. The idea of divine

aliens has been endlessly reprised in both nonfiction and fiction, from Erich
von Däniken's controversial work of pop archaeology, *Chariots of the Gods*
(1968), to science-fiction films such as *E.T.* (1982) and *Stargate* (1994), to actual UFO religions such as the Raëlians. Perhaps our nearly religious "alien-
longing" has a cultural source after all.

Whether as the result of science fiction, wish fulfillment or both, there is
currently tremendous public interest in life elsewhere in the universe. Moreover, this interest has had important public policy implications. For instance,
the NASA Astrobiology Roadmap was implemented in 2003 to guide research
in "astrobiology," or the science of life on other planets. NASA's justification
of the Roadmap taps into some of our cultural as well as scientific preoccupa-
tions. The document states that "the Roadmap embodies the efforts of more
than 200 scientists and technologists," and that among NASA's stated goals is
to discover information that would answer the question "What is the future of
life on Earth and beyond?"

"The future of life on Earth and beyond"—what can this phrase possibly mean
in this context? Does it imply that the American space program seeks information about the future of life on Earth by exploring life that lies beyond Earth? Or
does this curious question perhaps suggest that if we could only get far enough
into space, we would understand something about our own destiny, our future on
Earth and beyond Earth? Future space missions are cited as the means of acquiring the desired answer to what must be, however it is construed, a transcendent
question. NASA claims that one of the major incentives for the Roadmap project
was "a broad societal interest" in life on other planets. The polls cited above
would bear out this contention, but both they and the Roadmap beg the interesting question of the source of that "broad societal interest." Yet there is to be an
"inspirational" scientific payoff to space exploration as well. The search for such
life, says NASA, "will inspire the next generation of scientists, technologists and
informed citizens."[9]

The NASA statement stops short of asserting that NASA is actively searching for Spielberg-like aliens, but it is certainly reasonable to assume that major
cultural figures such as the scientist Sagan and moviemaker Spielberg have
contributed to the remarkable public interest in the idea that drives the Roadmap project. Indeed, another highly successful science-fiction moviemaker—
James Cameron of *Alien* and *Terminator 2* fame—sat on the NASA advisory

council for several years, while Spielberg himself has served on the corresponding panel for the prestigious Planetary Society, a group of scientists and other social leaders who promote space exploration.

Over the past several centuries, science fiction and the more speculative productions of scientists themselves have combined to create a virtually religious hope in aliens, space exploration, the future and the "next step" in human evolution. From the many cultural texts devoted to these and similar topics, from the surprising interest of the scientific community in such questions and from the positive public response to speculation on such issues, it seems apparent that we are witnessing nothing less than the emergence of new transcendent narratives—new myths—to answer our deepest questions. We appear to have entered a second pagan era, complete with a new mythology in which minor deities once again descend from the stars, seek intimate involvement in our lives, direct our course into the future, invite us to join them in the skies, and even interbreed with us to create a hybrid species capable of meeting the challenges of tomorrow.

Such observations might be of minor significance were it not for the fact that our mythologies—the narratives by means of which we make sense of our existence—have a way of shaping who we are and what we are becoming. Thus, our present search for new gods may influence a wide range of political, scientific and religious discussions and decisions. It is crucially important, therefore, to attend to the cultural sources that are delivering its new myths to Western culture. If we trivialize mythic tales of alien encounters, space exploration and human evolution as "merely" entertainment, if we dismiss all such stories as inconsequential cultural fluff, then we may find ourselves responding to these powerful narratives in another form—as public policies, social agendas and proselytizing religious movements.

NEW MYTHOLOGIES

Fictional as well as scientific discussions of life beyond Earth have a rather surprising tendency to turn toward discussions of religion. For instance, astronomer and historian Steven Dick, an expert on the extraterrestrial life debate, affirms the possibility of intelligent life on other planets. But he also affirms that aliens may have something to teach us about religion. "It may be," he writes, "that in learning of alien religions, of alien ways of relating to superior beings, the scope of terrestrial religion will be greatly expanded in ways that we cannot foresee."[10] Dick's easy logical leap from the mere possibility of intelligent entities on other planets to their likely religious insights is evidence of a major cultural development—a profound and persistent fascination with life elsewhere in the cosmos, and what "they" might teach us. Indeed, Dick admits as much. "It may even be that, as a search for superior beings, the quest for extraterrestrial intelligence is itself a kind of religion," he writes. If the "religious attitude" is itself a "striving for 'otherness,' for something beyond the individual that offers understanding and love," as Dick suggests it is, then the search for aliens may itself constitute the basis of a new religion, perhaps *the* new religion. Dick is surprisingly candid in this regard. Concerning the famous SETI (Search for Extraterrestrial Intelligence) project to which Carl Sagan lent so much support, Dick writes, "It may be that religion in a universal sense is defined as the never-ending search of each civilization for others more superior than itself. If this is true, then SETI may be science in search of religion."[11]

Other leading twentieth-century thinkers have also forged a link between extraterrestrials and our deepest questions. Consider the following remarkable statement about the possible origins of life on Earth by one of the intellectual leaders of the twentieth century:

> Could life have first started . . . on the planet of some distant star, perhaps 8 to 10 billion years ago? If so, a higher civilization, similar to ours, might have developed from it at about the time that the earth was formed. . . . Would they have had the urge and the technology to spread life through the wastes of space and seed these sterile planets, including our own? For such a job, bacteria are ideal. . . . They can be stored almost indefinitely at very low temperatures, and the chances are they would multiply easily in the "soup" of the primitive ocean.[12]

This suggestion that life on Earth may be the result of an extraterrestrial experiment in evolution is not drawn from a work of fiction. Rather, it is the opinion of the late Sir Francis Crick, codiscoverer along with James Watson of the double-helix structure of the DNA molecule. In the name of a hard-headed rationalist rejection of God, for he was an avowed atheist, Crick adopted the theory known as panspermia—the idea that the seeds of earthly life arrived here from outer space, perhaps by alien design. In other words, Crick believed in alien divinities bringing or sending life to Earth. As Mark Steyn writes in

The Atlantic Monthly: "And thus the Nobel Prize winner [Crick] embraced the theory that space aliens sent rocket ships to seed the earth."[13] Steyn observes that Crick advances a *theology* of human origins: "The man of science who confidently dismissed God . . . appears not to have noticed that he'd merely substituted for his culturally inherited monotheism a weary variant on Greco-Roman-Norse pantheism—the gods in the skies who fertilize the earth and then retreat to the heavens beyond our reach." Crick's scientific rationalism, continues Steyn, "took fifty years to lead him round to embracing a belief in a celestial creator of human life."[14] Eminent scientist that he was, Francis Crick's advocacy of panspermia suggests the subtly eroding distinctions among science, science fiction and spirituality.

A similar blurring of the lines is detected in the early works of the popular physicist Carl Sagan. Sagan argued that "advanced" aliens who were "motivated by benevolence" would help humanity. And why should they do this? Because they recognized that they themselves had once been "helped along" by even more advanced civilizations on other planets, and they knew that "this tradition is worthy of continuance."[15] Indeed, Sagan hoped that the entire galaxy might be united by an interconnected organization of civilizations, resulting in "the cultural homogenization of the galaxy" that would ultimately "unify . . . the cosmos."[16] Later in his career, Sagan was a driving force behind the massive SETI project; this Search for Extraterrestrial Intelligence is a network of radio telescopes waiting for messages from other planets. In Sagan's extraordinarily influential work over three decades, we find another source of the broad public expectation of extraterrestrial contact. Sagan announced themes that would become staples of much science fiction, some popular scientific writing and several religious organizations. He urged that knowledge gained from contact with alien civilizations would mark "the most profound single event in our history," and that information from aliens might be "the agency of our survival" and perhaps even "vital for the continuance of our civilization."[17] Highly advanced species on distant planets might have already achieved the status of "supercivilization gods."[18]

NEW GODS, NEW THEOLOGIES

How is it that in an age of rational dismissal of the Judeo-Christian God, other minor deities should appear on the scene with something of a free pass is-

sued by prominent scientists and other cultural leaders? Certainly the Western world's spiritual poverty has contributed to our cultural desire to "look
to the skies." Even secular authorities have observed this aspect of our alien
fascination. In a recently published book, Professor Susan Clancy, formerly of
Harvard University's psychology department, states that belief in aliens and
alien abduction reflects a growing desire for transcendence and spiritual significance. "Being abducted may be," she writes, "a baptism in a new religion of
this millennium."

Clancy argues that the narratives of popular culture, especially science-
fiction stories, are contributing to the development of a new spiritual outlook.
Specifically, she contends that people believe in aliens "to satisfy religious desires." "We want to believe there's something bigger and better than us out
there. And we want to believe that whatever it is cares about us, or at least is
paying attention to us."[19] Cultural observers from Jung to Clancy have recognized that a new spiritual hope is emerging in the West and, given the vast
power of the mass media for global dissemination of ideas, throughout the
world.

We could dismiss this propagation of spiritual ideas through science fiction and speculative science as an accident of entertainment, an unintended
consequence of telling arresting stories about flying saucers and aliens. However, comments such as the following from one of the most important cultural
leaders of our day suggest a different hypothesis. "I put the Force in the movie
to try to awaken a certain kind of spirituality in young people, more a belief in
God than in any particular religious system. I wanted to make it so that young
people would begin to ask questions about the mystery [of our existence]."
In this now-famous 1999 *Time* magazine interview, George Lucas presents
himself as a contemporary theological persuader employing the medium of
science fiction to "awaken a certain kind of spirituality in young people." And
in this he is not alone, as we have seen. Lucas continues, "I see *Star Wars* as
taking all the issues that religion represents and trying to distill them down
into a more modern and easily accessible construct."[20]

Developing new myths for a new age is not limited to the entertainment
industry. Cultural trendsetters, including scientists and even theologians,
have called the Western world to embrace a new theology to match emerging
insights from space exploration, likely alien contact, the prophecies of science-

fiction authors and revelations from physics and biology. Steven Dick, for instance, argues that the time is ripe for a "cosmotheology," a theology that prepares people to adjust their religious ideas to potential revelations from space exploration and even alien contact.

Dick, whose books are published by Cambridge University Press and who has worked as an astronomer of the United States Naval Observatory and as a historian for NASA, is not a voice from the fringe. He contends that space exploration will force a change in human consciousness itself, necessitating a new religious perspective. In short, old theologies will have to change in the light of what space will teach us. "With due respect for present religious traditions whose history stretches back four millennia," writes Dick, "the natural God of cosmic evolution and the biological universe, not the supernatural God of the ancient Near East, may be the god of the next millennia." A new unifying spiritual framework may transform the human race itself. When we consider "the fractious nature of religions and their accompanying theologies," we can only hope that "*Homo religiosus* also will be transformed" through new theological insights.

Dick believes that extraterrestrial aliens may be another potential component in bringing about the coming religious changes. Though he acknowledges that "extraterrestrial life is by no means proven," he also recognizes that such "is the view accepted by many" scientists. Dick introduces a paradigm he calls "the biological universe" to help propel a new way of thinking about the cosmos. "The central assumptions of the biological universe are that planetary systems are common, that life originates wherever conditions are favorable, and that evolution culminates with intelligence." The potential for communicating with alien life confronts us with "a new world view that theologies ignore at their peril and must eventually accommodate if they are to remain in touch with the real world." Interestingly, Dick contends that the social implications of cosmotheology have already been recognized by the United States government. He cites the NASA Astrobiology Roadmap as acknowledging "broad societal interest in our subject, especially in areas such as the search for extraterrestrial life and the potential to engineer new life forms adapted to live on other worlds."[21]

Dick cites Gallup polls indicating "that the majority of well-educated Americans today subscribe to the biological universe," a cosmos brimming with life, "and a large number even believe the aliens have arrived."[22] Dick acknowledges that among the factors shaping public appreciation of space exploration's implications is the enormously popular cultural phenomenon of science fiction. Indeed, the best science-fiction authors constitute a new class of pioneering theologians whose "imaginations . . . provide ample food for thought in the theological realm." Again, the twin probabilities of intelligent extraterrestrial life and communication with that life combine to create a world view "that *theologies* ignore at their peril."[23] It is a clash of theologies that Dick envisions.

THE FORCE OF SCIENCE FICTION IS WITH US

The extensive public interest in extraterrestrials and their potential connection to our social and spiritual progress provides evidence of the vast cultural impact of science fiction—a genre that only forty years ago was dismissed as shallow adventure stories by writers of marginal ability, composed for the entertainment of adolescent boys, and sold by the word to pulp magazines. Indeed, until relatively recently literary scholars regarded science fiction as unworthy of serious critical attention. Now that picture has changed, and both historians and scholars of popular culture are seeking to take the measure of the science-fiction juggernaut.

Science fiction has emerged as a formidable social force with a worldwide reach and an international audience in the hundreds of millions. Seven of the twenty most profitable movies ever produced fall within the science fiction genre. Indeed, the *New York Times* recently reported, "A genre that 80 years ago was on the margins is now, at least in its cinematic incarnations, at the very center of culture."[24] And if Steven Dick and George Lucas are right, science fiction is producing popular theologies. It is certainly not a new observation that science fiction can influence religious thought. In 1939 Christian apologist C. S. Lewis wrote in answer to a question about his first science-fiction work, *Out of the Silent Planet*, that "any amount of theology can now be smuggled into the reader's mind under cover of a good romance, without their knowing it."[25] Lewis's own concern about the theological implications of science-fiction works by Olaf Stapledon and H. G. Wells was among the factors prompting him to write his famous science-fiction Space Trilogy.

The intermingling of science fiction and theology—understanding the term broadly—is perhaps not as out of keeping with the genre as it might at first glance appear. Science-fiction author and critic Thomas Disch comments that "myths are everywhere in literature, but especially in science fiction," adding that "SF has been trafficking in magic and mythology since first it came into existence."[26] Indeed, Disch finds that among science fiction's "tasks" as a literary genre is "simply the custodial work of keeping the inherited body of myths alive."[27] Like Disch, science-fiction author Robert Sawyer observes that the genre addresses ultimate questions. Indeed, Sawyer calls science fiction—because of its close affiliation with science—"the most effective tool for exploring the deepest of all questions." Among the deep questions left to science and science fiction to address are these: Where did we come from, why are we here, what does it all mean, and, indeed, the biggest of them all, is there a God? Science fiction will "finally and at last, help humanity shuck off the last vestiges of the supernatural" by challenging earlier religious explanations while at the same time answering transcendent questions with a finality reflecting the borrowed authority of science.[28]

I will be arguing that science fiction does more than manage "inherited" myths; it also generates new ones. By its very nature, science fiction bursts the limits of space and time, bestows unimaginable powers on humans, transforms mortals into immortals, sends its heroes hurtling from star to star, and populates the cosmos with virtual gods called extraterrestrials and "advanced" humans. Moreover, science-fiction narratives often follow an essentially religious trajectory, exploring issues such as human origins and destiny, the nature of the divine, the possibility of redemption, and even what follows death. Is it any wonder that Disch can write of "the religious nature of SF fandom," that vast army of readers and viewers who wait breathlessly for each new science-fiction production? He comments offhandedly, "If you think about some of the purposes that religions serve for people, and try to think of how science fiction may serve those purposes for us, there is a rather large number."[29]

While the religious themes in a movie such as *The Matrix* (1999) are right on the surface, Arthur C. Clarke's assessment that he and Stanley Kubric had made a "ten-million-dollar religious movie" when they completed *2001: A Space Odyssey* in 1968 took some observers by surprise.[30] We have already heard director Lucas's comment that he sought to "awaken a certain kind of spirituality in young people" through *Star Wars*. Dick thinks that the popularity of movies such as those mentioned—as well as of *Close Encounters of* the *Third Kind* (1977), *E.T.* (1982), *Alien* (1979), *Independence Day* (1996) and *Contact* (1997), and the broad appeal of television shows such as *Star Trek* and *The X-Files*—"represent a phenomenon that is more than just entertainment." How are they to be best understood, if not as entertainment? Dick calls them "stories of mythic proportion" that "broaden our horizons" and "force us to consider our place in the universe," adding that they "make us realize that terrestrial concepts of God and theology are only a subset of the possible."[31]

Similarly, a Canadian journalist writing in *The Ottawa Citizen* affirms that the enormously popular science-fiction television series *The X-Files* "represents the state of beliefs and spirituality at the millennium." In a report titled "Why *The X-Files* is becoming our New Religion," Christopher Guly, citing media expert Daniel Noel, comments that "the proliferation of movies, TV shows, magazines, books and Internet sites devoted to the supernatural, aliens and apocalyptic themes" amounts to a powerful cultural phenomenon that has "proselytized people into a new way of believing" and is propagating "a different way of gaining religious knowledge."[32]

Surveying the many connections among science fiction, science and religion in recent decades, we are confronted with a bewilderingly vast and complex cultural territory that has not been adequately charted and where old boundary lines fail us. For example, we might take note of science-fiction writers who have transformed standard science-fiction components into religious narratives featuring distant planets, extraterrestrials, mysterious technologies and vast powers. The most prominent example is Scientology founder L. Ron Hubbard, an established science-fiction author of the 1940s and 1950s. In the opening years of the 1950s, Hubbard developed and promoted (with the assistance of science-fiction luminaries A. E. van Vogt and John Campbell) a set of self-help teachings known as Dianetics. A short time later he announced the new religion of Scientology, made famous today by celebrity adherents such as Tom Cruise and John Travolta.

Or we might consider the founders of UFO cults, including Marshall Applewhite of the notorious Heaven's Gate group, who have crafted ideas borrowed from science fiction into religions. Such organizations proliferated in the 1950s following the well-publicized Roswell, New Mexico, UFO "crash landing." In 1976 French journalist Claude Vorilhon reinvented himself as Raël, founding the Raëlian Religion on UFO teachings received during an alleged meeting with space aliens near the site of an extinct volcano in France. Vorilhon has invested heavily in human cloning research in a bid for immortality. Such UFO religions often claim that messages from "space brothers" teach the urgent need for global religious and political unity in order to avert nuclear holocaust or other disasters, a theme in some science-fiction movies and books such as *The Day the Earth Stood Still* (1951).

Then there are the many established scientists who have also written science fiction with spiritual themes and implications. Arthur C. Clarke's novel *Childhood's End*, the short story "The Sentinel" and the screenplay for *2001: A Space Odyssey* all feature advanced aliens that direct human history toward "the next stage." Carl Sagan's novel and movie *Contact* involve similarly "highly evolved" aliens who have moral insights for primitive humanity, as well as secrets to reveal about "the numinous." Controversial British physicist Fred Hoyle explored variations on the superintelligent extraterrestrial and origins of life themes in *The Black Cloud* (1957). Computer scientist Vernor Vinge wrote his ideas about posthumanity in a technological future into his science-fiction novel *Marooned in Realtime*.

THE NEED FOR A NEW FRAME

The literary and cinematic genre of science fiction—now also a major component in the world of video gaming—represents a phenomenon so diffuse and complex as to render risky any generalizations about its cultural purposes or impact. And yet, there is growing evidence that popular works of science fiction—along with the closely related genres of speculative scientific writing and works on "alien" religions—are shaping the worldview of a vast international reading and viewing public. A new perspective that helps us to account for the persuasive influence of science fiction is vital if we hope adequately to assess and respond to this potent cultural juggernaut. In a society inclined to dismiss the possible psychological influence of any experience that can be classed as entertainment, the task of reframing science fiction and related narratives is particularly crucial.

Literary critic Northrop Frye suggests that science fiction exhibits "a strong inherent tendency to myth."[33] Moreover, several of the basic mythic elements of science fiction are surprisingly consistent from one work to another and have begun to form into a more or less coherent worldview that is creating a community of belief. David Samuelson writes of "a genuine communal acceptance" within the science-fiction audience "of some of the basic principles making up the [science-fiction] cosmology, regardless of quibbling over details." Samuelson reports that among the elements constituting science-fiction cosmology, "travel to the stars, the existence of intelligent life elsewhere in the universe, and the desire of man to increase his knowledge and power are rather firm articles of faith." Such notions may be embraced "on the level of what Tolkien calls 'literary belief,' the acceptance of things as real within the fictional or Secondary World."[34] This particular "secondary world," I will argue, is the world that science fiction shares with much speculative scientific writing as well as with works on alien religions. Samuelson concludes that the "chief value" of science fiction for its audience "is *inspirational*," thus hinting at a religious or spiritual function in the genre.[35] Moreover, he finds in science fiction a potentially beneficial educational role. "By mapping out *possible* futures," the science-fiction writer "can do a great service to the community" by encouraging in readers "flexibility of mind, readiness to accept and even welcome changes—in one word *adaptability*."[36]

But training an audience toward any set of values may have a rhetorical or persuasive goal as well. Through its various elements—possible futures, alien life-forms, miraculous technologies, planetary travel and human evolution—science fiction prepares its readers' imaginations to entertain a worldview that they might not ordinarily have considered reasonable or even plausible. Noted science-fiction author Clarke explains that "science fiction encourages the cosmic viewpoint" and that the genre thus bothers those intellectually constricted readers who do not accept "the fact [sic] that man may not be the highest form of life in the universe."[37] In Clarke's estimation, then, science fiction "encourages," that is, trains, prepares or persuades—and its encouragements tend toward propagating something called "the cosmic viewpoint."

The striking comments of Samuelson, Clarke, Disch, Dick, Lucas, Sawyer and many others involved with the art form lead me to believe that science fiction is not principally an entertainment, as so many audiences take it to be. Rather, it is a mythmaking enterprise, a narrative project animated by cosmological and spiritual themes, an inherently persuasive literary and cinematic genre seeking to "prepare" its audiences. Indeed, science fiction's great cultural impact has often been due precisely to the fact that it is viewed as entertainment and thus not as myth. Science-fiction historian Robert Philmus writes of the genre's tendency to "transmute an abstract idea into a concrete myth."[38] So powerful is its persuasive appeal—as practitioners from Wells and Lewis to Heinlein and Lucas have fully recognized—that Philmus approaches science fiction as a narrative "strategy" and as highly "rhetorical" in its relationship to its audiences.[39] Indeed, science fiction and the speculative scientific writing to which it is so closely allied and the alien religious works that it has spawned have emerged as our most important popular sources of modern mythologies. Because of their similarity of transcendent theme and persuasive purpose, and because of the central validating role played by some conception of science in each, I will group them together under the heading "scientific mythologies."

Mythologies are transcendent stories that address ultimate questions and that typically also involve the interaction of deities with humanity. But our modern scientific mythologies are also crafted to be persuasive. When scientific mythologies address the origin and destiny of the human race, the human predicament and its resolution, methods of redemption or spiritual perfection, the problem of evil and the consummation of all things, they also seek to persuade their audiences to understand the universe in new ways. I will be arguing that our scientific mythologies are a powerful cultural engine for inventing and for propagating a worldview that stands in marked contrast to, and seeks to move its audiences away from, traditional monotheistic religious perspectives, in particular the Judeo-Christian tradition. When we consider the vast worldwide public that science fiction and related genres today regularly reach, as well as their enormous capacity for cultural and psychological shaping, this understanding of science fiction as mythic persuasion becomes enormously consequential. Before considering the historical development of specific components of our modern scientific mythologies, it will be helpful to look more carefully at the nature and cultural role of myths.

2

New Myths for a New Age

Professor Alexander, for example, in *Space, Time, and Deity,* suggests that
the end towards which "the whole creation groaneth and travaileth"
is the emergence of a new kind of being which will bear
the same relation to mind as do mind to life and life to matter. It is the
urge towards this which finds its expression in the higher forms of
religion. Without necessarily accepting such a view, one can
express some of its implications in a myth.

J. B. S. HALDANE, *ON BEING THE RIGHT SIZE*

Weichart was frank in his opinion.
"The whole idea is quite ridiculous," he said.
Marlowe shook his head. "This comes of reading science fiction."

FRED HOYLE, *THE BLACK CLOUD*

The universe is made of stories, not atoms.

MURIEL RUKEYSER

Though science fiction and speculative science have been important forces in
Western culture for centuries, their mythic impact has been felt most powerfully in the past one hundred years or so. Why should recent generations be
so interested in the new myths science and science fiction have to offer? Any
adequate answer to this question must take into account modern loss of enliv-
ening myths as a consequence of the rise of scientific materialism and biblical

criticism. Huston Smith, for instance, has observed, "The East and the West are going through a single common crisis whose cause is the spiritual condition of the modern world." Culturally, we are experiencing "the loss of religious certainties and of transcendence with its larger horizons." Smith identifies the ascendancy of a scientific worldview as the cultural point at which "meaning began to ebb and the stature of humanity to diminish."[1] Similarly, James Hollis writes that "the old authorities have lost their power and the maps are missing."[2] According to Lawrence Jaffe, "We are living in an era of unparalleled impoverishment and depreciation of the human soul. The collapse of our religious forms has been followed by a general demoralization of the dominant (Western) culture. No myths remain to sustain us."[3]

CREATING NEW MYTHS TO REPLACE OLD CREEDS

Stephen Rauch asserts that science-fiction graphic novelist Neil Gaiman creates new myths in his popular Sandman series. Rauch writes that "many of the old religious creeds now seem outdated, the products of another age, and it may seem that nothing has emerged to take their place." Moreover, he contends that "life without faith, without meaning, loses its essential vitality." Thus, new myths are a virtual necessity, perhaps especially for a rising generation.[4] Rauch quotes Smith to the effect that "the finitude of mundane existence cannot satisfy the human heart completely. Built into the human makeup is a longing for a 'more' that the world of everyday existence cannot requite."[5]

Rauch wonders how to make myth "relevant today," given religion scholar Joseph Campbell's observation that "the old forms do not work anymore." "If this is true," Rauch concludes, "then what is needed is a modern myth."[6] Campbell's own oft-cited definition of myth guides Rauch's analysis, as well as that of many other writers on similar subjects: "It would not be too much to say that myth is the secret opening through which the inexhaustible energies of the cosmos pour into human cultural manifestation."[7] It is well known that Campbell's vision of mythology inspired no less a crafter of science fiction than George Lucas, a topic to be explored in later chapters.

As the heaven of theology faded from view and the distant planets of science came into focus, new myths arose from exciting space-adventure stories exploiting public curiosity about the future, Martian canals and alien lifeforms. Talented writers exploring this genre—so new that it did not yet have a name—included George Edward Bulwer-Lytton (1803-1873), Jules Verne (1828-1905) and a little later, the young H. G. Wells (1866-1946). In the twentieth century, Wells would be followed by the likes of Edgar Rice Burroughs (1875-1950), David Lindsay (1876-1945) and Olaf Stapledon (1886-1950).

It often appeared that these authors had more in mind than simply writing captivating stories or even achieving commercial success. Robert Scholes reports that Stapledon, though certainly not the first to do so, was among the most talented writers to discover in science fiction the possibility for creating a new mythology. The purpose of his mythmaking—something Stapledon quite readily acknowledged—was to propagate in the public a new moral outlook. The great task of what Stapledon termed "the romance of the future" was "to attempt to see the human race in its cosmic setting, and to mould our hearts to entertain new values." Stapledon's interest in preparing his readers for "new values" drew him inexorably toward science fiction as modern myth. "Our aim is not merely to create aesthetically admirable fiction. We must achieve neither mere history, nor mere fiction, but myth," he wrote.[8] In a *Saturday Review* interview, influential science-fiction editor John Campbell argued that the genre's principal social role was as "prophecy"—by which he did not mean simply foretelling the future, but also preparing its audiences to embrace a particular vision of the future. The man who shaped the careers of such science-fiction greats as Asimov, Heinlein, van Vogt and Doc (E. E.) Smith assigned to science fiction an essentially moral or spiritual role.[9]

Philosopher of science Mary Midgley has written of the cultural power of the stories we hear repeatedly: "Involvement in the drama enslaves one to the myth."[10] Certainly we have been involved in the vast drama of science and science fiction; we have thus run the risk of enslavement to the myths both are generating as they have sought to serve as stand-ins for traditional religion. No corporate human action is undertaken without reference to some guiding story, either personal or societal. Myths are the carriers of our guiding values, the expression of our moral precepts, and the means by which imagination is shaped. Ideas and values move into the public mind and down the generations by the vehicle of narrative. A myth is a narrative engaging with timeless themes and seeking to define humanity's place in the larger scheme of things.

Today no type of story is more powerfully persuasive, more loaded with moral force, more intentionally mythic in character than are the stories of science fiction. Moreover, these stories often are reprised in nonfiction as the musings of a genre I will refer to as speculative science. For example, the melding of human and machine intelligence is a common theme of science fiction; it contributes to a rising myth concerning "improving" the human race. But inventor and author Ray Kurzweil in his best-selling nonfiction work *The Singularity Is Near*, refers to "the impending merger of our biological thinking with the nonbiological intelligence we are creating" as "the story I wish to tell in this book." Moreover, Kurzweil recognizes that "our ability to create models of reality in our mind" is what will allow us to grasp the "implications" of such a blending of biology and technology.[11] He clearly recognizes the power of story, not just to "create models of reality in our minds," but also to guide action as these models suggest the "implications" of new technologies. Kurzweil even cites Muriel Rukeyser to the effect that "the universe is made of stories, not atoms." This eminent investigator apparently understands the fundamental fact that science and technology do not speak for themselves; our storytellers speak for them. Nevertheless, Kurzweil writes that his book "*is* the story of the destiny of human-machine civilization," apparently not appreciating the fact that any story he tells will not so much *relate* as *shape* that destiny.[12] This inventor ought to perceive that stories also are inventions.

Mythology was poised to emerge as a topic of broad public attention when journalist and ordained Baptist minister Bill Moyers sat down to interview scholar and teacher Joseph Campbell at George Lucas's Skywalker Ranch during the summers of 1986 and 1987, shortly before the scholar's death. Lucas had often acknowledged his debt to Campbell's work on myth in creating the *Star Wars* films, a personal connection between the academy and Hollywood celebrated in a late 1990s Smithsonian Institution National Air and Space Museum exhibit titled "Star Wars: The Magic of Myth." The six-part PBS series *Joseph Campbell and The Power of Myth* aired in 1988 and was among the most popular series ever broadcast on public television. Moyers knew that the public's curiosity about myth was intense when an earlier televised interview with Campbell, author of *The Hero with a Thousand Faces*, resulted in fourteen thousand requests from viewers for transcripts. Why this explosive interest in mythology?

Mythology scholar Richard Cavendish writes that "interest in mythology has grown steadily throughout the last hundred years, powered by the realization that myths are not childish stories or mere pre-scientific explanations of the world, but serious insights into reality." Cavendish comments that myths offer a glimpse of what we value: "The things which people regard as important . . . find a place in their mythology." But myths also impose a system of valuation on our thinking. Cavendish is certainly correct in affirming that myths are "part of the fabric of human life, expressing beliefs, molding behavior and justifying institutions, customs and values." He concludes: "It is impossible to understand human beings without an understanding of their myths."[13] This is as true of contemporary cultures as it was of ancient ones with whom we are likely to associate the idea of mythology. We have our myths, though we call them by different names.

We live in a time when many traditional myths have been discarded. And as Cavendish perceives, "When old myths are lost, new ones are needed."[14] Myths shape perceptions of reality, and "people naturally interpret what happens to them in the light of their prevailing attitude to reality, which includes their mythology."[15] He suggests that renewed interest in mythology "has drawn strength from the feeling that scientific and technological man has lost his way and that a path to truth lies through the territory of myth."[16] This is almost certainly the case; but it is also clear that our path to *myth* lies through our current territory of *truth*: science and technology. Where are today's new myths coming from?

During the twentieth century the literary and cinematic genres of science fiction and speculative science spun out new mythologies at a remarkable rate. In the 1930s supermen with Anglo-Saxon surnames like Rogers, Gordon and Carter blasted their way from planet to planet, defeating evil geniuses, solving galactic problems, and saving beautiful princesses, employing intelligence, bravery and, when necessary, ray guns. More recently epic battles for Truth and Justice (and to save beautiful princesses) have been fought in Space by larger-than-life heroes named Kirk, Solo and Skywalker. Powerful Forces such as cosmic rays, dilithium crystals and The Force have been harnessed both for good and for ill. Astronomers have occasionally assisted the credibility of these mythic narratives by (erroneously) reporting atomic explosions on Mars, interplanetary radio messages and visible engineering feats on distant planets. For well over a century, famous scientists with names like Tesla, Flammarion, Lowell, Huxley, Hoyle, Sagan, Crick, Dyson and Hawking have captured the public imagination and provided a hyperspace boost for science fiction with their own speculative suggestions about space colonization, superintelligent extraterrestrials, life-giving organisms wafting through Space, synthetic spheres built around stars, and newfangled human beings produced in scientifically equipped rooms rather than old-fashioned wombs.

Many of the scientific mythologies often have been crafted principally for young people, those most likely to be searching for narratives to make sense of life. Clearly the new market force of youth culture aided proliferation of the new myths; mythology in the form of science fiction was suddenly profitable. In the 1940s Robert Heinlein switched from writing adult science fiction to writing what was then called juvenile science fiction. Science-fiction author and historian James Gunn reports that these books sold in much larger numbers than the adult books had and "brought him more income each year on each juvenile book than the total income from any of his adult science fiction novels."[17] Yet the appeal of these stories was not contained within a limited demographic.

In 1941, NBC radio introduced the first *adult* science-fiction radio series, *Latitude Zero.* An increasing number of science-fiction radio programs—including *Suspense, Destination X, X Minus One, Doc Savage* and *2000 Plus*—drew ever larger audiences of young people as well as adults from the early 1940s through the late 1950s.[18] Moreover, well-written radio plays such as *Donovan's Brain* (1944) and Ray Bradbury's *Mars Is Heaven* (1955) brought the mythic themes of science fiction to an enormous listening audience. In the narrative of *Donovan's Brain,* by the prolific German science-fiction and horror writer Curt Siodmak (1902-2000), a great scientist's brain is retrieved from his dying body and placed in a vat. The brain, however, has ideas of its own, and takes over the body of a human experimenter. Science-fiction radio programs dealt extensively with universal questions such as what it means to be human, the clash between science and religion, and the great discoveries just over the horizon in "the Future." Dramatic sound effects and exciting music enhanced the vocal acting of stars such as Orson Welles.

Young science fiction readers and listeners grew up, and in a number of prominent cases they carried ideas from the potent genre into important positions of leadership. A few examples may serve to illustrate the point. The Mars adventure stories of Edgar Rice Burroughs fueled the imagination of the young

Carl Sagan. In a remarkable turn of events, physicist Sagan's own science-fiction story *Contact* was an inspiration for astronomer Maggie Turnbull, a NASA astrobiology researcher. Filmmaker Lucas, one of the most influential artists alive today, read extensively in the science-fiction genre as a teenager. Another teenager, Wernher von Braun—later the inventor of the V-1 and V-2 rockets and architect of the American space program—read Jules Verne and assisted the rocket scientist Hermann Oberth with technical aspects of Fritz Lang's 1929 film *The Woman in the Moon.* But the greatest influence on his ideas about space travel was German science-fiction author Kurd Lasswitz. Physicist Dyson's thinking was guided by ideas discovered in a copy of Olaf Stapledon's *Star Maker* found in a railway station.

As the twentieth century progressed, mass media such as television, the movies, popular magazines, mass-marketed books and video games added even greater reach and force to mythic science-fiction stories and themes, in the process often blurring the lines differentiating science, science fiction and first-person narrative. The 1950s and 1960s witnessed a plethora of magazine, television and movie accounts of flying saucer sightings, UFO abductions, extraterrestrial visitations and the feasibility of spaceflight. Famed animator and media entrepreneur Walt Disney played a crucial role in promoting the idea of spaceflight as human destiny in the pubic mind through a series of television programs in the 1950s featuring von Braun himself.

The stage was being set for Hollywood to take the lead role as mythmaker to the Western world. A landmark event was the lavish 1950 movie production *Destination Moon,* an adaptation of rising science-fiction author Robert Heinlein's own novel *Rocket Ship Galileo* (1947). James Gunn writes, "Heinlein helped create a Hollywood market for serious science fiction and an atmosphere in which science fiction could be considered as serious fare for motion pictures."[19] But more than a market was being created; arguments were being crafted and myths fashioned. *Destination Moon,* like other 1950s science-fiction movies—including *Rocketship XM* (1950), *When Worlds Collide* (1951), *Conquest of Space* (1955) and Lang's much-earlier *Woman in the Moon*—were thinly disguised arguments for the necessity of space exploration and colonization. Their appeal was enhanced by the presence of heroic figures battling to "conquer the universe." The case for American involvement in space was dramatically underlined by the successful Russian launch of the first satellite

Sputnik in October 1957. Stories about space and the future, often depicted in film or glossy magazines, influenced public interpretation of stunning new knowledge about the stars and planets. With vastly more scientific information available to the public, the need for transcendent narratives and their guiding principles of information management and valuation grew ever more urgent.

The need for new myths was still more acute because religious faith, the traditional source of transcendent narratives, was under attack by scholars and even religious leaders. In this regard the situation in the Western world is unchanged, leading Midgley to declare that "in our age, when that jumble [of facts] is getting more and more confusing, the need for such principles of organization is not going away. It is increasing."[20] We are a culture awash in new knowledge and thus a culture hungry for new myths to manage the deluge. Stories do sort, order and evaluate as they entertain; yet audiences often only notice that entertainment is taking place.

Whence these new myths in a society prone to dispensing with the traditional stories of religion? In the early 1980s William Sims Bainbridge, a sociologist and member of the National Science Foundation, speculated that a new world religion he termed the Church of God Galactic would emerge in the near future. Bainbridge suggested that the "most likely origins" of this new faith "are in science fiction."[21] Though the Church of God Galactic is not yet a major social force, one thing seems clear: the myths we encounter today come more often from books, movies, graphic novels, television, video games and websites than they do from community traditions, religious documents and revered teachers. Consequently our modern myths may be barely recognizable as such; they develop out of the powerful systems of entertainment and science with which we have been slow to associate spirituality and transcendence. For example, though evolution is a widely debated scientific concept with clear public policy implications, few people would identify it as also a major cultural myth or an important religious notion. But in the mid-1980s philosopher of science Midgley correctly observed that "a surprising number of the elements which used to belong to traditional religion have regrouped themselves under the heading of science, mainly around the concept of evolution."[22] The same can be said for much of the modern science of cosmology, a great deal of popular writing about physics, as well as of much research in medicine. Science, the great edifice of rationalism and empiricism, is now among our principal myth-generating engines.

As the Western world has turned away from traditional religion, science fiction and speculative science have been quick to fill the resulting spiritual vacuum with ideas bearing little resemblance to those that were jettisoned. Orthodox theologian Seraphim Rose comments that in science fiction, "religion, in the traditional sense, is absent, or else present in a very incidental or artificial way." This is in part because "the literary form itself is obviously a product of the 'post-Christian' age." Moreover, the cosmos of science-fiction narratives is one in which God, "if mentioned at all, is a vague and impersonal power, not a personal being." According to Rose, "The increasing fascination" of the contemporary world with science fiction "is a direct reflection of the loss of traditional religious values."[23] This is because the transcendent narratives that organize and interpret experience are not an option, but a necessity. Although we may choose our myths for understanding our strange new quantum world, Midgley reminds us that "we do not have a choice of understanding it without using any myths or visions at all."[24] Thus, it is crucially important to consider the sources as well as the content of our modern myths, especially as they are being propagated by means of the West's incomparably powerful, hugely persuasive and globally potent mass media.

THE CROSSOVER PHENOMENON: BLURRING THE MYTHIC PICTURE

The myths shaping the public imagination today often are derived from a bewildering assortment of media sources blending well-substantiated facts with freewheeling speculation, scientific research with straight fiction, and objective observation with subjective worldview peddling. Popular books presenting accessible treatments of scientific findings offer, in addition, speculation about the future, arguments for interstellar space exploration, guesses about extraterrestrial life and opinions about the nature of the soul. Throughout the late nineteenth and early twentieth centuries, popular scientific writing became increasingly prone toward transcendent pronouncements, that is, toward mythmaking. Today a book that moves from a popular discussion of quantum physics to religious-sounding statements about the "soul of the cosmos" is not considered to have crossed any literary boundaries. The same is true of works on religion or spirituality that move back and forth between theological claims and the latest scientific speculations.

From the late nineteenth and through the twentieth century, scientists from Alfred Russell Wallace and Nicola Tesla to Fred Hoyle and Carl Sagan could be found advancing vast mythic narratives to accompany—or occasionally to contradict—powerful new scientific theories ranging from evolution to the Big Bang. Such narratives often involved "advanced" alien civilizations, "highly evolved" humans, fascinating technological solutions to perennial human problems, and even a conscious cosmos. Where did science end and fiction begin? Blurring the picture further was another remarkable crossover effect that brought the heroes of science-fiction narratives into the realm of popularized science. Thus, for example, the actor Patrick Stewart—*Star Trek: The Next Generation*'s (aired 1987-1994) Captain Jean-Luc Picard—was picked to narrate a 1994 educational video titled *From Here to Infinity: The Ultimate Voyage.*[25] The fact that Stewart's experience as an actor in a science-fiction series was deemed relevant to his credibility on matters of space is interesting in itself. But a strikingly incongruous aspect of the video makes Stewart's selection even more curious. *From Here to Infinity*, in addition to its Astronomy 101 discussion of comets, stars, planets and galaxies, includes a commendatory description of the SETI project, the Search for Extraterrestrial Intelligence. Stewart asks, "Will we discover that there are other intelligent beings in the universe, that we are not alone?" Stewart suggests that our failure to discover extraterrestrial intelligences would condemn us to cosmic loneliness; hence, science should be pressed into the service of answering the extraterrestrial question. All this points to scientific findings *and* powerful scientific mythologies as the animating presence in this documentary.

From Here to Infinity incorporates a mythic framework to assist its audience in interpreting scientific facts. Why do we want to understand space and its various components? In part because we want to know whether we are alone in the cosmos. Reversing the crossover equation, world-famous physicist Stephen Hawking appeared briefly in a 1993 episode of *Star Trek: The Next Generation* to explain some scientific principles. (For that matter, so did Sir Isaac Newton.)

No less intriguing in this regard is the famous opening installment of Carl Sagan's widely viewed 1980 television series *Cosmos*, which features Sagan seated at what can only be described as the control panel of a spaceship as he explores the universe while making the case for an intensified search for extraterrestrial life. In the odd opening installment of *Cosmos,* science and science fiction are freely mixed in a mythic collage that has scientist Sagan sailing into the limitless realm of space in his private starship as he searches the cosmos for signs of intelligent life. Are we watching Carl Sagan or Captain James T. Kirk, *Star Trek* or a PBS documentary?

Another fascinating example of the mythic crossing of science and science fiction occurs in a documentary by famed moviemaker and deep-sea explorer James Cameron, director of *Aliens, Terminator 2* and *The Abyss,* and until recently a member of the National Aeronautics and Space Administration (NASA) Advisory Council. In Cameron's 2005 Disney studios production *Aliens of the Deep,* a documentary about life in the deep oceans, Cameron openly advocates for a probe to be sent to the oceans presumed to lie under the thick ice of Jupiter's moon Europa. What organization would send such a probe if not NASA? Moreover, *Aliens of the Deep* subtly shifts from documentary to science fiction in its closing scenes, which feature an undersea city complete with intelligent residents. This deep-sea city bears a striking resemblance to one seen in the closing minutes of Cameron's own earlier science-fiction production *The Abyss* (1989). Cameron's trajectory from science-fiction filmmaker to advocate for space exploration projects and advisor to NASA seems powered less by science than by his association with a forceful mythology: that Space holds answers to our deepest questions.

For centuries, Christianity has provided the Western world with a coherent narrative that lent meaning, not just to religious and community life, but also to pursuits such as education, business and science. At this point in time, for more than three centuries we have been in the process of slowly dismantling and discarding traditional religious narratives that had provided purpose and dignity to individual and corporate human existence. In their place we have constructed a new set of myths transforming science into a spiritual project serving a vision of the future, suggesting that questionable benefits will arise from our involvement with unseen intelligences from other planets or dimensions or times, and even rendering the life of the individual person an inconsequential step along the way to something better.

A number of observers have recognized this trend toward myth in the twentieth-century's media products. For instance, the widely read science-fiction author Philip José Farmer (b. 1918) enjoyed a long career, during which he wrote an enormous number of books, many on essentially spiritual themes. Peter Nicholls writes of Farmer: "All his work is permeated with mythology."[26] Farmer—like other influential creators of science fiction, with George Lucas as the prime example—was greatly influenced by the famous popularizer of myth Joseph Campbell. "It is the idea of the Hero that fascinates Farmer," writes Nicholls, "and he has clearly used as one of his source books . . . Joseph Campbell's popular study in mythology, psychology, and anthropology: *The Hero with a Thousand Faces* (1949)."[27]

The mythic potential in science fiction was recognized at least as early as Mary Shelley's *Frankenstein* (1818). Shelley's "monster" is certainly more than that, despite the impression left by later cinematic interpretations: he is a new kind of human being in a new cosmos devoid of God. Poe, Verne, Wells and others continued the tradition of creating mythic tales in the genre, producing great social effect. But the reach and impact of science fiction increased dramatically as talented and well-funded filmmakers discovered the genre, often translating classic written texts for the screen. It was a formula for unprecedented commercial as well as cultural success. Dickens and Twain never enjoyed audiences rivaling those of Lucas and Spielberg. Moreover, blockbuster science-fiction movies reached audiences in every corner of the world, developing an international community of belief around their principal themes of interplanetary travel, intelligent extraterrestrials, human evolution and a miracle-filled future. As Steven Dick writes, "The adaptation of some of these [science-fiction] novels to visual media undoubtedly hastened science fiction's acceptance by the masses beyond the wildest dreams of its pioneers in the first half of the century."[28] But as Nicholls reminds us, science fiction "has always been a propaganda medium," a narrative form designed intentionally for persuading audiences to an author's point of view.[29]

Labels can be misleading, and the label *science fiction* tends artificially to bracket a type of imaginative entertainment dealing with the future, other planets, extraterrestrials and remarkable technologies. When viewed as "entertainment," science fiction can easily be dismissed as an unlikely source of religious or spiritual ideas. This is why journalists had such a difficult time interpreting the surprising results of the 2000 British census described in the previous chapter, in which nearly 400,000 Britons (and many more people than that worldwide) identified their religion as Jedi. How could mere entertainment create a community of religious belief? This must have been a hoax. Science fiction is not so much a type of entertainment—though it is clearly that—as a persuasive literary and visual style or strategy that can show up in various places: adventure fiction, religious literature, scientific writing and various entertainment formats, including video and online games. Among its persuasive purposes has been to propagate a kind of faith in a particular vision of the future and the cosmos, a vision that tends to contradict traditional religious ones.

Literary scholar David Samuelson wrote in 1975, immediately before the *Star Wars* phenomenon and the blockbuster science-fiction movies of Steven Spielberg, that what he termed "the science-fictional cosmology" already constituted "a genuine object of belief." He added that, for science fiction's many readers and viewers, there is a "communal acceptance of some of the basic principles making up the cosmology."[30] Samuelson spoke of science fiction as "the expression of a myth," albeit a myth "not yet in wide acceptance among the population at large."[31] Audiences found science fiction "inspirational" because it helped the public "to face the strange realities of the universe in which we live." It met an important social need: the genre promoted "flexibility of mind, readiness to accept and even welcome changes—in one word *adaptability*."[32] And if the cultural landscape coming into view in 1975 required anything, it was adaptability. We needed new myths to match new ideas, new discoveries, new technologies, a new way of life. More than thirty years later, in the wake of *Star Wars, Star Trek, Close Encounters, E.T., The X-Files, The Matrix, Babylon 5, Battlestar Galactica* and *Stargate*—not to mention an endless cascade of science-fiction-themed video games—the myths of science fiction are fully with us, a new worldview, indeed a new religion so familiar that it has spawned its own satirists and heretics. We live with the massive success of science fiction; we seldom recognize the implications of that success.

The following chapters explore the history, contemporary manifestations and possible social implications of several powerful scientific mythologies of our age. These narratives have originated in science fiction and popular scientific works that provide an explanation of everything from the conundrums of our daily lives to the complexities of our universe, from the human soul to human destiny. In the process of tracing out some of the sources of these new myths, I will be arguing that an alliance, persistent though uncoordinated, developed some centuries ago between speculative scientific writing and the hugely popular genre now known as science fiction. This alliance created a potent source of new mythic narratives for the Western world: scientific mythologies.

In some cases I will argue that stories of our origins and destiny, the design of the cosmos, new humans and beings from other planets, otherworldly sources of religious truth and spiritually advanced races—all need to be carefully assessed for their potential to re-create suspect and even dangerous mythic notions from the past. I will also contrast these new mythologies with the traditional narratives of the Judeo-Christian tradition that the West has turned away from as outdated or historically unfounded. Do our new myths represent an improvement over earlier narrative accounts suggesting what it means to be human, the nature of the universe we inhabit and our destiny? What is gained and what is lost as we look to science and science fiction for transcendent truth? These are the larger questions we will have before us as we examine today's scientific mythologies.

3

THE MYTH OF THE
EXTRATERRESTRIAL

Innumerable suns exist; innumerable earths revolve about
these suns in a manner similar to the way
the seven planets revolve around our sun.
Living beings inhabit these worlds.

GIORDANO BRUNO

Why should we, tucked away in some
forgotten corner of the Cosmos, be so fortunate?
To me, it seems far more likely
that the universe is brimming over with life.

CARL SAGAN

Many myths have a dream-like quality.
Strange distorted figures move through them,
monsters and hybrid beings. . . .
Women are impregnated and children born
in physically impossible ways.

RICHARD CAVENDISH

Probably the Overlords have their reasons
for keeping us in the nursery,
and probably they are excellent reasons.

ARTHUR C. CLARKE, *CHILDHOOD'S END*

In *Star Trek VIII: First Contact* (1996), the notion that contact with alien races will inaugurate a new age of peace and prosperity provides the plot's central premise. Captain Jean-Luc Picard and crew are transported back to the late twenty-first century in an effort to ensure that the first human-extraterrestrial contact not be missed. As one member of the crew explains, this contact is crucial because it will inaugurate an era during which warfare, poverty and disease will end. In fact, such a utopia will be achieved within a mere fifty years of "first contact." The crew of the *Enterprise* is willing to risk their lives and their ship to ensure that this first human-extraterrestrial meeting occurs, for it is the moment that ushers in, not only techno-utopia, but also unimagined relationship with numberless extraterrestrial civilizations. But such ideas were not new with *Star Trek* or even with the twentieth century. Precisely the same sentiment had been expressed a century earlier in the groundbreaking German science-fiction work *Auf zwei Planeten* (*On Two Planets*), in which one character tells another, "Admit . . . that for civilized humanity there has never before been a more significant event than that of the encounter with the inhabitants of Mars!"[1]

THE EXTRATERRESTRIAL IN POPULAR CULTURE

Science fiction imagined the intelligent extraterrestrial visitor at least as long ago as the seventeenth century. And science-fiction writers of later centuries have consistently added to alien lore, ensuring public acceptance of extraterrestrials despite any solid evidence of their existence. The twentieth century witnessed a veritable population explosion in the alien domain—both in number and type— and this with no help from the many scientists in hot pursuit of actual extraterrestrials. As Steven J. Dick reports, "If in the first half of the century science had come no closer to learning the truth about aliens, between Burroughs and Bradbury progress had surely been made in defining the possibilities."[2] Science-fiction works such as the entire *Star Trek* franchise from the first television episode in 1967 to the last movie installment, *Star Trek IX: Insurrection,* in 1998, also promoted the mythic idea that human contact with extraterrestrials will mark a stunning turning point in human history. In particular, science fiction often suggested that such contact would lead to remarkable technological advances for humanity and inaugurate a destined human-alien future.

Intelligent beings from outer space have played many roles in popular culture, from the friendly know-it-all alien uncle of television's *My Favorite Martian* (1963-1966) to the decidedly unfriendly Martian marauders of Steven Spielberg's screen adaptation of Wells's *War of the Worlds* (2005). But aliens have also been a regular feature of speculative scientific writing for more than two centuries, as is evident from the seventeenth-century works of astronomer Christian (Christiaan) Huygens (d. 1695) to the popular books and television specials of Carl Sagan (d. 1996). The extraterrestrials of both science fiction and speculative science may promise a New Age of human enlightenment, or seek human partners in order to develop a new species. Some godlike aliens observe the human race's progress from afar (Clarke's *Childhood's End* and "The Sentinel"), or from close range by living among us (television's *The Invaders*, 1967-1968). Other extraterrestrial visitors are angelic, even messianic in nature (e.g., *E.T.*, 1982).

Aliens come from beyond to bless, devour, breed, possess, educate and warn. In the 1942 radio play *Meteor Man*—an installment of the *Lights Out* program broadcast by WENR in Chicago starting in 1934—an extraterrestrial traverses the vastness of space inside a meteor for the sole purpose of satisfying his hunger by consuming humans! More professorial than predatory, the alien visitors featured on the cover of a 1960s *UFO Magazine*, however, are simply here "to tell us something." Rising even higher on the benevolence scale, the messianic alien Klaatu (a.k.a. Carpenter) of the popular film *The Day the Earth Stood Still* (1951) warns Earth's warlike residents against further warfare. (Somewhat incongruously, however, he cautions that Earth will be reduced to a "burned out cinder" by deadly robots if we break the no-war rule!) At the other end of the spiritual spectrum, demonic aliens in the low-budget 1953 science-fiction classic *Invaders from Mars* seek to take control of human minds, an idea reprised in the cult classic *Invasion of the Body Snatchers* (1956). Despite their disparate purposes, these mass-media extraterrestrials have one thing in common—all are portrayed as more "advanced" than the humans they seek either to consume, instruct or possess. Regardless of where one resides in the cosmos, evolution reigns supreme.

THE EXTRATERRESTRIAL OF SCIENCE

Despite our tendency to associate them with such relatively recent artifacts of popular culture, intelligent extraterrestrials are not the invention of twentieth-century or even of nineteenth-century science fiction. Indeed, such beings may not be an invention of fiction at all. The famous English astronomer Edmund Halley (1656-1742) could write in 1705 that "it is now taken for granted that the earth is one of the planets and they are all with reason supposed habitable, though we are not able to define by what sort of animals."[3] Taken for granted? Apparently the idea of planets with atmospheres, water and a temperature conducive to life was widely discussed as early as the sixteenth century, and perhaps much earlier. And Halley is speaking as a scientist rather than as a writer of fiction. He was reporting that habitable planets were taken to be *scientifically* likely by 1705, not just as notions in the fertile imaginations of Swift or Defoe.

Perhaps the reason why Halley could speak of extraterrestrial intelligence as taken for granted in 1705 is that the idea had been discussed in Europe long before that date. Nicholas of Cusa (Kues, Germany, 1401-1464) was a theologian who in *De docta ignorantia* endorsed the idea of other inhabited worlds in the mid-fifteenth century. Remarkably, Nicholas even affirmed that the inhabitants of other planets were superior to Earth's human residents. Following Nicholas's announcement of their presence, intelligent aliens were in the Western mind to stay. The fact that there was no evidence of their existence did not diminish their vitality. Nicholas's philosophy "fertilized the course of thought in Europe."[4] His extraterrestrials exceeded humans in intelligence and other capacities. "Perhaps the inhabitants of other stars are nobler than ourselves," he suggests. Even more remarkable, Nicholas hinted that the denizens of each world "are fitted to their habitation."[5] Thus, it appears that Nicholas anticipated the idea of aliens adapting to their different environments four centuries before Darwin wrote *On the Origin of the Species* (1859).

The most successful proponent of Nicholas's ideas was the controversial Renaissance astronomer and philosopher Giordano Bruno (1548-1600). Bruno argued that the cosmos was infinite and filled with inhabited planets.[6] This infinite universe was *causa sui*, capable of generating life; thus all the worlds of space were populated, not through the creative work of God, but through the generative ability of a living cosmos.

Bruno influenced many European intellectuals, including Francis Godwin (1562-1633), the author of one of the earliest works of science fiction. As a student Godwin likely heard Bruno lecture at Oxford in the 1580s.[7] In God-win's story *The Man in the Moone*, posthumously published in 1638, an early astronaut (bearing a striking resemblance to the diminutive Bruno) is pulled to the moon on a platform harnessed to a number of specially trained geese. Not surprisingly, as Bruno would have predicted, the moon-voyager finds intelligent life there.[8] Godwin's book was an instant success, went through three editions, and was translated into French. Like Bruno's cosmos, the Western imagination was being populated with extraterrestrials. English scientist and cleric John Wilkins (1614-1672), influenced by Bruno as well as by Godwin, wrote his own book on moon travel titled *Discovery of a World in the Moon* (1638). Wilkins was among the founders of modern science and helped to start The British Royal Society.

Bruno's thought had been shaped by Nicholas of Cusa, but Nicholas him-self had apparently borrowed ideas from "the philosophers of Islamic Spain, who themselves formed part of the wave of Islamic thought which during the centuries had swept from Persia and Asia Minor westward to the frontier of France."[9] Hence, early European theories about a populated cosmos, theories that led eventually to the extraterrestrials of science fiction, may not have originated in the West at all, but in medieval Islamic philosophy with its roots in even earlier Zoroastrianism and Persian astrology.

Two centuries later the famous German astronomer and mathematician Johannes Kepler (1570-1630) authored his own science-fiction novel, *Somnium* (1634), or *The Dream*, in which he also endorsed the likelihood of life on other planets. Kepler's narrative mixed astronomy with witchcraft to create a fan-tasy about travel to an inhabited moon. The protagonist is a young Icelander named Duracotus, whose space travels are made possible by his mother's mas-tery of witchcraft. Interestingly, Kepler's own mother was arrested and tried for witchcraft after the book's publication; Kepler took personal responsibility and arranged for her defense.

Thomas Burnet (1635-1715), chaplain to King William III of England, au-thored a book about life on other worlds: *The Sacred Theory of the Earth*. Pub-lished in Latin in 1681 and in English in 1689, the book was popular for well over a century.[10] The leading geological authority of his day, Burnet used his theories of Earth's formation to launch a series of speculations about inhabited planets. Employing an argument still common among those in the extraterrestrial-life debate, Burnet wrote that we must not suppose that "this great Universe was made only for the sake of Man, the meanest of all Intelligent Creatures that we know of." Burnet imagined the possibility of spaceflight to distant planets, and expressed confidence that humans would meet creatures there who would expand our notions about life. He speculated that angelic beings inhabited such distant planets, perhaps living alongside mortals. Other planets are "the habitation of Angels and glorified Spirits, as well as of mortal Men." Important lessons are to be learned from extraterrestrials, according to Burnet. If "we could waft ourselves over to our neighbouring Planets, we should meet with such varieties there . . . as would very much enlarge our thoughts and Souls."[11] In 1698 the Dutch astronomer and physicist Huygens's book *The Celestial Worlds Discover'd* argued that the expanse of the universe makes it likely that other planets are inhabited. Huygens accepted Bruno's contention that all planets were inhabited and went so far as to speculate about the forms such inhabitants might take.

With a growing understanding of astronomy, eighteenth- and nineteenth-century scientists spoke with increasing certainty about life on other planets. The astronomer William Herschel (1738-1822) expressed his belief in residents of the moon. The German astronomer Franz von Gruithuisen (1774-1852) claimed to have located a city on the moon as well as jungles on Venus, a planet whose residents celebrated festivals of fire. Later, astronomer Percival Lowell (1855-1916) confirmed the earlier "discovery" of canals on Mars, the work of intelligent beings. Given the rapidly growing social credibility of scientists in the late nineteenth century, as well as the burgeoning public interest in science fiction, the cultural influence of astronomers and biologists willing to speculate about life on other "worlds" was great. Religious leaders sometime seized on the idea. For example, Mormon prophet and Salt Lake City founder Brigham Young (1801-1877) expressed his belief in "moonmen" as well as residents of the sun. "Do you think it [the moon] is inhabited?" Young asked his readers in a Mormon publication. "I rather think it is. Do you think there is any life there? No question of it; it was not made in vain."[12]

THE ALIEN: AN INTERNATIONAL HOPE

The fruitful union of speculative science and very early science fiction was populating the cosmos. As Karl Guthke of Harvard University has written,

Victorian-era science lent the idea of extraterrestrial life "a previously un-imagined credibility that allow[ed] it to penetrate deep into the conscious-ness of the age."[13] And once it was firmly fixed in that consciousness, the idea was reinforced by numberless portrayals in books and magazines, later in movies and television programs, most recently in video games. The consis-tent assumption of those affirming the extraterrestrials' existence was that they would "represent more advanced stages of evolution than our own."[14] The Myth of the Extraterrestrial was, by the late nineteenth century, fully in place in the Western mind.

By the middle of the twentieth century—the precise cultural moment when UFOs invaded the popular imagination with the Roswell "crash landing" and widely publicized sightings over Washington State—life on Mars and other planets was a preoccupation of a number of American and Soviet scientists, some military officials and a large segment of the general public. In April and May of 1949 the *Saturday Evening Post* ran stories on UFO sightings and the military's response to them. The April 7, 1952, edition of *Life* magazine fea-tured a lengthy investigative story by H. B. Darrach and Robert Ginna: "Have We Visitors from Space?" The magazine left open the possibility that these reports "cannot be explained by present science as natural phenomena—but solely as artificial devices, created and operated by a high intelligence." *Life* reported that the public and the government were deeply concerned about this issue. Walter Sullivan writes that in 1962 "an American scientist suggested that flashes observed on Mars . . . might be atomic bomb explosions." This "far-fetched idea" was not announced in a pulp magazine, but in "so respect-able a journal as *Science*." Around the same time "a Soviet astrophysicist said the moons of Mars may be artificial, launched by an extinct civilization," while another Soviet authority "proposed that Mars may furnish us with 'cattle' of extraordinary usefulness."[15]

We must remind ourselves that these were *scientists*, not just science-fiction authors, who were writing in both popular and professional venues, with the apparent intent of persuading both the public and other scientists. Yet sci-entists had been commenting on intelligent aliens for centuries. The absence of actual evidence did not impede scientific or public enthusiasm for the idea of life on other planets, or hinder support for experimental efforts to find and communicate with such life. As scientists began to meet in international venues to discuss civilizations elsewhere in the cosmos, Sullivan remarks, "the participants shared a strong feeling that such civilizations exist."[16] The Myth of the Extraterrestrial had, for many members of the scientific community, apparently taken charge of their thinking, beliefs and goals.

During the 1960s interest in extraterrestrial life acquired greater scientific legitimacy and support; it received important boosts from the governments of both the United States and the Soviet Union. It was, after all, the National Aeronautics and Space Administration (NASA) that "transported origin-of-life studies—and their accompanying biologists—into outer space."[17] Moreover, the question of the origin of life was increasingly seen as a question to be answered by space exploration, a highly questionable proposition. Theories of evolution were also becoming more sophisticated, lending the extraterrestrial further scientific support. For example, George Gaylord Simpson's *The Meaning of Evolution* (1949) argued that chemical conditions on other planets might have been favorable to the emergence and development of life.[18]

Soviet scientists had a special interest in proving that life existed on other planets, one step in the proof that it originated by strictly naturalistic means. In this way they hoped to undermine the traditional religious explanations of life's origins.[19] Much of the active searching for extraterrestrial life forms in the 1960s and 1970s was undertaken by the Soviet Union. This is likely due to the influence of the famous Soviet scientist Iosif S. Shklovskii, who became an associate of the young American physicist Carl Sagan.[20] In 1962 the Soviet Academy of Sciences "published an entire book on the universality of intelligent life." Its principal author was Shklovskii, whom Sullivan describes as "one of the most brilliant theoretical radio astronomers alive." Sagan was among the most outspoken advocates of the intelligent-life position in the United States during the 1970s. In his book *The Dragons of Eden* (1977), for which he won a Pulitzer Prize, Sagan wrote: "Once life has started in a relatively benign environment and billions of years of evolutionary time are available, the expectation of many of us is that intelligent beings would develop."[21] Indeed, scientists meeting to discuss the possibility of life on other planets in the 1960s concluded that "perhaps a million technical civilizations existed in the Galaxy."[22] Sullivan asked of extraterrestrial life studies, "Why, in the second half of the 20th century, has this subject so abruptly become 'respectable,' after being so long corrupted and discredited by various science-fiction writers, comic strips and, more recently, television shows?"[23] Perhaps these popular media were not so much corrupting a subject as they were crafting a myth, one that had been lurking in the Western imagination for centuries: advanced civilizations in space. The dominance of that cultural myth was felt increasingly in scientific circles.

Much of speculative science and science fiction are driven by a vision of a new Holy Grail. A quantum leap forward in scientific knowledge, a breakthrough in understanding our place in the cosmos, an epoch-making change in the human condition—all are associated with the persistent myth of imminent human contact with intelligent extraterrestrials. In this quest for an interstellar community, the lines of influence running back and forth between science and science fiction have been intricate and difficult to trace. For instance, physicist Freeman Dyson was famous for speculating that an advanced civilization might construct a sphere around its sun in order to capture all of its energy. With little delay the Dyson Sphere showed up in the works of several authors of science fiction and was featured in an episode of *Star Trek*. And yet, Dyson has suggested that he originally found the idea in a work of science fiction: Stapledon's *Star Maker*.

Science-fiction portrayals of extraterrestrials have shaped scientists' ideas about likely alien life. Scientists often cite microbes or bacteria as the most likely forms of life to be encountered in Space. But single-celled life-forms certainly were not the intended audience for the intricate, meticulously engraved maps of our solar system, the recorded greetings in fifty-five human languages, a message from President Jimmy Carter, and the anatomically correct portrayal of a human couple carried on board both the *Voyager 1* and *Voyager 2* spacecrafts as they were blasted into Space to great media fanfare in 1977. Would we have witnessed such a strange intermingling of mass-media attention, general cultural acceptance, government backing and endorsement by the scientific establishment in the absence of a powerful cultural mythology regarding the existence and nature of intelligent life on other planets? By the way, one of the Voyager crafts also played a key role in *Star Trek: The Motion Picture* (1979). Later, a fictional Pioneer X NASA probe was also featured in the movie *Star Trek V: The Final Frontier*.

I have already mentioned that we exhibit a determined tendency to categorize our mass-media products as simply "entertainment," thus overlooking their powerful and persuasive effect as narratives. Yet clearly, science fiction's broad popularity and capacity for visualization have also shaped our beliefs and expectations regarding space aliens. Dick observes that visual media "brought the alien one step closer to the hearts of the masses, while the marriage to science verified the alien theme as a plausible reality." Scientists such as Hoyle, Clarke and Sagan "used fiction to speculate about alien contact." At the same time, "alien science fiction influenced many who actually became involved in scientific programs to search for extraterrestrials."[24]

This last comment from Dick underlines a fascinating fact about several major *scientific* efforts of the late twentieth century. Some of the scientists involved in the large and well-funded programs directed toward discovering life elsewhere in the cosmos—for example, the NASA astrobiology experiments—were themselves influenced by reading and watching works of science fiction featuring intelligent extraterrestrials. Thus it is not surprising that as the modern age progressed, science fiction notions merged with scientific speculation to engender a virtually apocalyptic expectation regarding extraterrestrials arriving from the skies. And increasingly, the international scientific community was ready to legitimize the search for intelligent extraterrestrials.

As this brief sketch suggests, the Myth of the Extraterrestrial—the idea that intelligent extraterrestrials exist and that interaction with them will inaugurate a new era in human existence—is at this point in our cultural history permanently entrenched in the Western mind. From our current vantage point, some degree of hope in extraterrestrial contact is widely manifested. As already recognized, polls suggest that a majority of Americans are "prepared for the discovery of extraterrestrial life" in the coming centuries, and that we also believe that these aliens will be both friendly and "more advanced." Moreover, we have invested a great deal of money and creativity in the effort to confirm what we apparently already believe—that we are not alone in the universe.

It is not the mere existence of intelligent life elsewhere in the cosmos that has characterized our search for E.T. We have also developed a strangely unfounded confidence in the aliens' desire to help humanity "progress." Yet we should recognize that aliens have received a mixed press, for in addition to advocating world peace and unity, they have also been portrayed as wishing to annihilate us, ingest us, enslave us, impregnate us, colonize our planet and kidnap beautiful members of our species for their entertainment. But the view of aliens that seems to have stuck most tenaciously in the Western conscious-ness is that aliens are heavenly agents of assistance, doe-eyed benevolent help-ers from on high, ready to lend a thin, pale hand whenever they can. Regardless of the form they have taken, science fiction and some speculative science—and not a few new religions and government programs—would have been robbed of their mass appeal without the mass-media character of the intelligent alien. There are now dozens of UFO religions founded on the idea of the intelligent extraterrestrial.

As we shall see, the Myth of the Extraterrestrial has a long history in the Western imagination. It has received frequent assistance in making its way into our corporate psyche through the works of both popular artists and pop-ularizing scientists. In the following pages, I will focus attention on several important efforts by both scientists and the creators of science fiction, efforts promoting the idea that the cosmos, indeed even our solar system, has its vari-ous intelligent extraterrestrial residents.

FONTENELLE IMAGINES THE INTELLIGENT ALIEN

Seventeenth- and eighteenth-century writers were not the first to imagine intelligent life on other worlds; the idea is of ancient origin. The Greek phi-losopher Thales (d. ca. 547 B.C.) "proposed that the stars are other worlds." His student Anaximander "appears to have been the first to elaborate the idea that the number of worlds is infinite, some of them in the process of birth, some dying." Anaximenes of Lampsacus (d. 320 B.C.), a friend of Alexander the Great, "told that warrior, to his astonishment, that he had conquered only one of many worlds."[25] Democritus (d. ca. 370 B.C.), inventor of the theory of atoms, argued that "there must now be, and always have been, an infinite number of other worlds in various stages of growth and decay." Similarly, the Roman poet Lucretius (d. ca. 55 B.C.) considers the idea in his *On the Nature of Things* and "expresses a view that still strongly influences those today who believe [that] life exists elsewhere than on earth, namely, that no phenomenon in na-ture, including the emergence of life on a planet, occurs only once."[26] He wrote that "in other regions there are other earths and various tribes of men and breeds of beasts." Aristarchus of Samos (d. 230 B.C.) engaged in "far-reaching philosophical speculations regarding the existence of other universes or other worlds."[27] The Roman satirist Lucian (d. A.D. 180) also wrote about the possibility of other habitable worlds. On this point at least some among the Chinese sages apparently also agreed. The philosopher Teng Mu (13th c. A.D.) affirmed "how unreasonable it would be to suppose that, besides the earth and the sky which we can see, there are no other skies and no other earths."[28]

But in the seventeenth century the intelligent space alien seeking communication with Earth-dwellers entered the mainstream of Western culture to stay. Its first sighting by a mass audience seems to have occurred in France in the 1680s. The scientist, playwright and poet Bernard le Bovier de Fontenelle (1657-1757) is best known for a remarkable French work of fiction that must be accounted among the earliest and most original tales of the extraterrestrial alien: *Conversations on the Plurality of Worlds* (1686). It was certainly the most culturally influential of the early alien tales. Knowledgeable in science and literature, Fontenelle's works captivated readers. So popular was *Conversations* that the book went through numerous editions, was translated into English in 1695, and maintained a steady audience in several countries for more than a century and a half.[29]

Fontenelle's imagined weeklong conversation between a male courtier and a noblewoman begins with the assertions that life likely exists on other planets and that "it would be very pleasant to see different Worlds." These ideas were to become the twin foundation stones of science fiction. Though actual space travel might be arduous and the residents of the other planets quite strange, still "it would be much better certainly than to go to Japan" and see "nothing but men."[30]

Fontenelle, a religious skeptic, realized that his suggestions about alien life would upset the Catholic Church hierarchy. If alien beings are not descended from Adam, then did God create them? And if so, are they also created in God's image? But there were scientific issues at stake as well in affirming life on other planets. For example, the concept of polygenism—multiple and separate origins for human life on Earth rather than the biblical single human beginning—was being widely debated in Fontenelle's day. The basic case for multiple origins had been set out in Isaac la Peyrere's controversial *Men Before Adam* (1655). For Fontenelle and his contemporaries, the issue of polygenism was not of merely academic interest but was also intimately tied to the question of whether the various human races were equal or even similar. Those accepting polygenism tended to argue that they were not equal or similar, and the inhabited-planets hypothesis certainly supported polygenism. Thus, planets might host various species of intelligent beings, and their relative intelligences might vary widely. In other words, some space aliens were likely superior to others, and to us. It seemed to follow that some races of people, originating in different regions of Earth, might also be superior to others.

Thus the view that "every star is a world" with intelligent inhabitants, though optimistic, was not necessarily benevolent.[31] The racist trajectory of polygenism quickly surfaces in *Conversations*. Fontenelle comments that though every land that human explorers have discovered has been inhabited, the residents often barely qualified as human. "In the lands that have been lately discovered, we can scarce call the Inhabitants Men; they are rather animals of human shape, and that too sometimes very imperfect, almost without human Reason." Fontenelle concludes: "He therefore who would travel to the moon, must not expect to find Men there."[32]

Fontenelle employed his early work of science fiction to weigh in on an important "scientific" idea of his day, and one that would have a long and troublesome life in Europe: that the various human races reflect a permanent hierarchy and may represent entirely different species with separate origins. Fontenelle's aliens became part of his polygenetic argument: intelligent species on other worlds support the idea that life originated in various places in the cosmos, and if in the cosmos then perhaps also on Earth. And there was no reason to assume that these various species had similar intellectual capacities. Whether humans were higher or lower in that hierarchy than the residents of other planets was a debatable question. But Europeans knew that they were a higher species than the "animals of human shape" existing in other parts of the Earth. Polygenetic theories were later used to support practices such as slavery and even genocide.

Fontenelle anticipated the themes of interplanetary travel and communication. "Shall any one say, There shall never be a communication between the Moon and the Earth?" Space travel is a challenge that humankind will meet, just as it met the challenge of the seas and of balloon flight, an innovation in Fontenelle's day.[33] "The art of flying is but newly invented; it will improve by degrees, and in time grow perfect; then we may fly as far as the moon."[34] Indeed, helpful aliens will themselves teach us the secrets of space-flight, our cultures will blend, and one day "we shall know the people in the

Moon as well as we do now the Antipodes."[35]

In this remarkable early effort in science fiction, Fontenelle combined the ideas of technological progress and inhabited planets to develop a narrative brimming with speculation about spaceflight, alien civilizations and even new religions. He demonstrated an astonishing capacity to anticipate the major themes of later science fiction, right down to the possibility of the phenomenon now known as abduction. Extraterrestrial "curiosity" about humans will cause them to "swim on the outward surface of our Air" and "angle or cast a Net for us, as for so many Fishes." His companion says in response to this exciting prospect, "For my part I would go into their nets of my own accord" just for "the pleasure of seeing such strange Fishermen."[36] Interplanetary colonization is also imagined: humans "might bring Mercury and Venus under our government." After all, "they are little planets, and cannot resist us."[37] Finally, deceased persons "may reside on other planets," perhaps even traveling from one planet to another.[38]

Fontenelle's views were exotic, occasionally troubling and persuasively presented. Nor can he be dismissed as an inconsequential voice. Voltaire dubbed him "the most universal genius that the age of Louis XIV has produced." In both the seventeenth and eighteenth centuries, *Conversations* was popular in France as well as in England.

More surprising was the impact the work had in Russia. Walter Sullivan adds this remarkable footnote to the story of Bernard de Fontenelle and his *Conversations*. "Fontenelle's concept of many worlds, expressed in so readable and popular a manner, excited people far and wide." M. V. Lomonosov, "the so-called father of Russian science, read the book in its French original and was deeply impressed." He then arranged for the publication of a Russian translation. Sullivan adds, "It might even be argued that seeds thus planted in 18th century Russia bore fruit in the work of Otto Struve after he came to America and presided over mankind's first serious attempt to reach out and make contact with intelligent beings elsewhere."[39] Struve was instrumental in promoting the first fledgling American SETI project, then under the direction of Francis Drake. Thus does Sullivan draw a direct line of influence from a foundational seventeenth-century science-fiction work on intelligent extraterrestrials onward to modern scientists' first efforts to contact these imaginary beings.

CAMILLE FLAMMARION AND
EXTRATERRESTRIAL MYSTICISM

As Western science developed, it threw its weight behind the Myth of the Extraterrestrial with surprising regularity. The famous French astronomer Camille
Flammarion (1842-1925), a brilliant scientist who worked for many years at the
Paris Observatory, authored a series of books that helped to popularize astronomy. At the tender age of sixteen, he had already completed a 500-page manuscript titled *Cosmologie universelle*. However, Flammarion is best known for
his passionate devotion to the idea of life on other planets and for his many
books that brought this idea persuasively before the public. Indeed, the scientist
Flammarion, who penned more than seventy books, did more than any other
writer to popularize the basic presuppositions of science fiction. Flammarion's
books likely inspired early French filmmaker George Méliès, whose flamboyant
and popular turn-of-the-century (1896-1914) silent movies dealt with futuristic
themes such as travel to the moon, sun and planets.

Flammarion applied Darwinian ideas on a cosmic scale, arguing as early
as 1875 that "all planets would attain life in due time."[40] His first book, *The
Plurality of Inhabited Worlds*, appeared in 1862 and was reprinted a remarkable thirty-three times by 1880. Extraordinarily popular on both sides of the
Atlantic, the book was still being printed as late as 1921.[41] But Flammarion's
most popular work appeared in 1880 under the title *Astronomie populaire* and
was translated into English in 1894. Selling in excess of a hundred thousand
copies, this work was a catalog of ideas about life on other worlds and clearly
exhibited the evolutionary view that such life would likely be "superior" to human beings.[42]

Among other durable notions, Flammarion popularized the theory that
an "advanced" civilization had constructed canals on Mars. Influenced by
reading Huygens's arguments about inhabited planets, Flammarion was inclined toward more metaphysical speculations about space and its inhabitants. John Clute describes him as an "astronomer, mystic and storyteller" who
was "obsessed by life after death, and on other worlds, and [who] seemed to
see no distinction between the two."[43] Thus, Flammarion actually incorporated inhabited planets into a new religious view centered on reincarnation.
He was particularly interested in the spiritual theories of his countryman Jean
Reynaud, who had speculated that spiritual perfection was not possible during

one lifetime, but might be possible over the course of many lifetimes. By such reincarnational evolution, the perfection of the human race was slowly but surely taking place. Flammarion even suggested that spiritual progress took place as souls migrated, not just from body to body, but also from planet to planet. Thus human beings are "citizens of the skies," and other planets are locations where spiritual progress takes place in evolving souls.

Not surprisingly for a man of his planetary and metaphysical interests, Flammarion also wrote science fiction, albeit with a decidedly spiritual quality. His novel *Lumen*, published in 1870, traced the travels of a spirit through space, transported—like Kepler's protagonist in *Somnium* centuries before and Burroughs's hero John Carter a few decades later—by occult powers. In another early work of science fiction, *Récits de l'infini* (1872), he traced the reincarnation of a soul on several planets. Later in his life, Flammarion turned his attention to spiritualism and psychical research, eventually publishing a three-volume work titled *Death and Its Mysteries* (1920-1921).

In his life and work, Flammarion represents the close relationship that was developing among science, science fiction and the spiritual. With great commercial success he blended scientific speculation with science fiction to propagate modern myths such as the notion that "superior" extraterrestrial species reside on numerous planets, and that the human soul evolves through cosmic reincarnation. Flammarion's influence was great, not just on the popular thought of his day, but also on later writers with similar interests and convictions.

NIKOLA TESLA: COMMUNICATING WITH MARTIANS

Serbian-born electrical genius Nikola Tesla (1846-1953) was another great turn-of-the-century scientist with extraterrestrial interests. His many patents, bold experiments, gigantic ego and flamboyant social life made him a famous figure in his day.[44] A friend of millionaire and science-fiction author John Jacob Astor, who occasionally funded his research, Tesla shared Astor's interests in life on other planets. Indeed, Tesla believed that he was the first to receive signals beamed to Earth from Mars. By means of his tireless promotion of the idea of radio contact with intelligent Martians, this towering scientific genius lent tremendous credibility to the Myth of the Extraterrestrial.[45]

Tesla is best known for his pioneering work on the mass production of electrical power, but he was also instrumental in developing long-distance radio communication. Recognizing before most scientists that radio communication was not limited by distance, Tesla immediately suggested the possibility of communicating with beings on other planets. Indeed, Tesla's convictions regarding alien communication led him to hopeful interpretations of his data, and eventually to the groundless claim that he was receiving radio signals from Mars. Before most authorities, this great scientist recognized that "a message could be sent to Mars almost as easily as to Chicago."[46] Tesla's ideas about alien communication may have been influenced by the science-fiction work of his friend Astor, who in 1893 had published a novel on interplanetary travel and visits with extraterrestrials. At this time, Tesla was living in Astor's famous Waldorf-Astoria Hotel.

For Tesla, a true believer in the Myth of the Extraterrestrial, human contact with intelligent aliens would usher in a Utopia on Earth. He considered the existence of intelligent Martians "a statistical certainty" and their superiority to humans equally likely. Tesla dreamed of a technological utopian future in which planet Earth would be "delivered from hunger and toil" and people would enjoy "easy world communications, control of weather, a bountiful supply of energy, limitless light, and . . . a link with the forms of life he was convinced existed on other planets."[47] To the very end of his life, Tesla held out the hope of interstellar communication, releasing a paper on the topic on the occasion of his eightieth birthday. He claimed to have drawn up plans for "devices" for "communicating with other worlds" and thus hoped to claim the 100,000-franc Pierre Guzman prize. He was "perfectly sure" the prize would be his. Tesla sought not the monetary reward but "the great historical honor of being the first to achieve this miracle," an achievement for which "I would be almost willing to give my life."[48]

For all of his tremendous brilliance, Tesla seemed at times to be living out a series of science-fiction fantasies. Indeed, science fiction was emerging as a popular genre in the 1890s, a fact of which Tesla could not have been unaware. The occult power called Vril depicted in Bulwer-Lytton's *The Coming Race* (1871) and the powerful cosmic rays of Blavatsky's Atlanteans provided an imaginative background for Tesla's own claim to be able to generate "a different kind of energy" from ordinary electricity. Tesla announced that this new energy could be transmitted as far as to other planets.[49] So powerful was this new force that Tesla worried lest he damage another planet by hitting it with a "needlepoint of tremendous energy." According to biographer Margaret Cheney, Tesla held that "advanced thinkers on other planets might even mistake the Tesla energy beam for some form of cosmic ray."[50] He also boasted that he could create a "teleforce" wall around the United States that would "melt airplanes at a distance of 250 miles."[51]

Like Flammarion, Tesla speculated about religion as well as science. He held that "the essences of Buddhism and Christianity would comprise the religion of the human race in 2100." Moreover, it was a near certainty that the science of eugenics would be practiced by advanced nations, and that the natural process by which "less desirable strains" were eliminated would be resumed.[52] Compassion had taken over societal planning, and a "new sense of pity" was impeding "the ruthless workings of nature," with the result that "the unfit were kept alive." Like many intellectuals of his day, Tesla held the selective breeding of human beings to be necessary and helpful. Preventing "the breeding of the unfit by sterilization and the deliberate guidance of the mating instinct" was vital to social progress. Tesla praised the "several European countries and a number of the states of the American Union" that had already begun programs of sterilization of "the criminal and the insane."[53]

As with Fontenelle, Tesla's interest in life on other worlds dovetailed naturally with potentially dangerous social views. Perhaps it is not surprising that Tesla imbibed some of his more extreme ideas from his friend the fascist poet George Sylvester Viereck, a German immigrant who dazzled New York socialites in the 1930s. In his later years, Tesla wrote that "man in the large is a mass being urged on by a force."[54] Traditional religious ideas impeded human progress, because progress depended upon such morally questionable but socially necessary practices as eugenics. For this reason, enlightened governments ought to establish bureaus to regulate marriages so as to improve the human race.[55] For Tesla, eugenics was just part of a progressive scientific social agenda that included communicating with advanced civilizations on other planets.

PERCIVAL LOWELL AND THE
CIVILIZATIONS OF MARS

As science fiction was beginning to achieve genuine cultural stature in the late 1800s under the influence of masters such as Verne and Wells, prominent scientists like Flammarion and Tesla were increasingly prone to lend their support to one of its foundational albeit unsupported tenets: the existence of intelligent extraterrestrials desirous of communicating with humans. Every year the case for extraterrestrial life seemed to gain some new piece of evidence in its support, each of which would eventually be overturned. In 1877 the Italian astronomer Giovanni Schiaparelli famously announced that he had observed *canali* on the planet Mars. His term, which literally meant "channels," was translated into English as "canals," a mistake perhaps influenced by the recent completion of the Suez Canal (in 1869).

The mistranslation of Schiaparelli's term *canali* launched an enormous public interest in the apparently technologically advanced Martians, who were developing such masterpieces of engineering. The German science-fiction author Kurd Lasswitz, under the influence of Schiaparelli's dramatic announcement, wrote one of the first novels featuring actual human contact with Martians in 1897. *On Two Planets (Auf zwei Planeten)* has German explorers discovering that Martians not only exist, but have already established colonies at both the North and South poles of Earth. Around the same time the distinguished astronomer Percival Lowell (1855-1916) claimed to have actually seen Schaparelli's canals on Mars. From his observatory in Arizona, Lowell spent years studying Mars and was taken with the idea that Mars had once sustained life. He advocated the notion in popular books including *Mars* (1895), *Mars and Its Canals* (1906) and *Mars as the Abode of Life* (1908). Lowell's argument for life on Mars was to have a profound influence on the developing genre of science fiction, particularly through the tireless work of editor, writer and inventor Hugo Gernsback, who read a German translation of Lowell's *Mars* as a child in his native Luxembourg. Gernsback's thoughts about the possibility of life on other planets were profoundly shaped by Lowell's speculations.

Lowell was drawn to Herbert Spencer's theories of social evolution and, following extensive travels and studies in Asia, concluded that Western culture was more advanced than Asian. Why not extend such thinking to civilizations on other planets? The idea that a "more advanced" civilization had once existed on another planet would have been in keeping with Lowell's basic view of life's development. His understanding of social evolution, would have prepared him to believe that, just as some human civilizations were superior to others, an advanced technological civilization had constructed the intricate system of canals on Mars.

Lowell's alleged confirmation of Schaparelli's canals launched what was perhaps the most popular series of stories in the history of science fiction: the Martian tales of Edgar Rice Burroughs (1875-1950), appearing with some regularity between about 1918 and 1955. James Gunn has written that Burroughs's Mars, or Barsoom, "bears a general relationship to the concept of Mars popularized by Percival Lowell in his books *Mars and Its Canals* (1906) and *Mars as the Abode of Life* (1908)."[56] Burroughs's stories set the stage for a large number of popular stories of Mars and its inhabitants. Among the most noteworthy was Stanley Weinbaum's 1934 short story, "Martian Odyssey," a work featuring a helpful alien named Tweel.

FRANK DRAKE AND OZMA

We can now bring the search for extraterrestrials and the closely related Myth of the Extraterrestrial into the second half of the twentieth century. Frank D. Drake was born in 1930 and received a Ph.D. in astronomy from Harvard in 1958. This eminent scientist writes, "Ever since I was eight years old, I had wondered about the origins of people and whether there could be others elsewhere in the universe."[57] Drake is credited with having mounted the first genuinely scientific effort to detect messages from intelligent aliens in space.

Working for the National Radio Astronomy Observatory at Green Bank, South Carolina, Drake in 1960 began searching the heavens with a single eighty-five-foot Howard Tatel radio telescope in hopes of receiving messages from outside our solar system. He referred to this effort as the Ozma Experiment, but it has usually been termed Project Ozma. Drake and several colleagues "worked out a mathematical equation designed to indicate the number of civilizations that may have evolved to the point where they can—and want to—communicate with other solar systems."[58] This formula, still referred to as the Drake Equation, provided the basis for Project Ozma. At around this same time, the early 1960s, Giuseppe Cocconi and Philip Morrison published a paper in *Nature* that proposed a search for signals from space, including a likely radio frequency for the search.[59]

As a newly minted Ph.D. working in an isolated location, Drake and his modest early effort received a surprising level of interest from members of the scientific and business communities. He was visited at his small outpost in South Carolina by the young Catholic theologian Theodore Hesburgh, already president of Notre Dame University. Hesburgh "felt that the search for extraterrestrial life was an inspiring and a very good thing to do." Forty years later Hesburgh would write the foreword to a book about SETI. In defense of his interest in SETI, Hesburgh wrote, "As a theologian, I would say that this proposed search for extraterrestrial intelligence (SETI) is also a search of knowing and understanding God through his works—especially those works that most reflect him. Finding others than ourselves would mean knowing Him better."[60]

Drake was also visited by John Lear, science editor of *Saturday Review* and one of the leading science writers in the country at that time. As Drake recalled later, "He wanted to see history made, and knew that the detection of another civilization would be HISTORY if it really happened."[61] Finally, Drake reports that he was also visited by the vice-president for research of Hewlett-Packard Corporation, Bernard Oliver, who "had thought about the means of detecting other civilizations for many years."[62] Such visits, particularly given the modest nature of Drake's experiment—one telescope being used as time allowed—point out the cultural power at that time of the Myth of the Extraterrestrial. The UFO craze was in full swing in 1960, science fiction had been ascendant for at least thirty years with alien-themed books and movies achieving enormous cultural acceptance, and Sputnik had been launched just two years earlier.

Perhaps most surprising, however, was the intense interest in Project Ozma by Otto Struve (1897-1963), the Russian émigré to America who was the most eminent astronomer of the 1940s and 1950s. Drake writes that Struve was "one of the few senior astronomers of that era who believed that intelligent life was abundant in the universe and felt that everything possible should be done to support any feasible searches for signals of extraterrestrial intelligent life."[63] Struve became the first scientist of international stature to throw his weight behind a SETI-type project, promoting Drake's experiment in prestigious public lectures at MIT. Remarkably, Struve had grown up in a famous family of astronomers who had been influenced by reading the Russian translation of Fontenelle's *Conversations* commissioned by Lomonosov.

In 1961, with the support of Struve, Drake helped to convene the first international conference on interplanetary communication, in West Virginia. A number of well-known scientists attended, including the young Carl Sagan. In 1964 Drake joined the faculty of Cornell University, where he held the Goldwin Smith Professorship of Astronomy in 1976-1984 and was director of the National Astronomy and Ionosphere Center in 1970-1981. His 1967 book *Intelligent Life in Space* is considered a landmark in the SETI field. Early SETI efforts were criticized by members of the astronomy establishment but then slowly gained broad acceptance. Sullivan reports that "Sir Bernard Lovell, director of what was then the largest [astronomical] instrument of this kind, at Jodrell Bank in England, was at first among the skeptics, but he modified his views."[64] The migration of the basic SETI approach from the fringes of science to a position considerably more in the mainstream is reflected in Lovell's comment: "I think that now one has to be sympathetic about an idea which only a few years ago would have seemed rather far-fetched."[65]

CARL SAGAN: IMAGINING CONTACT

No writer of the late twentieth century did more to propagate the Myth of the Extraterrestrial than physicist and author Carl Sagan, the David Duncan Professor of Astronomy and Space Sciences and director of the Laboratory for Planetary Studies at Cornell University. A Peabody and Emmy Award-winning television producer as well as a Pulitzer Prize-winning author on scientific issues, Sagan brought planetary science out of the observatory and into the living room. But Sagan (1934-1996) may be best remembered for his lifelong interest in communicating with intelligent beings on other planets. An enthusiastic backer of SETI, his passion for this project marked his academic and public career and also shaped public policy. Even his famous 1980 documentary TV series, *Cosmos*, was often a commercial for the possibility of extraterrestrial life and the pursuit of efforts to communicate with that life.

In addition to the tremendously popular *Cosmos* series, Sagan's fame was enhanced by his many popular scientific books such as *The Dragons of Eden* (1977), *The Demon-Haunted World* (1996), *Billions and Billions* (1997) and his best-selling science-fiction novel *Contact* (1985), which became the basis of a popular movie starring Jodi Foster. The 1980 book *Cosmos*, on which the *Cosmos* series was based, remains the most widely read science publication ever written in the English language. Sagan was also involved in the American space program for many years and received twenty-two honorary doctorates. He lived to see Harvard University establish the eight-million channel META/Sentinel survey and NASA begin an even more powerful program.[66]

Sagan frequently expressed the fervent faith that contact with extraterrestrial life forms was possible and would transform human history. Early books, such as *Intelligent Life in the Universe* (with I. S. Shklovskii, 1966) and *Communication with Extraterrestrial Intelligence* (1973), explored the idea of such contact. Sagan was not alone among twentieth-century scientists who held out this hope. For example, Philip Morrison of Cornell University was known for "his intense interest in the possibility of communicating with intelligent beings elsewhere."[67] And Drake and Struve were also prominent scientists who backed the basic idea of extraterrestrial communication. But Sagan was a gifted communicator with a flair for explaining difficult concepts in everyday language, and his frank and highly credible presentational style made him the leading public spokesperson for SETI and related ventures.

More than any other proponent of the late twentieth century, Sagan helped to propagate an elaborate narrative involving extraterrestrial intelligences, civilizations on distant planets, human communication with aliens, an extensive intergalactic network of civilizations, and human advancement to an unspecified "next stage" with the help of our benevolent cousins in space. The basic arguments of the first installment of *Cosmos* regarding extraterrestrial life—presented by Sagan seated at what can only be compared to the captain's chair of the Starship *Enterprise*—do not vary widely from the case made in the UFO-exploiting pseudo-documentary, developed by B-sci-fi filmmaker Ed Hunt, that appeared a year earlier, *UFOs Are Real!* (1979). In its broad outline the argument runs like this: (1) The universe is vast and contains an unimaginably large number of planets, many of which are likely habitable. (2) Probability, if nothing else, suggests that there must be other intelligent beings "out there." (3) These beings might be willing to communicate with humans. (4) They are more technologically and biologically "advanced" than we are. And (5) they may wish to help us to progress. Sagan successfully translated this extraordinarily popular and empirically unsubstantiated Myth of the Extraterrestrial into the highly credible language of science.

By 1973 Sagan published a brief and highly accessible book on the possibility of extraterrestrial life with the trendy title *The Cosmic Connection: An Extraterrestrial Perspective.* With characteristic confidence the young physicist announced that "after centuries of muddy surmise, unfettered speculation, stodgy conservatism, and unimaginative disinterest, the subject of extraterrestrial life has finally come of age." The search for such life "has now reached a practical stage where it can be pursued by rigorous scientific techniques, where it has achieved scientific respectability, and where its significance is widely understood. Extraterrestrial life," Sagan added in a characteristic flourish, "is an idea whose time has come."[68] As we have seen, Bernard de Fontenelle beat Sagan to the cosmic punch on this idea by exactly three centuries.

Sounding themes common during the Cold War, Sagan urged that "interstellar communication . . . may be the agency of our own survival."[69] Facing the various crises that technology presents us—ecological disaster, nuclear warfare, a growing gap between haves and have nots—we may need the help of civilizations that have already learned to live with advanced technology. Sagan's breathtaking narrative features aliens "motivated by benevolence" because they were themselves "helped along" and thus find this "a tradition worthy of continuance." Moreover, highly advanced civilizations, "hundreds or thousands or millions of years beyond us," likely possess "sciences and technologies so far beyond our present capabilities as to be indistinguishable from magic."[70] Alien signals may be "there for us to detect them—if only we know how."[71]

The goal of extraterrestrial communication is nothing less than galactic unity, what Sagan termed the "cultural homogenization of the Galaxy."[72] But we are not yet ready to enter such a galactic organization. In a dizzying rhetorical flourish, Sagan writes that the idea of "present Earth establishing radio contact and becoming a member of a galactic federation" is akin to "a blue jay or an armadillo applying to the United Nations for member-nation status."[73] After all, the beings we are imagining are highly cultured and "more advanced than we in science and technology, in politics, ethics, poetry, and music."[74] The science-fiction grammar of Sagan's musings, down to the use of terms such as "galactic federation," is reminiscent of Heinlein, Roddenberry and Asimov, and before them, Kurd Lasswitz. The line between speculative science and science fiction is blurred in some of Sagan's early works as it had been a century

earlier in the writings of Flammarion, Tesla and Lowell, and long before that
in Huygens and Burnet. Nevertheless, the SETI project eventually received
important support from prestigious organizations such as NASA.[75]

Some of the aliens that Sagan imagines achieve almost divine status: there
may be "supercivilization gods," beings so advanced that they have connected
a large number of civilizations that are working in concord to achieve total
galactic unity, thus "unifying the cosmos."[76] Sagan's novel *Contact* introduced
extraterrestrials with astonishing capabilities. Like those in Fred Hoyle's 1962
novel *A for Andromeda*, Sagan's aliens beam to Earth a set of instructions for
building a machine that finally makes the long human-alien "contact" a reality.
The aliens of Sagan's *Contact* are engaged in cooperative projects—manipu-
lating galaxies, for example—in keeping with his original vision of *The Cosmic Connection*.[77] Sagan acknowledged that "since no . . . contact has yet been
made," his thinking on the topic is "necessarily speculative."[78] Nevertheless, if
The Cosmic Connection promotes "public consideration of these exploratory
ventures, it will have served its purpose."[79] Thus, Sagan did hope to create public interest in extraterrestrial contact, a project that would certainly benefit
from public support.

Sagan acknowledged the influence on his thought of the most commercially
successful and unscientific of all of the early science-fiction writers, Edgar Rice
Burroughs. Burroughs's stories not only suggested the possibility of visiting
other planets. Sagan also was captivated by the thought that humans might
be related to the inhabitants of other worlds, though probably not Mars. "Possibly the most remarkable hypothesis proposed by Burroughs in these novels,"
he writes, "was that human beings and inhabitants of Mars could produce live
offspring—a biologically impossible proposition if the Martians and we are
imagined as having separate biological origins."[80] Sagan fails to mention that
the space hero John Carter's offspring, produced with a Martian woman, goes
through its entire gestation in a large egg.

As a footnote to SETI history, Sagan's extraterrestrial interests were originally pursued in concert with a group of Soviet scientists who took an early
interest in the question of intelligent extraterrestrial life. Among the most
visible proponents was Struve, whom we have already met. Physicist Iosif S.
Shklovskii became one of Sagan's early collaborators, accepting the idea of advanced civilizations on other planets. He also helped to formulate some of

the foundational theoretical assumptions for interstellar radio communication. Also worthy of mention is mathematician Matest M. Agrest, who in 1960 hypothesized that the destruction of Sodom and Gomorrah "was caused by a nuclear explosion when visitors from space destroyed their surplus nuclear fuel before leaving for their home planet."[81] Agrest entertained many other similar theories. By 1964 the Soviets were sponsoring their own conference on the search for extraterrestrial intelligence.

Soviet interest in the question of extraterrestrials was likely tied to the regime's investment in the evolutionary model, and especially in its progressive dimension, which was used as part of the argument for socialism. If advanced civilizations could be proved to exist on other planets, then this fact provided additional evidence for the Marxist notion that unseen forces are pushing social evolution forward toward a perfect state. For Shklovskii, life on other planets was a virtual Holy Grail, a spiritual quest for confirmation of basic Soviet assumptions. His 1962 publication, *Universe, Life, Intelligence*, became a major source of Soviet interest in the search for extraterrestrial life. The book was rewritten in 1966 with Sagan's aid. Indeed, Sagan added as many pages to the book as Shklovskii had written for the original. So solid was Shklovskii's scientific reputation that his announcement of belief in the possibility of human-alien communication gave the idea "immediate credibility." A similar credibility transfer had occurred when Struve, then the world's most famous astronomer, promoted the work of Drake. Shklovskii's enthusiasm for extraterrestrial life led other Soviet scientists into the search, most famously Nikolai Kardishev, who made "bold predictions" regarding extraterrestrial civilizations "billions of years more advanced than our own."[82] So powerful was the enchantment of civilizations in Space that Shklovskii and his colleague G. B. Sholomitskii made a worldwide announcement of alien "contact" in 1965 that actually turned out to be surprisingly regular radiation bursts from a distant pulsar, one already being studied by scientists at Cal Tech.

Carl Sagan looked forward to a day when the human race would make contact with intelligent extraterrestrials. His scientific knowledge lent the kind of credibility to his writing that would have been unavailable to someone of lesser accomplishments. No one else more forcefully articulated for late twentieth-century audiences the Myth of the Extraterrestrial.

STEVEN SPIELBERG'S
EXTRATERRESTRIAL VISION

In the dramatic closing scenes of Steven Spielberg's classic UFO film, *Close Encounters of the Third Kind* (1977), alien beings emerge from their gigantic craft bathed in brilliant light. In this cinematic rendition of the Myth of the Extraterrestrial, all of human history has led up to this moment of revelation: humanity's deliverance has finally arrived from the skies. One member of the hand-picked crowd of scientists and military personnel approaching the alien craft actually falls on his knees in reverent response to the enormous, illuminated spaceship that resembles a majestic heavenly city. Upon seeing the craft, another says, "Oh, my God."

Spielberg, fresh from his gigantic success with *Jaws*, invited moviegoers to behold the dazzling and angelic alien faces. These were not the hideous monsters of Wells's *War of the Worlds*—a Spielberg project that would have to wait another twenty-eight years—but what appear to be cosmic children. Moreover, these aliens actually vaguely resemble some, though certainly not all, of the members of the gathered and adoring humans. Spielberg's camera lingers on an alien face, and we notice its childlike high forehead, large eyes and small chin. The director's camera now focuses on particular human faces in the crowd. Again we are struck by the large eyes, the high foreheads and the receding chins of these special humans.

Through the juxtaposition of cinematic images, Spielberg—who personally authored the screenplay for *Close Encounters* after reading abduction accounts—suggests that extraterrestrials may reflect what the human race might look like somewhere in a distant evolutionary future. Moreover, it seems clear that Spielberg is suggesting that some of us—those who vaguely resemble the aliens?—have already taken important genetic steps in that evolutionary direction. Yet some of us most certainly have not taken any such steps. Alas, that is the way things happen in a Darwinian universe—the strong, or the highly intelligent, survive and reproduce; others do not.

Leaving aside this unpleasant fact, and allowing the evolutionary progress of humanoids to proceed on some distant planet for two or three hundred thousand more years, we might find ourselves face-to-face with nothing less than these minor gods—"advanced" beings here to save us from a newly defined fallenness, lost not in sin but in the early stages of physical and social evolution. If we doubt that these are divinities from afar, Spielberg reassures us that this is so. During a religious service being held on the landing site for the chosen few who will join the aliens as they depart into space, a robed Christian minister reads aloud from Psalm 91 a familiar verse, recited by the devil in the temptation of Christ: "He will give his angels charge over you" (Psalm 91:11 KJV).

The extraterrestrials of *Close Encounters* are angels of a new age, here to take charge of us, to teach us what we need to know to get ahead in an ever-evolving cosmos. As one of the stunned scientists says to his colleagues when first seeing the aliens' vast ship, "It's the first day of school, boys." Moreover, Christianity in the person of a priest hands over the human race to the greater truth for which Christianity could only be a temporary, preparatory spirituality; friendly deities from beyond our world will show us the way into our cultural and spiritual future.

Close Encounters was not Spielberg's only science-fiction myth. The film *E.T.: The Extraterrestrial* (1982) is a simple fable of an innocent visitor to Earth who prefers the company of other innocents—children. Possessing supernatural powers to heal and to fly, his identity with one human comrade—the boy Elliot—is so intimate that Elliot feels what E.T. feels. Indeed, their names are even similar. E.T. comes from above, befriends the marginalized, loses his life, regains it and ascends back into the heavenly "home" from whence he came. E.T.'s divinity, like that of the aliens of *Close Encounters*, is apparently a result of evolutionary advancement, the two notions being often conflated in science fiction and thus in the public mind. As in *Close Encounters,* evolution will eventually produce peaceful, godlike beings who possess a range of abilities that appear to us, in our embryonic state, as utterly miraculous. Is it any wonder that the dominant metaphors of both films are religious?

In an April 2005 interview with the German magazine *Der Spiegel*, Spielberg said of his early movies such as *Close Encounters* and *E.T.*, "I used to be the goodwill ambassador between the alien civilizations and our own, and did everything I could to prepare the ground for a peaceful encounter."[83] Obviously, the only ground Spielberg could imagine himself to be preparing would be the minds of his audiences, for presumably even his films have not reached other planets. In a much earlier (1978) *Rolling Stone* interview, Spielberg had said of *Close Encounters*: "The movie will only be successful if, when [people]

see it, they come out of the theater looking up at the sky."[84] Our brief survey
of the Myth of the Extraterrestrial in science fiction and speculative science
suggests that Spielberg and his colleagues in the extraterrestrial industry may
have been more successful in drawing public attention to the sky than they
could possibly have imagined.

THE SCIENCE/SCIENCE FICTION CYCLE

Government support for SETI was stopped in the early 1990s—but the project
lives on. Today major funding for SETI comes from private donors rather than
the government, especially a wealthy former computer industry executive. The
project "could have come to a grinding halt years ago without Paul Allen's
steadfast philanthropic support, according to a leader of the ambitious—and
occasionally controversial—enterprise." Allen, whose fortune resulted from
his involvement with Microsoft, the company he cofounded with Bill Gates,
"has always believed this is an important project," according to Jill Tarter, in
2007 the ongoing director of research for SETI. Indeed, the Allen Telescope
Array, 350 telescopes in the Hat Creek area of Northern California, bears his
name. Allen contributed $11.5 million toward the project, and additional
money came from other Microsoft investors. The telescope array "will be constantly dedicated to SETI," according to Woody Sullivan of the University of
Washington. Writer Tom Paulson adds that "recent discoveries of extrasolar
planets, the appearance of an ice-covered ocean on Jupiter's moon Europa, and
an expanded appreciation for the possibility of life in extreme environments
have lent credibility to the search for extraterrestrial life."[85]

Jill Tarter is the astronomer on whom Carl Sagan based the character Ellie Arroway in his novel *Contact*. The actress Jodi Foster actually spent several weeks getting to know Tarter before the filming of the movie version of
Contact. In April of 2007 scientists announced the discovery of a planet that
might possess an atmosphere similar to Earth's, once again raising hopes
that we might be a step closer to an extraterrestrial encounter. The planet
was dubbed 581c. Journalist Dick Gordon of National Public Radio chose
the occasion to interview Maggie Turnbull, a postdoctoral researcher with
NASA's astrobiology project. Turnbull told Gordon that her own interest in
the search for extraterrestrials was fired by seeing the move *Contact*. "That
is what I am supposed to do," she concluded. The cycle from science (Tarter)

to science fiction (Sagan) and back to science (Turnbull) continues unbroken. Turnbull calls her research "the most interesting thing in the whole universe."

During the interview, Gordon admits that his imagination "is either guided or limited by" science-fiction notions of extraterrestrials. What else would he or the rest of us have to go on? Turnbull acknowledges her own strong sense of the extraterrestrial presence. "I was sitting in the woods, and I was thinking, 'What do you guys look like?'" She has experienced "that feeling of just an awareness coming from somewhere else in the universe." Perhaps the awareness comes from somewhere closer to home, however. Turnbull notes, "I liked the *Star Wars* movies as well," for they have the effect of "unshackling our minds and thinking of the infinite possibilities of things." Is it not more likely that the *Star Wars* movies have had the effect, in the absence of scientific evidence, of suggesting both the presence and nature of aliens? Still, the hope remains that a Saganesque "contact" will be made. "We always make sure that, first of all, there's a bottle of champagne in the refrigerator." The interview concluded with the theme music to the original *Star Trek* television series, heroic strains signaling for all of us the ultimate human adventure.[86]

CONCLUSION

The idea that intelligent extraterrestrials exist, wish to communicate with us and perhaps want to help us has had its proponents for more than three centuries. Usually thought to be the domain of science-fiction writers and moviemakers, the idea often received highly credible public endorsement from scientists as well. As orthodox theologian Seraphim Rose has written, "Science fiction has given the images, 'evolution,' has produced the philosophy, and the technology of the 'space age' has supplied the plausibility for such encounters."[87] Sagan wrote that "the virtue of thinking about life elsewhere is that it forces us to stretch our imaginations."[88] But it is also true that this has never been just an exercise in interplanetary imagination. This chapter has shown that the intelligent extraterrestrial often has been a rhetorical invention that has placed powerful ideas into play, from polygenism to ongoing human evolution—ideas that had no other basis in scientific evidence.

To "stretch" the imagination may not always be a "virtue." It may be that some care needs to be exercised in the shaping of our corporate imagination. When speculative scientists trade in mythologies, the essence of their work becomes religious rather than scientific. Science-fiction writer, physician and moviemaker Michael Crichton, representing something of a minority voice from inside the science-fiction community, comments regarding the absence of evidence for extraterrestrial life: "The belief that there are other life forms in the universe is a matter of faith. There is not a single shred of evidence for any other life forms, and in forty years of searching, none has been discovered. There is absolutely no evidentiary reason to maintain this belief."[89] Some in the scientific community have voiced similar sentiments.

Given the mythic power of the extraterrestrial idea, Crichton's observation takes on an urgency it might not otherwise have. Facts and policies organize themselves around stories, and the Myth of the Extraterrestrial is a powerful story indeed. We have already made considerable commitments of public money and attention to the idea that human beings ought to seek to locate beings inhabiting other planets. Have such policy decisions been driven by a Myth? If so, our efforts to discover real E.T.s may have more to do with promoting a vision of salvation than with pursuing scientific investigation.

This Myth is certainly closely connected to, is perhaps the offspring of, the most powerful scientific idea of the last two hundred years: evolution. As Steven Dick observes, "In all cases the evolutionary worldview . . . played an important role in the birth of the alien."[90] If life evolved on Earth, then why not elsewhere in the universe? And if evolution is progressive—an idea popularly associated with Darwinism—then why should our own present form be the end of the story? The extraterrestrial often is us in future form, an idea that renders our present form inferior by comparison. Moreover, the "highly evolved" extraterrestrial, not the preexistent God of traditional faith, will deliver us through advanced technology, extraordinary spiritual insight and a boundless desire to help. Like the idols of the Old Testament, themselves minor deities with a type of salvation to offer, the extraterrestrials of today often hold out a false spiritual hope. On the biblical account, the human predicament is not one to be solved by any amount of alien advice; it requires the direct intervention of the God who created all of us, including any extraterrestrials that might exist, for that matter. "I lift up my eyes," said the psalmist. "From where will my help come?" The biblical answer remains the same through the ages:

"My help comes from the LORD" (Psalm 121:1-2).

The essence of the Myth of the Extraterrestrial is that our more advanced space cousins—indeed, our more advanced selves—are returning from the skies to save us from all that threatens to hinder or destroy, including our outdated religious delusions that suggest we cannot save ourselves. As we shall see, we are increasingly coming under the influence of not just one such myth, but a network of such allegedly scientific mythologies. We are in the presence of a new religion.

4

THE MYTH OF SPACE

Who are you? Where are you from?
I am a child of earth and of starry Heaven,
but my race is of Heaven alone.

ORPHIC LAMELLA

He called himself Man. He was one of the starfolk.
And he longed to return to the stars.

CARL SAGAN

The fact that man is the most adaptable and versatile
measuring instrument—and we mortals have an insatiable thirst
for knowledge and firsthand observation—
makes project Mercury a natural first step in the future manned
exploration of the solar system.

ERIC BERGAUST, *FIRST MEN IN SPACE*

Space—the final frontier.

STAR TREK, INTRODUCTION

During a June 2006 speech in Hong Kong, eminent physicist and Copley Prize-winner Stephen Hawking urged his audience that "it is important for the human race to spread out into space for the survival of the species." Hawking's rationale for this proclamation in favor of Space was that "life on Earth is at the ever-increasing risk of being wiped out by a disaster, such as sudden global warming, nuclear power, a genetically engineered virus, or other dangers we have not yet thought of." Hawking did not explain why humans in Space would not cause similar problems there. Another physicist remarked in response, "[Hawking] is certainly stepping outside his research domain" when speaking about space colonies.[1] A few months later Hawking told a BBC radio interviewer that "once we spread out into space and establish independent colonies, our future should be safe." He expressed his opinion that a *Star Trek*-style propulsion system would make space travel possible. "Science fiction has developed the idea of warp drive, which takes you instantly to your destination," adding, "unfortunately, this would violate the scientific law which says that nothing can travel faster than light."[2]

In November of 2006, President George W. Bush rekindled interest in manned space exploration by announcing that the United States should pursue plans to establish a permanent base at the moon's South Pole. It is not surprising that Space figures so importantly in our corporate cultural vision of the human future. After all, many of our media-inspired mental images of the future are set in that undefined realm known only as Space. Science and science fiction joined forces long ago to fix the idea of Space firmly in the Western imagination. We all are eye witnesses, via the skill of the special-effects artist, to spacecraft racing through space, epic battles in space, colonies well established on planets deep in space, lives lived out in the vacuum of space. Conquest of Space is the hallmark of the final human escape from the confines of Earth and all that it represents, including limitations on human knowledge.

Often religious images and language have been used to describe our relationship to Space. H. G. Wells wrote in his *New Worlds for Old* (1908) that one day humankind will "stand upon the earth as one stands upon a footstool, and laugh and reach out their hands amidst the stars." Carl Sagan's collaborator, and later his wife, Ann Druyan, commented on the messages the two helped send into space with the *Voyager* probes: "Those of us privileged to work on the making of the *Voyager* message did so with a sense of sacred purpose." She explained, "It was conceivable that, Noah-like, we were assembling the ark of human culture, the only artifact that would survive into the unimaginably distant future."[3] Because the probes and their carefully assembled messages were being launched into space, they took on sacred significance.

Whether we accept that in space exploration we will find salvation or the sacred, certainly many modern people accept the sentiment expressed in Gene Roddenberry's original *Star Trek* television series that space is "the final frontier," the last and ultimate domain of human exploration and conquest. For centuries now, space and science fiction have been inseparable. Into space, Jules Verne fired intrepid explorers from a gigantic cannon in *From the Earth to the Moon* in 1865, while from space came the devouring Martians of Wells's *War of the Worlds* in 1898. Into space the best of the human race escapes in the 1936 movie *Things to Come* (based on another Wells story), and from space the peace-loving alien of *The Day the Earth Stood Still* arrives in the classic 1951 film. Into space go the forty humans who will start a new civilization in the stylish 1955 film *When Worlds Collide*, and from the depths of space the destructive monsters of the 1996 blockbuster *Independence Day* descend on a hapless Earth. Into space are sent the ill-fated crew of *2001: A Space Odyssey* in 1968, and from space come the benevolent aliens of *Close Encounters* in 1977. Indeed, a dizzying traffic into and out of space has characterized science fiction since the seventeenth century, when Cyrano de Bergerac sent explorers up to the moon and the sun in the 1650s, and Bernard de Fontenelle imagined aliens descending from space to Earth in 1686.[4]

But space is vastly more than a "final frontier" in our modern scientific mythology, as is clearly evident in the *Star Trek* television series and movies themselves. Space is also a place for the resolution of ultimate questions, and for rendering more complex the important questions to which we thought we already had answers. For instance, in *Star Trek III: The Search for Spock* (1984), space is the setting for the creation of life on a dead planet, and for Mr. Spock's resurrection from death through a mysterious ritual on his home planet of Vulcan. Nor is space incidental to these fabulous activities; space is to the modern mind the proper setting for such wonders.

Space in science fiction is the location wherein, for unspecified reasons, deep spiritual questions are raised and, on occasion, provided definitive answers. Literally and metaphorically elevated, indeed suspended in the heavens, freed from the restraints of earthbound existence, physically closer to celestial sources of knowledge, space travelers enjoy a perspective that allows them to engage the transcendent and peer into the ultimate. Science-fictional astronauts regularly enjoy contact with beings farther along the biological and social evolutionary trails, and thus presumably in possession of truths unavailable to ordinary human beings sadly gravity-bound to their ancestral home-planet Earth.

Heaven, hell, life, death and even resurrection are issues to be managed in Space. In the climactic scenes of *Contact*, worm-hole traveler Jodi Foster finds herself in a celestial paradise, where she is reunited with what appears to be her deceased father. Is this an alien heaven? Other space travelers are catapulted into what can only be described as hell itself—as are the unfortunate space pioneers in the 1997 movie *Event Horizon*. They also meet deceased loved ones. The vast distances and extra dimensions of Space often seem to bring human beings into contact with friends or family members who have passed from this life. This theme marks the movie *Solaris* (1976, 1999) based on a Stanislav Lem novel by the same name. Or those presumed dead may be returned alive and unharmed to Earth from Space, as is the case in the closing scenes of Spielberg's *Close Encounters*. Here, in a latter-day resurrection marking the arrival of our saviors from Space, abductees emerge alive and unaged from the bowels of an alien ship, where presumably some have been kept for decades.

But it is not science-fiction writers alone who find space populated with those who have left earthly life. In the last chapter we saw that famed French astronomer Camille Flammarion explored the idea that the deceased might migrate from planet to planet in a reincarnational process. More recently, popular speculative scientific writer Gary Zukav has also remarked that souls of departed humans continue to evolve on other planets, an idea that caused great controversy when the deist Jacob Ilive proposed it in several speeches in 1740s London.[5] Mormon founder Joseph Smith also explored the possibility of postearthly life being pursued on other planets. Indeed, so pervasive is the idea that space and the deceased are somehow connected that it cannot clearly be said to belong to science fiction, science or religion. But it certainly is now well established as part of modern mythology.

The limitless vastness of Space, its endless emptiness, legitimates all manner of miracle. Space represents escape from earthly responsibility and from the constraints of time, energy, money, morality and even mortality. The distant planetary landscapes and high-tech spacecraft interiors of the science-fiction and scientific imaginations are the new geographies of human destiny. Not on Earth shall we achieve our evolutionary telos, but on all the planets of the universe and in all the gigantic vehicles floating freely in space. Indeed, in space we may become the saviors of that universe as we work to preserve it from slow but certain entropy.

Moreover, our dreams of space are easily transformed into a mythic quest for our own version of divinity. Space exploration may be justified in terms of scientific inquiry, but guided by the Myth of Space, the purpose of our pursuit of knowledge quickly becomes "not just science, but omniscience."[6] Space is to be conquered, as a children's book from 1960 unabashedly puts the goal of space exploration. With "permanent manned space stations, we will make efforts to fly farther away from earth—perhaps even to the vicinity of the Moon and the planets." Early efforts at spaceflight marked the beginning of "man's greatest challenge—the conquest of space."[7] As the American space program developed, the first people selected to be catapulted into space were idealized versions of ourselves. Despite the racial and ethnic diversity of one of the world's largest nations, the seven astronauts selected for the original Mercury missions were all relatively young white male military pilots with Anglo-Saxon surnames: Carpenter and Cooper; Glenn and Grissom; Slayton, Shepard and Schirra. Several were the sons of military officers, and popular books and magazine articles on these first astronauts told us their height, weight and even the color of their hair and eyes.[8] Why did space demand of us this kind of uniformity?

In the works of science fiction, the freedom of space has also meant moral license, unfettered scientific experimentation, religious exploration and escape from the limitations imposed by family, community and work. How strangely incongruous is the birthday message from mom and dad back on Earth being watched with insouciant half interest by a young astronaut on his way to Jupiter in Kubric and Clarke's *2001*. Earth is irrelevant in Space, along with birthdays, home, family and all other markers of a humanity trapped in the mundane existence of Earth.

Ironically, Earth is our home, our place of origin, and the setting in which the vast majority of us will live out our lives; yet according to the Myth, it is in Space where we will resolve human controversies, achieve limitless knowledge, discover our origins and our destiny. And perhaps most important, in Space we shall meet our divine deliverers, the extraterrestrials. Space has become the new heaven, complete with its own gods, its own highly evolved angels, and its distinctive forms of salvation. The Myth of Space has so completely captured the Western imagination over the past three centuries that it is now sufficient merely to claim to have been visited by beings from space, or to have visited space, in order to achieve *religious* credibility and have the right to speak of transcendent things with authority.

The Myth of Space is not of recent origin, nor has its propagation been limited to imaginative writers and popularizing scientists. Indeed, it shows up much earlier than we might expect and in some rather surprising places. This chapter examines several prominent sources and proponents of the Myth of Space, beginning in the eighteenth century and moving forward into our own. In these works we will witness the development of a modern mythic idea tied closely to scientific thought and propagated by many of our most popular products of mass media. In all of its cultural power, this Myth helped to propel the twentieth-century race into space. Today the myth remains a component in an emerging spirituality.

THOMAS PAINE: SPACE IN A SKEPTICAL AGE

The seventeenth and eighteenth centuries produced dozens of imaginative works about traveling to either the moon or the sun, many of them quite popular. During this period of rising skepticism about traditional religion, European readers were infatuated with space. The French writer Cyrano de Bergerac (1619-1655), a student of the skeptic Gassendi, was best known in his own day for his swashbuckling stories of space travel. And not only fictional journeys into space were shaping the Western imagination during the period; space and its possibilities were explored in scientific and religious works as well. Astronomers such as Christiaan Huygens in Holland published widely read scientific works on the stars and planets in the late seventeenth and early eighteenth centuries. More surprisingly, space was taking on religious significance as well. Two examples illustrate this rather surprising spiritual development in an age of unbelief.

Thomas Paine is best known today for his involvement as a pamphleteer in the American Revolution (1775-1783) and French Revolution (1789-1799). He was also a notorious critic of Christianity. But it appears that Paine was not without spiritual longings. Among his most influential works, the two-volume *Age of Reason* expresses how the writer's fervent devotion to "the infinity of space" filled him with religious awe.[9] Following a line of argument that had become commonplace by the late eighteenth century, Paine reasoned that because "no part of our earth is left unoccupied," the universe's many planets and stars were also home to intelligent residents.[10] And it seemed reasonable to Paine to assume that "the inhabitants of each of the worlds of which our system is composed enjoy the same opportunities of knowledge as we do."[11]

In keeping with the empirical spirit of the age, Paine claimed to be following science alone as he set out his hope in a universe filled with inhabited planets.[12] He even entertained the hope that this "fact" might be the foundation of a new and more-scientific religion. The prospect of humanity reaching out into space conjured up "the cheerful idea of a society of worlds," for Paine a vision more captivating than Christianity's "idea of only one world" no bigger than "twenty-five thousand miles." Paine asks, "What is this to the mighty ocean of space?"[13] For Paine, the Myth of Space enhanced human existence by situating us in a cosmos filled with innumerable inhabited planets, and thus holding out the possibility of a greatly expanded "society." Worshipful awe of Space and communion with its many inhabitants expanded human spiritual consciousness in a dawning scientific era, opening new realms of spiritual insight.

INVENTING SPACE AND SPACEFLIGHT

In the mid-nineteenth century, science-fiction writers such as the French master Jules Verne began to imagine something resembling actual spaceflight. No longer were individual humans carried into the void by geese (Godwin), the activity of the sun on dew drops (de Bergerac), or "in the spirit" (Emanuel Swedenborg). By the 1860s teams of people were being blasted into space in propelled vehicles resembling gigantic artillery shells, and eventually rockets.

As both the Myth of Space and available technology continued to develop, space was increasingly associated with human destiny. Permanent occupation of space, the "conquest of space," became the goal, not simply occasional visits to the moon or Mars. Space colonization was not originally a scientific idea, however, but rather a creation of the science-fiction imagination. Human residences in space began to be incorporated into science fiction with the publication of Edward Everett Hale's popular short story "The Brick Moon" in the December 1869 edition of *Atlantic Monthly*. Hale's story was simple and not particularly scientific. He imagined a hollow brick satellite two hundred feet in diameter "hurled into orbit, as an aid to navigation, by the use of two giant fly-wheels made of oak and pine hooped with iron." By accident, workmen living with their wives in the brick satellite while it is being constructed are sent into space, where they "raised food, communicated with Earth, and survived."[14] So influential was the story on visions of humanity in space that it is listed in the NASA timeline of important events in space history.

Not until the 1890s did the Russian scientist Konstantin Tsiolkovsky suggest the basic mechanics of the modern rocket. The ideas of space travel and space colonization, the inventions of fiction writers, now began to receive support from well-regarded scientists. The combination of vividly imagined fiction and scientific endorsement rendered the Myth of Space one of the most powerful narratives of the modern era. By 1900, Space was here to stay: at the Pan-American Exposition of 1901, held in Buffalo, New York, more than 400,000 visited the Trip to the Moon exhibit, where they rode aboard the wooden spaceship Luna.

Science and science fiction regarding spaceflight came together, as they so often would, in a single person who became crucial to promoting the Myth that human destiny was involved with our permanent presence in space. Austrian rocket scientist Max Valier (1895-1930) was both a visionary scientist and an avid author of science-fiction works. Valier was deeply influenced by his reading of German rocket scientist Hermann Orberth's groundbreaking theoretical work *The Rocket into Interplanetary Space* (1923). Valier recognized the brilliance of Oberth's work, but he also realized that the public would have to be convinced of the merits and feasibility of spaceflight. Thus, he sought to explain Oberth's ideas in a fashion accessible to the general reading public. In 1924 Oberth himself helped Valier to publish his suggestively titled book *The Advance into Space*. Valier's book was an immediate success, going through six editions before 1930. Other essays and books followed, including *A Daring Trip to Mars* (in a journal, 1928; as a book, 1931).

Valier's ideas formed the basis for a series of popular science-fiction works in Germany. These books by author Reinhold Eichacker include *The Flight for the Gold, Panic,* and *The Ride into Nothingness.* Featuring their hero-scientist Walter Werndt, Eichacker's novels present Valier's rocketry theories as facts of the not-too-distant futrue, and rocket scientists as Germany's economic saviors for bringing gold back to Earth from distant planets. But Werndt was after larger prey—nothing less than "the secret of the primal substance" of which the universe is composed. This unknown substance would bring its discoverer unlimited power.[15] Eichacker portrayed Space as a font of rich resources for humanity, as well as a location in which transcendent questions could be resolved. With the introduction of the "mystery substance," power had also entered the space equation to stay. All that was lacking was the actual technology for human conquest and colonization of space.

John Desmond Bernal (1901-1971) is ranked among the most brilliant intellectual figures of the twentieth century, a modern thinker who was as committed to scientific inquiry as he was opposed to traditional religion. Born in Ireland and educated in mathematics and science at Cambridge, Bernal is most famous for his development of x-ray crystallography and discovering the structure of graphite. In addition to his scientific work, which would have been sufficient to ensure his lasting fame, Bernal was a widely known political activist in Britain, and he helped plan the D-Day invasion of Normandy.

Bernal was also intensely interested in the exploration and colonization of space. In 1929, near the time of the British Planetary Society's founding, he suggested a structure that came to be known as the Bernal Sphere, an updated version of Hale's brick moon. The sphere was a habitat intended for long-term stays in space and the foundation for permanent space colonies. Bernal was motivated by more than scientific curiosity. He believed that the exploration of space would provide humanity with a sense of the limitless, a concept without which true intellectual development was not possible.

Indeed, in his dreams of Space, Bernal had something even grander in mind than intellectual development: human destiny itself. Human beings represent a force for change in the cosmos, and space is the launching pad for our transformative work. Bernal argued that humanity could not be satisfied with "repeating itself in circles," rehearsing the same old earthbound philosophical and religious ideas. Instead, we require "a real externalization" that can occur only "in the transforming of the universe" and thus of ourselves.[16] This ultimate "externalization" of both our thinking processes and our technological practices could only take place in Space. For Bernal, space colonization was a crucial component in realizing human destiny and cosmic transformation. To achieve this vision would require permanent human outposts in space.

But in his many popular essays about space, Bernal may have been passing

off a species of science fiction as scientific musings. He used his credibility as
a scientist to cover a literary sleight of hand; science fiction masquerading as
science became, for Bernal, a rhetorical strategy to sway the public. Bernal's
influence was greatest during the period when the British titans of science
fiction—H. G. Wells, Olaf Stapledon, C. S. Lewis, Arthur C. Clarke—were the
most active. Indeed, it was the widely discussed suggestion that human destiny
involved extending our influence throughout the galaxy—virtually a religious
vision for intellectuals such as Bernal and J. B. S. Haldane—that prompted
the Christian apologist Lewis to write his own science-fiction stories. Lewis, a
literary scholar and author of note, recognized the power of science fiction, in
the hands of a Wells or a Stapledon, to persuade the public to embrace a new
spiritual vision. Fallen humanity expanding endlessly into space with the goal
of redeeming the cosmos was just such a vision. Lewis began writing his own
space adventures as a response to what he perceived as the dangerous direction of Western scientific thought.

DESTINATION MOON (1950)

Science fiction as a rhetorical strategy has not been limited to popular books
by scientists and science-fiction authors, however. Hollywood produced
more than 130 science-fiction films in the 1950s alone. In the important
1950 movie *Destination Moon*, American audiences were introduced to the
concept of flight to the moon, complete with detailed explanations of how
rockets work and how a ship could reach and return from the moon. The
movie, which the *New York Times* listed as one of the year's ten best, was
an extended cinematic promotion for space exploration. After years of Buck
Rogers and Flash Gordon serials, scores of radio science-fiction broadcasts,
and thousands of pulp space stories published in the magazines of Gernsback
and Campbell, a 1949 poll still revealed that only 15 percent of the American
public thought that it would be possible to send people to the moon within
fifty years. Clearly, Americans were not yet convinced about Space as human
destiny; movies such as *Destination Moon* provided an important means of
accomplishing that goal.

Promotional materials built anticipation by announcing that production
of *Destination Moon* took two years. The resulting movie moved slowly; it
provided audiences with little action and no monsters from outer space. This

noteworthy departure from the usual science-fiction film fare was intentional: *Destination Moon* was argument rather than entertainment. The goal was to persuade the American public that our collective human future was in Space. Strangely, the film included a brief cartoon segment that featured Woody Woodpecker and in simple terms explained the basic concepts of rocketry. The movie was popular with audiences, and the phrase "Destination Moon" entered the American vocabulary to be used as a name for later documentary films, books about the space program and even an LP by the singing Ames Brothers in 1956.

Destination Moon was based on *Rocketship Galileo*, a short novel by science-fiction author Robert Heinlein, and Heinlein assisted with the film's writing and production. Hungarian-born producer George Pal spared no expense in ensuring that *Destination Moon* was authentic down to the last detail. Thus he recruited German-Hungarian rocket scientist Hermann Oberth to help design the movie's rocket ship.

This was not Oberth's first venture into science fiction. Earlier in Germany, he had worked with Fritz Lang as a technical consultant for the epic 1929 spaceflight film, *Die Frau im Mond (The Woman in the Moon)*. Lang's silent movie was an early effort to convince the German public of the feasibility of spaceflight; hence, rocket engineers were hired to design the movie's central feature, an extraordinarily detailed and futuristic spaceship. Lang's film cap-tivated the imagination of seventeen-year-old science prodigy Wernher von Braun (1912-1977)—a student of Oberth's and his assistant in designing the movie's rocket—inspiring the young man to pursue his history-making inter-est in rocketry. Von Braun would have a Woman in the Moon logo painted on the base of his V-2 rockets.

Other familiar names in the 1950s science-fiction and science matrix were also involved in making *Destination Moon*, including the famous art-ist and architect Chesley Bonestell. Woody Woodpecker, sharing the screen with a rocket designed by leading scientists and sets prepared by one of the world's most famous artists, would indeed be inexplicable if it were not for the fact that Heinlein, Pal, Oberth and Bonestell were pulling out all the stops to convince the American public of the need to aggressively pursue space exploration.

Destination Moon's purpose was persuasion, and it was highly effective.

The potential for science fiction to promote scientific projects and even to influence governmental policy was beginning to be fully understood. In several important cases, *Destination Moon* also influenced young people to pursue careers in the growing space-exploration industry. For instance, the NASA website records that space-shuttle payload specialist Roger Crouch made the decision to become an astronaut following a childhood viewing of the film. The NASA account states: "His interest in space flight began when he was in elementary school and watched a movie called *Destination: Moon.*" Crouch "was excited by the movie's fictional story of a trip to the moon, almost 20 years before people actually made it there." *Destination Moon* ends with the screen announcing: THIS IS THE END OF THE BEGINNING. Crouch comments, "I wanted to do something in my life that would be a lot of fun, so I wanted adventure. And when I saw that—'The End of the Beginning'—that just registered in my mind, that this really is the new frontier, space travel. So I said, 'I want to be part of that.'"[17]

With its realistic moonscapes, courtesy of Bonestell, its no-nonsense script and its patient explanations of rocketry, *Destination Moon* played an important role in moving spaceflight from pulp-fiction fantasy to feasible science in the public mind. Crouch was not the only one convinced by what he had just witnessed. Pal and Bonestell would team up at least one more time in the effort to promote the developing Myth of Space.

THE *COLLIER'S* SYMPOSIUM ON THE CONQUEST OF SPACE

A short time after the release of *Destination Moon*, Bonestell provided what would become legendary illustrations for an extremely popular series of articles that von Braun himself wrote for *Collier's Weekly* magazine between 1952 and 1954. In fact, the editor of *Collier's*, famed journalist Gordon Manning (1917-2006), introduced the two men for the purpose of a collaborative series on space exploration for the magazine. The eight *Collier's* illustrated essays constitute a remarkably effective effort on the part of scientists, journalists and artists to persuade the public to embrace an idea it was disinclined to accept—that spaceflight to the moon and distant planets was both possible and necessary.

The March 22, 1952, issue dubbed the series the "*Collier's* Symposium on the Conquest of Space," a name that at the time would have been reminiscent of the serialized *Flash Gordon Conquers the Univese*, which appeared in theaters only a few years earlier, in 1940. A more accurate title for the committee of eminent scientists, journalists and artists making up the Symposium might have been The Committee to Render Space Exploration Credible to a Dubious Public.[18] The *Collier's* project was a major factor in bringing the Myth of Space into the homes of millions of Americans just before the advent of television and its even-greater capacity for both visualization and the conditioning of public expectations.

Recruiting such scientific luminaries as Professor Fred Whipple, chair of the Department of Astronomy at Harvard, and with the full participation of von Braun himself, the *Collier's* essays described in exciting detail the process of flying to the moon in rocket ships, with a stop along the way at a permanent space station or space wheel. Even von Braun's old teacher from Germany, the great popularizer of science Willy Ley, was recruited for the *Collier's* project. One of the early installments was titled "Man on the Moon: Scientists Tell How We Can Land There in Our Lifetime." The March 22, 1952, issue explained how a space station would be built and staffed, complete with detailed cutaway drawings of its interior. "We will build a wheel-shaped structure 250 feet in diameter, . . . with a crew of 80," wrote von Braun. The wheel and the moonship appearing in *Collier's* were duplicates of the ships the public would see in the movie version of *Conquest of Space* in 1955. New York's Hayden Planetarium contributed its own persuasive power to the project of making space exploration appear inevitable and imminent by constructing a thirteen-foot-high detailed replica of von Braun's moonship for the public to visit. The rocket was "designed for Collier's by renowned rocket expert Wernher von Braun."[19] There was simply no escaping the encroachment of Space and its burgeoning mythology on daily life and thought.

Bonestell's photo-realistic illustrations were stunning, allowing the public to "see" von Braun's rockets in full color as they hung majestically in the exotic realm of Space. Space itself took on a life and look of its own: colorful planets tilted at dizzying angles in a sea of dazzling stars, while astronauts worked meaningfully in spectacular machines. Even the cartoons that *Collier's* ran in the same issues were designed to make the point that space exploration was a matter of human destiny, much like Columbus's own voyages of discovery. Indeed, one cartoon shows three spaceships heading to an unknown destination and labeled *Nina, Pinta* and *Santa Maria.*[20] *Collier's* serialized science-fiction stories by writers such as Ray Bradbury and Kurt Vonnegut during the same period.[21] *Collier's Weekly*, with a distribution of more than three million and an estimated readership of more than twelve million, was a major media force of the early 1950s.

Von Braun, brought to the United States following World War II through a secret program called "Operation Paperclip," eventually directed the Marshall Space Flight Center. Because of his involvement with the Nazis, von Braun was a controversial figure. The 1960 Columbia Studios film *I Aim at the Stars*, starring Curt Jürgens as von Braun, was intended to adjust public attitudes about the great scientist. One dubious reviewer who referred to von Braun as "the fabricator of the Nazis' deadliest missiles" also accused the film of being "conspicuously fuzzy" about the ethical issues surrounding von Braun.[22] Another suggested that the subtitle for *I Aim at the Stars* ought to have been *But Sometimes I Hit London*. Von Braun's rockets may have been responsible for the deaths of 67,000 citizens of that city. Nevertheless, in the eyes of many Americans, von Braun was transformed into a hero through the film. The *Collier's* pieces had an inestimable impact on public opinion about space exploration, and their impact sent shockwaves through American popular culture. Science-fiction author Andre Bormanis writes that von Braun's flare for public relations "attracted the attention of an even more successful showman—Walt Disney."

Starting in 1955, Disney invited von Braun to appear in three television films about manned spaceflight: *Man in Space* and *Man and the Moon* aired in 1955. The third, *Mars and Beyond*, was broadcast in 1957. The handsome von Braun was becoming a Hollywood celebrity and relished the role of Space's salesman. Later, von Braun assisted with designing the Trip to the Moon ride at Disney's Tomorrowland theme park.[23] Thus, the Myth of Space—a transcendent narrative announcing that human destiny was intertwined with realms beyond Earth—was persuasively presented to the American public well before President John F. Kennedy's famous challenge in his 1961 inaugural address. Kennedy called a nation to support a massive governmental project fueled by a dangerous international rivalry. But the West's spiritual conversion to faith in Space had already begun years before his speech.

CONQUEST OF SPACE
AND THE RELIGIOUS OBJECTION

The *Collier's* Symposium prepared the ground for another important Holly-wood contribution toward propagating the growing Myth of Space and refuting religious objections to that Myth. *Conquest of Space*, released in 1955, was also produced by Hungarian-born moviemaker George Pal and directed by Byron Haskin. In *Conquest of Space* five astronauts who think they are being trained for a mission to the moon find out that they are actually being sent to Mars. But problems ensue, largely due to the mission commander's religious convictions. The movie has been of continuing interest to historians of cinema because later directors freely borrowed from the Haskin vision of space. Scenes involving the two spacecraft in *Conquest of Space*—the same ones designed by von Braun for the *Collier's* pieces—are so reminiscent of similar scenes in Kubric's *2001* that the influence is unmistakable.

The lasting significance of *Conquest of Space* is due also to the movie's heavy-handed polemic quality. Viewers were exposed to a cinematic digest of several arguments in favor of human space exploration, especially the argument that Earth needs both the raw materials and extra real estate that space has to offer. Moreover, the central action and several statements by key figures in the film are intended to put to rest any religious objections to the project of space exploitation. Dismissed in the movie as backward, ill-informed and the products of unstable minds, religious reservations about space exploration receive harsh treatment and are counted as impediments to progress. The movie's principal figure, a daring space explorer, is overwhelmed by his religious convictions on the way to Mars. He actually tries to destroy himself and the rest of the crew—including his own son.

Conquest of Space was based on a 1949 nonfiction book by the same title, illustrated by Bonestell and written by German rocket scientist Willy Ley (1906-1969). Ley, a high profile proponent of space exploration in both Germany and the United States, did much to persuade the public that spaceflight was feasible and necessary. He had helped to found the famous German spaceflight organization *Verein für Raumschiffahrt* (VfR) in 1927, was one of von Braun's teachers, and wrote popular scientific works including *Journey into Space* (1926) and *The Possibility of Interplanetary Travel* (1928). After immigrating to the United States, he continued to write books promoting space exploration, including *Rockets: The Future of Travel Beyond the Stratosphere* (1944). But Ley is best known for *Conquest of Space.*

The film version of *Conquest of Space* is quite different from the original book from which much of its scientific material was drawn. The odd religious dementia of the movie's central character, General Merritt, was the screenwriters' effort to answer objections to space exploration raised by the popular Christian writer C. S. Lewis and expressed in both his science-fiction novels and his lengthy correspondence with Arthur C. Clarke. Lewis's own objections were in part a consequence of his reading of passages such as Psalm 115, which states, "The heavens are the LORD's heavens, but the earth he has given to human beings" (Psalm 115:16). Lewis was troubled by the increasingly popular vision of science-fiction writers who imagined an evolving humanity throwing itself out into space and ultimately claiming the entire universe for the human race. In *Conquest of Space*, the arguments between Christians and progressive thinkers are reduced to a simple contest between the maniacal religion of a benighted past and the sane science of an inevitable future. Science emerges as the clear winner. The devoutly religious General Merritt becomes increasingly unbalanced as the movie progresses, and he also develops a chemical addiction. Eventually his own son is forced to kill him or allow him to kill the rest of the crew. In this modern space fable, the son sacrifices his father in the name of a new generation's spiritual vision. Heaven, purged of religion, is transformed into Space.

THE PLANETARY SOCIETY:
SPACE EXPLORATION AND HUMAN NATURE

The Planetary Society was established in 1980 as a private effort to promote space exploration at a time when support for the American space program was lagging. Founded by Carl Sagan, Bruce Murray and Louis Friedman, the Planetary Society provides an example of how organizations, through their publicly available materials, seek to shape public attitudes and propagate new mythologies. The society's mission is "to inspire the people of Earth to explore other worlds, understand our own, and seek life elsewhere."[24] The Planetary Society's online justification for space exploration reflects a fully formed mythic account of humanity's relationship to space.

As with many sources on the topic, the argument for space exploration advanced by this prestigious group is based largely on human nature. Humans "in every age" express a "marvelous instinct" to explore. Once basic needs are met, humans "begin to create arts, to invent gods, to wonder and theorize about the universe." According to author James D. Burke,

> The line of descent from ancient legends to the modern quests of philosophy, religion, and science is direct and unequivocal. . . . It is a constant of humanity to reach toward the future, to want to visit the stars, to want to know itself. It seems that this drive is just something contained in the human mind—or, if you wish, placed by a Creator in the fabric of space-time where that mind resides. . . . [Why do humans] strive to understand our place in the heavens and seek other intelligences out there?[25]

An "instinct" to explore, including the desire to probe space, is here assumed to be innate in humans. Thus, the exploration of space is a natural drive: to thwart it would be wrong, unnatural and thus harmful. It is as basic and undeniable as our tendency "to create arts," "to invent gods" and to "seek other intelligences out there." Burke adds this intriguing anthropomorphic note to his argument: "Yes, the cosmos is calling." He then poses a crucial question: "How do we sophisticated humans reply?" We could simply "spend all our energies, skills, and resources on maintaining our beautiful home planet, relieving misery, educating each other, improving our civic behavior," but this kind of activity would simply ignore that ringing cosmic telephone.

Burke is not convinced by the argument from earthbound social responsibility. "In all parts of the world, including many places whose living standard is relatively low, humans share dreams of a wider future. Governments, however, are sometimes unresponsive to this fundamental human urge. In trying to respond to short-term crises, they lose sight of the deeper purposes of civilization." Burke argues as if even the Earth's poor are motivated by the Myth of Space, eager for their obtuse governments to recognize their desire to see space exploration move forward into a "wider future" so that the human urge to "seek intelligences out there" would be fulfilled.

Fortunately, there exists a counterweight to the inertia of "obtuse governments" such as the one that canceled funding for the SETI project in 1992. "The Planetary Society was founded to remedy this situation," the problem of lagging government support for space exploration. "In 1980 our

founders, Carl Sagan, Bruce Murray, and Louis Friedman, had a clear reason for launching the Society. They believed that people were ahead of their
governments in realizing the long-term importance of reaching out into the
starry void."

The emphasis on public demand for space exploration in Burke's document
amounts to an *ad populum* appeal that trumps the reluctance of governments
and the arguments of do-gooders who would divert funds to the poor. The
driving human sense, shared around the world, is that this simply has to be
done: Space must be explored. "Events soon proved [the founders] right. The
society grew explosively," writes Burke. "Only three years after its founding, it
was the world's largest space-advocacy organization." Members are provided
access to such information as "the *facts* about humanity's drive to explore the
Sun's realm, find planets of other stars, and seek other intelligences in the cosmos, but also the wonder, the mystery and the fun of responding to that drive"
(emphasis added).

Burke's argument is rooted in human nature, the nature of the cosmos, and
the relationship between the two. To this he adds a fundamentally moral or
spiritual argument, an argument from an internal, intuitive sense—though not
one shared by everyone—that exploring space is only "right." Burke writes:

> We deep-space explorers know that it is right for us to go on striving outward.
> We cannot articulate reasons that will satisfy everyone, and we do not know
> what we shall find. But we do know that we are part of some natural process, life
> seeking self-knowledge, life seeking other life. The Planetary Society gives us
> one way to express this ancient human impulse. We shall continue.[26]

The language of this Planetary Society document is strikingly religious
in tone, but without reference to God. A deep human impulse to seek other
life—timeless, immutable and fundamentally moral in nature—drives us out
of ourselves and into the cosmos. An undeniable natural process is at work,
even among the world's poor who might suffer; it is something built into
the essence, woven into the fabric of our being by some power greater than
ourselves. All of us are responding to a call from the cosmos. Our reply to
this call is creative, joyful, world-changing, worshipful. Governments may
oppose, unbelievers misunderstand, and reasons fail to convince, but "we
shall continue." Can there be any clearer evidence that we are in the presence

of a new religious quest, of a Myth so powerful that it claims universal allegiance transcending personal circumstance, national boundaries and even reason itself?

Gene Roddenberry, creator of the original *Star Trek* television series, is quoted on this Planetary Society website: "Why are we now traveling into space?" he asks. "Why indeed did we trouble to look past the next mountain?" Again, human nature is fulfilled through space exploration. The Planetary Society has been a major backer of the SETI project. On their webpage devoted to SETI, they rhetorically ask: "Could humans be the only intelligent beings in all the vastness of the universe? Or are we just one humble race, a member of a vast intergalactic fraternity of advanced civilizations?" Are these the only options, either to be alone in the universe, or to be in the awe-inspiring presence of "advanced civilizations" on other planets? Apparently so; and if so, we are really missing the boat into Space. Which alternative sounds more "fun and creative"? Again, as in the writing of speculative scientists, the science-fiction language of this document is palpable: "vast intergalactic fraternity of advanced civilizations," "homeworld," "deep-space explorers," "other intelligences in the universe."

SETI, according to the website, "is the scientific quest to answer these great unknowns." Religion certainly has tried to answer some of the same great questions. What makes SETI scientific is not the *absence* of propelling myths—for those are clearly at the forefront in SETI—but the *presence* of telescopes. That the quest for Space is religious in nature is beyond doubt. Nothing short of world transformation, reminiscent of J. D. Bernal's universal transformation, is at stake. "As of now all we have are questions, but we know that the answers, when they come, could transform our world." Since "the dawn of human consciousness," the society affirms, we have been asking, "Is anybody out there?"[27]

In addition to a number of well-regarded scientists, the Planetary Society Advisory Council includes such luminaries as astronaut Buzz Aldrin; science fiction author Ray Bradbury; scientist and science-fiction author David Byrne; astronaut Franklin Chang-Diaz; Arthur C. Clarke; Project Ozma founder and SETI Institute president Frank Drake; actor Robert Picardo, who appeared in one of the *Star Trek* movies; actor John Rhys-Davies; and science-fiction author Kim Stanley Robinson.

JAMES CAMERON:
FROM DEEP SEA TO DEEP SPACE

James Cameron is one of the most famous and successful directors in Hollywood. His blockbuster *Titanic* is the highest grossing film of all time and won eight Academy Awards in 1997. Earlier in his career, Cameron had written and directed such science-fiction classics as *Terminator 2* (1984), *Aliens* (1986) and *The Abyss* (1989). Cameron's interest in science fiction goes back to his college days. His first film, made as a student project, the twelve-minute-long *Xenogenesis* shows astronauts searching space for a place "to begin the cycle of creation again." Cameron has been searching for that place ever since.

Cameron's 2005 film for the Disney studios and Walden Media, *Aliens of the Deep*, presents itself as a documentary about life in the deeper reaches of the Earth's seas. The film is actually an argument for exploring space in search of life and its origins. Publicity for the movie reports that director Cameron was "inspired by concepts from the field of astrobiology," which is defined rather optimistically as "the study of life on other worlds." "Cameron explores the idea that the bizarre creatures living in the extreme environments found on the ocean floor might provide a blueprint for what life is like elsewhere in the universe."[28]

Astrobiology has been a focus of the NASA space program from its very inception in 1958. The idea of discovering life on other planets provided considerably greater public appeal than military applications of spaceflight. Indeed, the promotional literature for *Aliens of the Deep* indicates that director Cameron "is joined in the journey by a team of young marine biologists and NASA researchers who share his interests and excitement as they consider the correlation between life under water and the life we may one day find in outer space." Of particular importance here is the last word of the sentence: "space." Diving to the bottom of an ocean is a great adventure in itself and certainly can provide clues about the great variety of life-forms on Earth. But what does this adventure have to do with travel into space and in particular with discovering life in space? And yet, audiences are assumed to understand the connections immediately. "This adventure brings the audience face-to-face with what it might be like to travel far into Space and encounter life on other worlds," proclaim the promotional materials.

"These deep-ocean expeditions always seem like space missions to me," states Cameron, an avid deep-sea explorer. "So why not combine outer space and inner space? Sure, we'll take marine biologists, but why not take astrobi-ologists and space researchers?" We may discover "extremophiles very similar to the ones from our own planet in subterranean aquifers on Mars or on the ice moons of Jupiter."[29]

As the film eventually reveals, Cameron's hope is that a space mission will be sent to Jupiter's icy moon Europa. "How are we going to explore Europa?" Cam-eron asks, looking forward to "an expedition that might not take place for an-other twenty years or so."[30] Given his interest in astrobiology, "Cameron worked with researchers at NASA and the Jet Propulsion Laboratory (JPL) to find a proj-ect that would not only make an entertaining film but [also] bring the latest advances in the search for extraterrestrial life to audiences around the world."[31] We might be excused for wondering how we would recognize an "advance" in the search for extraterrestrial life. Nevertheless, Cameron applauds the scien-tists who are "working on the great questions of extraterrestrial life."[32]

Based on the discovery of colonies of sea life near deep ocean heat vents, *Aliens of the Deep* hypothesizes that Europa might be hiding life beneath a thick layer of ice covering extensive oceans. What specific goal justifies such extravagant and expensive projects in space, particularly given that there is no evidence that life would be discovered on one of Jupiter's frozen moons? The answer suggested in *Aliens of the Deep* is that, through space exploration, the human race might come to understand "what it is all about." In space we may discover answers to deep and ancient questions. The very questions that reli-gious faith has traditionally sought to answer are now the questions that sci-entific mythologies purport to address. Interestingly, Cameron does not leave the nature of life in Europa's oceans entirely to our imaginations. Indeed, the movie's closing scenes portray humans making contact with what appear to be highly intelligent sea-dwelling aliens beneath the ice of this ancient Jovian moon. These aliens closely resemble the benevolent alien deep-sea residents of Cameron's 1989 hit, *The Abyss*, who also seem to have something to tell us about the larger mysteries. Once again, the products of our mass media have blurred the lines between science, science fiction and the spiritual.

CONCLUSION

Our fascination with Space continues unabated. Recently chief NASA adminis-trator Mike Griffin announced that "our road to Mars goes through the Moon."

Making an odd distinction, Griffin is reported as affirming that "space exploration, not science, is the primary reason for returning to the Moon."[33] If space exploration is not science, then what is it? Apostles of the Myth of Space are certainly still present, and their pronouncements are no less certain than in past decades. For example, Professor J. Richard Gott III (b. 1947) of Princeton University has recently written, "Self-sustaining colonies in space would provide us with a life insurance policy against any catastrophes that might occur on Earth, a planet covered with the fossils of extinct species." He adds, "The goal of the human space-flight program should be to increase our survival prospects by colonizing space." Professor Gott believes that "since time is short, we should concentrate on establishing the first self-supporting colony in space as soon as possible." This is because the "existence of even one self-supporting colony in space might as much as double the long-term survival prospects of our species—by giving us two independent chances instead of one."[34]

Mars would be a likely place to begin. The so-called Mars Direct program proposed by another scientist, Robert Zubrin, thus plans: "Rather than bring astronauts back from Mars, we might choose to leave them there to multiply, living off indigenous materials. We want them on Mars. That's where they benefit human survivability."[35] Just as the beleaguered mission director of the *Rocketship XM* (1950) announces in the movie's closing lines that space exploration may bring "the salvation of our own world," Professor Gott and many others still advocate for a form of human salvation by casting ourselves out into space. Nevertheless, as others report, "the space community is painfully aware of the disappointing performance of the International Space Station, now circling the earth with little scientific value to show for its $100-plus billion cost."[36] But more to the point, survival is not salvation, and distance is not hope. No matter how long the human race survives, it will remain in a state of profound spiritual need. And no matter how far we cast ourselves from the Earth, we will come no closer to God.

But will we come closer to E.T.? Much of the initiative in contemporary space exploration comes from private entrepreneurs such as real estate magnate Robert T. Bigelow. Bigelow has already established a vast research facility in Nevada, and developed a prototype space station. His motivation is rooted in family reports of UFO sightings which he heard as a child. Bigelow has interviewed more than 230 people who claim to have seen UFOs or encountered extraterrestrials. He has also provided millions of dollars to help found the National Institute for Discover Science which investigates alien abduction accounts and other paranormal phenomena. The logo on Bigelow Aeronautics staff uniforms is the now familiar alien face.[37]

Sir Martin Rees, perhaps the world's leading astrophysicist and the Astronomer Royal of Great Britain, is also an avid advocate of space exploration and colonization. Because of "the ever-present slight risk of a global catastrophe," humans ought to be establishing colonies in space. "Humankind will remain vulnerable so long as it stays confined here on Earth," he writes. "Once self-sustaining communities exist away from Earth—on the Moon, on Mars, or freely floating in space—our species would be invulnerable to even the worst global disasters."[38] Yet Rees also believes that the greatest chance of a global disaster resides in the recklessness of human beings, something escape to Space does not change.

Finally, Carl Sagan held a similar view regarding space, writing that courageous exploration marked "the nations and epochs" exhibiting "the greatest cultural exuberance." Space holds out this possibility today, especially if that space brings encounters with higher cultures and thus "contact with new things, new ways of life, and new modes of thought unknown to a closed culture, with its vast energies turned inward."[39]

Space as human survival, Space as a font of resources, Space as spiritual expansion, Space as destiny, Space as a new heaven. Despite the enormous practical and ethical issues involved in establishing, sustaining and choosing the residents of space colonies, the idea has more—and more prominent—advocates now than perhaps ever before. And yet, what clearly have not changed are the humans who would be sent into Space and the humans who would do the sending. Why space should provide the answers to our woes is seldom clearly explained, and when it is, the reasoning seems to be driven by a mythical view of space suggesting that once we are there, we will know what to do. Given the history of human colonization of remote spots on this planet, one wonders why such confidence exists in our moral success in space. Spiritual fatigue is engendered by contending with intractable problems here on Earth, but looking to Space will neither solve those problems nor provide the solace we seek. Such comfort and direction are found in responding to the call of the Creator rather than to the call of the cosmos.

5

THE MYTH OF
THE NEW HUMANITY

Man, unconscious at first, begins now, in an individual here
and an individual there, to realize his possibilities
and dream of the greatness of his destiny.
A new phase of history is near its beginning.

H. G. WELLS

We will then be cyborgs, and from that foothold in our brains,
the nonbiological portion of our intelligence
will expand its powers exponentially.

RAY KURZWEIL

So God created humankind in his image, in the image of God
he created them; male and female he created them. . . .
God saw everything that he had made, and indeed, it was very good.

GENESIS 1:27, 31

Arthur C. Clarke is among the most respected and influential authors of
science fiction, with a career spanning more than five decades. In the 1950s,
Clarke's earliest stories, such as *Against the Fall of Night*, *Childhood's End*
and "The Sentinel," set a high standard of scientific integrity and solid story-
telling for an emerging popular genre. Though he is the author of dozens of

novels, Clarke is perhaps best known for an epoch-making screenplay that he authored with director Stanley Kubric for the movie *2001: A Space Odyssey* (1968). Based loosely on ideas that Clarke had explored in earlier works, *2001* imagined unidentified extraterrestrials guiding and tracking human evolution by means of mysterious black obelisks. In the movie's climactic closing scenes, a lone astronaut is selected, apparently without his consent, to take the next step in human progress toward some unspecified end point. At movie's end, with the triumphant strains of Richard Strauss's tone poem *Also sprach Zarathustra* playing appropriately in the background, a human fetus is pictured floating in space, symbol of humanity's birth into something grander and more highly evolved; something worthier of Space and the Future than the current specimens.

In a 1997 sequel, the novel *3001: The Final Odyssey*, Clarke hints at an even more "advanced" humanity, now disembodied and virtually divine. "Now they were Lords of the Galaxy, and could rove at will among the stars. . . . Though they were freed at last from the tyranny of matter, they had not wholly forgotten their origin, in the warm slime of a vanished sea."[1] Such themes in Clarke's work harken back to his earliest forays into the field of science fiction. In his early novel *Against the Fall of Night*, Clarke imagines an advanced human race ready to enter the universal drama on a level with the most highly evolved races to be found anywhere in Space. Humankind "could live forever, if he wished." Traveling "into the great spaces of the Galaxy," the human race "would meet as an equal the races of the worlds from which he had once turned aside. And he would play his full part in the story of the Universe."[2]

Arthur C. Clarke helped to popularize one of the more persistent myths of the modern age, and perhaps the most dangerous of our scientific mythologies: the Myth of the New Humanity. Crafted by science, envisioned in dreams of "conscious evolution," and propagated in the narratives of science fiction and speculative science, the New Humanity represents a secular hope for individual and societal salvation. As Seraphim Rose has written, "The center of the science-fiction universe (in place of the absent God) is . . . man as he will 'become' in the future."[3] This is the future-human of science and science fiction, a product of biotechnology and computer-brain interaction, the goal toward which life on Earth has been striving from the beginning. As such, the Myth of the New Humanity stands in sharp contrast to—perhaps as a counterfeit of—the Christian vision of a new human race spiritually transformed by the redemptive activity of God.

In the Myth of the New Humanity, the human race *evolves* progressively upward toward spiritual as well as physical transformation, or toward absorption into something even grander—a Cosmic Mind, a Conscious Universe, The One. Our evolutionary path takes us off our home planet and out toward the stars. Clarke did not invent the myth; it was given perhaps its greatest expression in Stapledon's *Last and First Men* (1930) and *Star Maker* (1937), is present even in some of the works of H. G. Wells, and is foreshadowed in Mary Shelley's *Frankenstein* (1818). The idea of a coming humanity persists in popular fiction. Science-fiction novelist and historian Brian Aldiss writes that the evolution of the human race into more advanced forms "remains one of the staples of SF."[4] The strong Darwinian impulse behind the Myth is clear and has historical roots. For instance, Wells in the 1880s was a student of the famous scientist Thomas H. Huxley, who was a personal friend and defender of the reclusive Charles Darwin. For Huxley and other Victorian intellectuals, human spiritual and physical evolution provided the foundation of the next great spiritual movement of the human race, for a new faith in Nature, which would displace Christianity. Shelley's inspiration for Frankenstein was an even earlier Darwin, Charles's grandfather Erasmus Darwin, who had propounded an early theory of evolution in works popular at the beginning of the nineteenth century.

Huxley's own grandson, Sir Julian Sorrel Huxley (1887-1975), would develop the idea of human progress through technologically assisted "conscious evolution" in his many books, essays and radio talks, dubbing it "Transhumanism" in his 1957 book *New Bottles for New Wine*.[5] Today The World Transhumanist Association, founded by Oxford University philosophers Nick Bostrom and David Pearce, states that it supports "the ethical use of technology to expand human capacities" and "the development of and access to new technologies that enable everyone to enjoy better minds, better bodies and better lives."[6] Present humanity is described as a "relatively early stage" of human development, with a more advanced humanity just over the horizon.

Also reflecting a hope in a scientifically engineered New Humanity, the Immortality Institute for Infinite Lifespans (ImmInst) exists "to conquer the blight of involuntary death." Founded by Bruce Klein and Ben Goertzel, the organization assumes that "the prospect of conscious post-death survival of the spiritual sort is improbable and non-reliable," and thus rejects "spiritual immortality" as having an "unfounded nature." The Institute's vision of a technologically achieved immortality is shaped by thinkers such as Dr. Aubrey de Grey, best known for his Strategies for Engineered Negligible Senescence (SENS).[7] The ImmInst enjoys significant financial support from figures such as PayPal cofounder Peter Thiel. In a similar vein, German philosopher Peter Sloterdijk has recently roused controversy with his claim that human beings "encounter nothing strange when they expose themselves to further creation and manipulation, and they do nothing perverse when they change themselves autotechnologically," because such operations occur "on so high a level of insight into the biological and social nature of man" that they become "coproductions with evolutionary potential."[8]

THE *ÜBERMENSCH* ON THE ESCALATOR

Evolution by means of natural selection was the nineteenth century's most powerful idea, and the gifted young science-fiction writer Wells emerged as evolution's greatest mythmaker. Wells's own philosophy moved in the direction of Nietzsche's superman, as did the thinking of other artistic luminaries such as George Bernard Shaw. In 1921 Shaw published the five plays that make up the *Back to Methuselah* series, his "Pentateuch," in which the eccentric Irish playwright imagined a superior human race to follow the present one. Christian apologist G. K. Chesterton wrote of his friend Shaw's disappointment with the public's unwillingness to embrace scientific progress as a source of spiritual hope: "If man, as we know him, is incapable of the philosophy of progress, Mr. Shaw asks, not for a new kind of philosophy, but for a new kind of man."[9]

Mary Midgley has coined the phrase "the Escalator Myth" to refer to the idea that humanity is riding an evolutionary escalator smoothly, progressively, ever upward toward some as yet only imagined state of perfection.[10] Moreover, this evolutionary escalator eventually will take us—or our robotic doubles—off this planet and out to the stars. Thus, this powerful myth dovetails in modern thought with the Myth of Space. No one "with a knowledge of the implications of modern physics," wrote Wells, "can believe that life is necessarily limited to this planet for ever."[11] Evolution is the engine of our destiny, and that destiny is the limitless expansion of a New Human race into Space. Perhaps because of this connection between the two powerful myths, William Shatner, the actor who played Captain James T. Kirk in the original *Star Trek* television series, was a keynote speaker at the 2007 World Transhumanist Association meeting in Chicago. The third day of the three-day conference was devoted entirely to the topic of the new humanity in space. Topics included Outer Space: Beyond the Planet, Future Humans, Colonizing Outer Space, Space Tourism and Future Civilizations. The title of the conference also linked the mythologies and suggested a spiritual dimension to the gathering as well, "Transhumanity Saving Humanity: Inner Space to Outer Space."[12]

Toward what specific future form is human evolution tending? Suggestions have included two or more divergent human species with specialized functions; beings with new senses to add to the original five; superhumans with enhanced intellect, beauty and physical strength; posthumans with exotic powers such as telepathy; blended mechanical-biological cyborgs; and disembodied virtual gods. Science fiction has a long history with such "progressive" understanding of human evolution, often portraying the current human race as but a step along the way to something grander. Though these future-human visions are not uniform endorsements of the New Humans, each does present dramatic changes to the human form and function as inevitable and desirable.

Adapted, enhanced or highly evolved humans are not new to science fiction; they have abounded in the genre for more than a century and a half, some versions predating Darwin. We have already noticed Shelley's highly intelligent and physically powerful monster in *Frankenstein* (1823), himself an enhanced human. J. D. Beresford's superintelligent Victor Stott in *The Hampdenshire Wonder* (1911) represents the "child prodigy as next step" theme in an early work of science fiction. Wells's *The Food of the Gods* (1904) explores what happens when, through a scientific experiment, a superior race of giants emerges out of the population of ordinary people. Philip Wylie introduces his own prototype scientifically enhanced superman in *Gladiator* (1930). E. E. "Doc" Smith explores the idea of selective breeding of humans to create a warrior race in his *Lensman* series of the 1940s and 1950s. Other examples include James Blish's adapted men in *The Seedling Stars* (1957), Robert Heinlein's "man from Mars" Valentine Michael Smith of *Stranger in a Strange Land* (1961), and the Mutants of *The X-Men* comics and movies. Science fiction has persistently prompted its readers to imagine what is next for humanity and to introduce possibilities.

The idea of a superhuman is not limited to the pages and screens of science fiction, however. The person of superior intellectual, spiritual or physical capacity has exercised extraordinary influence in a range of Western thought. French philosopher August Comte (1798-1857) believed that the future would produce "a new and more exalted type of human being."[13] Much modern thought about human advancement can be traced to the late nineteenth-century German philosopher Friedrich Nietzsche, who envisioned an *Übermensch*, or overman—the individual who rises above the run of ordinary humanity—in works such as his extremely popular *Thus Spoke Zarathustra* (1885). Nietzsche's idea—often treated as incapable of accurate interpretation, and equally often as forcefully persuasive—had a powerful effect over European and American intellectuals, lending scholarly credibility to a myth that was already much alive in the pages of literature.[14] Nevertheless, if supermen are possible, so are their opposites. The great English scientist and essayist J. B. S. Haldane referred to genetically determined "classes of mankind," fearing, along with many intellectual figures of his day, the destructive influence of too many "undermen."[15]

Also among the most influential thinkers of the nineteenth century, Herbert Spencer (1820-1903) envisioned inevitable social and biological progress. Though not a household name today, Spencer sold more books than any other author of nonfiction in his day. Inspired by the draconian economic theories of Thomas Robert Malthus (1766-1834), Spencer coined the famous phrase *survival of the fittest* and popularized the term *evolution* itself. He adopted the idea of social progress advanced by the utopian Romantic writer William Godwin (1756-1836) and the French naturalist Jean-Baptiste Lamarck (1744-1829). This idea came to be known as social evolution or social Darwinism. Spencer propagated a narrative in which the fittest are also the best—clearly not a conclusion derived strictly from scientific data. If we add the force of evolution, it is a short step to the conclusion that the best will give way to the Next Humans.

For many since Spencer, the vaguely formed idea of continual human evolutionary progress has been virtually a law of nature, even the dominant Rule of the Cosmos. As such, we are powerless to resist its operation; to attempt to impede evolutionary progress would constitute a sin against Nature. In the late nineteenth century, Francis Galton (1822-1911), founder of the eugenics movement and another grandson of Erasmus Darwin, insisted that the New Humans would emerge out of a process of selective breeding. Later, the eminent biologist Sir Julian Huxley, grandson of Thomas H. Huxley and the first head of UNESCO, argued that we must engineer the new humans ourselves in superlaboratories funded by massive government support. We exist solely so that one day they may exist; we are necessary only to ensure that they arrive and render us unnecessary. Whether they appear as the result of eugenics, as products of crossbreeding with aliens, or by means of simple evolutionary change—they are as inevitable as is the human colonization of Space.

There need be no preexistent creating God on a cosmic stage dominated by the New Humans. The cosmos is creating its own gods by the sure-fire method of evolution, now assisted by various technologies. In this way a crucial piece of a rising religious view has been put into place, a view in which our "highly evolved" descendants take both our place and the place of God. The following pages explore several important developments in the creation of the Myth of the New Humanity in speculative scientific writing as well as in popular science-fiction movies and books. This chapter considers how the mythic hope for New Humans clashes with Judeo-Christian conceptions of the human race.

FRANCIS GALTON
AND THE RELIGION OF EUGENICS

Francis Galton, cousin of Charles Darwin, was the English scientist who coined the word *eugenics*.[16] In books such as *Hereditary Genius* (1869), Galton applied Darwin's strategic analogy between evolution and animal husbandry to the breeding of humans. John W. Burrow writes, "One decided whom one wanted to breed and rear offspring and then tried to arrange the environment accordingly. It was akin to what Darwin in *The Origin* had called 'artificial selection.'" Such selective breeding of humans was to be overseen by "a rational elite."[17]

In his article "Hereditary Character and Talent" (1864-1865), Galton urged that if even a fraction of the money "spent on the improvement of the breed of horses and cattle" would be spent "for the improvement of the human race," we would soon create "a galaxy of genius." Indeed, a new religion would be born of this improved human race, complete with "prophets and high priests of civilization" rather than the current crop of "idiots" achieved "by mating cretins." The New Humans that "we might hope to bring into existence" are as far superior to the "men and women of the present day" as are "highly-bred varieties" of dogs to mere mongrels. Galton envisioned three stages of eugenics to achieve this goal. The first was the academic study of human improvement, the second involved introducing eugenics into law and policy, and the third occurred when eugenics was embraced "as a new religion." Humanity would save itself through scientific improvement of its genetic stock.

Galton considered that Darwin's *On the Origin of the Species* had fomented a religious as well as an intellectual revolution. *Origin*'s publication in 1859 affected Galton's "mental development" as it had "that of human thought generally," he wrote in a widely read series of essays published in *Macmillan's Magazine* in 1864 and 1865. The effect of natural selection was to "demolish a multitude of dogmatic barriers by a single stroke, and to arouse a spirit of rebellion against all ancient authorities whose . . . statements were contradicted by modern science." Galton made no secret of his own intellectual revolt against Christianity; he became a determined foe of the faith and a proponent of what he took to be its replacement: human improvement through eugenics.

We live, he wrote, "in want of master minds," and they can only be created through controlled breeding. The path to human perfection is to breed "talented men" with "talented women, of the same mental and physical characters as themselves," and to do this for "generation after generation" until we produce "a highly-bred human race, with no more tendency to revert to meaner ancestral types than is shown by our long-established breeds of race-horses and fox-hounds." The "law of natural selection" would "powerfully assist" in the improvement of the human race. Galton founded the Eugenics Society in 1907, an organization whose name was changed to the Galton Institute in 1989. Its members have included a number of British intellectual luminaries.[18] Though Charles Darwin never publicly endorsed Galton's program, Darwin's son Major Leonard Darwin (1850-1943) headed the Eugenics Society until 1928.

Progressive politicians and intellectual figures of the 1920s and 1930s often supported eugenics. The idea spread from England to other countries with the Galton Laboratory of National Eugenics established in 1907 and the First International Eugenics Congress convened in 1912. The powerful movement was especially strong in Germany, where in 1905 the German Society for Racial Hygiene was founded. Eugenics and "racial purification" often were related concerns in the early twentieth century—a formula for human disaster.

WELLS'S VISION OF A NEW HUMANITY

Freeman Dyson writes that H. G. Wells "was the first novelist to place his characters, with their individual passions and personalities, within the framework of biological evolution."[19] In his lifetime (1866-1946), Wells bridged the age of Victorian science fiction, of which he was the leading figure, and the era of the pulp magazines, to which he also contributed significantly. It is generally agreed that Wells was the greatest of the early science-fiction writers; some authorities consider him to be the greatest science-fiction author ever. John Clute calls Wells "the most important SF writer the genre has yet seen, although he never called his work Science Fiction."[20] The most famous of his more than eighty science-fiction books include *The Island of Doctor Moreau*, *The Invisible Man*, *War of the Worlds* and *The Time Machine*.

Wells's writing career began around 1885, when he was still a student at Thomas Huxley's Normal School of Science in London. Huxley was a towering scientific genius, and doubtless his views on evolution shaped those of the younger man. Wells reports that in his youth Huxley "became a great hero to me."[21] J. P. Vernier writes of "the impact of the theory of evolution" on Wells's thought. Evolution provided Wells "with the fundamental theme of his 'scientific romances' and of many of his short stories."[22] While attending Huxley's school, Wells published an early version of *The Time Machine* in the student newspaper. This story imagines the evolution of the human race into the far-distant future. Wells explored the theme of evolution in many of his works and, because he exercised such a profound influence on the genre, evolution became a major theme of later science fiction. As his long career progressed, his evolutionary views took a ruthless turn in the service of a new humanity. He became involved in political movements and tried to convince the British Labor Party to adopt his view of a coming "worldwide society of prosperity and peace."[23]

Huxley and his associates understood that Darwin's explosive theory had "pitchforked God out of the universe." England's intellectual elites were exuberant at the potential in Darwinism for both the death of traditional religion and the possibility of limitless human advancement. Indeed, progressive thinkers of the late nineteenth century saw in natural selection the seed of the next great spiritual movement. This new faith would rest, not on irrational revelation, but on the great Scientific Fact: life evolves, and as it evolves, it progresses. A morally and spiritually evolving human race would restore the sense of transcendence lost with God's disappearance from the cosmos. The New Humans themselves might provide the needed objects of worship for a new civilization founded on science. Wells envisioned the ultimate emergence of "a Titanic being" to which we are all "contributory units" and which will "eventually take hold of this planet."[24]

DEEP WELLS: BRIGHT GODS, DARK RACES

Wells's vision of the humanity to come is perhaps most passionately presented in a little-known book titled *The Food of the Gods* (1904). Two scientists discover a miraculous food that greatly enhances the size and strength of anything that consumes it—plant, animal or human. A race of giants emerges, and inevitable conflict ensues as the ordinary people see them as a threat. This is Wells's novel of "an astounding scientific experiment and the creation of a super-race," and Wells's sympathies are clearly on the side of the giants— a metaphor for all of humanity's great spirits who must contend against the "pigmies." As one character states, "You cannot have giants and pigmies in the same world together."[25] A spokesman for the giants refuses the offer of a homeland where giants can live out their lives in peace. The "food" would be destroyed, and there would be no more giants in the Earth. But the genie of racial superiority is out of the bottle, and "greatness is abroad . . . in the purpose of all things! It is in the nature of all things, it is part of space and time. To grow and still to grow, from first to last, that is Being, that is the law of life. What other law can there be?"[26] He declares, "We fight not for ourselves, but for growth, growth that goes on for ever." Then, clad in shining chain-mail armor and gesturing heroically toward Space, the giant shouts, "*There!*"[27] Space and the limitless expansion of a New Humanity are thus linked in this stirring narrative.

Biographer David Samuelson reports that Wells "had a need to be regarded as a significant social prophet."[28] At the very center of Wells's prophetic vision was evolution, with its "ultimate logic" that present humanity was passing off the scene in favor of something better. "Life," he writes in the semiauto-biographical *The World of William Clissold* (1926), "has been uninterruptedly progressive from its first beginning."[29] Above humanity stood something Wells referred to only as Mind, a powerful life force "in which exist science, history, and thought" and which "invades all our personalities." Humanity was slowly achieving an "adult mentality," which would be more "scientific and creative" than "anything that has gone before."[30] Evolving humanity will not remain fixed to this one planet, for "any one with a knowledge of the implications of modern physics" can no longer accept that life is "limited to this planet for ever."[31] Space is future-humanity's destiny.

But a sinister note haunted Wells's fanfare for an emerging humanity. He loathed "the masses" and believed that birth control was crucial to ensuring a brighter human future.[32] "As he saw it," writes John Carey, "the main prob-lem was the mass of low-grade humanity such as inhabits the underground in *When the Sleeper Wakes*." Enlightened governments had to take measures against the "great useless masses of people," whom he termed "People of the Abyss." The "nation that most resolutely picks over, educates, sterilizes, ex-ports, or poisons its People of the Abyss will be in the ascendant." The evolu-tionary vision animating his thought was ruthless in the extreme. If " 'a man's actions' show him to be unfit to live, the New Republicans will kill him." [33]

Wells's social "ethic" was based directly on the economics of Malthus and the biology of Darwin. Like many intellectuals of his day, Wells considered "black and brown races" to be "inferior to whites in intelligence and initiative." He declared that the "swarms of black, and brown, and dirty-white, and yellow people" who cannot keep pace with modern technological society will "have to go."[34] A small elite would control such decisions. "I look to the growth of a mi-nority of intelligent men and women for the real revolution before mankind," Wells writes. "I look for a ripening elite of mature and educated minds, and I do not believe progress can be anything more than casual and insecure until that elite has become . . . effective." Wells longed for "an increase in number of these exceptional types."[35] These were his giants, and he imagined himself to be one of them.

This view of the masses puts a new light on Wells's *War of the Worlds* (1898), in which members of the working class die by the thousands as victims of the invading Martians. John Carey observes that the "Martian invasion of the

earth is sited precisely in the areas of London's suburbs that had caused most
heartache to sensitive, thinking people in the later nineteenth century," including Wells.[36] According to Wells, Christianity was hindering the kind of
social advances that could come as the result of a truly scientific social agenda
that included reducing the numbers of the poor. In *Star Begotten*, Professor
Keppel exclaims, "I hate common humanity. . . . Clear the earth of them![37]

Though Wells advocated such ideas in his later fiction, he also sought "not
to be held accountable for them." Science fiction, which regularly "turns natural law to lawless ends," provided the ideal medium for him to advocate brutal
social policies.[38] In light of Wells's sentiments and the public's tendency to
underestimate science fiction's social importance, it is fascinating to see that
scientist Leo Szilard, "who worked on the Hiroshima bomb," claimed that "the
idea of chain reaction first came to him" while reading another Wells novel,
The World Set Free.[39] Vernier observes that "evolution, as presented by Wells,"
is a "mutation resulting in the confrontation of man with different species"
and is now well established as "one of the main themes of modern science
fiction."[40]

OLAF STAPLEDON: THE LAST MEN AS SALVATION

According to Samuel Moskowitz, an historian of science fiction, "the most
titanic imagination ever brought to science fiction undoubtedly belonged to
Olaf Stapledon."[41] Though his name is no longer widely recognized, no writer
of science fiction has had a greater impact on the genre's development than
the English writer William Olaf Stapledon (1886-1950). Born near Liverpool,
Stapledon's family moved to Egypt, where he lived until the age of six. During
World War I he served as an ambulance driver. Aristocratic and well educated,
Stapledon frequently lectured on topics ranging from English literature and
philosophy to industrial history. He wrote an early book on ethics and was influenced by the socialist views of Wells. In the late 1920s, Stapledon turned his
attention to writing a highly original type of science fiction that read like histories of the future. His most famous works include *Last and First Men* (1930),
Odd John (1936), *Star Maker* (1937) and *Sirius* (1944). Both *Last and First Men*
and *Star Maker* have been described by critics as the greatest science-fiction
works ever.

Stapledon inaugurated a more philosophical approach to science fiction; he was an avowed promoter of science fiction as mythology. His influence on the genre is inestimable, with Arthur C. Clarke saying of *Last and First Men* that "no book before or since has ever had such an impact on my imagination."[42] Stapledon is also credited with inventing many of the plot devices that became science-fiction's hallmarks. But as a crafter of mythology, Stapledon is without peer. In his works we find ourselves at the headwaters of much of the Western world's modern mythmaking.[43]

Stapledon was never a convinced Christian; he belonged to no church and referred to himself as an "agnostic mystic."[44] If he had a spiritual hope, it was in the evolutionary advancement of the human race as a whole and throughout the cosmos. For Stapledon, humanity was "the living germ which is destined to enliven the whole cosmos!"[45] A spiritual explorer, Stapledon viewed science as an instrument for addressing spiritual questions. Humanity was achieving new religious insights as "the intricate universe" of our current science was giving way to "an ampler, stranger universe." The present observable world is but "the threshold to another world."[46] Science was forcing a new spiritual outlook, one that required new mythologies. As a result, Stapledon sought to craft a "not wholly impossible account of the future of man" that would reflect "the change that is taking place today in man's outlook." Old mythologies would be rejected in light of new knowledge; new myths were needed. "Our aim," he wrote, "is not merely to create aesthetically admirable fiction. We must achieve neither mere history, nor mere fiction, but myth."[47]

For Stapledon, "a true myth" is one that captures "the highest admirations possible within that culture."[48] In Stapledon's mythic productions, two factors emerge as "the highest admirations possible": humanity as intelligence seeking progress, and spiritual evolution as that progress. As Gregory Benford writes, "Stapledon had studied the Darwin-Wallace idea of evolution, and projected it onto the vast scale of our future."[49] Indeed, Stapledon was preoccupied with evolution into a limitless future, to the extent that the present state of the human race seemed to be of no particular import. "Our whole present mentality is but a confused and halting first experiment."[50] A "highly advanced" human from the distant future can thus say to a present-day counterpart that "the loftier potencies of the spirit in you have not even begun to put forth buds."[51] Stapledon's future is so remarkably detailed, so dispassionately told, so comprehensive in its scope, that it emerges from his novels as an actual history of the future.

The ultimate goal of the Stapledon mythology is a new deity to replace the Christian God. Steven Dick observes, "Stapledon did not forget his purpose: the search for the spirit of the universe, what humans on Earth formerly called God."[52] This pantheistic divinity pushes human evolution forward until humanity itself becomes God. "The history of the race continues to reel off," writes Dick, until a humanity arises "incorporating the positive features of all previous races to crown the history of Man as the ultimate creation of that spirit which permeates the process of evolution in the universe."[53] Stapledon imagined a deity who "through mathematics, physics, and spiritual need, will fill the place that religion has reserved for God."[54] That deity is, however, itself a product of evolution. Perhaps for this reason "the ultimate salvation . . . rests in future man biologically improving the species."[55]

Stapledon read the best scientists of his day and was intrigued with their theories and speculation about the future. He communicated with J. B. S. Haldane, whose essay "The Last Judgment" "inspired parts of *Last and First Men*. In addition, *Star Maker* was shaped by prominent physicists and astronomers, including J. D. Bernal, Willem J. Luyten, Arthur Eddington and James Jeans.[56] Stapledon in turn helped to mold the imagination of a later generation of both scientists and science-fiction authors. His many original plot themes show up in subsequent science fiction, and through the popularity of that science fiction, they nurtured an emerging cultural vision: a cosmos filled with life, human communication with extraterrestrials, the evolution of the human race, and all this hinging on the exploration of space. Mythic narratives shape perception, and perception is the basis of action—including public policy.

Stapledon's academic training was in philosophy, a field in which he held a Ph.D. He thus was prepared to read a wide range of sources, including theologians such as Rudolph Otto. Indeed, *Star Maker* "replaces [a] loving God with one based partly on Rudolf Otto's *The Idea of the Holy*."[57] Stapledon's thinking was also likely influenced by the famed British historian Arnold Toynbee, especially his *A Study of History*, which included "the historian's discussion of civilizations beyond the Earth."[58] In turn, Stapledon's erudite prose influenced a generation of writers, including Arthur C. Clarke, John

Maynard Smith, Robert Heinlein, Isaac Asimov, Erik Frank Russell and Freeman Dyson. Steven Dick writes that "it is difficult to over-estimate the influence of his work, especially in Britain."[59]

Like so many Victorian intellectuals, Stapledon maintained an earnest interest in eugenics. Given the ruthless nature of Galton's program, it is shocking to read from someone of Stapledon's intellectual sensitivity: "Columbus found a new world; but Francis Galton found a new humanity."[60] Stapledon believed that "our conception of humanity must be fundamentally altered" in light of the work of Galton and Gregor Mendel. "Darwin showed that man is the result of evolution," he wrote. "Others have shown that he may direct his [own] evolution." Stapledon even adopted Galton's language in talking about eugenics. "In time it may be as possible to breed good men as it is possible to breed fast horses."[61]

For Stapledon, the improvement of the human race—even divinity—was "within our grasp." "Why is it sacrilegious to use direct means for the improvement of the human race?" he asked. "We have been given wherewithal to climb a little nearer to divinity."[62] The Christian apologist C. S. Lewis, a rough contemporary of Stapledon's, was concerned with Western society's increasingly religious trust in a scientifically empowered human race—a theme he found in Stapledon's fiction as well as in some works of Haldane, among other places. As Lewis saw it, the great danger lay in "the belief that the supreme moral end is the perpetuation of our own species, and that this is to be pursued even if . . . our species has to be stripped of all those things for which we value it—of pity, of happiness, and of freedom." For Lewis, himself a successful author of fiction, this idea was particularly dangerous as an embedded value in much popular writing. "I am not sure that you will find this belief formally asserted by any writer: such things creep in as assumed, and unstated, major premises."[63] Lewis's own works of science fiction—*Out of the Silent Planet*, *Perelandra* and *That Hideous Strength*—were written at least in part as a response to Stapledon and Haldane, whose books were having a powerful influence on public conceptions of the human future.

ARTHUR C. CLARKE ON
OUR DISEMBODIED FUTURE

Stapledon's influence on following generations of science-fiction writers has been great, with many of his emulators achieving a fame and social influence that never came to Stapledon himself. Most prominent among Stapledon's heirs is perhaps the greatest of the twentieth-century science-fiction visionaries, Sir Arthur C. Clarke (1917-2008). Of the array of Stapledon's ideas, Clarke has been particularly interested in exploring the concept of human experiment and evolution producing something beyond recognizable, embodied humanity. For example, Clarke's classic *Childhood's End* (1953) imagines a divine Overmind on a distant planet, a conscious cloud ruling numerous planets and absorbing into itself the intelligence and consciousness of the various races it selects for predation. Servants of this Overmind have been assigned to monitor the progress of human life on Earth, guiding it toward its ultimate destiny—absorption into the Overmind itself. Strangely, these servants appear in the unmistakable form of devils.

A number of other Clarke stories developed around a similar evolutionary theme: human progress toward a spiritual essence free of bodily constraints, a theme treated extensively by Stapledon. The extraordinarily popular movie *2001: A Space Odyssey*, created by Clarke in partnership with director Stanley Kubric, features a human selected by unknown forces to take the next step in evolution, pictured as a human fetus floating freely in space and observing the Earth of its origin.

But in one of his first science-fiction stories, *Against the Fall of Night* (1948)—written twenty years before the screenplay for *2001* and while Stapledon was still living—Clarke imagined a future in which "contact with other species" revealed to humanity the limitations of understanding the cosmos through a "physical body and the sense organs with which it was equipped." A better understanding was sought through "a pure mentality." He then adds that "this idea was common to most very ancient religions and was believed by many to be the goal of evolution."[64]

Experiments were begun to create such a disembodied mentality, and a "new race was born [that] had a potential intellect that could not even be measured."[65] Once accomplished, "the creation of pure mentalities was the greatest achievement of Galactic civilization: in it man played a major and perhaps dominant part."[66] Clarke's vision of the New Humanity has never been limited by current physical or mental models, but extends into a realm that can only be described as divinity itself.

TELEPATHY AND THE NEW HUMANITY

Powder is a 1999 science-fiction film by the controversial director Victor Salva. Following fifteen months in prison on a sexual molestation charge, Salva convinced Disney Studios to allow him to create this strange and compelling movie, for which he also wrote the screenplay. *Powder* explores the fate of a young albino man possessing extraordinary intellectual and psychic powers as a result of lightning striking his mother during her pregnancy with him. Growing up in a small Texas town, Jeremy "Powder" Reed faces rejection and torment because of his unusual appearance and uncanny mental abilities. But one of his teachers recognizes the truth: Jeremy represents an evolutionary advancement. Particularly noteworthy is Jeremy's capacity to read the thoughts, feelings and hidden history of others. It is this capacity that provides the central feature of Jeremy's unusual powers.

In his definitive study of the idea of telepathy, Roger Luckhurst writes that telepathy betokens a "utopian future in technology, science, and human sensitivity."[67] And he adds, "It has become a given in science fiction."[68] Where else has the idea flourished? The occult and science are the two other locations of intense interest in mental communication. Indeed, the very term *telepathy* arose out of late nineteenth-century efforts to investigate and establish the phenomenon on scientific grounds.[69] At the same time, those most actively involved in promoting the concept were associated with occult circles in Victorian London. Why should the idea that some individuals might know the thoughts and feelings of others at a distance find its cultural location in the worlds of science, science fiction and the occult? Why, again, the tendency of such apparently unrelated enterprises to delve into mysterious mental powers? The answer is found in the Western world's efforts to develop a new spiritual outlook in future humanity. The notion of ongoing human evolution is at the very heart of those efforts.

That there is a connection between "mental powers" such as telepathy and human evolution is not simply a concept of the science-fiction author but also a notion that has received considerable scientific interest. A number of leading late nineteenth-century scientists, including William Crookes, Francis Galton and Alfred Russell Wallace, sought to establish human "progress" on the fact of mental telepathy and other "spiritual" powers. Specifically, telepathy supposedly demonstrated that humanity was evolving spiritually, becoming increasingly attuned to a pantheistic cosmic force actively at work in all things. Science, it was thought, could assist such spiritual progress. In an 1871 essay titled "Experimental Investigation of a New Force," Crookes wrote that his own experiments established "a new force" that "in some unknown manner" operated in some people. "For the sake of convenience," he decided to dub this power "the Psychic Force."[70]

Crooke's experiments with the Psychic Force were part of a broad effort to establish spiritualism—contact with deceased individuals—on scientific grounds. New technologies were viewed by many even within the scientific community as means of gaining access to the spirit world. Indeed, virtually every new communication technology arising during the period from 1860 through 1930—telegraph, radio, telephone—were promoted as avenues into the spirit realm. Telephone inventor Alexander Graham Bell found inspiration for his experiments in the possibility of contacting deceased family members.[71] Bell's famous assistant, Thomas Watson, was a practicing spiritual medium who believed, as did many others, that electricity was an occult force that provided a means of contacting spirits. Some claimed to be "phone-voyants," specially gifted to talk with the dead through the telephone. Thomas Edison also saw the potential in new technologies for communicating with deceased persons.

Science and magic could be difficult to differentiate in Victorian England; technology often was closely associated with occult practices. One goal was shared: to control the "psychic force" so as to join the worlds of the living and the dead in a communication network. All minds are part of a vast cosmic fabric of consciousness. Science, through the proper course of research, might release this untapped potential of the Cosmic Mind, thus helping humanity realize the next stage of its evolutionary development. For Victorian scientists such as Frederic Myers, the reality of telepathic ability in some individuals "signaled a transition between evolutionary levels."[72]

Such "scientific" thinking often was clearly spiritual in nature. The evolutionary theorist Alfred Russell Wallace himself proposed a "continuity" of mind under the control of "higher intelligences or of one Supreme Intelligence."[73] The public, mired in an "outdated" Christian worldview suspicious of psychic phenomena, needed to be persuaded to accept such progressive ideas. Popular works such as *The Unseen Universe* (1875) argued for the essentially spiritual nature of the new forces that science was investigating. A new

scientific-religious age was dawning as science was enthusiastically spiritualized. Discoveries such as x-rays, black light and radio were heralded as much
for their potential to reveal secrets of the spirit world as for their capacity to
enhance life.

Science fiction quickly incorporated the closely related scientific ideas of
mysterious forces and telepathy, particularly in its discussion of "advanced"
humans. It was a short step from scientific talk of sensitive minds united by a
pervasive "psychic force" to the powerful force dubbed Vril in Bulwer-Lytton's
The Coming Race, the occult interplanetary transportation of Edgar Rice Burroughs's hero John Carter, and through the influence of Burroughs and others,
to the Force of *Star Wars* fame. Telepathy is a capacity enjoyed by Valentine
Michael Smith in Heinlein's *Stranger in a Strange Land*, Dr. Jean Grey of the
highly evolved mutants in *The X-Men* movies, members of the Psycore in the
Babylon 5 narratives, as well as *Star Trek*'s Mr. Spock, who joins his mind to
other minds through physical touch. Any feature of the science and science-
fiction connection will also show up in UFO religions, so it is no surprise that
Raëlian literature makes frequent reference to extraterrestrials communicating with Raël through telepathy.[74]

Once scientists endorsed the idea of telepathy, telepathic contact with deceased individuals was easily accepted. As scientist J. J. Thomson wrote, "Telepathy with the dead would present apparently little difficulty when it is ad-
mitted as regards the living."[75] Contemporary science fiction is in apparent
agreement with such logic. In the *Star Wars* franchise, mastery of the Force
may allow mental influence to pass between two living individuals (for example, the Jedi knight Qui-Gon Jinn and the leader of the Gungan people in
The Phantom Menace), or between living Jedi such as Luke Skywalker and
the deceased Jedi master Obi-Wan Kenobi. The odd assumption that spirits
exploit new technologies to speak with the living also continues to have its
science-fiction adherents, as suggested by movies such as the science-fiction
thriller *White Noise* (2005).

J. B. RHINE AND THE
SCIENCE OF PARAPSYCHOLOGY

Perhaps the most extensive effort to prove telepathy on scientific grounds occurred in the United States in the early twentieth century. Duke University

psychologist Joseph B. Rhine (1895-1980) was the most important academic advocate of the idea. In a series of experiments carried out in the 1920s and 1930s, Rhine sought to establish the existence of what he called ESP (extrasensory perception) in some individuals. In this work he was encouraged by the maverick Scottish psychologist William McDougal (1871-1938), then chair of Rhine's department at Duke.

In his book *New Frontiers of the Mind* (1937), Rhine traces the history of mind reading to the Austrian mentalist Franz Mesmer (1734-1815) and various hypnotists and mystics of the past who "took over the earlier view that the mind could go out through space and bring back knowledge of events which the senses could not possibly reveal or the reason infer."[76] Such theories clearly had roots in the works of Swedenborg and other self-styled mystics. Prominent nineteenth-century occultist Madame Blavatsky (1831-1891) made similar assertions: while residing in London she claimed to remain in mental contact with distant ascended Tibetan masters.

Despite the occult nature of their origins, scientists were eager to investigate claims of mental telepathy and related paranormal phenomena. Study groups were established, including The English Society for Psychical Research, founded in 1882.[77] Vast public interest in the various phenomena was propagated in popular books such as novelist Upton Sinclair's reports of his own telepathic experiments in *Mental Radio: Does It Work, and How?* (1930).[78] Sinclair argued that his wife, Mary Craig Kimbrough, possessed telepathic abilities. Kimbrough was a devotee of the occult, an interest she shared with her husband. The book's preface was penned by none other than Albert Einstein! Though scientists are skeptical, writes Einstein, "it is out of the question in the case of so conscientious an observer and writer as Upton Sinclair that he is carrying on a conscious deception of the reading world; his good faith and dependability are not to be doubted."[79]

William McDougall was a controversial figure who founded the department of psychical research at Duke, providing important support for Rhine's ESP experiments. McDougall, himself "a veteran . . . of psychic research," was also a devotee of eugenics. His interest in telepathy was directly connected to his confidence in the potential for scientific improvement of the human race.[80] McDougall was convinced of the Lamarckian view of evolution, that traits acquired during life could be passed to one's progeny and that "certain training effects are inheritable."[81] Thus, if Rhine could actually cultivate the ability to read minds in his subjects—or just locate individuals in which the ability was present—they might become the vanguard of a new humanity possessing expanded mental abilities.

PARAPSYCHOLOGY AS NEW RELIGION

Rhine's own interest in telepathy was more religious in nature. He writes, "My interest in psychic research had grown out of my desire, common, I think, to thousands of people, to find a satisfactory philosophy of life, one that could be regarded as scientifically sound and yet could answer some of the urgent questions regarding the nature of man and his place in the natural world." Rhine was "dissatisfied with the orthodox religious belief which had at one time impelled me toward the ministry," and thus was "ready to investigate any challenging fact that might hold possibilities of new insight into human personality and its relations to the universe." Rhine searched for spiritual truth to replace the Christian view he had abandoned.[82]

Indeed, Rhine concluded that "the mysterious capacities" claimed by psychic researchers provided "the very substance of most religious belief, stripped, of course, of theological trappings." In earlier times people "relied greatly on the strange occurrences that today would be called psychic in forming their concepts of man, his spiritual make-up, and his powers over nature." Thus, Rhine sought to reintroduce a primitive spiritual experience to the Western world. "I wondered if we were throwing away too much in outgrowing these old beliefs." Rhine searched for "illumination" and in his search "turned eagerly toward this realm of mysterious happenings, real or imaginary."[83]

Through his popular books, Rhine had a surprising impact on popular culture for someone who saw himself as a research scientist. He also influenced the scientific community. A number of prominent scientists took an interest in ESP, including Sir Oliver Lodge, Sir William Barrett and Sir William Crookes. These and many other scientists "proposed a theory or in some other way turned their attention to the infant science of parapsychology."[84] Finally, through a remarkable coincidence, Rhine's influence extended directly into the genre of science fiction as well. The famous science-fiction editor John W. Campbell had been a student at Duke in the early 1930s and was intrigued by Rhine's work. Campbell developed an interest in the topics of telepathy and

parapsychology that he maintained throughout his life. The persistent telepathic theme in later science fiction may be explained in part through Rhine's
shaping influence on Campbell's thought.

Many of us remain believers in some form of telepathy. A 2002 CBS national poll of 861 randomly selected Americans revealed that 57 percent said
that they believed in mental telepathy or similar phenomena "that can't be
explained by normal means." Belief in ESP was highest among younger respondents. Even among the religious faithful, two-thirds of Catholics and half
of Protestants accepted ESP as true.[85] Since ESP lacks scientific foundation, in
what is this rather widespread belief rooted? One possible answer is popular
narratives that feature mental telepathy, often as a characteristic of "advanced"
humans. This section opens with a reference to the movie *Powder*, which features a mind-reading boy who also represents a genetic advancement over his
peers. Many other examples could be adduced; the capacity to enter into another's mental world remains a staple of the science-fiction genre, where it is
characteristically a sign of evolutionary advancement.

Today the idea that we might have access to extrasensory information continues to receive scientific support from Rupert Sheldrake, a self-styled expert
on paranormal phenomena. According to Sheldrake, we all inhabit invisible
"morphic fields," which make it possible to "unconsciously transmit and receive information." He sometimes refers to this phenomenon as "the extended
mind" and has published ten books on his findings. To prove his hypothesis,
Sheldrake has conducted literally "thousands of experiments." In some of
these tests, subjects appear to have access to information for which they have
no sensory experience. Sheldrake's experiments have received funding from
universities, and he is trying to involve large corporations in his research.[86]

PHILIP WYLIE'S *GLADIATOR*:
PROTOTYPE OF THE EUGENIC SUPERMAN

American author Philip Wylie (1902-1971) is the father of modern superman stories. The son of a Presbyterian minister and a writer, Wylie studied at
Princeton University in the early 1920s. A prolific writer, he produced numerous books, essays, and Hollywood screenplays. Wylie also advised the Joint
Committee for Atomic Energy for a period of time. Several of Wylie's stories
are considered science fiction, including two of his best-known books, *Glad-*

iator (1930) and *The Disappearance* (1951). Wylie also wrote *When Worlds Collide* (1933), which became the basis of a major Hollywood science-fiction movie in 1951.

Wylie's book *Gladiator* is the story of a young man of superhuman strength and his painful existence in a world unprepared to deal with a superman.[87] Hugo Danner acquires his strength as the result of an experiment his father performs on his mother while Hugo is in the womb. Wylie's interest in eugenics and suspicion of religious objections are both present in the story: Hugo's pious and rigid mother claims that it is "wicked to tamper with God's creatures," but her opinion is dismissed.[88] His physically diminutive father announces that Hugo will be "the first of a new and glorious race. A race that doesn't have to fear—because it cannot know harm. No man can hurt him, no man can vanquish him. He will be mightier than any circumstances." Wylie adds that Danner's biologist father had "stood like a prophet and spoken words of fire."[89] Indeed, Hugo is so strong as to find no practical limits to his capacities. He nearly single-handedly defeats a German army in World War I, kills a giant shark with his bare hands, rips the door from a safe in which a man is trapped, and dispatches a charging bull with a single blow from his powerful fist.

While still a boy, Wylie's protagonist recognizes that he is a superhuman. "It was a rapturous discovery. He knew at that hour that his strength was not a curse. He had inklings of his invulnerability."[90] The connection between Wylie's Hugo and the later superman stories of comic-book and television fame is clear in several passages. For instance, Hugo tells his father: "It seem like there isn't any stopping me. I can go on—far as I like. Runnin'. Jumpin'. . . . I can jump higher'n a house. I can run faster'n a train. I can pull up big trees an' push 'em over."[91] But Hugo's life is often unpleasant precisely because he is a superman: he is rejected by people of lesser gifts.

The idea of a superman intrigued Wylie. He was famous for rejecting the "emasculating" influence of "Momism," the American tendency to worship mothers. *Gladiator* is a musing on what might be accomplished by a man with no such limitations on his strength and, when his emotions are aroused, no limits to his personal violence. Wylie's account of Hugo's massacre of thousands of German soldiers in the trenches of France is horrific. But like Wells's beautiful and powerful giants in *Food of the Gods*, Hugo does not belong in a world of ordinary people; he is a new human. "The stronger, the greater, you are, the harder life is for you," says his father. "And you're the strongest of them all, Hugo." Does this mean that Hugo rivals even God himself? He asks his father, "And what about God?" The elder Danner dismissively replies, "I don't know much about Him."[92] The question is not addressed again in the book. But Wylie writes that Hugo's father "worshiped his son" that he had created.[93] And well he might, for Hugo grows into "a man vehemently alive, a man with the promise of a young God."[94]

Hugo's strength comes from his father's bold and godless experiments in the "biochemistry of cellular structure" and the "production of energy in cells."[95] Wylie does not repudiate the idea of such a scientifically crafted superman, though he does plot out the personal difficulties of living as the first of a new and better species of human being. Hugo is a man who in war became "a machine that killed quickly and remorselessly—a black warrior from a distant realm of the universe where the gods had bred another kind of man."[96] Still, ordinary men were not ready for superman to arrive. Thus, "his deeds frightened men or made them jealous," and "when he conceived a fine thing, the masses individually or collectively, transformed it into something cheap."[97] Alas, superman is always held back by the masses of ordinary men. "People! Human beings! How he hated them!"[98]

Wylie apparently found in Hugo an actual possibility were it not for the fact that the pace of evolution was so slow and social mores so inclined to hinder scientific experiments with the human being. Thus, real human "growth . . . must remain a problem for thousands and tens of thousands of years."[99] Wylie eventually comes down on the side of science as the only realm large and bold enough to develop the superman. Hugo realizes that "of all human beings alive, the scientists were the only ones who retained imagination, ideals, and a sincere interest in the larger world. It was to them he should give his allegiance, not to the statesmen, not to industry or commerce or war."[100]

During an archaeological dig in Central America, Hugo understands that ancient people had already arrived at "the secret of human strength—his secret!" The scientist leading the dig explains that Hugo must realize that he has suffered, not because there is anything wrong with him, but because he is the first of a new race of men. What is coming is "other men like you. Not one or two. Scores, hundreds. And women. All picked with the utmost care. Eugenic offspring." These new people, "children of the best parents," will be "cultivated

THE MYTH OF THE NEW HUMANITY

and reared in secret by a society for the purpose." They will possess "perfect bodies, intellectual minds, your strength." A scientist reveals the truth of his destiny to Hugo. "Don't you see it, Hugo? You are not the reformer of the old world. You are the beginning of the new. We begin with a thousand of you. . . . The new Titans! Then—slowly—you dominate the world. Conquer and stamp out all these things to which you and I and all men of intelligence object. In the end—you are alone and supreme."[101]

Far from repudiating such a power-crazed vision, Hugo is convinced. "'I must go back and begin this work,' he told himself. 'I have found a friend!'" Doubts eventually assail him as he imagines that breeding a race of supermen is "folly in the face of God." Nevertheless, "they will make the earth beautiful."[102] *Gladiator* ends on this equivocal note, and Hugo dies in a lightning storm before his plan can be carried out. The scientist's reasoning about a race of Titans is never refuted, simply confronted in Hugo's mind with the religious attitudes that earlier had caused his devout and benighted mother to confront his agnostic and visionary father. The more vigorous voices of *Gladiator* all are on the side of science, eugenics and the brave new human future.

SUPERMEN AND SUPERCHILDREN

The New Humanity must, it would seem, begin with new children—advanced members of the human race who show up either as natural products of evolution, as members of a technologically modified new species, or as the offspring of human and alien parents. The idea that in their strange behavior certain children reveal the appearance or abilities of the next stage in human evolution is a frequently repeated theme in science fiction. Just a few of many examples that could be advanced include Wells's *Food of the Gods*, Beresford's *The Hampdenshire Wonder* (1911), Wylie's *Gladiator*, Stapledon's *Odd John* (1935), A. E. van Vogt's *Slan* (1946), Madeleine L'Engle's *Wrinkle in Time* (1962), Philip K. Dick's *Martian Time-Slip* (1964) and Greg Bear's *Darwin's Children* (2003). Many comic-book superheroes are children with "advanced" abilities such as telepathy, enormous strength, telekinetic powers or extremely high intelligence. The first of the *Matrix* (1999) movies features specially gifted children who attend the figure known only as The Oracle, while *X2: X-Men United* (2003) also incorporates the idea of children with remarkable powers— mutants—who, according to the movie's narrator, represent an evolutionary advance over ordinary human beings. The same theme animates the popular television series *Heroes*.

To take just one of these examples, Beresford's protagonist is a child named Victor Stott, born with an extremely large head and brain to match. However, Stott's body is weaker than those of his counterparts in the normal human community. Stott is truly a superman, a bridge between current humanity and a humanity to come, a superintelligent individual with a capacity to control the actions of others. The novel—much like *Gladiator* and *Food of the Gods*—explores the implications of such a new human in ordinary human society. Beresford's "next human" is an evolutionary prodigy born to an ordinary mother.

Beresford (1873-1947) helped to launch the subgenre of the superchild, putting in play an idea to be developed in a number of later novels, movies and comic books. He also fictionalized an idea that had been alive in the minds of many once the implications of Darwin's theory became commonly known and the possibility of scientific eugenics had been widely discussed. In the strange story *Odd John*, Stapledon breaks with his usual practice of writing vast imaginary histories of the cosmos and humanity and "narrows his focus to the life of one superhuman being, John Wainwright," who creates a remote colony of young people like himself. Their purpose becomes to "devote themselves to understanding and worshipping the spirit of the universe."[103]

The idea of a special group of children ushering in a new humanity has its real-life manifestation as well. *The Indigo Children: The New Kids Have Arrived*, is a book by Lee Carroll, a channeler for an entity that he calls Kryon, and Carroll's wife, Jan Tober.[104] Though some claim that the Indigo Children phenomenon was foretold by self-styled clairvoyant Edgar Cayce in the opening decades of the twentieth century, the term Indigo Child actually originated with the psychic Nancy Ann Tappe. Tappe claimed to be able to classify people according to the color of their "auras." On her theory, each age of humanity reflects a preponderance of people with a particular aural color. Most adults today are either Blue or Violet, the two colors with the attributes most needed in this Violet Age of transition. During the next age, the Indigo Age, Indigo colors will be the norm.[105]

Tappe taught that a new predominant color had emerged of late, reflected especially in the Indigo Children. Eventually, according to her predication, the

Indigos "will replace all other colors." As small children, she writes, "Indigo's are easy to recognize by their unusually large, clear eyes." Characteristics include being "extremely bright, precocious children with an amazing memory and a strong desire to live instinctively." In addition, "these children of the next millennium are sensitive, gifted souls with an evolved consciousness who have come here to help change the vibrations of our lives and create one land, one globe and one species." Indigos are "our bridge to the future."[106] The number of Indigo Children is said to be increasing rapidly around the globe.

With the advent of the notion of Indigo Children, the Myth of the New Humanity has manifested itself on the cultural scene as an active interpretive mechanism. Children displaying unusual characteristics, or who have such characteristics attributed to them, are seen through the lens of a powerful mythic narrative that has taken centuries to develop.

RAY KURZWEIL AND THE COMING BIOTECH HUMANITY

One of the most important recent nonfiction visions of a new humanity is found in Ray Kurzweil's 2005 book, *The Singularity Is Near: When Humans Transcend Biology*.[107] As a successful inventor and a widely recognized futurist, Kurzweil (b. 1948) has long theorized about the relationship between biological and technological evolution. He is an advocate of human enhancement through the blending of brain and machine processes, and he emerges as a staunch advocate for the Myth of the New Humanity.

Kurzweil's provocative concept, the Singularity, is the point in the near future when technological development occurs at such a rapid rate that a "rupture" occurs in human history. Because technological change occurs exponentially, "we won't experience 100 years of progress in the 21st century—it will be more like 20,000 years of progress (at today's rate)." Kurzweil, who has spent his adult life immersed in the world of computer technology, prophesies that the merging of "machine intelligence" and "human intelligence" will bring about the Singularity. In keeping with the dominant theme of both science and science fiction, the Singularity is an inevitable consequence of evolutionary forces. "The Singularity denotes an event that will take place in the material world, the inevitable next step in the evolutionary process that started with biological evolution and has extended through human-directed technological evolution."[108]

The ultimate outcome of this evolutionary biotech merger will be "immortal software-based humans, and ultra-high levels of intelligence that expand outward in the universe at the speed of light."[109] The bodies of these new humans will be nearly impervious to disease, making possible incredibly long life spans. Virtual immortality, employing technology to live as long as one chooses, is among Kurzweil's principal concerns. Microscopic "nanobots" will circulate through the body to repair damage. As befits a technoprophet, Kurzweil writes with religious conviction of the coming changes to humanity. Because "our bodies are governed by obsolete genetic programs that evolved in a bygone era," we will need "to overcome our genetic heritage" through advanced technology, much of it already available. Kurzweil adds that changing the basic building blocks of the human is "something I am committed to doing." The key to all of the envisioned changes is "to vastly expand our mental faculties by merging with our technology."[110] There is essentially no limit to the potential expansion of human intelligence when it becomes linked to machine intelligence.

Kurzweil's vision certainly raises important moral questions. For example, who will be assigned the task of determining the direction of our future development as the new biotech humans emerge from the ranks of "unenhanced biological humanity"? Kurzweil apparently trusts that the Singularity itself will choose in the direction of the good and the just. "As a consummation of the evolution in our midst, the Singularity will deepen all . . . manifestations of transcendence." These manifestations include, among other things, "art, culture, technology, and emotional and spiritual expression."[111] Current unenhanced humanity is merely a moral starting point: "Our technology will match and then vastly exceed the refinement and suppleness of what we regard as the best human traits." For Kurzweil, this is "the most important implication" of the Singularity.[112] Nothing, it seems, whether human beings or the cosmos itself, will be beyond the improving reach of the divine Singularity.

In the introduction to this book, I cited Kurzweil as asserting that explosive technological change will demand a "new religion" to help us comprehend the spiritual dimensions of technological advancement.[113] The spiritual implications of his vision are clear to Kurzweil as they would be to anyone encountering his ideas. For example, the Singularity will "allow us to transcend these limitations of our biological bodies and brains. We will gain power over our fates. Our mortality will be in our own hands."[114] The very nature of reality and experience will be altered by the coming modifications to the human body and brain. "There will be no distinction post-Singularity between human and machine or between physical and virtual reality."[115]

Nevertheless, the Singularity vision does not stop at either immortality or subjective experience of reality. A Singularity-enhanced humanity will change the nature of the universe itself, indeed, will awaken a sleeping universe into consciousness. Through our technologically acquired omniscience and omnipresence, "the matter and energy in our vicinity will become infused with the intelligence, knowledge, creativity, beauty, and emotional intelligence (the ability to love, for example) of our human-machine civilization."[116] Kurzweil's utter confidence in the human capacity for ultimate moral transcendence—many would say despite the obvious evidence to the contrary—is nothing short of breathtaking. "Our civilization will . . . expand outward, turning all the dumb matter and energy we encounter into sublimely intelligent—transcendent—matter and energy. So, in a sense, we can say that the Singularity will ultimately infuse the universe with spirit."[117]

Kurzweil can write this way because he holds to a spiritualized view of evolution, the engine driving all transformations in the Scientific Mythologies. In a formulation that sounds more like a religious creed than a scientific law, Kurzweil writes: "Evolution moves toward greater complexity, greater elegance, greater knowledge, greater intelligence, greater beauty, greater creativity, and greater levels of subtle attributes such as love." As Kurzweil is well aware, he has substituted evolution for traditional conceptions of God. "In every monotheistic tradition, God is likewise described as all of these qualities." Today we recognize that "evolution moves inexorably toward this conception of God, although never quite reaching this ideal." Most remarkable is Kurzweil's final statement on the issue of the Singularity's ultimate goal: freeing humanity from the restraints of the biological. "We can regard, therefore, the freeing of our thinking from the severe limitations of its biological form to be an essentially spiritual undertaking."[118]

As revealed in *The Singularity Is Now*, the specific spiritual project of Kurzweil's New Humanity is to awaken a sleeping universe to conscious life during a rapidly approaching period he terms the Sixth Epoch. Writing that "we can consider the universe to be God," Kurzweil adds that the universe is "not conscious—yet." But as a New Humanity extends its reach into the universe, infusing it with intelligence and knowledge, Kurzweil expects that "the universe will become sublimely intelligent and will wake up."[119] In contrast to the traditional, preexistent creator God, Kurzweil's lower deity of evolution first draws human consciousness out of inanimate matter, and then through the apocalyptic event called Singularity, bestows upon this consciousness the capacity to awaken god itself: to animate the sleeping universe. In Kurzweil the Myth of the New Humanity achieves perhaps its highest development.

CONCLUSION

The early twentieth-century racial theorist and eugenicist Oscar Levy wrote that "the successful breeding of men can only be brought about by religious or philosophic faith," pointing up once again the crucial role played by our dominant mythologies in directing our cultural practices.[120] It is not laboratory "advances" that will produce the Next Human, but a narrative: Levy's "religious or philosophic faith," Kurzweil's "new religion." Scientific data do not speak for themselves, and the blueprint for an improved humanity cannot be assembled from a mountain of facts about computer capacity and the human genome. A transcendent story about humanity and its destiny—a myth—will guide the creation of the New Humans. It is that myth which this chapter has explored.

Historian Francis Fukuyama has recently argued that "contemporary biotechnology" now raises "the possibility that it will alter human nature and thereby move us into a 'posthuman' stage of history." He cautions that this "possibility" poses real dangers because human nature is, "conjointly with religion, what defines our most basic values." Human nature also "shapes and constrains the possible kinds of political regimes," and as a result "a technology powerful enough to reshape what we are will have possibly malign consequences" in the political realm. Fukuyama adds, "One of the reasons I am not quite so sanguine is that biotechnology, in contrast to many other scientific advances, mixes obvious benefits with subtle harms in one seamless package."[121] In the advocates of a New Humanity, one does detect a determined avoidance of discussing potential dangers inherent in their project.

Mary Midgley observes that the escalator myth, the story of an ever-evolving and ever-improving human race, can lead to "a contempt for existing people, excused by a somewhat theoretical attachment to people who are not yet."[122] This simple but profound observation demands the attention of people of faith, particularly at present. The Christian tradition elevates the present human as created in the image of God and thereby of inexpressible value. Thus, this tradition recognizes and protects the weak, the poor and the marginalized as "neighbor." Christianity has nothing to say about supposedly superior human beings, those standing out from the crowd because of their remarkable strength, talent, beauty or intellect. It certainly has nothing to say about an idealized "highly evolved" future humanoid that, if it could be accurately imagined and a program for its creation established, would have to be classed as an idol—an object of veneration detracting from our vision of God and his creation.

Writing in the 1940s, the Christian apologist C. S. Lewis was already contemplating the human moral catastrophe that would follow the technological alteration of human nature. In his book *The Abolition of Man*, Lewis writes, "Man's conquest of Nature, if the dreams of some scientific planners are realized, means the rule of a few hundreds of men over billions upon billions of men."[123] The planners who develop the New Humans will have control over all subsequent generations of human beings, "for the power of Man to make himself what he pleases means . . . the power of some men to make other men what *they* please." Lewis cautions: "The final stage is come when Man by eugenics, by pre-natal conditioning, and by education and propaganda based on a perfect applied psychology, has obtained full control over himself. Human nature will be the last part of Nature to surrender to man. The battle will then be won."[124] So many have shown themselves willing to step into this role of "planner," yet with no evident concern that their own moral limitations might infect the outcome of their program for the New Humans.

Any story suggesting that an improved human is either desirable or inevitable—an evolved second Adam, crafted in our image—stands as a challenge to the Judeo-Christian theology's conception of both God and humanity. And yet, no idea is more central to contemporary dreams of both science fiction and speculative science than is a New Humanity, the inevitable consequence of directed evolutionary "progress." Could Christ's death to redeem the human race have been avoided if we had simply waited long enough for an "improved" version of humanity to arrive on the scene?

Future-human hopes represent our own technological and educational efforts to iron out the moral and physical flaws in ourselves, flaws of which we are painfully aware. Indeed, if we were not aware that something was wrong with present humanity, the Next Humans would not have occurred to us. Our longings reflect our failings. But the strange vision of improved people created by unimproved people suggests a deep problem of analysis: Humanity's spiritual need is not addressed in stronger or smarter or morally better people. It is addressed only in individual spiritual transformation. Christian theology teaches that no humanly invented iron is powerful enough for that job; it can only be accomplished through the intervening work of God. The notion that we might achieve spiritual salvation by "moving beyond" the present human race means attempting a technological end run around the problem we recognize in ourselves. This strategy, though tempting because of our magnificent sciences, is futile because of our moral state. We simply are not capable of creating, through any sort of education or technology, a race of people morally superior to ourselves. At the top of the escalator is a mirror.

Christianity reflects a determined insistence on both our moral incapacity in our fallen state, and our moral value as what we are: human. The very idea of a genetically perfectible human race carries with it the corresponding assumption that *some* human qualities—intellect, physical beauty, strength— are most worth perfecting, that a certain few of our characteristics are truly desirable and thus worth saving. But there is much more to being human than our capacity for cognition or cutting a striking physical figure; indeed, much more than we can know through any scientific endeavor. Phrases such as "the best and the brightest" roll easily off our tongues, and just as easily obscure the fact that God also created and seeks to save "the worst and the dimmest." Indeed, the Scriptures of Judaism and Christianity are insistent that God is no respecter of persons and does not favor the rich, the intelligent, the culturally privileged, the artistically gifted or, presumably, the genetically enhanced. Each of these qualities, so appealing to us in our fallen state, in God's eyes renders other people potential rivals for loyalty to himself. In the New Humanity we are tempted to reject the worship of the God who created us for venerating an idealized version of ourselves.

What sort of narrative led some of us to the conclusion that all of us needed to be improved, or to the even more stunning conclusion that our current lives are insignificant in comparison to the promise of the coming New Humanity?

All dreams of future-humans relegate ordinary present-people to the status of means to an end, props on a stage set for the arrival of a superrace of beautiful semidivine telepathic geniuses, a spiritual-cultural elite prepared to lead us into the future they choose for us. We are the victims of our fictions; for well over a century, our popular stories have argued that the future was pregnant with something beyond the human, something requiring our assistance to be birthed. Speculative science as well has helped to popularize and propagate this myth of the miracle baby, fruit of science and nature, citizen of the future, destined for space.

We are no longer the pinnacle of a divine act of creation, the specific flesh in which God chose to clothe himself. We are now instrumental people, no longer flesh, but stepping-stones to something more important, indeed, something divine. Nature and Science groan in anxious yearning for the revealing of the future-humans, a pagan apocalypse. We are haunted by the idea, confirmed in our own experience, that something *is* wrong with us, something that desperately needs fixing. But only a peculiarly human blend of vulnerability and hubris, nakedness and pride, leads us to conclude that we can do the fixing ourselves, thus missing the great historical Fact that the fixing has already been done. In the final analysis, each of the Scientific Mythologies discussed in this book imitates and thus seeks to replace a Christian truth. The Myth of a New Humanity counterfeits the Christian vision of a redeemed human race, spiritually transformed at the initiative of God and restored to its original glory through incomprehensible divine sacrifice. Christianity's redeemed humanity served as the living model for the laboratory mannequin called enhanced humanity. But scientific visions of immortal geniuses striving for divinity are dangerous precisely because they represent a hubristic human imitation of a divine purpose—to restore spiritually and physically a fallen human race. This restoration required, not the genetic invention of a superman, but the death and resurrection of the Divine Man.

6

THE MYTH OF THE FUTURE

Now the last barriers can be swept aside and our two races can move
together into the Future—whatever it may bring.

ARTHUR C. CLARKE, *AGAINST THE FALL OF NIGHT*

Scientists all over the world are united in a culture that
gives hope of a better future for all of us.

FREEMAN DYSON

Today's fiction—Tomorrow's Facts

FROM THE DUST JACKET TO *TRIAD: THREE COMPLETE
SCIENCE FICTION NOVELS*
BY A. E. VAN VOGT

Blessed are those who read SF, for they shall inherit the future.

THOMAS DISCH, *ON SF*

It is impossible to imagine science fiction without the future. Indeed, historian
of the genre John Clute writes, "What SF does is train its readers to look for
the future."[1] Clute's metaphor of audience "training" once again underlines the
inherently persuasive nature of science fiction. The two greatest figures of the
modern era of science fiction, Robert Heinlein (1907-1988) and Isaac Asimov
(1920-1992), were best known for their books of "future history." Heinlein was

particularly skilled at bringing an imagined human future into clear view for his readers. According to science-fiction historian James Gunn, Heinlein "created in the reader a feeling not of wonder but of reality. He gave the reader the conviction that this was the future that lay ahead, else how could he evoke it so casually and describe it so minutely." Gunn adds, "And if this was the future, the reader was forced to take it seriously." Writers such as Heinlein "mastered the technique of creating 'interlocking details' that created this strong sense of presence and the conviction that one was seeing the future, and that the future [that] one was seeing was a good deal more exciting and even more relevant than the present or the past." Gunn perceptively adds, "What escaped the reader's attention was that this Future was strictly a matter of the author's imaginative invention."[2] Perhaps to ensure that their remarkable accomplishment not escape our attention, the Science Fiction Hall of Fame in Seattle is devoted to commemorating the "science fiction legends and luminaries [Heinlein and Asimov among them] who have shaped our conception of the future."[3]

Among the many science-fiction writers who created a future vision for their readers, several distinguished themselves by specializing in the history of the future. In addition to Asimov and Heinlein, John Clute includes Stapledon's vast future history in *Last and First Men* (1931) and *Star Maker* (1937); Paol Anderson's (1926-2001) *Psychotechnic League* stories (1953-1957); Larry Niven's *Tales of Known Space,* including his *Ringworld* and *Man-Kzin Wars* stories (1970-2004); and Stephen Baxter's *Xeelee Sequence,* including *Raft* and many other stories (1991-2006).[4] Each writer advances what we might term a New Future, one that differs markedly from the unchanging futures of the past. Because a New Future offers humanity something entirely different in character, it requires prophets or visionaries to describe it for us. Longstanding analogies of the future to the past have been broken by the unpredictability and power of scientific advances.

Though we often associate the activity with late twentieth-century science-fiction writing, imagining the future is not an activity belonging strictly to the present, or just to science fiction. In 1893 the popular journal *McClure's Magazine* ran a series of articles on the future, preparing the public to embrace a host of new technologies—and attitudes to match—that would change their lives. The articles were grouped under the title "On the Edge of the Future" and featured interviews with such scientific luminaries as Thomas Edison and Alexander Graham Bell.[5] But Bell was not simply talking about his recent invention, the telephone. He was at that very moment in the process of "experimenting with helmets designed to pick up and transfer 'cerebral sensations' to distant receivers."[6] Similarly, the great scientist Nicola Tesla was conducting experiments with thought transfer, convinced that in the rapidly approaching future humans would communicate at great distances without the aid of wires and receivers. Both men were conducting scientific experiments in telepathy, a fact of the future, they thought.

Though the allegation violates textbook treatments of the great inventors, Bell's and Tesla's interests were not strictly scientific. Bell frequently attended séances and sought technological means of enhancing communication with the dead. Tesla, whose ideas were influenced by his interests in the esoteric system known as Theosophy, believed he was in radio contact with Martians. As with these two great scientists and advocates of the Future, technological progress has often been understood in spiritual as well as scientific terms. A century ago, at the dawn of the age of great scientific advances, conceptions of the future often involved what historian Roger Luckhurst has called a "hybridizing" of "speculative elements" from the "technological and psychical" realms, while popular authors couched the results in scientific jargon.[7] This tendency to blend science and the occult led one observer in Victorian London to comment that "there are few steps between the laboratory and the séance."[8]

Artists often joined scientists in creating this strange but popular hybrid for the reading public. Literary luminaries of the late nineteenth and early twentieth centuries, including Robert Louis Stevenson and Rudyard Kipling, often connected technological progress and occult spirituality in books and short stories.[9] What author Erik Davis has recently dubbed "TechGnosis" was a regular component of visions of the Future as the twentieth century opened.[10] Luckhurst also remarks on "how waves of technological innovation through the twentieth century" tended to produce new types of "occult belief."[11] Arthur C. Clarke develops this theme in his famous work *Childhood's End*. In the story, advanced extraterrestrials called The Overlords are in charge of humanity's development on Earth. Oddly, these scientifically advanced beings have a decided interest in books on the occult. As one human character states in bewilderment, "I mean, it seems so hard to reconcile the

Overlord's science with an interest in the occult."[12]

This science-séance intersection is still evident in science-fiction texts such as *The Matrix* and *Star Wars*, where strange and unseen forces are employed for good and evil alongside the most highly sophisticated machinery imaginable. The same mix of empiricism and spiritualism is also clearly present, however, in such works of speculative science as Jeremy Narby's and Francis Huxley's *Shamans Through Time: 500 Years on the Path to Knowledge*, in which scientists are invited to bring research questions to the attention of spirits, and in the alien abduction studies of Harvard psychiatrist John Mack.[13]

One of today's leading futurists, inventor Ray Kurzweil, also chooses the metaphor of magic to describe the biotechnological Future. He writes that J. K. Rowling's Harry Potter stories "may be imaginary, but they are not unreasonable visions of our world as it will exist only a few decades from now. Essentially all of the Potter 'magic' will be realized through . . . technologies." Harry Potter "unleashes his magic by uttering the right incantation," Kurzweil observes and then comments, "That process is precisely our experience with technology. Our incantations are the formulas and algorithms underlying our modern-day magic." The metaphor of magic applied to the Future is revealing. It is pervaded by a Faustian hubris regarding our inevitable technological mastery over nature, by a longing for the limitless power to be obtained through the worshipful cultivation of Science—a force greater even than magic. As Kurzweil remarks, "I have discovered that unlike mere tricks, technology does not lose its transcendent power when its secrets are revealed."[14] Kurzweil cites Arthur C. Clarke's celebrated "third law," which states: "Any sufficiently advanced technology is indistinguishable from magic."[15]

Though there can be no Future in the modern sense without imagined new technologies, the Future has seldom been presented to the public as merely a matter of wonderful new tools to enhance our lives. Rather, the Future often appears in Western popular writing as a scientifically unveiled technospiritual frontier, a New World in search of a New Worldview to guide the use of science's powerful and spiritually suggestive discoveries. It is this now well-established view of science and the Future that accounts for the enormous popularity of such science-as-spiritual-power movies as *What the Bleep Do We Know?* (2004) and books by authors such as the physicists Fred Alan Wolf and Amit Goswami, both of whom also appear in the movie as experts on the spiritual implications of science. In *What the Bleep?* and its sequel, *What the Bleep!? Down the Rabbit Hole* (2006), projects backed by New Age channeler JZ Knight, science is elevated as a source of limitless *spiritual* insight.

As the scientific age dawned, Friedrich Nietzsche (d. 1900) declared the God of the Bible dead. For more than a century, scientists, philosophers, religion-inventors and artists alike have been searching for his replacement. This work of god-seeking has required fashioning new mythologies, especially a mythology of the Future. In place of the God of the past, new "god terms" were deployed to describe the religion of a dawning technological age. Chief among the deities of the new pantheon were technology, progress, advancement, evolution, power, humanity, civilization and above them all, Science. Like living entities, these god-concepts have been incorporated into a guiding narrative intended to bring order to life in a marvelous scientistic-spiritualistic New Age.

As the scientific age dawned, Science was systematically mythologized as civilization's guide to a Future in which technology would not simply enhance life, but would also open the doors to an invisible world of unimaginable powers. Scientists were no longer simply investigators of observable physical phenomena, if they ever had been. They emerged as a new class of priests versed in the secrets of a "new unseen" to rival the invisible God of the Bible—x-rays, radio waves, electricity and subatomic particles, but also psychic forces, the ether, cosmic rays, extra dimensions, planetary civilizations—all were within the reach and realm of Science. Visionaries with a prophetic portrait of the Future propagated it through published books and journals, in the persuasive effort to, as one Victorian proponent of the new Future put it, "train readers to appreciate the marvels of science."[16] As part of their literary "training," readers' imaginations were shaped by a vision of tomorrow owing more to the visionaries' metaphysical beliefs than to any actual science—or any likely future. The future in question was often one in which spiritual notions and technological developments were inseparably linked in a mythic drama of a dominant Western civilization, driven ever forward by invisible forces such as evolution and progress. In helping to craft a mythic narrative of the Future, the rising popular genre of science fiction happily incorporated every imagined accoutrement of the coming Science—from cosmic rays to alien civilizations.

Among the ideas most readers of science fiction counted as certainties was that human beings were making continuous scientific and social progress, that we were constantly increasing our store of knowledge, and that this knowledge was leading to improvements in our lives. Clute writes of the widespread expectation of many at the opening of the twentieth century that "the world is surely going to continue to improve. It will become a healthier place to live, a happier place to raise children, a planet of marvels."[17] Moreover, there was no conceivable end to this process. In 1900 the highly regarded psychologist Frederic Myers wrote that "the small problems of this Earth—population, subsistence, political power—will be settled and gone by; when Science will be the absolutely dominant interest." Myers and many others of his day looked beyond a science that investigated physical phenomena to one that plumbed the depths of the psychic and the spiritual. In the future, "science will be directed mainly towards the unraveling of the secrets of the Unseen."[18] The future will be ushered in by science, but not the science we know. The exponentially explosive technology of the Future—Kurzweil's Singularity—is a comprehensive redemptive force capable of "transforming every institution and aspect of human life, from sexuality to spirituality."[19]

Science-fiction writers intimately linked the ideas of progress and the Future. The Future became more important than the present and—even when fraught with its own challenges—certainly preferable to the past. Gunn comments, "Although science fiction writers may toy with time, putter about in the past, or transport themselves to alternate worlds, their real home is the future."[20] Science-fiction authors as well as speculative scientific writers have often sought to propagate the Myth of the Future as a vision of spiritual hope in technologies sure to accompany our corporate "tomorrow," a hope that permeates even dystopian science-fiction futures. Somehow we can forget that the future might be bleak beyond imagining, but we cannot forget the devices and enhancements promised us. Warnings of the type conveyed in movies from Fritz Lang's 1926 *Metropolis* to Steven Spielberg's 2002 *Minority Report*—and any number of dystopian novels—have persuaded few modern viewers or inventors, let alone modern nations, to question the wisdom of technological "advancement." Even when the Future is dark, it still beckons.

Technology, frequently coupled with spiritual forces, will render the Future a more enthralling location than is the tedious present of jobs and families. Perhaps for this reason the Science Fiction Museum and Hall of Fame in Seattle groups all future metropolises, from the hellish future Los Angeles of *Bladerunner* to the cartoon utopia of *The Jetsons,* under the uncritical heading "Cities of Tomorrow." And though the specter of human mutants with virtually divine powers might prompt an array of nightmarish scenarios in a sane mind, Professor X (Patrick Stewart) assures audiences in the closing scenes of *X-Men 2* that protecting such a possibility will mean "a better future for us all."

Contemporary writer Max More's philosophy of Extropy is a future-oriented view that affirms, among other values, "Perpetual Progress." His organization's website announces, "Extropy means seeking more intelligence, wisdom, and effectiveness, an open-ended lifespan, and the removal of political, cultural, biological, and psychological limits to continuing development. [By] perpetually overcoming constraints on our progress and possibilities as individuals, as organizations, and as a species," we will continue "growing in healthy directions without bound." Ultimately, the future holds out the possibility of what the Extropy Institute calls Self-Transformation. This value is enacted by "affirming continual ethical, intellectual, and physical self-improvement," which will involve "experimentation" and "using technology . . . to seek physiological and neurological augmentation along with emotional and psychological refinement."[21] The New Human is the citizen of the New Future.

The Future, though it is always only imagined, has been an integral part of the modern experience. Indeed, some historians mark the beginning of modernity from the time Western writers such as Francis Bacon started imagining progress as a new, unifying source of cultural hope in works such as *New Atlantis* (1626). Certainly speculation about a technologically enhanced Future has accompanied the development of Western science. Walter Sullivan records that the seventeenth-century writer John Wilkins (1614-1672) "proposed the use of submarines (as yet uninvented) for voyages under the polar ice and helped organize weekly meetings of savants to explore the exciting avenues of scientific speculation opened to them by what they called the New Philosophy." Moreover, Wilkins "proudly predicted that the first flag to fly on the moon would be British—in contradiction to the claim of another imaginative scientist, Johannes Kepler, that the first flag there would be Germanic."[22] The New Future involves the Conquest of Space.

The Future in the narratives of popular culture is not monolithic: here a technological utopia, there a terrifying scenario of technology run amok. Nor is "the future" always ahead of us in time; it also can appear as a return to a grander past age. Léon Poliakov observes the close relationship between a distant utopian past and an imagined utopian future in the Myth of the Future. He writes that "the Golden Age, which occurred before the Fall," was in some modern narratives "transferred to the future."[23] Richard Cavendish explains that modern narratives of endless progress have "transformed the old myth of a golden age in the past into a new myth of a utopian future."[24] Thus, the future can acquire a religious quality, a vision of a better world to come that is modeled on a perfect world of the past. Wells demonstrated that "science and the future could be the subject of literature."[25] But the Future was more than just a literary subject. Wells and Stapledon were preoccupied with the future, arrested as by a vision, imagining that their Future was more than speculation, that it was narrative prophecy with spiritual legitimacy. They were "*prophets* primarily in the sense in which serious poets are so— spiritual guides, people with insight about the present and the universal, rather than literal predictors."[26]

The Myth of the Future fixes our attention on what our evolving civilization is destined to become. It thus renders the present—life as actually lived—irrelevant in light of the more-important question of what is ahead of us. Current problems fade into insignificance, paling in comparison with the vision of the Future, where they will be resolved or no longer matter. Limitations that beset us now will be overcome in the Future. This continuous focus on the time to come distracts from the present as well as the past. The Future drives the present, as when Carl Sagan warns: "There will be a time in our future history when the Solar System will be explored and inhabited. . . . The present moment will be a pivotal instant in the history of mankind. There are not many generations given an opportunity as historically significant as this one. The opportunity is ours, if we but grasp it."[27] The present is significant only in its service to the Future.

Science fiction has propagated the Myth of the Future and is the only literary and cinematic genre utterly dependent on this myth's continued existence in the public mind. Science fiction has shaped popular conceptions of what the Future must look like, from robots in the home and office to spaceships in the heavens above. As early as 1886, the French writer Villiers de l'Isle-Adam published a popular story about a female robot entitled *L'Eve future*. Robots remained a feature of the Future through a series of widely read works, including Czech author Karel Čapek's play *R.U.R (Rossum's Universal Robots)* (1923), where the term "robot" was first used to describe a mechanical worker. But the great master of a robotic future was the American science-fiction writer Isaac Asimov. In books such as the collection *I, Robot* (1950), Asimov explored every dimension of a future "peopled" with mechanical companions. He dedicated the book to his mentor, legendary science-fiction editor John Campbell, "who godfathered the robots."[28]

Late nineteenth-century literary giants such as Mark Twain, Robert Louis Stevenson and Rudyard Kipling also experimented with future narratives of their own. So successful were Kipling's *With the Night Mail* (1905) and several other futuristic stories that some experts credit him with inventing modern science fiction. His story "Wireless" incorporated the occult theme of mental telepathy into a story of technological progress and was directly influenced by a conversation with radio pioneer Guglielmo Marconi. But perhaps no writer had more influence on shaping popular conceptions of the future than did Hugo Gernsback (1884-1967), "the father of science fiction." Gernsback immigrated to the United States from his native Luxembourg, where as a child of nine, his lasting interest in life on other planets was kindled by reading *Mars*, by the famous American astronomer Percival Lowell. Gernsback became a scientist, inventor and writer who made his living selling devices such as batteries and small radios sets in New York City. He wrote and edited a popular radio magazine entitled *Modern Electrics* and was instrumental in establishing the first television station in New York City in 1928.

Gernsback occasionally published stories about the future in his *Modern Electrics*, dubbing these "prophetic" stories "Scientifiction," the term that eventually yielded to "science fiction." His vision of the future was filled with mechanical wonders, and his narratives provided the basis for the first science-fiction magazine, *Amazing Stories*, presented to the public for the first time in 1926.[29] T. O'Connor Sloane, a relative of Thomas Edison, was the magazine's first editor. Gernsback's influence on science fiction was enormous, in particular his interest in the technological advancements the future was certain to hold. And Gernsback proved to be remarkably capable of predicting what some of those advancements might be. His famous 1925 story *Ralph 124C 41+*:

A Romance of the Year 2660 predicted such wonders as radar, fluorescent lights and plastic. The great popularity of *Amazing Stories* helped to cultivate in the public an intense interest in everything and anything to do with the future. Gernsback permanently cemented science fiction's identity to his conception of the future as a place marked principally by technological progress.

The motto of the 1933 World's Fair announced with perhaps unintended menace, "Science Discovers, Industry Applies, Man Conforms." The Fair's official title was A Century of Progress International Exhibition. Progress, science and human conformity were joined in an imagined dawning age known only as the Future. Resistance was futile for the estimated 48 million attendees over a two-year run. The Future was also the theme of the 1939 New York City World's Fair. Its central attractions were General Motor's Futurama exhibit, a 700-foot-tall space needle, and a 200-foot-wide sphere called the Perisphere. Each attendee received a button announcing, "I have seen the future." The genre of science fiction, hugely popular in the 1930s, inspired much that the fair had to offer. Gunn comments that the futuristic exhibitions were "straight out of science fiction." He adds, "Hope for the future had begun to create what eventually would be recognized as a science fiction world."[30] Yet it was science fiction and its allied genre of speculative science that had first created that future hope. This chapter explores a few steps along the way to the Future, and in the process sketches the contours of one of the subtler scientific mythologies, the Myth of the Future.

FRANCIS BACON'S *THE NEW ATLANTIS*

Francis Bacon (1561-1626) provides an early example of a respected scientist who turned to popular fiction to propagate his speculative ideas. His famous fictional work *The New Atlantis* tells the story of sailors arriving at an island on which a variety of scientific advances have created a futuristic utopia. Written in 1623-1624, the book was not published until 1627, one year after the author's death. Though Bacon's utopia is set in an imaginary present, his narrative provided the basis for subsequent works about a future in which science has been allowed the resources it needs to deliver humanity from its most pressing problems. Moreover, the technological utopia of *The New Atlantis* is framed in spiritual terms. The true spiritual wisdom of the ages is recast as tending toward unlimited scientific investigation. In this way Bacon antic-

ipated—or set the direction for—speculative writing in which the science of
the future achieves human spiritual deliverance.

Bacon was convinced that science would create a better world and thus was
one of the principal early prophets of the Myth of the Future. His mythical
Island of Bensalem has developed to a high level of technological sophistication, as possible through the work of unfettered scientists associated with an
organization known as Salomon's House. A vast research facility, the House of
Salomon has ushered in the future that Bacon imagined for Europe. Bacon's
capacity to imagine scientific developments is remarkable, all of them based in
his guiding premise that humanity must master nature. In *The New Atlantis*,
Bacon also suggests that freedom from religious restraint may be the price
that has to be paid for a future scientific utopia.

The New Atlantis begins with a group of sailors setting off from Peru on a
voyage into the South Seas. After a long time at sea, they come upon an island,
Bensalem, populated with enlightened and generous inhabitants. There they
learn that long ago, following the death and resurrection of Jesus, the island's
residents witnessed "a great pillar of light . . . in form of a column, or cylinder,
rising from the sea, a great way up toward heaven." At the top of this mysterious pillar of light "was seen a large cross of light, more bright and resplendent
than the body of the pillar."

The association of this pillar of light with spiritual insight is significant, for
the light becomes a source of scientific rather than spiritual wisdom. When
the light disappeared, the residents discovered a "small ark or chest of cedar,"
and inside a book and a letter from one Bartholomew, "a servant of the Highest, and apostle of Jesus Christ." In a vision Bartholomew has been instructed
by an angel "that I should commit this ark to the floods of the sea." God has
delivered to the residents of Bensalem a new spiritual wisdom: Science. The
sailors are told that three thousand years earlier the great civilizations of the
Earth enjoyed a high state of technological advancement. This was the age of
Atlantis, the technologically advanced island paradise destroyed by an earthquake. A few people survived to rebuild civilization.

A great king named Salomon arose and established Salomon's House, a facility "dedicated to the study of the works and creatures of God." The name
Salomon is, it turns out, a corrupted version of Solomon. Thus, spiritual wisdom is again transformed into modern scientific knowledge. Salomon sought

knowledge from the ends of the earth, regularly sending out investigators to gather information and bring it back to the island. "Every twelve years" the king sent out "two ships, appointed to several voyages," with explorers who sought out "knowledge of . . . the sciences, arts, manufactures, and inventions of all the world." This whole social plan for Bensalem was originally suggested by the cabala (kabbalah), or secret writings of Moses.

Bacon's vision of what the residents of Bensalem have achieved is indeed remarkable. They build "high towers" up to "about half a mile in height," which are used for "insulation, refrigeration, conservation, and for the view of diverse meteors—as winds, rain, snow, hail, and some of the fiery meteors also." They have also developed "great lakes, both salt and fresh," which are used for conducting various kinds of experiments. Similarly they have built great rivers and waterfalls as well as "engines for multiplying and enforcing of winds." Experiments are being conducted on "vitriol, sulphur, steel, brass, lead, nitre, and other minerals." Through such experiments they have discovered drugs that improve health and prolong life.

The islanders have actually erected huge laboratories called houses for conducting a wide range of experiments. These "great and spacious houses" are used for gaining knowledge about everything from the weather to medicine. In addition, great parks have been established for studying "beasts and birds"; through "dissections and trials," they learn about the "body of man." In some of these experiments, animals that appear to be dead are actually brought back to life. Medicines are also tested on the animals. More astonishing is the idea that the islanders "by art" can make animals "greater or smaller than their kind," as well as different "in color, shape, [and] activity." Indeed, through "commixtures and copulations of diverse kinds," the residents of Bensalem "have produced many new kinds" of animal species that are "not barren, as the general opinion is." They boast that they can "make a number of kinds of serpents, worms, flies, fishes, . . . whereof some are advanced (in effect) to be perfect creatures, like beasts or birds, and have sexes, and do propagate." And this is not done "by chance, but we know beforehand of what matter and commixture, what kind of those creatures will arise." The island of Dr. Bacon begins to sound something like the later island laboratory of Dr. Moreau, as imagined by H. G. Wells. The islanders are also experimenting with "all lights and radiations," including lights that can be shone "to great distance" and made "so sharp as to discern small points and lines." Sounds and smells are also subjects of inquiry. "We multiply smells which may seem strange: we imitate smells, making all smells to breathe out of other mixtures than those that give them."

Applied technology on the island includes "engines and instruments for all sorts of motions," including "swifter motions" than are known outside the island, even swifter than a bullet from a musket and more powerful than "your greatest cannons and basilisks." Experiments are being conducted in both flight and submarine travel. "We have ships and boats for going under water," the islanders boast. "These are, my son, the riches of Salomon's House," says their guide. The sailors are also shown a great gallery in which scientists and explorers are honored with great statues and paintings, including Columbus and "your monk [Roger Bacon] that was the inventor of ordnance and of gunpowder."

The New Atlantis is an early work of science fiction in which Francis Bacon imagines a scientific future where research is pursued free of religious restraint, and where science has become the new religion. Human ills are conquered through the new Salomonic wisdom of a New Age. Disease is conquered, travel perfected, new animal species developed, social arrangements improved—all through the good offices of unfettered Science. The possibility that such knowledge would be misused or that human hubris might corrupt the course of science does not seem to occur to Bacon. In *The New Atlantis*, Francis Bacon crafted an early and highly influential version of the Myth of the Future—that given sufficient time and freedom, science would deliver humanity from all of its ills.[31]

MERCIER AND COMTE:
THE FUTURE AS SCIENTIFIC UTOPIA

The Future became an important component in the popular art of the eighteenth century, with tens of thousands of copies of fiction about the future being sold and read. Louis-Sébastien Mercier (1740-1814) was a French writer credited with creating the first fictional account of the future. His popular novel *L'An 2440 (The Year 2440)*, published in 1771, went through at least twenty-five editions. It is estimated that the book sold more than sixty thousand copies in the early years of its release, and it was translated into several languages—despite the fact that it was banned in France almost as soon as it was published. An English translation was published in America in 1795, making Mercier's future world available to a much broader audience.[32] Washington and Jefferson had copies of Mercier's early science-fiction work in their private libraries. *L'An 2440* is considered by most authorities to be the first utopian novel actually set in the future. An unnamed protagonist falls into a deep sleep and finds himself in a future world in which many social problems have been solved.

The French philosopher Auguste Comte (1798-1857) introduced the actual worship of scientific progress, the worship of the Future. In progress, humanity would discover what it fruitlessly sought in religion: deliverance, peace, liberation, justice. Not unlike Ray Kurzweil's vision of the Future in *The Singularity Is Near*, Comte believed that humanity was progressing through various distinct stages, each stage representing an advance over the previous one. The first and lowest stage is the theological, which, as the name implies, presents God as the cause of everything. The second is the metaphysical, in which humanity dispenses with the theological explanation in favor of philosophical ones. Both the theological and the metaphysical are mere steppingstones to the final stage, which Comte called the positivist, the highest achievement in human thinking. During this stage only scientific explanations are accepted as rational. Science has exposed the workings of the cosmos and brought nature under control.[33] For Comte, science was a new religion to replace Christianity, literally the religion of the Future. Science was the supreme font of knowledge, a new source of transcendence, and a path to a higher order of existence.

Historian James Turner writes that Comte "literally made a cult of science."[34] In the Future he envisioned, we will revere great thinkers, not religious prophets. This idea provided a model for a new calendar. "The year is divided into thirteen lunar months, each named after some great man." Feast days are celebrated to honor great minds, "just like a calendar of the Saints." Comtean churches sprang up in London and other cities, Comte himself "preached and performed marriages and burial services," and a faith of the Future developed called "the Religion of Humanity."[35] Comte was not fully devoted to the new faith, which apparently did not satisfy his deeper spiritual longings. He began to worship his deceased mistress, Madame de Vaux, and prayed to her on a regular basis.[36]

EDWARD BELLAMY'S *LOOKING BACKWARD:*
THE COMING ECONOMIC UTOPIA

The idea of a perfect future society continued to attract followers, largely because of its periodic presentation in a popular novel or play. More vibrant with each passing year, the Future was becoming recognizable, inevitable and alluring. Edward Bellamy's (1850-1898) *Looking Backward: 2000-1887*, published in 1888, was among the most popular of the late nineteenth-century utopian science-fiction stories.[37] Through narrator Julian West, readers were introduced into the socialistic utopia of the year 2000. In particular, Bellamy sought to address the terrible problems that resulted from the inequitable distribution of wealth in his day, and there was no better way than to imagine a trip into the Future. An insomniac, West constructs an underground room in which to sleep. In keeping with the times, he also contacts the famous mesmerist, Doctor Pillsbury, to put him into a hypnotic dream state. However, a fire destroys his home, leaving West alive but inanimate in his sleeping chamber. Friends and family assume that he has died in the fire. A century later, West is discovered—still alive. He has not aged, is revived by a Doctor Leete, and is then given a guided tour of late-twentieth-century society.

Given Bellamy's personal interests in social justice, it is not surprising that economic arrangements are the focus of much of *Looking Backward*. In the Future, a benevolent socialism has replaced heartless capitalism. Factories are owned by the government, and profits are distributed equitably among the citizenry. Other services such as education are also fairly distributed. There is no poverty or injustice, and everyone enjoys a leisurely and pleasant retirement at the age of forty-five. For Bellamy, the Future was not simply a fictional invention, but the result of inexorable processes. The Future, like human beings and everything else in this progressive thinker's universe, is shaped by evolutionary processes. Bellamy imagined social evolution at work, with the result being a socialist utopia he referred to as the Kingdom of God on Earth.

Bellamy's future was so appealing to readers that "Bellamy" or "Nationalist" clubs formed in many American cities. *Looking Backward* sold more than a million copies, was translated into twenty languages, and shaped public policy decisions in America and abroad. Many readers reported that reading Bellamy's book constituted for them a religious experience. So vivid was Bellamy's portrayal of the Future that it was taken by many to be an actual portrait of what was to come. David Samuelson writes that "a large number of utopian and anti-utopian novels seem to have been inspired by the need to support or rebut" Bellamy's story.[38] Perhaps more important than the specific social agenda of the movement was the growing belief, propagated through popular literature, that the Future is the ultimate laboratory for testing the merits of ideas, and that progress is its dominant characteristic. The Future was acquiring mythic status.

KURD LASSWITZ AND *ON TWO PLANETS:* MARS AS FUTURE BLUEPRINT

The year 1897 saw the publication of one of the most remarkable science-fiction works ever penned: Kurd Lasswitz's *Auf zwei Planeten (On Two Planets).* Lasswitz (1848-1910), a philosopher and mathematician intrigued with Schiaparelli's claims about Martian canals, created an engaging imaginative work about the first contact between Martians and the residents of Earth. *On Two Planets* was an immediate and enormous success, having a greater impact on European scientists than did any other fictional work of the late nineteenth century. Due to Lasswitz's unusual ability to explain scientific theories in a work of fiction, especially principles that would be involved in spaceflight, *Two Planets* represented a new phase of science-fiction writing. The contrast between Lasswitz's sophisticated work and, for example, Hale's scientifically primitive *The Brick Moon,* written only thirty years earlier, could not be greater. In a surprisingly realistic and prescient treatment, science had arrived in science fiction, putting in the shade even such venerated writers as Verne and the early Wells.

So stunningly conceived is Lasswitz's vision of interplanetary travel—which incorporates spaceships and wheel-shaped space stations—that the young Werhner von Braun, by his own testimony, determined to devote his life to rocketry after reading *On Two Planets.* The book provided a virtual blueprint to the future for a generation of German rocket scientists. Von Braun's own plan for spaceflight to the moon, as described in the mid 1950s *Colliers* series, involved both a space wheel and spaceship, as suggested by Lasswitz. Mark Hillegas writes, "In particular [*On Two Planets*] had an influence on the scientists and engineers at Peenemunde [the Nazi rocket development facility] who, fleeing the Russians at the end of World War II, surrendered to the Americans

and came to play a major role in this country's developing space program."
Hillegas adds the fascinating observation that "many of them seem to have
grown up on the book, which was widely read from the time of its publication
in 1897 well into the twentieth century."[39] In this way were the imaginations
of the world's leading rocket scientists shaped by a skillfully wrought work
of fiction. *On Two Planets'* popularity in Europe was as great among the general reading pubic as it was among scientists; the book was eventually translated into French, Danish, Italian, Norwegian, Swedish, Polish, Hungarian and
Czech.[40] Oddly, *On Two Planets* was not translated into English until 1971,
and then retitled *Two Planets.*

Lasswitz's *On Two Planets* is significant for other reasons: the work reveals
that several leading scientific myths were already well installed in the European imagination by the late nineteenth century. Lasswitz skillfully works each
into his extraordinarily influential tale. The Myth of the Extraterrestrial, for
instance, is clearly present in embryonic form in *On Two Planets.* The plot develops around the surprisingly familial first meeting of Martians and humans.
Physically, Lasswitz's Martians anticipate later extraterrestrial iterations: humanoid, they have large heads to accommodate their equally large brains. And
though his Martians resemble humans sufficiently to encourage romantic
relationships—indeed, interbreeding—Martian eyes are considerably larger
than human eyes. Moreover, in keeping with the Myth, these extraterrestrials
recognize a moral duty to assist the social development of other intelligent
beings they encounter in their interplanetary travels. Lasswitz, in this respect,
anticipates with remarkable accuracy the speculations of later writers such as
Sagan and Clarke about human-extraterrestrial interaction. Or perhaps we
should say that he gives early voice to several scientific mythologies that were
reiterated throughout the twentieth century.

Like so many other early authors of science fiction, Lasswitz was devoted to
an evolutionary view of both physical and social progress, following Darwin,
Spencer and Kant. A distinctly late nineteenth-century European racial hierarchy pervades *On Two Planets,* one that would mark some later science fiction, with Eskimos (the first humans Martians encounter) representing a low
level of human development, Germans a much-higher level, and the Martians
themselves ("with large heads, very light, nearly white hair; shining, powerful, piercing eyes") representing what humanity might become in the distant

future.[41] The Martians observe that, "compared with the small Eskimos, the tall, stately Europeans appeared as beings of higher development."[42] Human visitors to Mars read an angry newspaper editorial referring to earthlings as a "race [that] can only be tolerated by us as useful domesticated animals!"[43]

Importantly, it is not merely physical evolution that we encounter on Mars, for the peace-loving, law-revering Martians represent a future stage of moral or spiritual attainment as well. Lasswitz suggested that the Future would bring humans to such a point if impediments such as religion and nationalism did not prevent it. Mars has allowed "the development of culture and civilization to a much higher degree than the conditions of Earth."[44] Models of evolutionary progress were already present on the scene. Lasswitz hints that the Germans are the most spiritually advanced of all European groups. They are more accepting of the Martians than are the English, and the Martians find it easy to learn German. Lasswitz informs his readers that Martian is a "spiritually" advanced language, and that "German as a language of a highly developed people was a great deal closer to the intellectual level of the Martians than the primitive language of the Eskimos."[45] Such evolutionary thinking about language was common in his day.

And certainly, the Myth of Space is clearly present in On Two Planets. Lasswitz takes for granted that his Martians' technological advancement leads directly to conquest of space, thus rendering space exploration a human telos, or destiny. The ultimate purpose of technology is to leave Earth and make contact with extraterrestrials, a theme that science fiction has never abandoned. Lasswitz assumes that it is human destiny to explore Space, led there by a highly developed extraterrestrial race. Moreover, religious themes color the first human encounter with deep space. As they enter space for the first time aboard a Martian ship, humans revere the creation itself: Earth and Mars, sun and stars. But space is also a place for achieving social perfection. Lasswitz's heroes, German explorers who originally discover the Martians setting up a station at the North Pole, eventually experience a Martian technological utopia. In Space, secrets are revealed to humans that would have been impossible to imagine on Earth: global unity, political justice, egalitarian economics. Lasswitz's Mars resembles Bellamy's future Earth; each is a laboratory for observing inevitable social evolution.

Lasswitz's particular interest, however, is the Future. And though he does a remarkable job of anticipating developments in science fiction and thus in Western mythology, this author's principal interest is in advocating his own Kantian philosophy of human progress. *On Two Planets* is, more than anything else, a narrative hymn to a possible—perhaps even inevitable—future, one built around "the humanizing potential of science and technology."[46] On their older and thus more socially evolved planet, Martians live in the technologically enhanced and philosophically enlightened future that humans may, if cards are played right, achieve. When German explorers enter one of the Martian Earth bases for the first time, "the miracles of technology . . . transferred them into a new world." Lasswitz writes, "They felt as if they were in the enviable position of humans who had been carried by a powerful magician away from the present into a distant future, when humanity reached the apex of civilization."[47] That Lasswitz chooses the metaphor of a magician carrying these men into the future is suggestive, for—as already noted—progress, magic and the Future were inseparable ideas for many late nineteenth-century European intellectuals.

Lasswitz's interest in the Future was clear from very early in his writing career. His first novel, written when he was only twenty-three years old, was a projection of life on Earth in the year 2371.[48] In the more successful *On Two Planets*, Martians travel on superhighways in high-speed cars, fly through the atmosphere in supersonic airplanes, and travel to distant planets with the aid of antigravity spaceships and wheel-shaped permanent space stations. They have also achieved a social and economic equity that would be the envy of the most liberal of Western democracies. Indeed, still widely read in the 1930s, the Nazis suppressed publication of *Auf zwei Planeten* as being excessively democratic.

Much of the novel *On Two Planets* is devoted to an adventure and love story relating the slow domination of the Earth by the Martians and the Earth's eventual liberation through human ingenuity. The book's conclusion is striking, particularly given the powerful influence Lasswitz's novel had on World War II-era German rocket engineers. An international team of engineers, guided by a handful of Germans familiar with Martian technology, direct American industrialists in secretly developing spaceships used to throw off Martian rule. Thus, German technological know-how combined with unlimited American capital opens humanity's way into Space and thus into the Future. "So it happened that without the knowledge of the Martians, the United States had a fleet of warships at their disposal that were not inferior in any respect to those of the Martians."[49] The fact that the young Wernher von Braun and his colleagues at Peenemunde, the future architects of the American space program, were deeply moved by this story is surely a remarkable instance of life imitating art. Von Braun in particular, like Lasswitz, was profoundly influenced by his reading of Kant on the inevitability of human progress. In Lasswitz's novel, the young scientist found the themes of progress, space, technology and the future woven into an appealing and compelling narrative. Thus, *On Two Planets* stands as profound testimony to the power of fiction to shape cultural mythology and thus to transform society.

J. B. S. HALDANE ON
SCIENCE AND HUMAN DESTINY

Walter Sullivan writes that "it is probably more than a coincidence that contemporary discussion of the manner in which life could have come into being on our own planet was initiated by two students of the writing of Friedrich Engels, cofounder of communism." One of these two figures was A. I. Oparin, who published his classic work *The Origin of Life* in 1936. The other was the brilliant British scientist and public intellectual J. B. S. Haldane (1892-1964).[50] Haldane, a polymath and a prolific writer, "made major contributions to neurobiology, genetics, population biology, and evolution."[51] And Haldane was keenly interested in humanity's future. Physicist Freeman Dyson writes that "after Wells, the next visionary who dreamed of the future was the biologist J. B. S. Haldane."[52] It is intriguing that Dyson places a leading writer of science fiction and a major scientist next to one another as the two leading future visionaries of the early twentieth century. This eminent scientist seems to take for granted that envisioning the Future belongs equally to both endeavors.

Haldane was an extraordinarily popular speaker and writer on scientific and social themes in the early twentieth century. His many essays and books made him the greatest popularizer of science of his day, the Carl Sagan of the 1920s and 1930s. A captivating speaker, talented writer and tireless proponent of new ideas, Haldane's influence on the intellectual and artistic figures of his day was enormous. And his vision of the Future was unconstrained by traditional mores. He suggested the genetic engineering of babies, who would then be artificially produced outside the womb, "a move which Aldous Huxley satirized in *Brave New World.*"[53] In addition, Haldane admired both Soviet political arrangements and Eastern religions. He propagated the Myth of the Future, recognizing that he represented a tradition of attributing religious significance to progress. "Renan," he wrote, "suggested that science would progress so far that our successors would be able to reconstruct the past in complete detail, . . . thus achieving the resurrection of the just."[54]

Haldane was a prophet proclaiming the message that scientific progress would usher in a New Age of human peace, health and social equality. His many newspaper and magazine essays "had a powerful influence on public opinion."[55] Among various future "advances," Haldane advocated colonizing space, recording the genetic makeup of all newborns, and intentionally directing human evolution.[56] His speculations about space colonization and human evolution apparently persuaded contemporary science-fiction author Olaf Stapledon. In one particularly popular essay, *Possible Worlds*—written in the style of science fiction—Haldane imagines a human race that begins by colonizing space and ends as a limitless cosmic force. Space colonization was a religious hope; humanity "will certainly attempt to leave the Earth," and colonies will be established on other planets. Even that is not the end of progress: "After the immense efforts of the first colonizers, we have settled down as members of a super-organism with no limits to its possible progress." Thus, "there is no theoretical limit to man's material progress but the subjugation to complete conscious control of every atom and every quantum of radiation in the universe. There is, perhaps, no limit at all to his intellectual and spiritual progress."[57]

Humans are destined to become gods, or parts of a god, according to a message we receive from some unknown cosmic source. He declares, "We can never close our consciousness to those wave-lengths on which we are told of our nature as components of a super-organism or deity, possibly the only one in space-time, and of its past, present, and future."[58] The source of this message is not made clear. Nevertheless, Haldane's future human race must strive to achieve its destiny of galactic dominance—albeit in a form perhaps unrecognizable to present humans. Before the present galaxy comes to an end, "it is our ideal that all the matter in it available for life should be within the power of the heirs of the species whose original home has just been destroyed." And he says, "There are other galaxies."[59] The Future knows no limits to the cosmic human advance.

It was precisely this hubristic vision of the human future that prompted C. S. Lewis to write his own science-fiction works. Lewis had recognized the great scientist's tendency to couch his grandiose vision of the Future in spiritual terms, and the scientist Weston in Lewis's space trilogy speaks in similar terms about scientific progress and human destiny. Haldane wrote that the "use, however haltingly, of our imaginations upon the possibilities of the future is a valuable spiritual exercise."[60] The Future was the new religion. "For one of the essential elements of religion," he wrote, "is an emotional attitude towards the universe as a whole." And once we realize "the unimaginable vastness of the possibilities of time and space," we will begin to see our future and what "purposes may be developed in the universe that we are beginning to apprehend."[61] Our "destiny is in eternity and infinity," and "the value of the individual is negligible in comparison with that destiny." Haldane brought Bacon's religious hope in human scientific progress well into the twentieth century, placing "humanity" firmly in control of its spiritual as well as its physical destiny.[62] The individual's destiny was less certain.

FREEMAN DYSON:
THE FUTURE AS MYTHIC SYNTHESIS

One of the leading scientific minds of the twentieth century, physicist Freeman Dyson (b. 1923), has often expressed his hope that in the future humanity will find a kind of final deliverance. In Dyson's future, progressive thinkers willing to embrace evolutionary advances will find themselves locked in battle with those recalcitrant few committed to older forms of thought characteristic of the past. Thus, "societies of collective minds will be battling against old-fashioned individuals. Big brains will be battling against little brains." And he adds, "Devotees of artificial intelligence will be battling against devotees of natural wisdom." Dyson warns, somewhat unaccountably, that "such battles may lead to wars of genocide."[63]

Dyson himself is evidence of that symbiosis between science and science fiction that has had such a profound effect on the Western world over the past several centuries. He is a great fan of Olaf Stapledon, especially his *Last and First Men*, *Star Maker* and *Sirius*. In his introduction to a 2004 reissue of *Star*

Maker, Patrick A. McCarthy writes that Dyson "has traced the concept of the Dyson Sphere, an artificial biosphere designed to capture energy from a sun, to 'a tattered copy of Stapledon's *Star Maker* which I picked up in Paddington Station in London in 1945.'"[64] To complete the science/science fiction circle, the Dyson Sphere was prominently featured in an episode of the television series *Star Trek.* In this case an idea has run from the science fiction of Stapledon to the science of Dyson, and back to science fiction in *Star Trek.* In Dyson's future-vision we discover a synthesis of mythic themes about space, new humans, extraterrestrials and scientific progress.

So profound is Dyson's confidence in the human future that he has affirmed, "Six hundred years is plenty of time for the social problems of our own era to be solved, for the history of divisive struggles between nations and races to be forgotten, and for the spark of human individuality to be extinguished." In that same period of time, "we shall have achieved the age-old dreams of perpetual peace and the greatest happiness of the greatest number." There will be some sacrifices to be made, such as "intellectual curiosity and political discontent," as well as "the personal ambitions that cause us to fight and quarrel and stir up revolutions." Also to be sacrificed are "the three ungovernable passions that brought us too much grief in the past: science, art, and religion."[65] The Future will transcend even science.

Dyson is certainly willing to state his vision of the Future boldly, no matter how strange the details. For instance, he envisions that fundamental changes to the basic cerebral equipment of humans are in the offing, and in the process he revives Victorian dreams of telepathy. "Radiotelepathy," the capacity to communicate silently with other individuals via a device added to the brain, may characterize future humans. Radiotelepathy, "if it is possible, could grow out of the science of neurophysiology just as genetic engineering grew out of molecular biology." Again, this idea was suggested to Dyson by Stapledon. "The idea of radiotelepathy first appeared, so far as I know, in the science-fiction novel *Last and First Men,* written by Olaf Stapledon in 1931." Stapledon had imagined a symbiotic relationship developing between humans and a type of life from Mars in which "the cells of a multicellular creature communicate with each other by means of electric and magnetic fields instead of by physical contact and chemical exchange."[66] All that would be needed to make such communication possible is "a technology that allows us to build and deploy large arrays of small transmitters inside a living brain."[67] This should be within the reach of future technologies: when "we know how to put into a brain transmitters translating neural processes into radio signals, we shall also know how to insert receivers translating radio signals back into neural processes."[68] Bell and Tesla had attempted a form of radiotelepathy before 1931, employing helmets rather than chips, and the idea of telepathy itself originated in the world of the medium, the mesmerist and the hypnotist. The triad of science, magic and the future appear together again in radiotelepathy, as they did in Victorian psychic experiments. Dyson is aware that such a fundamental change in the human condition would raise crucial ethical issues. Nevertheless, he argues that "big jumps in technology or in evolution always have costs that are incalculable."[69]

Technological evolution on the order of Kurzweil's Singularity is also a major force in Dyson's future vision. "Compared with the slow pace of natural evolution, our technological evolution is like an explosion." As for Wells, Haldane and Kurzweil, Space plays a role in this endless evolutionary progress that will mark the Future. Thus, "when life and industrial activities are spread out over the solar system, there is no compelling reason for growth to stop."[70] And the New Humanity makes an appearance in Dyson's Future as well. The next millennium will bring "many opportunities for experiments in the radical reconstruction of human beings." Indeed, "some of these experiments may succeed. When they succeed, our descendants may be born with mental qualities different from ours." Exploring these changes "will be as great a challenge as the exploration of the physical universe." Sounding another Victorian theme—the pervasive psychic force—Dyson predicts that we may experience "collective memory and collective consciousness" that will "enormously enlarge the scope of art, science, religion, and history." But why stop here? "Other experiments in collective consciousness may link human brains with those of dolphins and whales, lions and chimpanzees and eagles, breaking down barriers not only between individuals but [also] between species."[71]

Following closely a theme that Stapledon introduced, Dyson envisions even a type of immortality arising out of the possibility of "group mind." And "those who have been part of an immortal group-mind," he writes, "may find it difficult to communicate with ordinary mortals." Thus, divisions will occur between progressing future humans, and humans who have failed to adapt and are mired in old modes of existence. "The most serious conflicts of the next thousand years will probably be biological battles, fought between different conceptions of what a human being ought to be." Indeed, "such battles may lead to wars of genocide." However, Space will come to our rescue, for "the vast expanses of space beyond the earth offer a way to resolve such biological battles peacefully." Disagreeing groups may begin "migrating to opposite ends of the solar system. Space is big enough to have room for them all."[72] When disagreements arise in the Future, we simply learn to avoid one another in the void of Space. One is reminded of the residents of hell in C. S. Lewis's *The Great Divorce:* when differences arise, they simply move further apart in the infinite territory of the abyss.

A "golden age of science" will be marked by "mental exploration," taking us "in many directions that we cannot yet imagine."[73] Some of us may even achieve immortality, a concept associated with Space, but "it would be wise to keep a population of mortal humans on Earth, so that some contact with the reality of death will not be lost." Volunteers? Religion under such circumstances would certainly look different. "Our descendants may, as Olaf Stapledon imagined, refresh their spirits with a 'Cult of Evanescence,' a form of religion or artistic creation in which the tragedy and beauty of short-lived creatures is given the highest value."[74] Earth would be preserved as "a cultural museum."[75]

Finally, Lasswitz-like benevolent and advanced extraterrestrials enter Dyson's future vision as well. "If we are lucky," he writes, "our history may be enriched by a multitude of alien cultures and traditions. The aliens will probably have notions of good and evil very different from ours. We will have much to teach and much to learn."[76] Let's hope their "notions of good and evil" aren't *too* different from ours. These aliens may, in a million years, join our descendants in "the intelligent intervention of life in the evolution of the universe as a whole."[77] The final triumph will be a "universal Gaia"—something akin to Kurzweil's humanly awakened universe—doing the work of "regulating life in every corner of the cosmos."[78] The final chapter of Dyson's future vision brings us around to a new deity, which actually is an ancient pagan one: Gaia, the soul of a living earth and universe.

MARTIN REES ON OUR FUTURE REFUGE IN SPACE

British Astronomer Royal Martin Rees is among the most widely read and influential science writers of recent years. His theories about multiple universes and the numerical basis of all physical reality have created controversy and earned him a devoted following. He has also recently written about the human future in a way that has attracted the attention of scholars and the general public alike.

Rees envisions the future as offering a kind of salvation for threatened humanity, if it is used well. After outlining many of the dangers facing us, Rees writes of the future as a "continuing process" that brings significance to our lives and validates our accomplishments. "Most of us care about the future," he writes, "not just because of a personal concern with children and grandchildren, but because all our efforts would be devalued if they were not part of a continuing process, if they did not have consequences that resonated into the far future."

The Future, as we have come to expect even of serious scientists like Hawking, Dyson and Rees, involves Space—our guarantee of survival for both our accomplishments and for the human race itself. Rees writes, "Even a few pioneering groups, living independently of Earth, would offer a safeguard against the worst possible disaster—the foreclosure of intelligent life's future through the extinction of all humankind." Because of the activities of human beings, Earth is not safe, but somehow human beings in the Future and in Space can be relied on to avoid disastrous cataclysms. "Once self-sustaining communities exist away from Earth—on the Moon, on Mars, or freely floating in space—our species would be invulnerable to even the worst global disasters."[79]

Looking "still further ahead, in future centuries," as Rees imagines, "robots and fabricators could have pervaded the entire solar system." Some of these essentially living machines, "unconstrained by any restrictions," would likely "exploit the full range of genetic techniques and diverge into new species."[80] All such development requires, however, our entry into Space—our last resort. "Once the threshold is crossed when there is a self-sustaining level of life in space, then life's long-range future will be secure irrespective of any of the risks on Earth (with the single exception of the catastrophic destruction of space itself)."[81]

A New Humanity is also part of Rees's larger vision of Space and the Future. Genetic duplication of humans could take place "on promising planets," thus guaranteeing "a diffusion through the entire Galaxy." Rees adds that "this would be as epochal an evolutionary transition as that which led to land-based life on Earth. But it could still be just the beginning of cosmic evolution."[82] Quoting Nobel Prize-winning medical researcher Christian de Duve (b. 1917) to the effect that the future depends upon human decision-making, for we now "have the power of decisively influencing the future of life and human-kind on Earth."[83] The human race has "a near-infinite future" to look forward to, so long as we master such complexities as "wormholes, extra dimensions and quantum computers," which "open up speculative scenarios that could transform our entire universe eventually into a 'living cosmos.'" In that Future we in our present form may no longer exist, a fate some of us might try to prevent. But there is no need to worry, for Rees imagines a "post-human potential . . . so immense that not even the most misanthropic amongst us would countenance its being foreclosed by human actions."[84]

Rees's integration of narrative constructions such as the Future, Space and the New Humanity illustrates how scientific mythologies constitute, not just isolated components of popular, scientific or religious culture, but also an overarching system of belief that, like a religious vision, can create a unifying worldview capable of bridging the gaps among various cultures. In this way such mythologies comprise a narrative force powerful enough to change the face of human society on an international scale.

CONCLUSION

Rees's vision of a limitless human future on various planets with human DNA wafting through the cosmos and sentient machines exploring the galaxy in search of habitable worlds provides a fitting summary of the topic of this chapter. His vision is not taken to be certain: Rees knows he is speculating. But neither is it considered as an expression of human hubris; this future-vision is presented as a distinct and desirable possibility, given the trajectory of technology and the virtually limitless capacities of the human mind. Science and science fiction have prepared us to accept such portrayals of the Future in which we are in control of our own fate, crafting our destiny out of technology and a scientifically inspired moral frame. The Tower of Babel notwithstanding, we are again reaching up into the heavens with great confidence, having finally rid that realm of its excessively restrictive Sovereign (though it is still not clear how that particular feat was accomplished). Nothing shall be beyond us, not even eternal life, according to Rees.

The Future is always with us, and it shows no signs of diminishing in its cultural influence. In the hands of some writers, the Future promises us divine qualities, producing superbeings or supermachines by the operations of technologically enhanced and consciously guided evolution. Thus, physicist Frank J. Tipler (b. 1947), in books such as *The Physics of Immortality*, has argued that the universe is heading inexorably toward something he terms Omega Point, a future moment at which immortality will be achieved by means of artificial intelligence. Kurzweil called this point the Singularity; Tipler identifies it as God, using phrases such as "the resurrection of the dead" to refer to the culmination of all things in everlasting technological existence.[85] The Future means progress, and the end point of progress, its telos, is an everlasting equilibrium in which the ultimate technology, an Artificial Intelligence god, overtakes and conquers death or entropy itself.

It is at precisely this point that the clash between biblical conceptions of the future and technological dreams of godlike control over *Life, the Universe and Everything*—to borrow satirist Douglas Adams's title—come into clash. In the biblical vision, the future, like all of time and space, is under the sovereign control of the God who created all that exists. Whatever occurs in the future will be determined, not by technological advances under the control of human intellect and perhaps unseen forces such as evolution or the Life Force, but by the will of God. The biblical tradition's insistence that God holds the past, present and future is as uncompromising as is its insistence that God did not arise out of nature. No human activity of any kind—spiritual, scientific or cataclysmic—will affect either the arrival or the shape of that future. The ownership of the future—human or divine?—is perhaps the central point of contention between its Judeo-Christian presentation and the Myth of the Future.

Moreover, the traditional religious vision of time past and time to come is part of an overarching narrative of redemption through God's intervention in the order of things. The centerpiece of this narrative of redemption is God's incarnation rather than humanity's innovation. No amount of technological advancement, no genetic enhancement of the human race, and no evolutionary telos is understood in this vision as resolving the human predicament by delivering us into a redeeming Future. Rather, the biblical concept of the final unveiling of God's predetermined culmination of human history, and the establishment of an eternally constituted divine order—as in the Apocalypse—stands in contrast to all other portraits of the future. Such contrasting visions include the gradualist depictions of the future as an inexorable outworking of a scientistic-spiritualistic course of research, portraits affording a commanding place to human intellect.

Why has the Future been so often presented as more relevant than, and even preferable to, the present? The answer is likely discovered in the powerful idea of progress, which has become coterminous with the future in Western thought. It is progress that has justified our grandest cultural project—science—and science that promises us the Future. Without the Future, where is science? But in the process of inventing a future worthy of a project the size of science, we also turned the Future into a powerful myth that has displaced sacred narratives urging us to inhabit the present, attending faithfully to its demands, addressing its injustices, and simply living with hope in its reality—a reality the Future, always an imagined abstraction, can never attain.

7

THE MYTH OF THE SPIRITUAL RACE

It may be that after much labour and many catastrophes in time,
there will arise a splendid race of men,
far wiser than we can hope to be, and far greater hearted.

OLAF STAPLEDON, "THE SPLENDID RACE"

Many great men of history, known as adepts,
leaders and reformers, belonged to other worlds.
Even now they serve in every field of endeavor: they are scientists,
inventors, writers, ministers, students, teachers,
electronic engineers, speakers and farmers!
They have infiltrated everywhere and only wait for the day of
The Telling to make themselves known.

GEORGE HUNT WILLIAMSON

I teach you the superman.
Man is something that is to be surpassed.

FRIEDRICH NIETZSCHE

Science . . . will be harnessed to the service of the Superman.
Thus Nietzsche's true leaders, the men of strong and beautiful bodies,
wills and intellects, will be developed.

PAUL COHN

In Christ . . . there is no Jew or Greek.

GALATIANS 3:26-28

By far the most influential editor in the history of science fiction was John W. Campbell, the man who presided over *Astounding Science Fiction* during its "golden years," 1938-1945. Campbell mentored such science-fiction greats as A. E. van Vogt, Isaac Asimov, Robert Heinlein and L. Ron Hubbard. But over time Campbell's own exotic theories about religion, psychology, sociology and "strange, undiscovered powers" began to creep into science fiction through his editorial hand.[1] For a time he promoted mental forces he called "psi" powers, and he was one of the first advocates of Hubbard's science of Dianetics.

Campbell, as might be expected of a man in his profession, was a true believer in the capacity of science to solve human problems and answer ultimate questions. But his faith in science had a dark side that was interpreted by some who knew him as reflecting an extreme brand of social conservatism. One of Campbell's biographers points out that "many of the leading intellects post-Darwin found themselves convinced that certain genetic groups [races?] had evolved higher up the ladder of evolution."[2] In particular, Campbell's "feelings towards Jews" are difficult to unravel, though they may provide a key to some of his thinking. Philip Klass recalls having lunch with Campbell "shortly after the Holocaust camps had been discovered." During the lunch, "Campbell expressed sympathy and his secret belief that the Jews were '*Homo superiorus.*'" But "this idea of an evolutionary ladder didn't sit well with Klass, and he told Campbell that separating out the Jews was racist, which confused Campbell since he thought that they were superior, which Campbell thought was a compliment."[3] Yet if one race was at the top of this imaginary racial ladder, other races must have been positioned on rungs further down.

This brief account from the life of John Campbell points toward the fact that science fiction has had a long and sometimes uneasy relationship with questions of race. Whether we are reading the disturbing Aryan dreams of Bulwer-Lytton's *The Coming Race* (1871), experiencing the shocking anti-Semitism of M. P. Shiel's *Lord of the Sea* (a 1901 work of science fiction "that provokes comparison with Hitler's *Mein Kampf* [*My Struggle*]"), contending with H. P. Lovecraft's early twentieth-century disgust at the "alien hordes" entering New York City or H. G. Wells's similar concern for London, imagining the millennia-long development of a master military race in E. E. "Doc" Smith's *Lensman* series of the 1930s and 1940s, pondering Robert Heinlein's shocking 1964 *Farnham's Freehold* with its cannibalistic black slave owners, noting with surprise that the "highly evolved" godlike character Q should be a white male in the *Star Trek* series, or questioning why Jar-Jar Binks should speak in a Jamaican pidgin and make himself the servant of a white male Jedi in *Star Wars: The Phantom Menace*—we recognize that science fiction has often dealt clumsily and occasionally dangerously with issues of race.[4]

And certainly, Western speculative science has not been free from the taint of racialism, making qualitative distinctions among people based on race. Racially charged eugenics theories were a virtual preoccupation of late nineteenth-century scientists, including Charles Darwin's cousin Francis Galton, while Darwin's chief defender in Germany, the naturalist Ernst Haeckel, was an avowed racist who advocated the elimination of "inferior" racial groups. Dan Stone writes that eugenics theory was not developed as "a way of benefiting everybody," but rather as a means of "realizing afresh social hierarchies" and to "justify class and race prejudices."[5]

For some proponents, the eugenics movement of the late nineteenth and early twentieth centuries was the scientific effort to produce "better" people. But to others it was clearly more than that. Eugenics was a religious quest to create the Superman: the race of people to transcend Homo sapiens, not just physically, but also morally or spiritually. This latter goal is reflected in the title of a widely read essay published in the first edition of the periodical *Eugenics Review* by the late nineteenth-century eugenic theorist Maximilian Mugge: "Eugenics and the Superman: A Racial Science and a Racial Religion." Mugge idolized the philosopher Friedrich Nietzsche as the intellectual leader who had "founded a Eugenic Religion, a valuable ally of the Eugenic Science."[6] A. R. Orage, an early twentieth-century proponent of Theosophy, stated that the main challenge confronting "mystics of all ages" was "how to become supermen" by developing a "superconsciousness."[7]

Why should many take the search for a new race or physically and morally superior people as a religious quest? And why was a science aimed at engineering a superior race of people thought to need a new religion as its ally? Popular fiction around 1900 promoted such racially charged thinking, including Wells's *The New Machiavelli* and Shaw's *Man and Superman*. Hitler's celebrated propagandist Leni Riefenstahl, creator of the legendary propaganda film *Triumph of the Will*, referred to the *Führer* as "the Coming Man," a phrase eerily reminiscent of Bulwer-Lytton's *The Coming Race*. Even the Superman of comic-book fame was referred to in serialized animations at the outbreak of World War II as "The Man of Tomorrow." As Nazi racial philosophy became better known to American audiences, the phrase was dropped.

Eugenic theories continued to maintain some popularity beyond the middle of the twentieth century. The 1956 Nobel laureate in physics and codeveloper of the transistor, William Shockley (1910-1989), spent the last years of his life advocating "dysgenics," a racial theory about intelligence. Shockley went so far as to advocate sterilization for those with an IQ below 100. He also famously donated samples of his own semen to the so-called Nobel sperm bank in an effort to ensure the perpetuation of great genius such as his own.[8] At his death he was reputed to have esteemed his work on intelligence more highly than his work in physics. Even relatively recent developments such as the publication of 1994 bestseller by Charles Murray and Richard J. Herrnstein, *The Bell Curve*, have posited a statistically based connection between racial distinctions and differences in intelligence, suggesting the existence of a "cognitive elite."[9] Moreover, in October of 2007 Nobel Laureate and DNA pioneer James Watson ignited controversy with statements suggesting that different races possessed differing levels of intelligence.

This chapter does not focus on racial theories broadly construed, nor is its topic human enhancement, which has already been discussed. Rather, our focus in the following pages is a species of fictional racial construction found in the pages of some speculative scientific writing and some science fiction. The Myth of the Spiritual Race carries forward the notion that there exists, at one time existed, will someday exist, or ought to be created—whether on Earth or on a distant planet—an aristocratic race possessing remarkable spiritual insights, powers and purposes. This spiritual race is, in some tellings of the myth, unspeakably ancient, either maintaining its "purity" through the millennia or perhaps being in need of racial revival.

A large number of science-fiction narratives incorporate an ancient, highly advanced and remarkably enlightened race. The Vorlons of the popular television science-fiction series *Babylon 5* represent such an ancient race possessing moral insight and, in some cases, the power even to restore life. They appear as pure light in the shape of angels (when not wearing their "encounter suits"), leading to their erroneous inclusion in many human religions. The Old Ones mentioned in Robert Heinlein's *Stranger in a Strange Land* are a similar type of advanced race, controlling events according to their own insights from behind the scenes. In other cases the special race, perhaps not quite so ancient, has been prepared for leadership or dominance through advanced genetic crafting. Frank Herbert's *Dune* series (1965-1985), for instance, features a carefully monitored eugenics project resulting in certain spiritually advanced members of the House Atreides, in particular the spiritually gifted messianic figure Paul Atreides.

In *The Aryan Myth*, Léon Poliakov chronicles the Western world's long history of racial mythologizing. Virtually every country in Europe has propagated myths about its own people's origins and relative moral superiority to surrounding people groups. The Nazi catastrophe in Western culture virtually put an end to public discussion of racial hierarchies and associated narratives, and scientific theories that sought to justify such ordering were quickly shelved. Nevertheless, racial mythologies have deep roots indeed in Western culture and, despite being discredited, have never completely vanished from the intellectual and cultural landscape. Often these mythologies have included claims about the special race's unusual spiritual capacities or unique spiritual destiny.

Where racial superiority is a theme, racial hierarchy will certainly also constitute a central concern. Stories about lost races in possession of a great secret, wandering races seeking a place to establish a new spiritual order, gifted races genetically descended from spiritually advanced ancestors, races specially created to perform a particular historical task, or prehistoric master races awaiting their time to reemerge onto the world scene—such stories are as charged with the spirit of racial hierarchy as are the rambling polemics of a racial supremacist. When the spirit of hierarchy appears in its most pernicious form, racial myths trade in megalomaniacal notions such as the right to rule other races, the possession of mystical power over other races, even the right to destroy inferior races.

So-called advanced races in popular narratives often reflect great spiritual capacities that include apprehending a grander human vision, ruling over other races with extraordinary wisdom, waging and winning the ultimate struggle against evil, possessing an ancient spiritual secret, or leading the human race to its destiny. The spiritually gifted race has been portrayed

as proving its superiority to mere humans by braving a great passage, endur-
ing a terrible struggle, or participating in an epic battle. The Great Race de-
scends from a high mountain, crosses a vast sea, wages an unimaginably costly
war against inferior foes (who sometimes prevail), or endures a great journey
across time or through Space. Indeed, Thomas Jefferson suggested that Americans might reflect the traits of such a race; he recommended "marking the seal
of the United States with portrayals of the two great ancestral crossings, that
of the sea by Hengist and Horsa, the Saxon chiefs, and that of the desert by the
children of Israel."[10]

Myths of the Spiritual Race, seldom the stuff of public discussion today,
have nevertheless reasserted themselves in important works of science fiction,
in some religious narratives that incorporate science-fiction motifs, and even
in some speculative scientific writing that projects virtual divinity through
science for at least some humans. Though most modern people recognize that
racial theories of the past contributed to dangerous political and military conflicts, the same modern readers and moviegoers may be unaware that racial
myths—even contemporary ones—often have a spiritual component that can
also be used to establish hierarchies.[11] Moreover, this connecting of race and
spirituality opened the way in Western thought to positing a biological basis for spiritual insight, and an evolutionary path to spiritual awareness and
power.

But has not the Western world with its Enlightenment heritage and scientific achievements moved beyond such antiquated notions about race and the
human spirit? On the contrary, Enlightenment and science have often aided
in perpetuating racial myths. For example, Poliakov writes that "some of the
most notable champions of the Enlightenment laid the foundations of the scientific racism which was to follow in the next century." In particular, Poliakov
reports that the prime symbol of the Enlightenment, Voltaire himself, wrote
in a viciously anti-Semitic vein and spoke of other races in "contemptuous language." Poliakov attributes much of this scientifically inspired racism to "crude
notions of progress" as well as other questionable ideas that were passed off as
science.[12] Among the most damaging was the once-widespread "scientific" belief that different human races originated in different parts of the world and at
different times, a theory known as polygenism. Poliakov states that the theory
of polygenism, which Voltaire "in particular advocated during the Age of En-

lightenment, early on claimed the status of a purely scientific doctrine."[13]

Strangely, the idea of a spiritually enlightened race is still with us in a number of highly influential popular narratives. This chapter examines a persistent theme in some science fiction, speculative science and certain new religious movements. I have chosen to label this theme the Myth of the Spiritual Race. Briefly, the Myth suggests that one race, whether real or imagined, exhibits a greater capacity for spiritual insight, supernatural power or moral development than do other races. To understand the nature and dangers of the Myth of the Spiritual Race, we need to search out some of its cultural roots as well as its manifestations in popular forms. How did we arrive at the idea that a particular group of people—often people of the past, the future, a lost land or another planet—should have greater spiritual capacities than the ordinary run of the human race? And how should people of faith respond to this persistent theme of our popular culture?

FROM INDIA AND ISRAEL TO
EUROPE AND AMERICA—AND INTO SPACE

During the course of the nineteenth century, racial theories were hotly debated among European intellectuals. Much attention was focused on India in the search for what was presumed to be the source of a proto-European race. Somehow the idea of the great height of India's many mountains came to be associated with superiority in racial character, particularly spiritual capacity or insight.[14] A writer named Johann-Gottfried Herder introduced the passion for India as a racial fountainhead into European, especially German, thinking. Many among the nineteenth-century Romantics were also prompted to write about Mother India. Herder urged his readers to "scale the mountain laboriously to the summit of Asia" in order to find their racial origins, which meant also the source of their spiritual superiority to other peoples. Christianity was sometimes viewed as a hindrance to the spiritual development of the German people. Poliakov writes that Germany, "striving to extricate herself from Judaeo-Christian fetters," sought an intellectual connection through Schopenhauer with "India and Buddhism" and through Nietzsche with Persia and Zarathustra.[15]

The interests of European racial theorists during the middle decades of the nineteenth century seldom were strictly academic. Instead, many sought a justification for racial and spiritual superiority of the white European race and began propagating the theory that a superior race had migrated westward out of India. "According to this new theory, it was not the whole human race but one particular race—a white race which subsequently became Christian—which had descended from the mountains of Asia to colonize and populate the West."[16] These imagined people formed the basis of the Aryan myth. Writers like Friedrich Schlegel were "able to galvanize German youth with the myth of an Aryan race" emerging from India. As Poliakov writes, Schlegel "boldly portrayed columns of masterful men marching down from the roof of the world, founding empires and civilizing the West."[17] Later in the chapter we will trace the Aryan myth into the twentieth century.

An entirely different version of the Myth of the Spiritual Race was emerging on American soil in the eighteenth and nineteenth centuries. The presence of Native Americans raised a number of racially related questions: Who were they? To what other races were they related? Did they possess special racial knowledge of spiritual matters? Various theories developed around the pre-Columbian residents of the New World. For instance, Joseph Smith (1805-1844), founder of Mormonism, suggested in the *Book of Mormon* that certain Semitic peoples—the Jaredites, Mulekites, Lamanites and Nephites—journeyed in the seventh and sixth centuries B.C. to the shores of America on large boats or "barges," where they functioned as keepers of important spiritual knowledge unknown to the rest of humanity. Several such migrations occurred at different times, and it is supposed that these peoples landed somewhere in Central America or southern Mexico. Supernatural signs attended at least some of these travelers. Indeed, they made the journey with the assistance of a navigational device or compass called the Liahona, which itself possessed special spiritual powers.[18] Two needles or "spindles" on the Liahona pointed out the way to the New World, while legible writing on the device changed periodically to provide messages from God for the prophet Lehi. Moreover, miraculous lights were provided for the interior of the boats of a different leader, Moriancumer, through sixteen divinely illuminated volcanic stones.

Some of the spiritual knowledge of these Semitic peoples was already in their possession before their departure from the shores of ancient Israel, while more was delivered later through spirit messengers and eventually through the resurrected Christ appearing in what is now Central America. Some of the members of these spiritually enlightened people remained true to divine teachings; others did not. This disparity in spiritual attunement among early residents of America eventually raised serious racial questions.

The issue of skin color and spiritual rectitude troubles these narratives, with dark skin typically being a sign of spiritual error as in the case of the errant Lamanites.[19] Repentance among these people was sometimes associated with a lightening of the skin, further unfaithfulness with its darkening. It appears, then, that in early Mormon teaching the racial marking of skin color was directly associated with spiritual faithfulness or unfaithfulness.[20] Eventually the unfaithful Lamanites (often viewed as the ancestors of the Native Americans) destroyed the faithful Nephites in a series of great battles.

Similar theories about the origins of some of America's early residents had been circulated since at least the early seventeenth century. Later, in 1823, Ethan Smith—not related to Joseph—published a popular book titled *View of the Hebrews*, which advocated a Semitic origin for Native Americans. The idea that Semitic peoples journeyed to North America in ancient times is of vital importance to Mormonism but has also always been a matter of debate.[21] Non-Mormon scholars have found little support for such a migration. Regardless, the story is clearly another important instance of the persistent Myth of the Spiritual Race, a narrative of mythic power woven into the fabric of pioneer-era American thought.

England developed its own version of a Lost Tribes of Israel mythology. The poet William Blake, for instance, celebrated the possibility that the English people were themselves a racial remnant of Israel:

And thus the Voice Divine went forth upon the rocks of Albion:
I elected Albion for my glory: I gave to him the Nations,
Of the whole Earth; He was the angel of my Presence, and all
The sons of God were Albion's sons, and Jerusalem was my joy.[22]

Much earlier the theologian Bede believed the English to be a special people chosen by God to establish a new kind of government and form of worship on Earth.[23] Moreover, Cromwell's associate John Sadler "tried to show that Anglo-Saxon laws were derived from Talmudic law and wondered whether the British Isles were not first populated by Phoenicians and if the Druids were not indeed Canaanites."[24] The late seventeenth-century skeptic John Toland, himself a Druid, also accepted the myth of a Hebrew history for the British Isles. Toland wrote that, when driven from Palestine, "a great number of 'em [the Jews] fled to Scotland." His evidence consisted of the fact that "so many in that part of the Island have such a remarkable aversion to pork and black puddings to this day, not to insist on some other resemblances easily observable."[25]

That the English were descended from ancient migrating Hebrews became the foundation of a considerable religious movement known as Anglo-Israelism. This belief, like so many other racial myths, rendered the English a spiritually superior race with a mandate for delivering other races from spiritual darkness. As Poliakov writes, English belief in "a physical link with the Jews" provided a foundation for the closely related idea of "spiritual descent." This strange concept eventuated in "the birth of a movement, that of the British Israelites, which numbered hundreds of thousands."[26] Such exotic ideas about spiritually gifted races strike many modern readers as odd holdovers from an earlier time. Yet the persistent idea that one obscure corner of the Earth, or galaxy, should produce a racial group of superior spiritual insight can still be found in popular narratives and religious thought.

In one of the more remarkable science-fiction adaptations of religious teachings, the popular television and movie franchise *Battlestar Galactica* incorporated several important components of the Mormon spiritual race narrative. The television series, written by veteran television writer and producer Glen Larson, a devout Mormon, began in 1978 and continues in movies, books, video games and on television.

In the *Battlestar* stories, humans in the distant future are at war in space with beings of their own creation, the Cyclons. Once created as androids or advanced robots, the Cyclons have evolved into sentient beings, albeit lacking a human soul. The Cyclons eventually destroy the members of the twelve human colonies, the only humans to escape the attack being a remnant of fifty thousand, who are searching for the legendary thirteenth colony known as Earth. Unknown centuries earlier, Earth and the other twelve colonies had been populated by émigrés from a distant planetary system. The remnant's leader is Captain Adamus, and the group hails from the same planetary system as their ancient ancestors. It is called Kobol in the *Battlestar* series—a name clearly reminiscent of Smith's Kolob, the star closest to the throne of God.

Literally preserving the spirit of the human race in opposition to the soulless Cyclons—and worshiping a pantheon of gods called the Lords of Kobol rather than the Cyclons' one God—this spiritual remnant, like Smith's La-manites and Mulekites sailing for North America, makes an arduous journey in search of its true homeland of Earth. *Battlestar Galactica,* a modern version of the Myth of the Spiritual Race, presented in a skillfully produced series of television and movie productions, reached audiences of millions. As we shall see in the following pages, the captivating possibility of a special race, a race above other races, is a motif that has a long history in popular works of both science and science fiction.

BULWER-LYTTON'S
SUBTERRANEAN MASTER RACE

As we have already seen, by the late nineteenth century, science fiction was a well-developed literary genre with numerous titles appearing in Europe and the United States. The century's leading science-fiction author was the famous Frenchman Jules Verne, most of whose eighty books—including *Journey to the Center of the Earth* (1864), *20,000 Leagues Under the Sea* (1870) and *Around the World in Eighty Days* (1875)—were published before 1900. Verne's great popularity helped to establish science fiction as a powerful cultural force. Other leading science-fiction titles appearing before the end of the nineteenth century include Samuel Butler's *Erehwon* (1872), W. H. Hudson's *A Crystal Age* (1887), and William Morris's *News from Nowhere* (1890). On the European continent major science-fiction works of the late nineteenth and early twen-tieth centuries included Villiers de l'Isle-Adam's *L'Eve future* (1886), Gustave Meyrink's *Der Golem* (1915), and *The Created Legend* (1906-1913) by the Rus-sian novelist Sologub.

Given the wide social interest in questions of race, racial theories occa-sionally appeared in the rising science-fiction genre of the nineteenth century, often substantiated by an appeal to social and natural sciences. The prolific Victorian writer George Edward Bulwer-Lytton (1798-1873), for example, "was inspired by the theory of evolution to write a utopian novel called *The Coming Race* (1871)," an early work of science fiction. Bulwer-Lytton's advanced race, the Vril-ya, were driven underground at the time of Noah's flood and "had evolved from men above into an intellectual, self-controlled race surpassing ours in the same ways we surpass the savages."[27] Again, racial hierarchies are unavoidable when discussing spiritually advanced races. Bulwer-Lytton refers to this nearly divine race as "Aryans," appropriating a term already employed in European intellectual circles to identify a supposed master race of the past. *The Coming Race* struck a nerve with readers; it was extremely popular and caused a considerable stir when it first appeared in the early 1870s. A skilled storyteller and author of more than fifty books, Bulwer-Lytton combined scientific theories of race and evolution, speculation about ancient Egypt, and a love story to create a captivating but troubling work of racially charged fiction.

In *The Coming Race*, a young American explorer falls through a chasm in the lower reaches of an abandoned mineshaft. The unnamed protagonist finds himself in a new world inhabited by a race of physically perfect, extraordinarily intelligent angelic creatures capable of flight with artificial wings. The Vril-ya remind the narrator "of symbolical images of Genius or Demon" found on ancient relics, "images that borrow the outlines of man, and are yet of another race."[28] Though human in form, these beings are "of a type of man distinct from our known extant races."[29] They are "sculptured gods" who constitute "a race akin to man's, but infinitely stronger of form and grander of aspect, and inspiring [an] unutterable feeling of dread."[30] It is important to the story that the Vril-ya have evolved in isolation from other races of people, a meaningful fact to readers familiar with the ideas of Francis Galton and other eugenicists who bemoaned racial mixing as a hindrance to evolutionary advance. The Vril-ya have also mastered a mysterious power known as Vril, an invisible energy that, like the volcanic stones lighting the barges of Joseph Smith's Semitic exiles, illuminates their dark world, powers their air and land vehicles, and provides them with potent weapons. Recognizing their superiority to surface-dwelling races, their right and destiny is to return to the Earth's surface, annihilate the inferior human species living there, and populate the lands thus acquired.

In *The Coming Race* Bulwer-Lytton envisions a spiritually evolved Aryan master race destined to rule lesser races. He was not the first to imagine such a race, though he was among the first to use the powerful medium of the novel to propagate the idea. In 1855, sixteen years before the publication of *The Coming Race*, the French intellectual Arthur de Gobineau published a highly influential theory of Aryan racial superiority in his *On the Inequality of the Races of Man.* Other works with similar themes flowed from the pens of Europe's leading scientific writers. The sociologist George Chatterton-Hill, influenced by reading Nietzsche (as were many leading European intellectuals of the day), wrote that both animals and "the lower races of mankind give way before the evolution of superior races."[31] Racial hierarchy and destiny became widely accepted ideas on both sides of the Atlantic, with alleged evidence ranging from linguistic studies to cranial measurements. Moreover, racial hierarchies were not strictly physical in nature: "higher" races exhibited psychological, sociological and spiritual advances as well.[32]

Thus, Bulwer-Lytton, while providing master-race theory the persuasive force and cultural reach of a captivating narrative, had not invented but merely appropriated an accepted *scientific* theory. At the same time, Francis Galton was proposing similar ideas as the basis of a religion. Madame H. P. Blavatsky (1831-1891), the founder of Theosophy and an advocate of science (as she understood the term), admired *The Coming Race.* She also had advanced a theory of racial development from "root races." Vril Societies formed in England and on the European Continent, some lasting well into the twentieth century. The Vril Society of Munich attracted several members who were later prominent figures in Hitler's National Socialist party. Richard Wagner's opera *Rienzi* (1840), reported to be a favorite of Hitler himself, was based on the Bulwer-Lytton novel of the same title (1835). This book developed racial assumptions similar to those of *The Coming Race*, focusing this time on the leaders of ancient Rome and Renaissance Italy rather than an imagined subterranean race.

LOST RACES: MU, ATLANTIS AND AFRICA

Some spiritual races, as we have seen, travel widely—across continents, oceans and space itself. Others are isolated underground, on a vast island, in an impenetrable jungle or inaccessible mountain valley, in a distant monastery or on an even more distant planet. These "lost" races often develop amazing technologies, while at the same time guarding a deep spiritual secret. In modern renditions of the story of a great ancient race, documents recounting this group's hidden history may be recovered through the happy accident of an unsuspecting scholar poking through an ancient library, a traveler's chance encounter in a distant land with a knowledgeable person, or direct contact with supernatural or extraterrestrial beings. As fanciful as these tales usually are, they have had their cultural impact and continue to fascinate readers and viewers. Lost-race narratives suggest that important secrets of human origins or destiny are available to the studious investigator, and that personal spiritual insight is a matter of apprehending these secrets.

One of the more-popular, long-lived and influential of such lost-race stories was told over a period of several decades from about 1870 until 1930 by James P. Churchward (1852-1936), a colonel in the British army who wrote on a range of anthropological and occult themes. Churchward's national origin, social status and apparent interests would have placed him in the path of ideas originating with writers such as Blavatsky and Bulwer-Lytton. Churchward was assigned to duty in India, where he befriended an Indian priest, or Rishi, who told him stories of the lost continent of Mu, an incredibly vast island with more than sixty million residents, located in what is now the Pacific Ocean. In this respect the stories of Mu resemble Blavatsky's myths of the lost continent of Lemuria, as well as the many Atlantis myths.

Churchward claimed that while in India he was shown ancient documents, one hundred and twenty-five tablets, hidden in a monastery and written in a mysterious language. After learning to translate the documents' ancient language, Churchward found that they revealed amazing details about the lost civilization of Mu that flourished from about 200,000 years ago until about 25,000 years ago, when the island was destroyed by earthquake. The tireless residents of Mu were, according to Churchward, spiritually advanced humans who provided the core ideas for all of the world's religions—including such apparently disparate faiths as Christianity and Freemasonry—as well as intrepid colonizers who founded all of the world's great civilizations.

Churchward spent most of his adult life developing a fictional language, geography, religion and history for the citizens of Mu, and his many books on the topic found a large audience. Indeed, so popular were Churchward's accounts that during the mid 1920s he hosted a radio program on WNYC in New York, during which he lectured on Mu as well as on other topics. A series of children's books on the ancient civilization was also produced under the title *Jungle Tales for the Kiddies*. These books portrayed, among other marvels, the life and teachings of Jesus while residing in India, a land often associated with esoteric spiritual lore and European racial origins.

Much like Bulwer-Lytton's Vril-ya, the residents of Mu were monists, believers that all things consist of a single substance or energy. In Churchward's famous phrase, "There is one great infinite force that governs all." As is typical of such histories of spiritually "advanced" people, the residents of Mu were alleged to have mastered scientific techniques that allowed them to accomplish a wide range of remarkable feats. In large measure their power is attributed to an inexhaustible source of cosmic or universal energy, much like the Vril of Bulwer-Lytton's Vril-ya. Churchward's own amateur anthropological work led him to conclude that all ancient people claimed descent from a single early civilization. In a series of popular books, Churchward claimed to recount the history of this first human civilization. These books include *The Lost Continent of Mu: The Motherland of Man* (1926), *The Children of Mu* (1931), *The Sacred Symbols of Mu* (1933) and *Cosmic Forces of Mu* (1934).[33]

Churchward's Muans—true to a version of the Myth that blends the isolated-race and wandering-race motifs—were forced to travel when it became evident that their island paradise was about to be destroyed by volcanoes and earthquakes. They navigated the world's oceans on ships, establishing both the great civilizations of the ancient world as well as all of the major religions. Churchward rejected the Darwinian notion of evolution, probably because it contradicted his own theories of highly advanced human races already existing in incredibly distant prehistoric times.

Churchward's ideas reflect a popular theme in late nineteenth- and early twentieth-century fiction—ancient, highly advanced, isolated races predating all known civilizations. This arresting notion, which seemed to validate all manner of secret spiritual insight, was also a feature of Madame Blavatsky's Theosophy, as well as the popular spiritual works of American clairvoyant Edgar Cayce (1877-1945). From Blavatsky, Cayce and other popular psychics and occult authors, the Atlanteans and their technology found their way into science fiction. Cayce taught, for example, that the residents of Atlantis had possessed a Great Crystal called the *Tuaoi Stone* and "said it was a huge cylindrical prism that was used to gather and focus 'energy,' allowing the Atlanteans to do all kinds of fantastic things."[34] This stone may have been the source of the "death ray" that Cayce claimed the Atlanteans possessed. When it came to lost races and their discoveries, the lines between spiritual writing and science fiction were again blurred.

Another version of the Myth of the Spiritual Race involved discovering

lost civilizations still existing in some remote part of the Earth. Sir Henry
Rider Haggard (1856-1925) authored a long series of extremely popular adventure novels between 1880 and 1920, several of which developed this theme. A
friend of Rudyard Kipling, Haggard in the late 1870s moved to South Africa,
where he grew to admire the courage of the Zulu warriors, eventually becoming a devoted student of their culture. Rider's stories always attracted a large
and devoted readership on both sides of the Atlantic. *The Popular Magazine*,
an early twentieth-century publisher of fantasy, adventure and science fiction,
increased its circulation from 75,000 to 250,000 after acquiring the rights to
Ryder Haggard's *Ayesha*, the sequel to *She*.[35]

Haggard wrote more than eighty books, but *King Solomon's Mines* (1885)
brought him his greatest fame. This book introduced Haggard's famous hero
Allan Quatermain, the protagonist of several subsequent novels. Haggard spe-
cialized in the adventure story set in an exotic location such as sub-Saharan
Africa, Iceland, Mexico or the South Seas. He had a devoted following in both
England and America and was among the most popular writers of his day.

Haggard perfected the lost-race adventure story, and his novels propagated
the idea that great races possessing astonishing powers and spiritual insights
were hidden in various corners of the Earth. Despite their obvious entertainment quality, some of Haggard's ideas also attracted the attention of scholars.
For example, Carl Jung referred to the central character in the novel *She* as
an example of *anima:* an individual with insights into the spirit realm. Indeed, several of Haggard's more than forty books feature female characters
with profound spiritual wisdom and extraordinary powers. In addition to
She (1887), these include *Montezuma's Daughter* (1894), *Pearl Maiden* (1903),
Ayesha (1905), *Queen Sheba's Ring* (1910) and *The Virgin of the Sun* (1922).

In *She*, Leo Vincey travels to Africa in search of clues about a mysterious
ancestor known only as Kallikrates. Not surprisingly, Egyptian lore plays a
major role in this story of magic, love, immortality and an ancient priestess
known as She-Who-Must-Be-Obeyed. The story has a decidedly religious
interest, with Christianity being relegated to the status of one among many
historical artifacts of the yearning human spirit. "The religions come and the
religions pass," says Ayesha, "and naught endures but the world and human
nature." Ayesha is virtually immortal and is given renewed life by entering "a
pure cold flame into which she steps for revivification."[36]

Several movie versions of the Haggard myth of She-Who-Must-Be-Obeyed were developed, some of them surprisingly early. Indeed, the film that may qualify as the very first science-fiction film, an 1899 production, was based on the character of Ayesha.[37] The most famous cinematic version of *She* was a 1935 version produced by Merian C. Cooper and directed by Irving Pichel and Lansing C. Holden. Cooper had also been involved with the film adaptation of Bulwer-Lytton's *The Last Days of Pompeii*, another of his master-race myths. Cooper set Haggard's African adventure story in the Arctic, another common location for hidden races, extraterrestrial outposts and discovering spiritual secrets.

Haggard's disillusionment with Western culture and the Christian faith are evident in many of his works, as is the search for a more esoteric spiritual outlook. His pursuit of spiritual insight led him to write about spiritualism, magic and even hallucinogenic drugs in novels such as *Allan and the Ice Gods* (1927). In Haggard's stories, lost civilizations are employed much like distant planets in later science fiction: places where great adventures occur, spiritual insights are achieved, and advanced races live.

Haggard had many imitators, and lost races led by mysterious women became a staple of 1920s, 1930s and 1940s science-fiction books as well as movies.[38] Most notable, perhaps, was Pierre Benoit's phenomenally popular 1919 novel, *L'Atlantide.* This story of a powerful and ageless queen of a lost civilization kept alive the idea of highly advanced ancient civilizations led by minor deities. *L'Atlantide* spawned film versions in 1920 and 1932.[39] The *L'Atlantide* phenomenon, though largely forgotten today, was a major cultural event and a milestone in modern mythmaking. Similar stories were also extremely popular in Germany. The large number of German books and films dealing with advanced civilizations with mysterious powers and powerful weapons during the 1920s and 1930s suggests that science fiction may have prepared the public to accept the notion of a modern "advanced" and "scientific" civilization. Indeed, Lasswitz's extremely popular *On Two Planets* (1897) begins with German explorers discovering a technological civilization at the North Pole; they turn out to be Martians.

H. Ryder Haggard inspired, among others, the most successful of the science-fiction writers: Edgar Rice Burroughs. Burroughs's extraordinarily popular books helped to secure a place within American literature for the exotic adventure story set in space or a lost land. Moreover, Burroughs was a major influence on several prominent scientists who read his Martian adventures during their adolescence, most notably Carl Sagan. Haggard also appears to have influenced the Cthulhu stories of H. P. Lovecraft, another great American mythmaker. Haggard was knighted by the British Empire in 1912 for work he had done on issues of social welfare. His most lasting legacy, however, is his powerful presentation of the lost and spiritually enlightened race to the Western imagination.

SCIENCE AND ARYAN MYTHOLOGY

Any discussion of racial myths and their propagation in the modern West must take into account the most notorious of all such stories: the Aryan myth. According to a leading authority on the topic, Léon Poliakov, the conceptions of race that fomented mayhem in Europe were propped up by Enlightenment rejection of the idea that all humans are descended from the same parents. Once scientific criticism destroyed the biblical "unbroken line and succession" for all humanity, Enlightenment theories of human origins gave rise "in due course to the Aryan myth."[40] The infamous theory of a dominant Indo-European race, the Aryans, rests in part on speculative science. Aryanism was once a nineteenth-century scientific mythology, and the Aryans were not simply a more-intelligent race, but also a morally or spiritually superior race. The apogee of human development was taken to be a distinct racial group possessing unusual spiritual awareness and inner strength, a race thus destined to subdue and lead other races.

Toward the end of the eighteenth and beginning of the nineteenth centuries, European scholars invented, not just the Aryans, but also an original point of geographical origin, and a path of transit into Europe for the master race. Thus, "long before Gobineau" (1816-1882), the most widely known of the Aryan race theorists, this scientific version of the Myth of a Spiritual Race was taking shape and having its influence throughout Europe.[41] The myth migrated quickly from science to literature. As early as 1801, the Romantic writer Friedrich Schiller (1759-1805) referred to the Germans as having been "elected by the universal spirit to strive eternally for the education of the human race." Another German writer, Heinrich von Kleist (1777-1811), affirmed that "the gods" had preserved "the original image of the human species with greater purity" in the Germans than in any other national or racial group.[42]

Such spiritualizing of race continued unabated in scientific and literary circles throughout the nineteenth century. But mythic descriptions of the German people in particular had much earlier, prescientific manifestations as well. Ulrich von Hutten (1488-1523) affirmed that "the free and noble German people were the natural lords of the universe *(weltherrschendes Volk)*."[43] A surprisingly similar view of a spiritually superior Nordic-Germanic race was still being expressed four centuries later; in 1899 the Englishman turned German citizen Houston Stewart Chamberlain set out a refurbished theory of the superior Aryan race in his *Foundations of the Twentieth Century*. Hitler himself called Chamberlain, Wagner's son-in-law, a "prophet" for his work on race. The persistent use of spiritual language regarding race underlines an important fact: European racial myths typically were not merely biological but also spiritual in nature.

Narratives regarding the destiny of the superior German race sometimes were strikingly reminiscent of the manner in which Bulwer-Lytton's Aryans described their own destiny. Recall that these highly evolved subterranean superhumans assured their surface-born guest in *The Coming Race* that they would rise to the Earth's surface and destroy all inferior races. Compare this idea to a remarkably similar view expressed by a nineteenth-century racial theorist: "We Germans are free, we are all noble; we have ruled and taken possession of the whole earth by force and before long, with God's help, we shall bring the world into submission to the ancient order."[44]

Hitler's reading of the philosopher Fichte provided further support for his own spiritualized views about race.[45] Timothy Ryback writes that Fichte "peeled away the spiritual trappings of the Holy Trinity, positing the Father as 'a natural universal force,' the Son as the 'physical embodiment of this force,' and the Holy Ghost as an expression of the 'light of reason.'" In his personal copy of Fichte's book, "Hitler not only underlined the entire passage but [also] placed a thick vertical line in the margin, and added an exclamation point for good measure." Hitler was thinking in spiritual terms of the new Germany, a nation consisting of one race embodying the "natural universal force." Fichte solved another problem for European racial theorists by eliminating the link between Jesus and the Jews, a race the philosopher considered spiritually inferior. As Poliakov writes, it was Fichte "who was the first to question the ethnic

origin of Jesus of Nazareth and to conclude that he was not perhaps of Jewish
stock, thus sweeping aside the greatest obstacle in the quest for an authenti-
cally German religion."[46] Ryback adds to this observation the striking fact that
"Hitler was seeking a path to the divine," literally a connection between divinity and himself. He found the key to this connection in Fichte: "Fichte asked,
'Where did Jesus derive the power that has held his followers for all eternity?'
Hitler drew a dense line beneath the answer: 'Through his absolute identifica-
tion with God.'"[47]

In his private library Hitler also kept a number of volumes on occult subjects. Ryback was struck by one of these works in particular. He writes that
"among the numerous volumes dealing with the spiritual, the mystical, and
the occult I found a typewritten manuscript that could well have served as a
blueprint for Hitler's theology." The book in question was a "bound 230-page
treatise titled *The Law of the World: The Coming Religion,* written by a resident
of Munich named Maximilian Reidel." Reidel's book, its title reminiscent of
Bulwer-Lytton's *The Power of Vril: The Coming Race*—a fact of which Ryback
was apparently unaware—was of special import to Hitler. He "not only received
the Reidel manuscript but also read it carefully with pencil in hand." Indeed,
"individual sentences and entire paragraphs are underlined, sometimes twice
or even three times." Reidel had "established the groundwork" for a system he
termed a "new religion," one that would replace the old Western religion based
on the Christian Trinity.[48] Hitler apparently embraced the religion-making
project as his own and saw himself as the new object of worship.

Hitler's efforts to spiritualize a race and craft a religion became a personal
passion inspired in part by his exposure to artists and intellectuals then shaping German culture. According to John Carey, "Nietzsche was often on his
lips, and he could quote Schopenhauer by the page." In addition, Hitler "idolized Wagner," whose most famous opera presented figures such as Parsifal as
an Aryan Christ.[49] He considered that a great artistic achievement such as that
of Wagner "effectively establishes the supremacy of the Aryan race."[50] In Hitler's view, "only the Aryan race has . . . produced great artists and writers," and
thus "the cultural achievements of the West" proved that the Aryan race is, in
Hitler's own words, "the highest image of God among his creatures."[51]

But Carey's argument is not merely that Hitler proclaimed the Aryan race
as superior, nor even that Hitler understood this superiority principally in

spiritual terms. These ideas are well known. Rather, Carey also argues that the tendency to enshrine a *spiritually* superior race characterized much of late nineteenth- and early twentieth-century thought and art in both Europe and America. He writes that the idea of a "natural aristocrat" who is superior to "the mass," an idea that is a "large element of Hitler's thought," also "finds a counterpart in twentieth-century intellectual orthodoxy." A component of that orthodoxy is that "the creative act of genius is 'always a protest against the inertia of the mass [of people].'"[52] It is perhaps not surprising then, that this kind of thinking about spirituality and race trickled down to more popular forms of writing such as science fiction.

European race theories did not arise in a spiritual vacuum, nor were they strictly an interest of artists and intellectuals. Modern racial mythmaking in Germany was also closely connected with "the disconcerting phenomenon of German neo-Paganism," which was characterized as a distinctly "German Christianity."[53] Reducing Christianity to a species of paganism tended to reduce the power of foundational Christian teachings, such as the common parenthood of the human race. European racial ideologies of the 1920s and 1930s drew on deeply rooted cultural myths, propagated in some popular fiction such as *The Coming Race*. These same myths were propped up by a speculative racial science that also spawned eugenics. Finally, these sources coalesced into a religion of race so deeply rooted and so powerful that only a fully formed Christian theology could have stood as an effective bulwark against it.

STAR TREK: TO DIVINITY AND BEYOND

Star Trek is arguably the most popular, long-lasting and influential mass-media phenomenon in history. Inestimably vast has been the cultural influence of the six different iterations of the *Star Trek* television programs, beginning with the original version in 1966: scores of Star Trek books, ten movies with an eleventh on the drawing board, and a series of video games. *Star Trek* has even shaped the English language, adding terms and phrases such as "warp speed," "Beam me up" and "phaser," to name only a few.

Despite the wide cultural adulation for this brainchild of science-fiction writer Gene Roddenberry (1921-1991), *Trek* has also generated controversy in its treatment of the evolutionary human future. Media scholar Daniel Bernardi has examined in particular how *Star Trek* has addressed the topic of

evolution's relationship to race. That *Star Trek* creator Roddenberry spiritualized evolution seems clear. Under a doctrine termed "parallel evolution"—the
notion that humanoid beings on other planets have evolved at a rate approxi-
mately that of humans on Earth—Roddenberry and later writers often speculated about where humanity was headed, both physically and spiritually.[54] The
ultimate goal of evolution is, apparently, divinity. In an interview, Roddenberry once affirmed his conviction that the "intelligent beings on this planet
are all a piece of God, are becoming God," a belief occasionally reflected in
Star Trek itself.[55]

It is to be expected that evolution would play a central role in *Star Trek*
mythology, as it does in much science fiction. Bernardi observes that evolution's influence on *Star Trek* stories is "perhaps most obvious in the titles of
various episodes, including 'Evolution' (1989); 'Unnatural Selection' (1989), . . .
[and] 'Genesis' (1994), which involves the crew of the *Enterprise* 'de-evolving'
into primitive life forms."[56] Nor is Roddenberry's view of evolution's end point
surprising given science fiction's history with the question of the distant human future. Still, it is worth recognizing that this most popular of all science-
fiction narratives repeatedly imagines not just physical and cognitive changes
in the human being but also a divine future for distant descendents of the
human race. Moreover, lurking in the background of some *Trek* stories are
humanoids in other parts of the galaxy who have already completed the evolutionary journey to godhood.

In several *Star Trek* episodes a godlike race known as the Organians "take
humanoid form," suggesting a possible trajectory for future-humans. Regarding these "advanced" beings, Mr. Spock comments: "I should say the
Organians are as far above us on the evolutionary scale as we are above the
amoeba." Such "Escalatorology," to borrow Midgley's term, is in keeping with
the general *Star Trek* account of human origins and trajectory. In the *Star
Trek* mythology, advanced aliens seeded the Earth's oceans with their DNA
in the distant past. In a *Next Generation* episode titled "The Chase," a holo-
graphic image of an early humanoid explains that "the seed codes directed
your evolution toward a physical form resembling ours." Thus, the human
race is created in the image of a dying race of aliens anxious to perpetuate themselves throughout the galaxy. Similar themes animate a number of
other science-fiction works, including the movie *Mission to Mars* (2000), in

which an almost identical secret is revealed in a similar fashion.

If this is where we started, the character Q may be where we are destined to arrive in the *Trek's* telling of the Myth of the Spiritual Race. "The pinnacle of evolution in *Trek* is a creature who looks white and becomes god-like."[57] Indeed, the very first episode of the television series *Star Trek: The Next Generation* features Q, an "omniscient being who can manipulate the space-time continuum with the snap of a finger."[58] This Q also makes appearances in *Star Trek: Deep Space Nine* and *Star Trek: Voyager.* Played in memorable fashion by actor John de Lancie, Q is an arrogant minor god who represents the evolutionary apex of a humanoid species that apparently started its cosmic climb from a point of departure similar to that of present-day human beings. In episodes featuring the immortal Q, the *Trek* stories suggest that human beings also are embarked on a spiritual evolutionary journey that will culminate in beings resembling members of a guild of gods known as The Q Continuum. The Q Continuum represents an "elder race" lurking in the cosmic background, advanced beings possessing godlike qualities.

The immortal, invisible Arisians of E. E. "Doc" Smith's *Lensman* series may be the origin not only of *Star Trek's* Q Continuum but also of the disembodied Vorlons of the *Babylon 5* saga, and the good side of the Force in *Star Wars.* J. Michael Straczynski, creator of *Babylon 5*, is a fan of Smith's *Lensman* series, which he calls "one of the true milestones in science fiction literature."[59] George Lucas reportedly labeled the good side of the Force "Arisian" in early versions of his story. Smith, in turn, was a devoted reader of H. Ryder Haggard, claiming to have read all of his novels. Haggard's spiritually advanced and immortal characters may be prototypes for Smith's highly evolved, behind-the-scenes races.

Star Trek stories frequently introduce new humanoid species from various parts of the galaxy; the theme of what will follow the current human stage of evolutionary development is common. Such is the stuff of much science fiction. But given science fiction's troubling history of portraying "the next step" as brilliant, powerful or gigantic white men, it is surprising that even as recently as the 1980s and 1990s, "the evolution of the humanoid life-form . . . takes the figure of a white-humanoid with divine powers."[60] Also surprising is the fact that the official *Star Trek* website, maintained by CBS Studios and Paramount Pictures, describes the members of the Q Continuum as "a super-race."[61] In *Star Trek*, "Q almost always takes the form of a white male; indeed all members of the Q Continuum represented in *The Next Generation*, whether male or female, have chosen the white way."[62] At least some of the *Star Trek* tellings of the Myth of the Spiritual Race reflect the influence of a problematic Western cultural and scientific heritage regarding the notion of a superrace. This heritage developed in much early science fiction, its roots sunk deeply into evolutionary theory, eugenics and visions of supermen.

STAR WARS AND SPIRITUAL RACE

George Lucas, creator of *Star Wars*, was an avid reader of science fiction from his youth. During a long convalescence from a serious automobile accident in his teens, he was reading the leading authors of the genre. One of the masters of the genre, E. E. "Doc" Smith (1890-1965), set out in his stories an epic pattern not unlike Lucas's own stories written for the *Star Wars* movies. Smith is credited with developing the science fiction subgenre known as space opera: an adventure story set in space, developing over an extremely long period of time, and built around godlike heroes locked in a titanic struggle between good and evil. While in college, Lucas also began to read the works of comparative religions scholar Joseph Campbell, particularly his classic work *The Hero with a Thousand Faces* (1948). Campbell, who more than any other figure explained and advocated the mechanics of mythology to the American public, exercised a decisive influence on Lucas and *Star Wars*. In 1976, combining his interests in science fiction, myth and film, Lucas wrote a screenplay he called *The Star Wars*, a cinematic space opera that harkened back to earlier science fiction, including the Smith stories and the serialized Buck Rogers short movies.

In his groundbreaking work, Campbell affirmed that "myth is the secret opening through which the inexhaustible energies of the cosmos pour into human culture."[63] Lucas came to see his *Star Wars* movies as developing a new iteration of the ancient hero mythology the aging scholar had described. Interestingly, Campbell interpreted the Lucas movies in this way as well, as he would relate to journalist Bill Moyers in a famous series of interviews filmed during 1986 and 1987 that aired on Public Broadcasting Service in 1988, shortly after Campbell's death. Campbell and Lucas eventually became friends, Lucas at one point referring to the erudite professor as "my personal Yoda."

No doubt Lucas meant this comment to be a profound compliment to

Campbell, and perhaps something of a compliment to himself as well. But Campbell was in some respects a controversial figure with a checkered scholarly past. Campbell's friend, the art critic Brendan Gill, suggested that Campbell was an anti-Semite and a reactionary in a now-famous essay appearing in the *New York Review of Books* in 1989.[64] Gill went on to argue that Campbell belonged to that group of American intellectuals—celebrated by Ayn Rand in her novel *Fountainhead* and including Frank Lloyd Wright—who disparaged "the masses" and held out for the existence of a social elite of gifted artists. In *Atlas Shrugged*, Rand develops a heavily didactic story about social hierarchies centered around a gifted elite constituting the creative and intellectual soul of America. In a controversial speech given in 1941, Campbell had cautioned the students of Sarah Lawrence College (where he taught) not to overreact to the rise of Hitler in Europe. True artists and intellectuals were not to be distracted from their high calling by the swirl of mere worldly events.

The Lucas films have been as culturally influential as have the *Star Trek* productions, likewise creating a vocabulary of their own. Light-sabers are as familiar as phasers, and hyperspace is widely understood as warp speed. But the Lucas *Star Wars* films are best known for introducing a mysterious cosmic life force known only as The Force. Lucas's purposes in developing the idea of the Force went beyond providing his films with an intriguing spiritual plot device; his goals were at least in part spiritual and evangelistic in nature. In a now-famous 1999 interview, he told *Time* magazine, "I put the force into the movies to awaken a certain kind of spirituality in young people, not a belief in any particular religion, more a belief in god."[65] In this first of the *Star Wars* movies, the elder Jedi, Obi-Wan Kenobi, describes the Force as "an energy field created by all living things." He adds, "It surrounds us, penetrates us, and binds the galaxy together."

The Force, with its good and bad (or "dark") sides clearly has both spiritual origins and implications. The idea of opposed light and dark forces is found in ancient Zoroastrianism, where Ahura Mazda, or the force of light and creation, and Angrha Mainyu, or the force of darkness and destruction, carry on an eternal cosmic competition. In an earlier chapter we also noticed the pervasive influence of the idea of a universal psychic force that was thought to allow for such phenomena as telepathy. Bulwer-Lytton's Vril was also a powerful force apparently found in all living things. And "vitalist" views of evolution posit a "life force" pushing the cosmos toward higher and higher levels of intellectual achievement. In a recent interview, Lucas said, "The idea behind the force was universal: similar phrases have been used extensively by many people for the last 15,000 years to describe the 'life force.'"[66]

The Force became a popular if invisible member of the cast, playing the central role in the plot's development and final resolution. It was also central to the "certain kind of spirituality" Lucas hoped the movies would "awaken." In the first *Star Wars* movie, protagonist Luke Skywalker studies under master Yoda's direction until he is able to control the Force. Yoda is not human, and so it is clear that control of the Force does not belong to one species.

The *Star Wars* series suggests that in learning the secrets of the Force, disciples take an important step toward spiritual insight and control. But another suggestion of the movies is of particular importance to the role of *Star Wars* in propagating the Myth of the Spiritual Race. Luke Skywalker—as well as his father, Anakin Skywalker, later revealed as Darth Vader—is descended from a select group known as Jedi Knights. It is this special pedigree that enables Luke to master the secrets of the Force. *Star Wars* implies throughout that an ordinary human, or member of some other sentient though less-developed species, might not possess the spiritual capacity to control the Force. But do the Jedi, who apparently incorporate different species among their ranks, qualify as a spiritually gifted race, or just carefully trained disciples of a religion?

One possible answer to this question comes in the *Star Wars* installment *The Phantom Menace* (1999). In this episode, chronologically the first in the series, audiences are introduced to Anakin Skywalker, the child who will one day become Darth Vader, father of Luke Skywalker. During a visit from two Jedi Knights—Qui-Gon Jinn played by Irish actor Liam Neeson and Obi-Wan Kenobi played by Scottish actor Ewan McGregor—to the remote planet where the young Anakin lives with his mother (who admits that Anakin is the product of a fatherless if not virgin birth), it is discovered that his blood contains an unusually high number of "medi-chlorines." These undefined but apparently microscopic organisms allow a few individuals to gain an unusually high degree of control over the Force, and thus extraordinary power. Thus, two distinctly British male Jedis, complete with unmistakable accents, discover an important biological fact about a miraculously born white male child, a fact that speaks to his remarkable capacity for dominating the Force. The evil Sith-

Lord Senator Palpatine, another great master of the Force, is also played by a British actor, Ian McDiarmid, while the voice of Yoda himself comes from the English actor Frank Oz. And the elder Obi-Wan Kenobi of the original 1977 *Star Wars* was acted by the great English master Alec Guinness. The preference for British adepts of the Force is remarkable.

The important discovery about young Anakin's blood chemistry constitutes a turning point in the six-film series; it has much to do with the outcome of the extended Lucas-Campbell myth that is *Star Wars*. But in attributing extraordinary control of the Force to a biologically based capacity, which the *Phantom Menace* clearly does, *Star Wars* hints at a contemporary version of the Myth of the Spiritual Race. Mastery of the Force, the ultimate spiritual power in the universe, is not, it turns out, simply a matter of careful study and arduous discipline. Spiritual power is literally in the blood of a genetically select group. Neither skin color nor species marks the spiritually gifted Jedi (or their evil counterparts the Sith), but medi-chlorine count apparently does. In this way the Jedi/Sith are presented to moviegoing audiences as a genetically prepared, species-transcending, advanced spiritual race of characters that carry their spiritual capacity literally in their blood.

ABDUCTEES AS SPIRITUAL RACE

The closing decades of the twentieth century witnessed an increasing number of UFO abductee accounts and a somewhat surprising scientific effort to document and assess them. While such reports had constituted merely "a minor diversion to the UFO theme" during the 1950s and 1960s, by the 1970s and 1980s they were a cultural preoccupation. Scholars at prestigious universities studied the phenomenon, garnering much media attention in the process. Indeed, in the 1990s, Harvard University had two separate research groups devoted to the UFO abduction phenomenon. Some of these researchers came to the surprising conclusion that "the phenomenon could not be explained psychiatrically, was not possible within the framework of the modern scientific worldview, and was in all likelihood truly explained by alien abduction."[67]

Steven Dick, an historian of the extraterrestrial life debate, has written that "the phenomenal popularity" of abduction reports "demonstrated the continued willingness of the public to accept, without physical evidence, even the most extreme beliefs of the extraterrestrial hypothesis . . . or at least to use them for entertainment value." He concludes that "such beliefs demonstrated allegiance to a different worldview than the scientific, as normally understood." Some suggested, on the other hand, that the abduction phenomenon was merely awaiting a worldview broad enough to accommodate it, just as "a twentieth-century science has encompassed the aurora borealis, a feat unimaginable to nineteenth-century science, which likewise was incapable of explaining how the sun and stars shine."[68] Still others were content to relegate the phenomenon to the realm of the tall tale, psychotic delusion or simple efforts to gain media attention.

The late Professor John Mack of the Harvard University Medical School was perhaps an unlikely expert on the experiences of individuals who claimed to have been abducted by aliens. Nevertheless, Mack's bestselling 1995 book, *Abduction: Human Encounters with Aliens*, reports his interviews with dozens of persons who allege that beings from another dimension or another planet have contacted and even kidnapped them.[69] But Mack's most striking claim was the suggestion that abductees might constitute a spiritually enlightened race, a vanguard in humanity's quest to understand its place in the cosmos.

Mack believed that he was encountering something other than ordinary memories in his interviews with the abducted. He thus argued, not that abduction experiences were concocted, but that we needed a broader definition of memory. "In this context," he writes, "thinking of memory too literally as 'true' or 'false' may restrict what we can learn about human consciousness from the abduction experiences I recount in the pages that follow."[70] On the basis of his extensive interviews of UFO abductees, Mack concluded, "We participate in a universe or universes that are filled with intelligences from which we have cut ourselves off, having lost the senses by which we might know them."[71] In Mack's universe, behind-the-scenes intelligences became a reality.

According to Mack, science does not help us to comprehend the full significance of the abduction phenomenon. For deeper insight we must turn to religion and mythology. The "connection between humans and beings from other dimensions has been illustrated in myths and stories from various cultures for millennia," he wrote.[72] UFO abductees "are continuing an amply documented tradition of ascent and extraterrestrial communication."[73] For John Mack, abductees become a spiritually attuned group capable of communicating with higher intelligences and gleaning spiritual truths from them. They are people equipped with the additional senses necessary to perceive what the rest of us miss and therefore assume not to exist. Mack concluded that "contemporary examples of such entities" as the aliens of the abductee accounts include the "spirit guides that are reported by many individuals."[74] Some extraordinary quality prepares abductees for encounters with otherwise inaccessible intelligent beings.

Mack's invisible "intelligences," the aliens of abduction accounts, are actively seeking to influence the human race, choosing to do so through spiritually sensitive people who may bear a special, perhaps genetic, capacity for spiritual openness. The abductees thus parallel the shamans and mystics of earlier ages. "The UFO abduction experience" can be seen to resemble "other dramatic, transformative experiences undergone by shamans, mystics, and ordinary citizens who have had encounters with the paranormal."[75] Abductees are thus conduits of otherwise inaccessible knowledge from higher intelligences. The abductee receives "a new dimension of experience or knowledge."[76] Abductees, for Mack, were a select group possessing a peculiar openness to other dimensions of experience. They exhibited unique spiritual qualities; they are "unusually open and intuitive individuals" and "more flexible in accepting diversity and the unusual experiences of other people."[77] Thus, abductees are a distinct group living among us, sensitive to a wider range of experience and mentally more flexible than ordinary humans. Abductees represent nothing less than a new type of human being.

Indeed, Mack suggested that abductees are of an entirely different genetic type than the rest of us, a result of human and alien interaction. "Some abductees report being told by an alien female that she was their true mother, and they even feel that in some vague but deep way that this is actually true, i.e., that they are not 'from here' and that the Earth mother and father are not their true parents."[78] Mack transforms abductees into a spiritually gifted race, a special breed of humans who may have a parent from space, or perhaps from another dimension. If this were the case, abductees would constitute a distinct race, blending human and alien elements in some unexplained way.

In his unique version of the Myth of the Spiritual Race, Dr. John Mack posits the presence among us of a sensitive human species capable of drawing insights from other realms, and thus bringing moral knowledge to those of us less spiritually acute. In this way the UFO abductee is reminiscent of a mystic such as Emanuel Swedenborg, who likewise claimed spiritual contact with beings associated with other planets. Mack's abductees also take on some of the characteristics of the telepathic "sensitives" of the Victorian period, possessing innate senses and capacities beyond the normal that render them the recipients of otherwise inaccessible knowledge. A connection with science fiction is also evident in Mack's suggestion that abductees may actually have extraterrestrial parentage, or at least that they have been under the intimate influence of aliens from a very early age. The notion that the mixing of extraterrestrial and human will produce a remarkable leap forward in human development is a theme in science fiction that runs at least from Kurd Lasswitz's *On Two Planets*, which features a half-Martian half-human character, to the half-Vulcan half-human Mr. Spock of *Star Trek*.

CONCLUSION

An early twentieth-century proponent of racial advancement through scientifically applied eugenics looked forward to a day when "Science . . . will be harnessed to the service of the Superman."[79] Though he was borrowing the term *Superman* from Friedrich Nietzsche, the comment does bring to mind the more familiar Superman of contemporary popular culture. Can the two be related?

In the successful 2006 movie *Superman Returns* (as in the original 1978 movie, *Superman: The Movie*) a morally advanced extraterrestrial sends his son to Earth as the home planet is disintegrating. Reared by human parents of modest means, the young alien slowly discovers that he possesses remarkable powers. In adult life he receives spiritual instruction from his father, who was in heaven; assumes his appointed role of humanity's "savior"; hovers in space to hear the prayers of ordinary huddled masses in the cities below; and rescues them from crimes and other disasters. Eventually he must struggle against and defeat ultimate and personified evil; in the process he is slain—his side is pierced. He falls back into the Earth in cruciform posture and then rises triumphant to an even more divine and more powerful existence. This Superman—not one of the clearly implied "submen," and in all senses of the term "above" the rest of us—has bred with a human woman who bears him a similarly gifted offspring, the first of a new spiritual race, semihuman and semidivine.

Clearly the superman of *Superman Returns*, as in the many iterations of the
Superman story, is not a Christ figure, at least not in the Christian meaning of
that term. Rather, he is a counterfeit of Christ, a mythic substitute for the Suffering Servant. He is a genetically "advanced" extraterrestrial, descendant of a
superior race of space aliens, progenitor of a new breed of a gifted human-alien
hybrid, and bringer of salvation from space. Superman's impressive physical
dimensions (discussed in precise detail in *Superman Returns* and in the original 1978 film) as well as his piercing blue eyes and shimmering white skin,
betoken a traditional Western conception of "highly evolved" Aryan superman. This version of the New Man is borrowed from Homer and Wagner, not
Jesus and Paul. Superman is not a man of sorrows and acquainted with grief;
he *has* form and comeliness that we should desire him. And he has begotten
similarly gifted offspring with a human woman. The resulting spiritual race,
genetically prepared through the mixing of alien and human DNA, shall be
propagated and shall realize the destiny long prepared for it in the Western
imagination. Moreover, they alone will have access to the deep wisdom, the
spiritual memory of Superman's original alien race, through visits to the secret
chambers of The Fortress of Solitude.

The idea that a particular race or group has unusual access to spiritual secrets, possesses an extraordinary capacity for spiritual insight, or is morally
superior to other human groups has been a persistent—and sometimes dangerous—notion in Western culture. Contemporary minds have a difficult time
accepting that science could endorse such an idea; yet historically, we are not
far removed from the end of the Aryan myth era. Indeed, one can to this day
find adherents of superior race ideology in Europe and the Americas, such beliefs typically involving spiritual capacities such as "racial memory," great inner strength, superior will and insights into ancient mysteries. Whether in the
ancient anthropology of Joseph Smith, the operas of Richard Wagner, the lost-
race narratives of James Churchward, the UFO-abductee interviews of John
Mack, or the Force-driven narratives of George Lucas in which biologically
prepared Jedi Knights identify their own with a blood test—in all these forms,
spiritual races have made and continue to make their many appearances in
Western popular, scientific and religious culture.

Is it any wonder that eugenics theorist Thomas Common (1850-1919) and
other advocates of the coming "splendid race" identified Christianity, with its

maddening insistence on human equality before God, as the great enemy of scientific racial advancement? For many advocates of eugenics, Christianity was nothing more than an evolutionary invention of the weak to perpetuate their weaknesses in the human genetic line. Common wrote: "From the standpoint of all Darwinian philosophy of history, we now regard Christianity as an artful device for enabling inferior human beings to maintain themselves in the struggle for existence."[80] Dan Stone adds that because eugenicists such as Common viewed Christianity as "the prop of the weak," they thus also believed that a progressive culture would have to "do away with it." Such thinking arose from "connecting Darwin with Nietzsche" in the service of developing a superior race of people, a worldview understood in some circles at the beginning of the twentieth century as "the height of avant-garde sophistication."[81] Nor was this a minority view among early twentieth-century intellectuals and artists. As Stone points out, "Many thinkers . . . deduced human inequality from the writings of Darwin and Nietzsche." Just as many, following the same logic, saw Christianity as the great obstacle to human progress.[82]

The search for a superior race took on the qualities of a religion in the modern period, providing an ultimate purpose for human existence and a source of spiritual inspiration. As an early commentator on Nietzsche's thought wrote, "The ultimate justifications of humanity, the new 'wherefore?' is to be found in the development of a superior race, a new and higher type of humanity, physically, intellectually and morally—a type as far above the man of today as he is above the ape."[83] Moreover, notwithstanding scholarship that through a selective review of the evidence seeks to preserve the progressive image of renowned intellectuals and artists, this particular religion was invariably founded on what Stone terms "a racist worldview."[84] He worries that eugenics is returning, but in forms that appear unobjectionable, even benevolent: choosing a child's traits before birth, through abortion selecting out infants with physical or mental handicaps.

As the twentieth century opened, two worldviews stood in direct opposition to one another, each telling a different story concerning the human condition and each envisioning a different human future. Christianity required regard for all individuals as created in God's image, but "the theory of evolution points the way to the very opposite of democracy, to an aristocracy in the true sense, if the human race is to progress and be at its best."[85] And Nietzsche's popular *Thus Spoke Zarathustra* provided the narrative force necessary to propel the idea of superior humans into the public imagination.

Social theories founded on the ideas of Darwin, Spencer and Nietzsche venerate the supposed central natural law of biology and society: survival of the fittest. They thus sacralize nature and hence stand in direct opposition to the Christian insistence that only the God who created nature deserves human worship. The Myth of a Spiritual Race, intolerant of Christian thought and intolerable to Christian thought, must situate itself elsewhere—on pantheistic assumptions about a "life force" propelling nature's inherent trajectory toward an "aristocratic race."[86] For this reason the Myth of the Spiritual Race must oppose Christianity as an impediment to the essential progress of Nature itself.

The Judeo-Christian tradition presents a global picture of both spiritual need and spiritual redemption. No human group is exempt from this need, and no racial criteria are involved in who may carry, receive or benefit from the message of redemption. People of every tribe, tongue and nation gather around the throne of God, who created and is not contained within the cosmos (Revelation 7:9-17). The Bible also clearly presents a single point of origin for the entire human race, a single set of original human parents, and a single destiny of standing before the creating and redeeming Deity. The Holy Spirit, the Divine Presence of redemption, is poured out in a cacophony of voices representing many human nations. In writing that "in Christ . . . there is no longer Jew or Greek, . . . slave or free, . . . male or female," the apostle Paul affirms the unity of all races within the body of Christ (Galatians 3:26-28). Racialism, whatever its source and however persistent its existence in Western culture, is not a biblical idea. Its source lies elsewhere, in spiritual systems that Christianity has worked to banish from the human conceptual repertory. Its reappearance in new mythic forms needs to be recognized and addressed by people of faith as what it is: an ancient mistake that sets up false distinctions among us, sets false objects of worship before us, and thus separates us from one another and from the God who made us.

8

THE MYTH OF SPACE RELIGION

One of the greatest challenges to science in our time is from
modern superstitions such as UFO cults and people
who are beginning to take instruction from space brothers.

WHITLEY STRIEBER

It may even be that, as a search for superior beings,
the quest for extraterrestrial intelligence is itself a kind of religion.

STEVEN DICK

There is no need to kneel down or to lie down
with your face in the dirt, . . . but rather to look up at the sky,
standing proud, . . . living in this day and age when
we are able to understand and show love for our creators,
who have given us the fantastic potential to create life.

RAËL

For what can be known about God is plain to them,
because God has shown it to them.

ROMANS 1:19

In his 1985 science-fiction novel *Contact*, author Carl Sagan's protagonist Ellie Arroway asks the first alien she meets at the end of an arduous journey: "I
want to know about your myths, your religions. What fills you with awe? Or
are those who make the numinous unable to feel it?" Why do these particular

questions take center stage during the first meeting between a human being and an intelligent alien? It somehow seems natural in the era of scientific mythologies for a space traveler encountering an alien to ask a question about the ultimate, the transcendent, the numinous. Should not an alien, a resident of Space, a being more "advanced" than humans, know the answers to ultimate questions? What do virtual gods think about God? What do "those who make the numinous" think about religion? Sagan, like many other authors of science fiction, turns to the ultimate authorities—aliens—to answer these questions.

For well over a century, a persistent theme in science fiction has been the notion that alien beings possess spiritual or religious truth beyond that of Earth's residents, and that we can learn something about true religion from contact with them. Why this should be the case is seldom made explicit; in keeping with the Myth of Space and the Myth of the Spiritual Race, simply hailing from another planet and being highly evolved guarantee all manner of insight: technological, social, religious.

That there is a connection between space and extraterrestrials on the one hand, and religion and spiritual truth on the other, is an assumption that manifests itself in various ways in fiction, speculative scientific writing and religious works. Several specific assumptions recur about how extraterrestrials and space are involved with religion. One is simply the notion that religious truth and space exploration are complementary, that through space exploration we will acquire knowledge that alters how we understand religion. A second view suggests that the most advanced human religions are those ready to accommodate the discovery of aliens and truths they might convey to us. Third, some fictional narratives and religious works suggest that world unity depends on humanity's accepting a universal religion as revealed by residents of space. A more exotic belief about a connection between extraterrestrials and religion is that human religions had their origins in human-alien contact during humanity's ancient past. Finally, a closely related belief is that aliens were mistaken for angels, demons or gods in ancient times, and that these visitors to the human race brought messages regarding our welfare, origins or destiny. In some important instances, these ancient "gods" actually created the human race.

The idea that aliens and religion are somehow linked assumed a wider appeal in the second half of the twentieth century, following a long period of religious and biblical criticism in the West. The old systems of religion seemed to be crumbling under the weight of academic investigation and changing social arrangements. A new kind of religious authority attended the various UFO religions that began to spring up in the 1940s and 1950s as many people claimed to have received religious messages from space inhabitants. Most of these groups were clearly influenced by the language and motifs of science fiction, and a number by other sources, including popular scientific writing and occult literature. A few examples help to illustrate the movement's tendencies as a Myth of Space Religion emerged in popular culture.

A BRIEF HISTORY OF
EXTRATERRESTRIAL RELIGIONS

Hard on the heels of the Washington State UFO sightings and the famed Roswell flying-saucer incident, Daniel Fry claimed direct contact with spacemen in New Mexico. He authored a book in 1954 titled *The White Sands Incident*. Fry described his conversations with A-Lan, a prophetic figure from space who came to inform humanity about an "ancient civilization" on Earth that destroyed itself with nuclear weapons. A-Lan, like the alien Klaatu in the movie *The Day the Earth Stood Still* (1951), had come to caution modern humans about the dangers of nuclear weapons. In another manifestation of the alien-religion connection, Dr. William Sadler founded The Urantia Brotherhood in 1955. The group unveiled a sacred text titled *The Urantia Book*, or UB, alleged to have been dictated between 1928 and 1935 by superhuman entities. A second group, Unarius—not to be confused with Sadler's Urantia Brotherhood—was started by Ernest and Ruth Norman in 1954. Unarius (Universal Articulate Interdimensional Understanding of Science) sponsored The Unarius Academy of Science, an educational organization. Seeing themselves as "Cosmic Visionaries," the Normans claimed connection to the Space Brothers—highly advanced galactic intelligences (spiritual races) invariably mentioned by UFO groups, and reminiscent of Blavatsky's Ascended Masters and Great White Brotherhood. Unarius teaching was "the basis of the galactic intelligence."[1]

Other organizations arising in the 1950s and 1960s claimed extraterrestrial origins for many human religions, perhaps all of them—the same claim that James Churchward had made regarding the ancient spiritual race of Mu. For instance, the Aetherius Society, founded by George King in 1954, accommodated all of the major world religions. Science played a role in King's teaching, as did occultism, but many of the Aetherius Society's core religious teachings originated with a group of extraterrestrials called the Cosmic Masters. The Masters had a hand in the foundation of all of the major world religions. Many others claimed that religious knowledge was coming to them directly from aliens, who seemed to have a great deal to say on the topic of spirituality. Extraterrestrials were the new Ascended Masters, in constant telepathic contact with their chosen mouthpieces.

Perhaps the most influential of all the alien religionists, writer and self-styled psychic Jane Roberts (1929-1984) was known for "channeling" the religious messages of an alien named Seth. She had also worked as a spiritual medium, had a strong interest in ESP, and wrote entire books on her spiritual encounters with William James, Paul Cezanne and Rembrandt. But her principal contact was an extraterrestrial named Seth. The so-called Seth Materials came to her between 1968 and her death in 1984 and are considered by some to mark the start of the New Age movement. Roberts taught that we create our own mental reality, that all physical reality is generated by private and corporate consciousness, and that all things are one thing: consciousness. In this respect her teaching bore some resemblance to ideas contained in Robert Heinlein's popular novel *Stranger in a Strange Land* (1961), which was having its greatest cultural influence around 1968. Specifically religious questions were the central focus of what was to become Heinlein's most famous novel. The "man from Mars," Valentine Michael Smith, turns out to be a latter-day messiah preaching the message "Thou art God."[2]

A corollary of both the Myth of Space and the Myth of the Extraterrestrial, the Myth of Space Religion presents Space as a source of limitless spiritual potential for a humanity locked within the confines of Earth, mired in Earth's persistent problems, and limited by the constricting teachings of Earth's religions. But how did this myth attain cultural prominence and influence? Mass-media promotion provides at least a partial answer to this question.

James R. Lewis, one of the leading authorities on UFO culture, points out that, starting in the 1970s, all things UFO—including UFOs linked with alien religions—moved rapidly from the hidden fringe of popular culture to the mainstream. This movement occurred largely as the result of Hollywood's promotion of the culture's central themes in blockbuster films such as Steven Spielberg's *Close Encounters of the Third Kind* (1977), based on Spielberg's reading of abduction narratives; and *E.T.* (1982), which elevated the benevolent, semidivine alien. Later media productions, including television programs such as the same director's *Taken* (2002), also attracted large audiences. These and many other science-fiction narratives—such as the Sci-Fi Channel's production of Frank Herbert's *Dune* (2000), the *Stargate* movie (1994) and television programs (1997-2007), *Babylon 5* (1993-1998), the television and cinema iterations of *Battlestar Galactica* (with various interruptions, between 1978 and 2004), and television's series *The X-Files* (1993-2002), to name only a few— often had explicitly religious themes.

Stargate, to take one example, has enjoyed lengthy popularity on television and in movie theaters. The central premise is a fundamentally religious one: Alien beings have employed interplanetary "stargates" in the past to direct the evolution of primitive cultures throughout the universe. The aliens have ruled various civilizations literally as gods and were the source of the various religions now familiar to us. The movie's nemesis is an alien god named Ra, modeled on an ancient Egyptian deity. The television program moved beyond the Egyptian pantheon to include deities from a number of ancient faiths, including the Old Testament false deity knows as Baal. *Stargate* is in this way reminiscent of several novels of the science-fiction writer Roger Zelazny (1937-1995), in which mythic figures and themes from Hinduism, Buddhism and ancient Greek mythology animate the narratives. His award-winning novel *Lord of Light* (1968), for example, develops around Eastern religious ideas and deities, though in a distant future and on a different planet.

Has Western society come to accept that religion's biggest questions— Where did we come from? Where are we heading? What is our greatest need? How is that need satisfied?—are now often answered by science fiction, speculative science, and extraterrestrial religions? Few ideas are more important to science fiction and to other contemporary mythic writing than the idea of alien involvement in the origins, progress and even destiny of the human race. The many gods of the ancients, banished from Western culture by the advent first of Christianity and later of empirical science, have found their way back into the popular mind by the vehicle of the flying saucer. This chapter considers how the Myth of Space Religion has worked its way into Western thought over the past several centuries.

WILLIAM DERHAM'S *ASTRO-THEOLOGY*

As we have noticed in earlier chapters, speculation about life on other planets was common in the eighteenth century and indeed much earlier. Interest in the question is clear from one of the more intriguing and influential works of that period, William Derham's *Astro-Theology*, published in 1715.[3] A member of the Royal Society—which scientist, cleric and early science-fiction author John Wilkins helped to found—Derham (1657-1735) was an Oxford-educated Anglican clergyman and famous enough as an astronomer to have presented the prestigious Boyle Lectures of 1712-1713. Derham's books included *The Artificial Clockmaker* (1696), *Physico-Theology* (1713), *Astro-Theology* (1714) and *Christo-Theology* (1730). A polymath, Derham was an expert on astronomy, telescopes, clocks, history, meteorology, entomology, theology, physics and various kinds of scientific measurement devices.[4] He was also known for his list of sixteen nebulous stars.

On the basis of theology and astronomy, Derham was convinced that all stars have planets; indeed, he believed this to be the consensus view among the great scholars of his century. "The best and most learned modern astronomers," he wrote, "do generally suppose the great multitude of Fixt Stars we see [are] . . . each of them encompassed with a system of Planets like our Sun."[5] This opinion was reiterated by other eighteenth-century astronomers, including Edmond Halley and Benjamin Banneker. More powerful telescopes were revealing a complex and fascinating universe and in turn generating speculation about space's residents. Following the Dutch astronomer Christiaan Huygens, Derham affirmed that many planets were graced with "Land and Water, Hills and valleys, having atmosphere about them, and being enlightened, warmed and influenced by the Sun."[6] The only purpose of "so many Planets" is that the universe is widely inhabited by intelligent beings. Derham believed that through his enormous telescopes, Huygens had actually *seen* humanlike beings moving about on several planets!

The idea of intelligent life on other planets threatened prevailing religious ideas: if such beings existed, no longer was the human relationship with God unique. Would Christianity have to adjust to the new facts about space and its inhabitants? Derham moved seamlessly from science into the realm of religion; he affirmed that some of the many planets, comets and stars were places of torment for disobedient souls. This idea was reiterated thirty years later by the popular skeptic Jacob Ilive, who cited Derham as an authority on space and theology.[7] Inhabited planets fired the mythic imagination; the Myth of Space Religion was forming in response to the arresting idea that we are not alone in the universe. New religious views were being shaped around the concept of a vast and inhabited universe—an idea whose popularity dated back at least a century to Bruno. Was it not obvious that God would not create so vast a universe with only a single inhabited world? Only those who were "so stupid, so vile, so infatuated with their own vices" could deny that God had created numerous worlds, each with its own residents. No evidence then or now supported the idea, but this did not prevent Derham from making theological claims based on his scientific speculation about space and its populations.

SWEDENBORG VISITS SPACE

A famous eighteenth-century writer propagated a religious perspective on space and space travel that would prove widely influential. Swedish scientist, engineer and mystic Emanuel Swedenborg (1688-1772) is a writer little known today, but he wielded substantial influence over a variety of nineteenth-century cultural leaders, including Ralph Waldo Emerson and Joseph Smith. Despite his scientific training and practical inclinations, Swedenborg insisted that many of his religious insights resulted from daily episodes of direct contact with "spirits," by which he meant the spirits of people who had died. One of Swedenborg's important works, *The Worlds in Space*, records alleged out-of-body journeys through space, during which he conversed with spirits from various planets in our solar system and beyond—beings who had lived out their lives on other planets. Swedenborg's planetary conversations form part of the foundation of the first space-oriented religion of the modern period. Others would follow.

The Worlds in Space was published anonymously in Latin in 1758; the first English translation appeared in London in 1787. Widely read throughout the eighteenth and nineteenth centuries, the book is still available through the Swedenborg Society. The fact that Swedenborg chose spiritual space travel as a means of acquiring religious revelations suggests that the Myth of Space Religion was taking shape at the height of the Enlightenment period. To venture into Space, to visit other planets, was already in the 1750s a means of achieving *spiritual* credibility.

Swedenborg, apparently recognizing the power that space wielded over the imagination, claimed to be "enabled to talk with spirits and angels, not only those in the vicinity of our earth, but also those near other worlds."[8] These other worlds included Mars, Venus, Saturn, Mercury and Jupiter, planets well known to eighteenth-century astronomers. Again, Swedenborg claimed that his space travel was spiritual in nature and that he could thus travel incomprehensible distances in mere hours or days.[9] By entering an altered mental state, a trance, Swedenborg moved freely "in spirit" and "through space." Moreover, both "the outward and return journeys" required "continuous guidance" from spirits, for sense impressions of the physical world were unavailable to him.[10]

The spirits in space inform Swedenborg that "the universe contains very many worlds inhabited by human beings."[11] He sometimes communicates with these spirits through a medium he calls "thought activation," apparently a form of telepathy or direct mental transference of thought.[12] This would remain a preferred method for communicating with space beings. When the spirits encounter a living human being, they "review everything in his memory, calling up from it whatever suits them," an idea remarkably similar to the "downloading" of memory engaged in by extraterrestrials in recent science-fiction works such as Sagan's *Contact*. In these and other ways, Swedenborg anticipated many of the themes of later science fiction, yet in a book still treated by some as a work of religious revelation.

While in Space, Swedenborg receives religious instruction from spiritual beings, including spirits and angels. His space quest was intended principally to increase his store of religious knowledge—in particular, knowledge of what happens to people following death—which is then communicated to Earth's residents. The planetary spirits with whom he communicates also correct the many false teachings of Christianity. They also take a rather dim view of mere scientific knowledge, which is doomed to pass away with the temporary physical world. By rendering space the location for acquiring pure spiritual truth, Swedenborg helped to shape the Myth of Space Religion.

ELLEN G. WHITE: SPACE VALIDATES RELIGION

The Myth of Space Religion was rapidly developing as a peculiar fascination of the Western imagination, evident in the fact that the very mention of planets and space carried the capacity to validate religious ideas. It was vastly more credible to claim that an entity one came across in space disclosed an important insight or that it was discovered during a visit to a distant planet, than it was to claim that one's neighbor related the idea or that it was learned during a trip to Philadelphia. As we saw in the discussion of Emanuel Swedenborg, the mystic took spiritual journeys into space that justified his religious ideas, and with lasting effect on other religious figures. Joseph Smith also worked planetary notions into foundational concepts of Mormonism.

The history of American religion provides other examples of prophets who employed space and planetary themes in making their case for the authenticity of a new revelation. For example, Ellen G. White (1827-1915), founder of the Seventh-Day Adventists, also claimed to have made interior journeys into "space." White occasionally discussed her experiences of near distant planets that she visited while in a trance state. Her most widely reported claims of this type seem to have been limited to a particular set of incidents occurring in the spring of 1846, while she was trying to convince wealthy sea captain Joseph Bates to support her struggling new religious movement. White frequently claimed spiritual visions, and Bates was known to have an intense interest in astronomy. As a sea captain, Bates had studied the various stars and planets, becoming in this way familiar with the principles of astronomy. Bates had discussed his interests with Mrs. White and others. "We all knew that Captain Bates was a great lover of astronomy," writes one contemporary, "as he would often locate many of the heavenly bodies for our instruction."[13] In the presence of Bates and others, White experienced a series of visions that involved visits to planets such as Jupiter and Saturn.

During a later meeting at a conference in Topsham, Maine, in November 1846, White went into a trance and talked about planets, moons and stars that she was apparently visiting. Bates was again present and was allowed to draw conclusions such as "She is viewing Jupiter" and "She is describing Saturn." White added to the drama of the event by making motions that suggested she was flying through space. She reported the number of moons she was seeing around various unidentified planets. Bates happily supplied the planets' names based on then-current but erroneous astronomical knowledge. White also mentioned a "gap" in space near the Orion constellation, a phenomenon that Bates had earlier said he witnessed while viewing the night skies and that had been reported by a British astronomer named William Parsons. As a final embellishment, White reported of Jupiter, "The inhabitants are a tall, majestic people, so unlike the inhabitants of earth. Sin has never entered here."[14] It appears that Jupiter has produced a spiritual race. This detail could not have been the result of simply viewing a distant planet; White wished to suggest some level of actual involvement with the planet's inhabitants. Bates was convinced to support the Adventists, perhaps saving the movement from oblivion. Clearly, Ellen G. White understood the growing religious power of Space. In this respect she was prophetic.

JOHN JACOB ASTOR: SPIRITUAL EVOLUTION AS SPACE RELIGION

The Myth of Space Religion was not the product of religion alone, however; the idea quickly made inroads into the emerging genre of science fiction in the late nineteenth century. Spiritualism was wildly popular in Victorian England and America. Newspapers almost daily reported on spiritualistic phenomena such as haunted houses, séances and visitations by ghosts. Among the varied efforts to promote the idea of contact between the living and the dead, science fiction must be counted as having been quite significant between 1870 and 1920. Several popular writers pressed the genre into the service of spiritualism. And the dead often were assumed to have acquired religious insight and even to be able to travel at will throughout the cosmos. The combination of spiritualism and science fiction undoubtedly helped to shape popular mythologies.

For instance, though he is known principally for his detective novels featuring the supersleuth Sherlock Holmes, Sir Arthur Conan Doyle (1859-1930) was fonder of his science-fiction works. These novels recount the adventures of Professor Challenger; to entertain friends, Doyle would dress up as this character. The Professor Challenger books include *The Lost World* (1912), *The Poison Belt* (1913) and *When the World Screamed* (1929). In *The Lost World*, Conan Doyle explores the lost-race theme so popular with Victorian readers. *The Poison Belt* finds virtually the entire human race wiped out by a toxic gas from outer space. More clearly reflecting Conan Doyle's persistent interest in spiritual themes, however, is *When the World Screamed*, the story of a living earth with a spirit and emotional feeling. Challenger discovers this fact for himself while drilling a deep shaft into the earth's crust—the living earth lets out a bloodcurdling scream. Perhaps more reflective of Conan Doyle's per-

sonal convictions, however, is *The Land of Mist* (1927). In this novel, Professor
Challenger is contacted by his deceased wife and comes to believe in spiritualism. Conan Doyle was a well-known devotee of spiritualism and spent many
years trying to establish contact with his own deceased son.

Less well known today is John Jacob Astor IV, a wealthy American tycoon
who perished in 1912 on the *Titanic*. Astor devoted much of his leisure time to
writing science-fiction novels, and in 1894 published a space story in which intrepid planetary explorers encounter alien intelligences who advocate, among
other things, scientific progress and spiritual exploration. Of his several
science-fiction novels, *A Journey in Other Worlds* is Astor's best known. Not
surprisingly, given the rising influence of the Myth of Space Religion, the book's
intrepid space explorers are as interested in religion as they are in space, perhaps more so. Religious questions come to provide the book's central theme.
In keeping with this interest, spirit beings inhabiting distant planets communicate with the human explorers of Space and give them religious guidance on
many weighty matters.[15]

In Astor's Darwinian solar system, the various planets saw life evolve and
develop at different times. Thus, on a visit to Jupiter, the explorer Cortlandt
reports that the planet has as yet not produced "even so much as a monkey"—
a rather different Jupiter than that visited by Ellen G. White a few decades
earlier.[16] Other planets, by contrast, are home to highly advanced beings who
have transcended the limitations of time and the body: according to Astor,
evolution implies both biological and spiritual advancement.

Astor's *A Journey in Other Worlds* is clearly the work of an amateur; it lacks
the subtlety and literary skill of his younger British contemporary H. G. Wells.
The novel is also heavy-handedly didactic. But what he lacked in ability, Astor made up for with a capacity to anticipate important trends in later science
fiction. He explored evolutionary themes that later authors would popularize:
highly evolved species from an old world direct or assist the evolution of life
in a younger world; the building blocks of life are taken from one planet and
are used to jump-start evolution on another. These and related ideas would
show up in such influential works of science fiction as Stapledon's *Star Maker*,
Clarke's *Childhood's End* and Spielberg's *Close Encounters of the Third Kind*.

Astor also explores moral questions arising at the intersection of evolution
and space travel. For example, his heroes observe that Jupiter is "admirably

suited" for the propagation of living species "developed somewhere else." Indeed, these voyagers are morally required to assist the evolutionary life force that will eventually produce and develop life on Jupiter. "It would be an awful shame if we allowed it to lie unimproved 'til it produces appreciative inhabitants of its own."[17] Astor's two astronauts thus appear on Jupiter as life-giving gods from the sky.

As highly evolved as these human space travelers are, they welcome guidance from beings even higher up on the great evolutionary ladder. Regular visits from highly evolved "spirit beings" on one planet—spiritual existence being merely a stage in evolutionary development—provide the interplanetary explorers with answers to their deepest *religious* questions. Indeed, *A Journey in Other Worlds* eventually *de*volves into a preachy primer in late nineteenth-century progressive religious thought. One planetary spirit assures the earth astronauts that "a man's soul can never die" and that each human's consciousness will "live forever." Moreover, as humanity progresses in consciousness, individual human spiritual powers will also increase. The spirit employs a surprising example to justify this principle: a child develops "the power to move its hand or a material object . . . before it can become the medium in a psychological séance."[18]

As in Swedenborg, the scientific and the spiritual are parts of the same whole in *A Journey in Other Worlds*, as spiritual principles parallel scientific insights. But occasionally Astor's scientific reasoning about spiritual matters takes a bizarre twist. One advanced spirit affirms that just as heat enlarges physical objects, so spiritual heat must enlarge a soul's capacity to understand truth. Consequently, "souls in Hell" experiencing spiritual heat have their spiritual vision "magnified." And the principles of evolution, "invariable throughout the universe," apply even in Heaven and Hell.[19]

Following the Myth of Space Religion, Astor's planetary spirits—"angels of light" inhabiting a paradise called "the seventh heaven"—speak with an authority higher than human knowledge. And their central teaching is that human spiritual evolution will continue to improve the race, eventuating in "a new era" on Earth.[20]

Staking out a position that would endear him to science-fiction authors past and present, Astor writes that the human imagination is the key to the future and places us "almost on a plane with angels." Through the imagina-

tion, humans have already "visited Jupiter and Saturn." Through the exercise
of scientific imagination, "it is impossible that man should remain chained to
the earth during the entire life of his race."[21] As contact with planetary spirits
reveals to humans the vast powers of the physical and spiritual worlds, and
as through the technological use of these secrets we travel to distant planets,
we will "attain a much higher civilization."[22] And in keeping with the Myth
of Space Religion, our new religion will be shaped by our discoveries in space.
Eventually the key to immortality, the "Fountain of Youth," will be discovered,
thus scientifically bringing about "Christ's second visible advent on Earth."[23]

BAHA'I AND THE SPACE CONNECTION

By the late nineteenth century a number of religions that presented themselves as forward looking and modern took account of life on other planets.
The Myth of the Extraterrestrial had joined evolutionary thinking to create a
widespread belief in "more-advanced" space aliens. And was it not likely that
these advanced beings were in possession of knowledge beyond that of mere
earthbound humans, including religious knowledge? The Myth of Space Religion was not limited to Europe and America but apparently also had advocates
in other parts of the world. Cross-fertilization of religious ideas was becoming
more common across international boundaries. American religions, such as
Mormonism, were sending missionaries abroad, and the World Parliament of
Religion in Chicago in 1893 brought the religions of the East to America.

In his unpublished essay titled "Intelligent Life in the Universe and Exotheology in Christianity and the Baha'i Writings," author Duane Troxel reports
a substantial interest in extraterrestrial life within the history of Baha'i.[24] The
prophet Bahá'u'lláh (1817-1892) was apparently a believer in extraterrestrials
who had adapted to conditions on various planets. For instance, in his work
Gleanings the prophet wrote, "Know thou that every fixed star hath its own
planets, and every planet its own creatures, whose number no man can com-
pute." Troxel goes on to point out that "the Bahá'í Writings contain many
statements that implicitly and explicitly point to the existence of not only extraterrestrial life-forms but [also] to extraterrestrial intelligence (ETI) as well."
The Baha'i faith has sought to present itself as a modern religion friendly to
science, emphasizing that Baha'i teachings "expressly support the notion of
the agreement of science with religion and vice versa."[25] Troxel adds that "a

clear logical deduction of the existence of ETI can be drawn from statements of 'Abdu'l-Bahá," a revered Baha'i teacher.[26]

Bahá'u'lláh apparently taught the eternal existence of the human race, which virtually necessitated other inhabited planets: before the Earth's existence, people must have lived somewhere. Troxel writes that the Prophet's teaching "implies the existence of men somewhere at all times!"[27] The Prophet had taught that "there are creatures in every planet," and another Baha'i teacher added, "It remains for science to discover one day the exact nature of these creatures."[28] In another place, Bahá'u'lláh had written, "Verily I say, the creation of God embraceth worlds besides this world, and creatures apart from these creatures."[29] The teacher Shoghi Effendi also commented that "there are other worlds than ours which are inhabited by beings capable of knowing God."[30]

An evolutionary view marks the Baha'i vision of planetary inhabitants. According to Troxel, some Baha'i teaching suggests that "the form" of beings on other planets "exhibit[s] the power of adaptation and environment moulds their bodies and states of consciousness, just as our bodies and minds are suited to our planet."[31] Troxel's study of Baha'i writings leads to the suggestion that "sentient beings on other planets have evolved in a different time frame and have different capabilities than us"; or perhaps they are "at nearly the same evolutionary state that we are." The eventual goal of the evolutionary process is "planetary unity" through the "founding of a world civilization and culture."[32] The prophet Bahá'u'lláh is believed to have inaugurated a "cycle" of 500,000 years, leading to the question, "What comes after the achievement of planetary unity? . . . Inter-planetary unity?"[33] After all, the Prophet spoke of "His appearance in 'other worlds,'" but the meaning of the phrase is unclear.[34] "Nevertheless," adds Troxel, "Shoghi Effendi does not limit the Revelation of Bahá'u'lláh to our star system alone."

Troxel notices "the remarkable flexibility of Bahá'í Exotheology," that is, religious insights originating in planetary exploration or theories about space. As for other, less-flexible faiths, Troxel is confident that "discovery of extrasolar sentient life-forms will require a significant recasting of traditional dogma before the majority of faithful Catholics—for example—can fit such a conception within its worldview." Among the doctrines that may need revising in light of extraterrestrial intelligence are original sin, incarnation, atonement and resurrection. "There will need to be," for example, "a considerable shift in the existing Catholic exotheological paradigm to accommodate such an understanding." Faiths that can accommodate extraterrestrials will have an easier time facing the inevitable interplanetary future.

WHITLEY STRIEBER'S *COMMUNION:* FOUNDATIONS OF THE NEXT RELIGION?

It is indeed surprising that a story written by an established science-fiction author about being visited by diminutive extraterrestrials should have been accepted by millions of readers as nonfiction in the thoroughly modern year 1987. And yet, Whitley Strieber's book *Communion: A True Story* sat atop the bestseller list for several weeks that year. The book also spawned a broad cultural discussion of the possibility that alien visitors were indeed interested in the human race, and perhaps even desirous of interbreeding with us. In *Communion*, novelist Strieber describes in detail what he alleges to be his own dramatic encounter with aliens. Strieber relates in graphic and chilling detail the highly invasive, disturbing, often sexually related nature of his interactions with and interrogations by the highly advanced beings encountered by him and his family during a stay in the mountains of upstate New York. A movie followed in 1989, with the screenplay written by Strieber himself.

Strieber sounds many of the themes of the now-familiar alien abduction story. But his most engaging contributions to the literature of alien encounters are his speculations about where aliens come from and their possible connection to religion. In this respect, Strieber stands exactly on the thin line separating science fiction from religious speculation. The very title of his book, *Communion*, suggests immediately that religious themes will be at the center of his concerns. Moreover, one of Strieber's sharpest critics, science-fiction writer Thomas Disch, virtually accused Strieber of seeking to start a religion with his tales of alien abduction.

Strieber refers to the aliens in question as "the visitors," describing them as small, gray and smelling like "smoldering cardboard." The visitors perform various kinds of invasive procedures on Strieber and members of his family. Strieber's speculations about the purposes of the visits are decidedly religious in nature. Among Strieber's conjectures about the aliens' origins, we read that they may be from another dimension, from a different time, or perhaps from another region of space. But Strieber extends these guesses to suggest that the visitors are based on human belief in gods, fairies, elves and a host of other elusive, supernatural beings reported by human beings throughout history.

Communion, presented as a factual narrative but often suspected of being largely fictional, relates a series of incidents in which Strieber is contacted by extraterrestrial or extradimensional beings. But this is no simple story of witnessing aliens emerge from a flying saucer. A distinctly messianic tone is struck when, on more than one occasion, Strieber is told, "You are our chosen one."[35] Strieber speculates about the possible origins and message of the beings who have sought him out. He connects his experience with fairy stories and related mythic narratives from earlier times, seeing the alien phenomenon as a continuation of an ancient connection between humans and beings from other realms.

Strieber claims that these aliens have a specific interest in what humans term religion, and that through prolonged human contact with them we may be "dealing with a new system of beliefs on its way to becoming fixed into religious dogma." This new perspective is perhaps being implanted "right into the middle of a mind with no obvious allegiance to it at all." The dogmas of alien religion may even have a biological basis in the human brain itself, resulting from "a totally misunderstood biological process," something akin to but "far more concrete than" Jung's collective unconscious. In dramatic fashion Strieber warns that this new religious experience—"something else" issuing forth from a new breed of religious prophets—"is a power within us, maybe some central power of the soul." Consequently, "we had best try to understand it before it overcomes objective efforts to control it."[36]

The blending of traditional religious motifs and science-fiction concepts marks Strieber's narrative throughout. Thus, he affirms that "visitors" might reach "the center of the soul and enter its reality, being too experienced to be interested in any but the deepest essence of our beings." If this were the case, "they might well seem to be part of our mythology, part of the basis of being human."[37] We carry trace memories in our culture of such encounters in the past. The ancient goddess Ishtar, for instance, bears a striking resemblance to the physical descriptions coming from allegedly firsthand reports of encounters with aliens. Of Ishtar he writes, "Paint her eyes entirely black, remove her hair, and there is my image as it hangs before me now in my mind's eye, the ancient and terrible one, the bringer of wisdom, the ruthless questioner."[38] "Perhaps," writes Strieber, "the visitors are the gods." Indeed, "maybe they created us." Strieber reports that "Robert [sic; Francis] Crick, renowned discoverer of the double helix, has postulated that the genetic structure of life is so intricate that it seems designed."[39] We may be on the threshold of a spiritual breakthrough with which the aliens are hoping to assist us. "Maybe the ancient and revered concept of human spiritual transformation relates to the emergence of the adult from the larva."[40]

Strieber's hypothesis is similar to that discovered in John Mack's abductee interviews, the documents of UFO religions, and a number of science-fiction narratives: aliens of unknown origin are the source of human ideas about deities, and they are the harbingers of a new spirituality. Strieber's narratives have done much to popularize the already-widespread mythology that extraterrestrials have been intimately involved with humans throughout our history, and that they have shaped our religions.

THE INTERNATIONAL RAËLIAN MOVEMENT: RELIGION FROM SPACE

French journalist Claude Vorilhon claims that on the morning of December 13, 1973, he was driving near Clermont-Ferrand, France, where he worked as a writer for a racing publication. Feeling called to drive past his office, Vorilhon ended up at a local extinct volcano in Auvergne. Here he saw a saucer-shaped space vehicle hovering overhead. After it landed, the saucer produced a small humanoid figure four feet tall, with green skin and almond-shaped eyes. A conversation ensued in which Vorilhon, renamed Raël, was entrusted with a variety of religious truths updated for modern people. Raël now heads a religious organization—The International Raëlian Movement—claiming more than fifty thousand adherents, and he is the source of financing behind the human cloning effort known as Clonaid.[41]

The space-being, a member of an advanced alien race known as the "Elohim," had instructions for Vorilhon: "You will tell human beings about this meeting but you will tell them the truth about what they are, and about what we are." They have sought out Vorilhon because they needed a messenger who "is a free thinker without being anti-religious." Vorilhon claims to have met with the aliens five more times, each time receiving important teachings, including the text of a commentary on portions of the Bible, which the Elohim say is a book containing some traces of the truth, but that has often been misinterpreted. New and true interpretations are offered through the Elohim. Thus, Genesis 1:2, "The spirit of Elohim moved across the waters," means that extraterrestrial "scientists made reconnaissance flights, and what you might call artificial satellites were placed in orbit around the Earth to study its constitution and atmosphere." The foundational text that emerged from these conversations is titled *The True Face of God.*[42] A number of other books have followed, including *The Final Message* and *Intelligent Design.*

Raël teaches that scientists on another planet sought out a suitable world for their experiments in creating life. They located the Earth where, after breaking into "small research teams," they created all of the plants and animals, and human beings.[43] Because separate acts of creation were taking place in different parts of the Earth, different races of humans were created, some more intelligent than others. The "most intelligent race" was "the people of Israel," a human group created by the most talented alien research team.[44] We recognize that this essentially polygenetic theory of human origins, with different human groups arising independently of one another in different parts of the Earth, harkens back to earlier French writers, including Voltaire, and even to the seventeenth-century science fiction of Bernard de Fontenelle. This elevated view of the people of Israel may explain why Raël, whose father was Jewish, desires to build an embassy in Jerusalem, to welcome the extraterrestrials when they arrive.

Following a narrative structure common in science fiction for over a century—one is reminded of the explorers in Astor's *A Journey in Other Worlds* contemplating creating life on Jupiter—the extraterrestrials explain that they designed "all life on Earth." Humans, however, mistook these alien creators for gods, which is the "origin of your main religions." Now that we have reached the appropriate level of evolutionary advance, our alien creators wish to reestablish contact through embassies on Earth, the first to be built in Jerusalem. The embassies will show that we are prepared for the actual return of the Elohim to Earth, at which time they will provide us with technological information that will allow us to progress to the next evolutionary plane. However, in keeping with the theme of many 1950s and 1960s science-fiction narratives, the Elohim are waiting for peace to reign on Earth before they return. Like the Overlords in Clarke's *Childhood's End*, the Elohim are "monitoring" our progress toward maturity as a species. This monitoring seems to involve using a giant computer to keep track of every human being's activities. Nevertheless, "the created do not have the right to judge their creator."[45]

The Myth of Space Religion typically envisions a single, unifying, enlightened religious view, revealed by extraterrestrials, as reigning throughout the Earth. Raël supports this vision of religious unity. Throughout human history the Elohim maintained contact with humanity through various "prophets," including Buddha, Moses, Muhammad and Jesus, all of whom were "specially chosen and educated by them." Thus, our various religions developed. Jesus plays a key role since his father was Eloha, apparently an important figure among the Elohim. His task was to prepare the world for the Age of Revelation, which has now arrived because of the advanced state of human scientific progress. But Raël has been selected by the Elohim as the "prophet of prophets" and "the last prophet," the Raëlian movement is the "religion of religions," and science is now "the most important thing for all of humanity." In fact, "Science should be your religion, for the Elohim created you scientifically."[46]

Perhaps because of his interest in scientific advancement, Raël teaches that only the highly intelligent should be allowed to govern, and only those of above-average intellect should be allowed to vote. He calls this view "geniocracy," or "selective democracy." Only government by geniuses will allow humanity "to progress." This also has been revealed by the Elohim from Space, scientist-gods who suffer not fools gladly. There may be fewer geniuses ready to govern in Asia, for "the people of the East have not accomplished one tenth of what the people of the West have achieved."[47]

This dominating interest in science is fed by Raël's vision of "scientific reincarnation," a process by means of which immortality is achieved by technology that allows transferring consciousness from one cloned body to another. Indeed, Raël requests that members of his organization arrange that, upon their death, "at least one square centimeter" of their skulls will be sent to the Raëlian embassy as a guarantee that their genetic material will be secure. The faithful "will be re-created from the cells that they have left in our embassy."[48] Raël refers to scientific reincarnation as "the reward" for those who "help the Guide of Guides to accomplish his mission." Those receiving the reward will experience eternal pleasure on "the planet of the eternals." It is clear from

Raël's writings that the word "pleasure" for him refers to sexual pleasure, a topic on which he has much to say. And again, famous science-fiction works of the 1960s and 1970s lurk in the background. The centrality of unfettered sexual experience to the International Raëlian Movement's message is strongly reminiscent of Valentine Michael Smith's libertine Church of All Worlds in Heinlein's *Stranger in a Strange Land*. If eternal sexual experience is the reward of the faithful, those who oppose "the Guide of Guides," another of Raël's titles, will "see their lives become hell."[49] Apparently neither the Elohim nor Raël accept the scientific method's insistence on rigorous testing of hypotheses.

The Raëlians now claim to have sixty thousand adherents worldwide, but actual numbers are difficult to determine. At this point in time, the largest numbers of Raëlians are concentrated in France, Canada and Japan, but outreach continues in the United States, Australia, Southeast Asia, Latin America, Africa, Britain and Europe. A growing trained clergy, known as Guides, also characterizes the group. The group's funds seem disproportionate to its membership, suggesting that many members must possess unusual wealth. The Raëlians have raised millions of dollars for the construction of the Jerusalem embassy. The fact that Raël's original symbol for his movement was a swastika inscribed in the Star of David (as revealed by the Elohim) certainly contributed to the reluctance of the Israeli government to allow construction of the embassy. Requests to build the proposed embassy in Jerusalem continue to be denied by the Israeli government. Other sites are now being considered. The symbol was changed in 1991 to eliminate the offending swastika. However, in January of 2007 the swastika design was reintroduced. Today, we "no longer have an excuse to believe in the 'God' that [our] primitive ancestors believed in."[50] We can now embrace the scientific religion from Space.

CONCLUSION

Space and its residents are a source of indisputable religious truth for a New Age, or so the Myth of Space Religion would suggest. Whether in the form of a twentieth-century UFO religion or a long-established organization such as Seventh-Day Adventism or Baha'i, involvement with space and distant planets is a feature, not just of science fiction, but of some religious thought as well. We have always had a fascination with the stars and planets, often imagining that beings there must possess truths beyond those available to us. This assumption, bolstered in recent centuries by scientific speculation about space's residents, manifests itself culturally in narratives involving telepathic messages from space, contact with religiously minded extraterrestrials, religious truth obtained during space exploration, flexible faiths that will accommodate space and its denizens, or simply that visiting Space makes one a credible source of religious ideas.

Today a religious claim may be based on little more than the assertion that it has some association with Space. This conviction is intimately connected with the persistent idea that "advanced" extraterrestrials are beings more "highly evolved" than we, are residents of Space, and have as a result of these factors also achieved extraordinary religious insight. This certainly assumes a great deal: that these intelligent extraterrestrials exist; that, like travelers arriving on an earlier flight, they are somewhere higher up on the evolutionary escalator; that this elevated perspective allows them clearer religious vision; that they even have an interest in what we term "religion"; that living on a different planet is a distinct advantage for the religious seeker; and that what we know of religious truth is inadequate or primitive, since living on Earth is a distinct disadvantage for the religious seeker. But none of these assumptions receives any actual support from space religionists; they are simply offered up as unsubstantiated guesses. It certainly seems a mistake of sober judgment to jettison, or even to prepare to jettison, established religious traditions in response to such surmises, particularly since their source is often found in the imagination of a fiction writer or religion inventor. There is certainly no good reason that Christianity, a religion with its roots in recorded historical events and deriving its foundational doctrines from a human being who insisted that he *was* a human being, is subject to revision or abandonment based on a telepathic message from an invisible space brother on another planet or even a visitor in a saucer.

Though the allure of Space seems to enhance spiritual claims, there are currently no religions founded on messages from extraterrestrials, or with theories about inhabited planets, that have produced either the alien messenger or evidence of the inhabited planets in question—and this is true despite the fact that religions of Space are allegedly more scientific than the old-fashioned, earthbound kind. The opposite is the case: the religions of Space are less scientific. Space religions invariably fall back on a writer's imagination, the word of a self-styled prophet regarding an extraordinary encounter, or an unsubstanti-ated theory of intelligent life on distant planets for their support.

By contrast, Christianity offers the life and teachings of its founder for our scrutiny, a man who was on the human scene in a single locale for more than thirty years, with written records of his life still available from other human be-ings who actually knew him. Jesus taught on his own authority, and—whether they believed him or not—his teaching was received that way by those who heard him. Why is a religion featuring planets or their residents *rationally* preferable to a faith established by a human being who was on the scene long enough for his claims to be believed by some and doubted by others? And why should interplanetary racists in saucers, voyeuristic aliens from another di-mension, or pop-philosopher spirits on another planet be considered credible sources of religious ideas in the first place? A credible religious claim should originate in a believable source, match closely with lived experience, and con-stitute part of a worldview that provides answers to the deep spiritual ques-tions that must occur to each of us at some point. The tenets of space religion satisfy none of these criteria.

The only validating credentials for extraterrestrial space religions are the extraterrestrials and Space, the former invisible and the latter a void. Distance from Earth does not confirm religious claims, and other planets remain an unknown quantity. There is little if anything in Christian teaching to disallow the possibility of life on another planet. But regardless of what space explora-tion reveals, the Christian faith continues to announce truths that resonate with the human spirit and that no contact with alien intelligences can over-turn: truths that the heavens as well as the Earth were created by a preexistent and loving God, that it is not possible to flee from that God's presence, and that his will is and ever will be the rule of the cosmos.

9

THE MYTH OF ALIEN GNOSIS

We did not fall because of a moral error;
we fell because of an intellectual error: that of taking the phenomenal
world as real. Therefore we are morally innocent.

PHILIP K. DICK

They are telling Man that he is truly a god in his own right!
This knowledge came to a selected few so that they could
open the way for the world to awaken to a New Age.

GEORGE HUNT WILLIAMSON

The Dead Sea Scrolls present graphic evidence
that the Qumranic sect looked for rescue to come
from the skies beyond the earth.

JOHN L. LASH

We declare to you what was from the beginning, what we have heard,
what we have seen with our eyes, what we have looked at
and touched with our hands, concerning the word of life.

1 JOHN 1:1

John Lash is a scholar, religious advocate and self-described "exponent of
the practice of mythology." Lash advocates a new Gnosticism which, he hopes,
will replace Christianity, Islam and other traditional monotheistic religions.
Counting the ancient Gnostic masters as "the elite of Pagan intellectuals,"

Lash calls their writings "the explosive charge that can blow the institution of Faith off its foundations, for good and all." His recent book *Not in His Image* decries "the wholesale genocide of Pagan culture" by Christianity and Islam and calls for Gnostic revival. Lash affirms that this new religion, founded on ancient secrets that allow humans to achieve divinity, is "not a call to faith in God, but faith in the human species."

Identifying what he terms the "sci-fi theology" of the ancient Gnostics as the basis of this liberating new faith, Lash equates the "archons," or guardian demons, of early Gnosticism with modern-day extraterrestrial sightings. These troublesome spiritual entities are on the scene at the present historical moment, "not to destroy us, . . . but to deviate us from our proper course of evolution," which Gnostic wisdom would make possible.[1] Apparently as support for his hypothesis, Lash adds: "It is worth noting that the first great UFO wave of the twentieth century occurred in the summer and fall of 1947, when Jean Doresse was in Cairo examining the Nag Hammadi Codices, at the very moment the first Dead Sea Scrolls were found."[2] The rediscovery of ancient Gnostic texts and the coincident proliferation of alien and UFO sightings mark the reemergence of a religion centered, not on "salvation by superhuman powers," but rather on "the divine potential innate to humanity and aligned with Sophia," the feminine wisdom goddess of the ancient Gnostics.[3] Knowledge of humanity's true and divine nature has been lost to us through trickery, illusion and spiritual blindness. Our membership in "the cosmic community at large" can be recognized through the exercise of "mythic imagination," which is our "innate power to see for ourselves how the cosmos works."[4]

That there is a hidden history of the human race, a deep spiritual secret known to only a few, since the many are perennially lost in a deep and permanent delusion, is a persistent myth of Western culture. The idea of *gnosis* (Greek: *gnōsis*, esoteric knowledge)—a secret explanation of the human predicament, usually involving a struggle between a good force associated with the spiritual realm and an evil force that created the physical—has in the past century experienced something of a renaissance. In gnostic systems, to know and embrace gnosis is to find salvation; increasingly in the artifacts of our popular culture, gnosis has come to be associated with extraterrestrials or other nonhuman entities. Gnosis has proved to be a particularly popular motif in science-fiction novels and movies, where alien beings or highly evolved humans are the guardians of gnosis.

We will be considering several examples in the pages that follow. However, the Myth of Alien Gnosis does not belong solely to science fiction. For instance, astronomer Martin Rees has advanced a startling multiverse view of reality that possesses its own remarkably gnostic qualities. Rees's argument runs something like this, as summarized by Freeman Dyson: "If a multitude of universes exists, then some of them are likely to allow the evolution of life-forms with mental processes far more advanced than ours." And if this is the case, then "a super-intelligent life-form might be capable of simulating in its brain or in a super-computer the complex history of another universe with a lower degree of complexity." Rees asks whether we and the universe we inhabit might be simulations, mock-ups lacking any real physical substance and existing only as mental constructions in the minds of our superintelligent colleagues, the alien beings who sort of "created" us. In his essay "Living in a Multiverse," Rees imagines virtual alien deities traveling through time, rerunning the past when needed, and in this and other ways controlling time and existence.[5] Rees's superintelligent aliens conduct experiments in "universe simulation," and we may all be their subjects, or guinea pigs. Here is gnosis revisited for a scientific age: our lives are not what they appear to be, reality is an illusion, and a gifted elite recognizes these facts.[6]

Dyson, a scientist who has always kept one foot planted firmly in the world of science fiction, adds this intriguing comment regarding Rees's new alien Gnosticism: "Now comes the big surprise. The proposal of Martin Rees, imagining our universe to be a simulation in the minds of intelligent aliens, is very similar to the proposal of Olaf Stapledon, imaging our universe to be an artifact of the Star Maker."[7] Dyson finds that Stapledon's anticipation of a new scientific gnosis "is not the first time that a writer of science fiction has leapt ahead to a new vision of reality that only becomes a part of the discourse of respectable scientists half a century later." Other examples include "Jules Verne's Captain Nemo" and H. G. Wells's Doctor Moreau.[8] It does not appear to trouble either Dyson or Rees that there is no evidence to support speculation about superintelligent aliens creating us as part of a thought experiment, or that such an idea might have had its origins in a work of science fiction.

Rees's gnostic narrative addresses perhaps the greatest mystery human beings face: our origins. This question has been a consistent theme of religion from time immemorial. But it has also proved to be a durable theme of both science fiction and speculative scientific writing. Whether the writers of a *Star Trek* screenplay speculate that, eons ago, advanced aliens seeded the oceans of a primitive Earth with DNA; or in his *Cosmos* book and television series, Carl Sagan suggests that we are "star folk," made of "star stuff"—science fiction and speculative science have taken a decided interest in questions that once were firmly within the realms of myth and religion.

In the movie *Mission to Mars* (2000), a group of human astronauts discovers the secret, heavenly origins of the human race: we are descended from the race of Martians who were forced to leave their dying planet, a "secret origins" theme that has been endlessly reprised in works of science fiction and often hinted at in the works of speculative science. The previous year, the sixth season of *The X-Files* concluded with episodes titled "The Sixth Extinction" and "Biogenesis." Agent Mulder discovers the same strange fact revealed in *Mission to Mars:* Martians brought life to Earth ages ago, a fact to be revealed to humanity "in the fullness of time," as a flying saucer revealing the grand secret of our origins is unearthed in Africa.

Marshall Applewhite, leader of the deadly Heaven's Gate UFO cult, taught his followers that the Hale-Bopp comet signaled the arrival of a vehicle from another dimension that would usher "a select group" of followers to their destiny in the stars.[9] For more than twenty years, Applewhite had been sharing his secret knowledge with a few devotees. Recruits were "highly evolved" and thus were among the "chosen ones." Applewhite "believed that he and his followers were aliens who had been planted [on Earth] years ago."[10] Descending from "a level above human in distant space," they sought to return to "their world" or the place of their cosmic origin by following secret teachings and—unfortunately for his followers—destroying their "material containers" or bodies.

This chapter examines the Myth of Alien Gnosis: the idea that our origins, predicament and destiny are not widely known, and that the truth about the human past and future is to be revealed by beings from other planets, another dimension or the future. We will consider various versions of this basic myth in several important works of science fiction as well as in other genres of popular literature, including speculative scientific writing and contemporary religious texts. Modern myths proclaiming a hidden alien history of the human race and a true reality just outside the present illusion we all inhabit have, as we shall see, had a peculiarly broad appeal in modern culture. As the next section suggests, this myth is not of recent origin in popular Western literature.

JACOB ILIVE AND THE EARTH AS HELL

In the 1730s and 1740s, a printer named Jacob Ilive (1705-1763) lectured widely in London about a theory that had come to him through study of the Bible and other ancient texts. Ilive believed that he had discovered the hidden spiritual history of the human race, and he propagated his insight tirelessly.[11] According to Ilive, the planet on which we live is hell, and each of us is a fallen angel imprisoned in a human body.[12] Ilive's strange religious ideas found a ready audience among London's working class; his speeches and books often took on a quality that today would be associated with science fiction: minor gods locked in cosmic conflict, a titanic struggle for control of Heaven, defeated souls being confined to prison planets.

Ilive freely appropriated biblical characters to people his fantasies: A divine being called Lucifer battled a rival named Jesus. Lucifer and his minions lost this epic heavenly war and were forced into fleshly bodies, "little Places of Confinement," and made to live on the prison planet Earth.[13] However, a higher god intent on "bringing back again the rebellious and apostate angels" decided to put the fallen "angelic host" through a series of purgatorial exercises on their new planet. Thus arose the human race, and the lives we live on Earth are planned drills meant to redeem us and to allow a return to a higher spiritual life.

Ilive's religious imagination did not limit itself to a single planet, and by projecting the question of human origins into space, he helped to invent the Myth of Alien Gnosis. Numerous inhabited planets—the "Celestial Mansions" mentioned in the Bible (John 14:2 KJV)—became the homes of ascended spirit beings who had achieved significant progress toward redemption. A vast network of inhabited planets formed a cosmic ladder of spiritual ascent. With great spiritual advancement, a spirit being might even be rewarded with dominion over an entire planet. Still, for those of us just starting the journey, "that Globe we now inhabit" is hell, and we are fallen angels held "in Prison."[14]

Ilive updated for his eighteenth-century audiences a gnostic recasting of several New Testament themes. We all are embodied fallen angels in need of the secrets that restore our former glory.

Such was Jacob Ilive's planetary gnosis, a secret spiritual history of the human race unknown to, or perhaps repressed by, established religion. This captivating spiritual narrative proved remarkably popular well into the nineteenth century, and his association of secret human origins with a pantheon in space and spiritual ascent toward divinity opened the way to later mythologies that would develop the Myth of Alien Gnosis.

JOSEPH SMITH'S PLANETARY GNOSIS

In early nineteenth-century America, a planetary gnosis similar in some respects to Ilive's was disseminated broadly in the teachings of Mormon prophet and founder Joseph Smith. Smith, an emphatic polytheist, rejected the monotheism of Christianity as unbiblical and misleading. In one famous sermon of 1844, he announced, "I will preach on the plurality of Gods"—and he did not mean just on that occasion. The three persons of the Christian Trinity were, for Smith, three distinct gods. "I have always declared God to be a distinct personage, Jesus Christ a separate and distinct personage from God the Father, and that the Holy Ghost was a distinct personage and a Spirit: and these three constitute three distinct personages and three Gods." Indeed, Jesus was actually the son of God the Father, a spirit child of a higher god. Clearly, Smith was not simply revising Christian theology—he was starting over.

There was more to Smith's differences with the established church than his polytheism. In the 1830s and early 1840s, he had developed a gnostic perspective on the spiritual history of the cosmos. Gods have arisen by a progressive process of "enlargement," in which human beings can participate. But as with Ilive, spiritual progress means taking on a body. A first step in progress toward godhood is for a spirit being to enter a physical body and live on a material planet for a period of time. Thus, "the head God" did not create the universe ex nihilo, but "organized the heavens and the earth" out of existing physical matter. Many gods gathered in a "Council of Gods," and "the head one of the Gods said, Let us make a man in our own image." The process of spirit embodiment was about to begin on Earth.

Smith was adamant that the Bible itself "shows there is a plurality of Gods beyond the power of refutation." These gods are arranged in a nearly infinite hierarchy, or as Smith put the point, these "Intelligences exist one above another, so that there is no end to them." Near the top of this progression, a council that Smith called "the heads of the Gods" assigned "one God for us," a deity to rule over the Earth. The Council of the Gods existed in space on a planet near a star called Kolob, and it deputized Adam and Eve to colonize the Earth for the purpose of allowing the birth into bodies of eternal spirit beings.

Where did Smith learn this gnosis, this secret knowledge of human origins and human nature? He asserted that much of what he had to say on this subject was garnered from his translation of "the papyrus which is now in my house." Smith claimed a special ability to interpret the mysterious symbols on the fragment of Egyptian papyrus, which some scholars say is a page from the Egyptian Book of the Dead. It subsequently became the foundation of the Book of Abraham, to which Smith often referred.

The charismatic Smith believed that "the Church is being purged" of its corrupted theology by his new gnosis involving many gods, physically embodied spirit beings, and the possibility of ascent toward divinity. But there was more to the vision, for "every man [apparently males] who reigns in celestial glory is a God to his dominions," his own planet.[15] Unfortunately, "the great majority of mankind do not comprehend . . . their relationship to God," presumably because of the bad teachings of the Christian church, and so they miss this opportunity. To "comprehend themselves" as people, they must "comprehend the character of God." God is simply an ascended person who now has responsibility for a planet—ours. For this reason "He interferes with the affairs of man." Indeed, "God himself was once as we are now, and is an exalted man, and sits enthroned in yonder heavens! That is the great secret." God has a body and the "very form as a man."

Smith was urgent in instructing his followers how to begin the process toward planetary godhood, since that is "how God came to be God." God did not exist "from all eternity," as Christians taught. "I will refute that idea, and take away the veil, so that you may see." The gnosis of human and divine origin and destiny is being revealed in the Latter Days. God "was once a man like us," indeed he "dwelt on an earth." Smith's wording is important—the god we now serve once lived as a man on a planet—he "dwelt on an earth." How did he get where he is, then? Smith's answer places him squarely within the Gnostic tradition, in which each individual possesses something of the divine that wishes to ascend. "You have got to learn how to be gods yourselves," Smith insisted, just "as all gods have done before you, namely, by going from one small degree to another, and from a small capacity to a great one." Godhood is achieved through spiritual progress by those possessing the new gnosis.

Through correct teaching and practice, you will "inherit the same power, the same glory and the same exaltation, until you arrive at the station of a god, and ascend the throne of eternal power, the same as those who have gone before." These teachings were not a mere footnote to his theology; Smith referred to them as "the first principles of the gospel." We are currently planetary gods in embryo, and "when you climb up a ladder, you must begin at the bottom, and ascend step by step, until you arrive at the top. . . . You must begin with the first, and go on until you learn all the principles of exaltation." This is how all of the "Gods in the grand council" achieved their status. "In the beginning, the head of the Gods called a council of the Gods; and they came together and concocted a plan to create the world and people it. When we begin to learn this way, we begin to learn . . . what kind of a being we have got to worship." That being is a highly evolved extraterrestrial who happens to be in charge of Earth, and who "organize[d] the world out of chaos—chaotic matter, which is element," or physical matter.

For Joseph Smith, human beings "exist upon the same principles" as God. We are a physical body that God "put a spirit into," the process that continues today at any human birth. An eternal spirit being takes up residence in a baby's body in order to begin the process of spiritual ascent. Thus, "the mind or the intelligence which man possesses is co-equal with God himself." And the "intelligence of spirits had no beginning; neither will it have an end": we are eternal spirits currently in bodies. Smith reiterates that God's creative activity is limited to organizing matter; he cannot create the human spirit, it is eternal. "God never had the power to create the spirit of man at all." The cosmos is itself filled with intelligence, and "Intelligence is eternal." But for such intelligence to become a "living soul," it must have a body. "All the minds and spirits that God ever sent into the world are susceptible of enlargement." God, a "more intelligent" spirit, "saw proper to institute laws whereby the rest could have a privilege to advance like himself." By this process of enlargement of our living soul through "advancement in knowledge," we can gain the knowledge necessary "in order to save them in the world of spirits."[16] Joseph Smith's planetary gnosis belongs in the tradition of Jacob Ilive and is a stark departure from traditional Christian theology.

H. P. LOVECRAFT: THE CULT OF CTHULHU

Born in Providence, Rhode Island, in 1890, H. P. Lovecraft was one of the most enigmatic of American popular writers.[17] His literary model was Edgar Allan Poe, whom Lovecraft referred to as the "God of Fiction." He was also a devoted student of the novelist Lord Dunsany. Never achieving much fame during his short life, Lovecraft is today credited with a number of innovations in both the horror story and science fiction. Lovecraft sought in his strange stories to create a sense of wonder lacking in the spiritless naturalism that he embraced. In 1933 he wrote that he sought "to achieve, momentarily, the illusion of some strange suspension or violation of the galling limitations of time, space, and natural law which forever imprison us and frustrate our curiosity about the infinite cosmic spaces beyond the radius of our sight and analysis."[18]

Like a true Gnostic revolting against the limitations of mundane existence through the imaginative creation of a transcendent gnosis, Lovecraft sought through his stories to escape the physical. His narrative "revolt against time, space, and matter" would not be "overtly incompatible with what is known of reality" because he would create "*supplements* rather than *contradictions* of the visible and measurable universe."[19] His stories would be strange but believable, otherworldly but connected to ordinary experience. Several of Lovecraft's most successful stories fit the genre of science fiction and appeared in *Amazing Stories* and *Astounding Stories*. Among these were "The Call of Cthulhu," "The Colour out of Space," "At the Mountain of Madness" and "The Shadow out of Time."

Perhaps Lovecraft's most influential story was "The Call of Cthulhu," written between 1925 and 1926 and published in *Weird Stories* in February of 1928. Some components of the exotic plot were based on a dream he had in 1920, to which Lovecraft added elements of Theosophy. S. T. Joshi observes that, though Lovecraft did not accept Theosophy as true, he "found many of its cosmic speculations imaginatively stimulating."[20] "Theosophists," Lovecraft wrote, "have guessed at the awesome grandeur of the cosmic cycle wherein our world and human race form transient incidents." Larger, hidden truths lurk in the background of ordinary experience, which traditional religion knows nothing of. A self-professed agnostic, Lovecraft followed no religion. Nevertheless, much of his fiction speculates about alien deities coming to Earth, and in this way he has influenced subsequent science fiction and propagated the alien-deity myth. His influence on the work of Arthur C. Clarke seems especially evident in this regard.

Steeped in the literature of magic, witchcraft and shamanism, Lovecraft was also intimately familiar with works on the "lost" continents of Lemuria and Atlantis. He often cites anthropological authorities such as Sir James George Frazier *(The Golden Bough)* and Margaret A. Murray *(The Witch Cult)*. Fascinated by the idea of an ancient race of alien or prehuman beings who possessed deep spiritual secrets, he incorporated the idea into stories such as "The Temple" and "Dagon." Lovecraft was particularly taken with Murray's notion of "a pre-Aryan race that was driven underground but continued to lurk in the hidden corners of the earth."[21] The possibility of such a master race, a feature of Bulwer-Lytton's *The Coming Race*, would have appealed to Lovecraft, whose own racism was well known.

In "The Call of Cthulhu," a mysterious, dangerous worldwide cult develops around strange objects of worship, including a small idol carved from an unknown type of stone. Large pillars appear mysteriously in various part of the world. Professor Angell has investigated the Cthulhu Cult, and the narrator, the Professor's grandnephew, sets about solving the mystery of the deadly religion. Members of an ancient nonhuman alien race that once "ruled on the earth" have embedded themselves in subterranean crypts and are awaiting the appropriate time to rise and destroy humanity. In the intervening eons, certain members of the human race continue to worship this alien race of demonic divinities, who demand human sacrifice. The human leaders of the cult are reputed to be "undying" and "living in the mountains of China," a clear parallel to Blavatsky's Tibetan ascended masters. Alien entities communicate with a few humans through the medium of "transmitted thought" in dreams. "In the elder time chosen men had talked with the entombed Old Ones in dreams," a reference to an ancient extraterrestrial race possessing secret truths.[22]

These eternal and malevolent deities from distant stars "knew all that was occurring in the universe" and communicated various secrets during the earliest days of humankind to "sensitive" members of the human race. The idea that certain individuals are capable, through special spiritual sensitivity, of hearing messages from superior beings, apparently borrowed from Blavatsky, is also a common theme in UFO mythology and some science fiction. Finally, the aliens' "great stone city of R'lyeh, with its monoliths and sepulchers," had long ago "sunk beneath the waves," thus cutting off the possibility of further telepathic messages.[23] This element in the Cthulhu narrative is reminiscent of the Lemuria and Atlantis legends.

The Cthulhu myth became part of the foundation of modern science fiction. David E. Schultz has referred to the sort of reverse religious thought found in Lovecraft's stories as "antimythology," but it can also be seen as the coalescing of a new set of mythologies that turn Christian theology on its head. Joshi explains that while religion has often sought to "reconcile human beings with the cosmos by depicting a close, benign relationship between man and god," Lovecraft's peculiar form of myth "brutally shows that man is *not* the center of the universe, that the 'gods' care nothing for him, and that the earth and all its inhabitants are but a momentary incident in the unending cyclical chaos of the universe."[24] Lovecraft leaves readers with the sense that the cosmos is fundamentally an unfriendly and dangerous place, that any deities that exist are not interested in the good of humanity, and that we know neither our origins nor our destiny. As the narrator of "The Call of Cthulhu" puts the point, "I shall never sleep calmly again when I think of the horrors that lurk ceaselessly behind life in time and space, and of those unhallowed blasphemies from elder stars which dream beneath the sea."[25] Lovecraft evokes the spiritual hopelessness of a cosmos devoid of God, but home to minor and malevolent deities.

GEORGE HUNT WILLIAMSON: WORLD UNITY THROUGH ALIEN GNOSIS

The 1950s witnessed a proliferation of flying-saucer and extraterrestrial religious organizations, usually founded by an individual claiming contact with intelligent aliens. Dr. George Hunt Williamson (1926-1986), for instance, wrote extensively on the topic of contact with entities from space. Williamson, a devoted student of the occult, helped to popularize belief in flying saucers and to connect such belief with secret systems, such as magic.

In 1953 Williamson published his most popular work, *Other Tongues, Other Flesh*. This odd book was a sequel to his earlier published account of UFO encounters titled *The Saucers Speak!* Among other things, Williamson claimed that radio messages from extraterrestrials were received throughout the world in the 1920s and 1930s. Ongoing contact with aliens was occurring "by code and voice." These messages were often explicitly religious and tended

to correct erroneous ideas about religion—a preoccupation of religious extraterrestrials. Williamson was particularly interested in the theme of world
unity in alien religion. Though human beings constantly divide themselves
into separate groups, and though we "set up artificial lines to separate and
segregate," the aliens are telling us that "the Infinite Father" is a unity and that
earthly religious doctrines are "man made" and work against unity.[26]

Williamson proposed using science to test religious doctrine, for "science
and religion are one, just as everything in the Omniverse is ONE!" Science
and religion are "the two great fields of human endeavor," and thus teach
complementary truths. But Williamson's pure scientific religion consisted of
neither traditional religion nor orthodox science, for orthodox theology "has
failed also to satisfy their deep longings, and orthodox science presents only
cold, bare materialism." A New Age or "Golden Dawn" would be ushered in by
extraterrestrials. People will enjoy religious insight, better health and "right
thinking." Intriguingly, in this New Age, every individual "will be a scientist,
even as space visitors are true scientists: utilizing the Forces of the Universe
in the ever upward, spiraling climb toward divinity and the Father." Jesus was
"The Elder Brother" who said, "Know ye not that ye are Gods?" Once we accept this fact, we will "leave the pupa of ignorance, superstition, dogma, [and]
orthodoxy," emerging ultimately as a "Son of God."[27]

"Son of God" was not a randomly chosen religious term for Williamson. In
his telling of the story of human origins, "a great migration of souls known as
the 'Sons of God' arrived on Earth when the evolution of its indigenous life was
progressing and incarnated in certain animal forms." It was this invasion from
space that "caused the basic difference between the human and other mam-
mal forms." Certain of the available "ape-forms" on Earth "were borrowed for
incarnation by the spirit-souls arriving from outer space," and these combined
beings "supplied the original expressions of the human." Out of the various
kinds of alien-ape beings, "the races of man" emerged. The "physical attributes"
of people were drawn from the apes, while "the spiritual attributes belonged to
the migration which came from the planets of the star-sun Sirius." This joining
of earthly and extraterrestrial species produced the strange fossil remains that
continue to confuse scientists. According to Williams, this genetic entrance
of the alien into life on Earth was a "spiritual link" between Earth and space
beings. The space beings were gods breeding with earthly apes.

In his strange narrative of human origins, Williamson blended Darwinian thinking with the Myth of the Extraterrestrial to create a new gnosis, with spirit from above and matter from below, a secret creation story known only to him and his readers. As in Ilive's planetary gnosticism, our embodiment is not spiritual in Williamson's account. Moreover, the body is to be jettisoned when the right time arrives. Each of us is "a prisoner of pain." The human soul is "heavenly in divine creation," while our bodies are "physically handicapped by weight." The human "came from races of angels mixed with beasts, and he is now engaged in separating the brute from the angel." Through our struggle with the flesh, we "become a fit subject for higher planes."[28]

FRED HOYLE ON THE SEEDING OF EARTH

One version of the modern Myth of Alien Gnosis is known as the panspermia hypothesis, the idea that bacterial and viral spores float through Space from one planet to another, seeding life as they go. The theory is attributed to the Swedish scientist Svante August Arrhenius (1859-1927), one of the first winners of the Nobel Prize in chemistry. According to Walter Sullivan, Arrhenius "tried to get around the problem [of life's origin] by proposing that the earth's life came from elsewhere in the form of spores wafted across interplanetary or interstellar distances by light pressure. When the hypothesis was put forth at the turn of the century, Clerk Maxwell had already discovered that electromagnetic radiation (that is, light) exerts a pressure, although it is so weak as to be unobservable under normal laboratory conditions."[29]

Panspermia has had its share of distinguished defenders, not the least being Sir Francis Crick of Watson and Crick fame. But the scientist who did the most to popularize the idea in the twentieth century was Sir Fred Hoyle (1915-2001). Hoyle was among the most gifted and controversial scientific figures of the mid-twentieth century. An astronomer and longtime director of the Institute of Astronomy at Cambridge, Hoyle is perhaps best known for his arguments against both the "Big Bang," a term he coined, and the Darwinian conception of evolution. Hoyle argued that the universe existed in a "steady state"; though individual atoms come into existence at a point in time, the universe itself has no beginning. The discovery of background microwave radiation in the universe tended to prove the Big Bang, however, and Hoyle's theory was relegated to the status of an interesting footnote to cosmology.

Like Arthur C. Clarke and Carl Sagan, Hoyle was a highly trained and re-spected scientist who wrote both nonfiction and science-fiction works. Hoyle's partners in a series of experiments predicting the energy levels in the carbon nucleus won the Nobel Prize, and it has remained a mystery why Hoyle was not also so honored. He was, nevertheless, the recipient of numerous other scientific awards, including the Gold Medal of the Royal Astronomical Society in 1968 and Crafoord Prize in 1997.

Nevertheless, Hoyle's most controversial theory was an intentional version of the panspermia hypothesis, which he advocated in a series of books with his coauthor, Chandra Wickramasinghe. Believing that there has not been time for life to have evolved from chemicals existing on the Earth's surface, Hoyle hypothesized that the cosmos—actually intelligent beings in the cosmos—was continuously bombarding the surface of the Earth with bacteria and viruses. These microscopic organisms from Space, according to Hoyle, account for both life's origins and its continuously changing quality. He labeled the theory of chance occurrence of life from a primordial soup as "nonsense of a high order." Hoyle is also the originator of the oft-repeated analogy that Darwin's theory is comparable to believing that "a tornado sweeping through a junk-yard might assemble a Boeing 747 from the materials therein."

Hoyle also wrote science fiction: his story *A for Andromeda* ran briefly as a BBC television series in the early 1960s. In this story, aliens from deep in Space beam to Earth the instructions for constructing a machine that would allow humans to communicate with them. This basic concept may have inspired a later physicist-turned-science-fiction-author, Carl Sagan, in developing his story *Contact*. Other well-known fictional works include Hoyle's *Ossian's Ride* (1959), *October the First Is Too Late* (1966), and *Comet Halley* (1985). Among his many nonfiction works are *Astronomy and Cosmology: A Modern Course* (1975), *The Intelligent Universe* (1983) and *Evolution from Space: A Theory of Cosmic Creationism* (1984).

Hoyle's best-known science-fiction work is his first; *The Black Cloud*, pub-lished in 1957, suggests that intelligent life might exist in forms radically dif-ferent from our own embodied state. Indeed, an intelligent entity might take the form of an extended interstellar cosmic cloud. Hoyle referred to his un-orthodox view of the universe and the origins of life on Earth as a "sort of re-ligion with me" and "the Word of God."[30] An outspoken opponent of Darwinism, he argued that "terrestrial biology has been spurred on through evolution by a force outside the Earth itself," and the purely natural scheme of Darwin as "the purposeless outlook of orthodox opinion." Interestingly, Hoyle felt that scientists resisted his ideas "because there might turn out to be . . . religious connotations," which they sought to avoid at all costs.[31]

Indeed, Hoyle's scientifically unorthodox theories reflect a mythic view of the universe. He argued, for instance, that "genes, the components of life, are assembled on Earth from elsewhere, from space."[32] As a result, we are "descendents of life seeded from the depths of space."[33] Rejecting as "too cautious" the idea that comets might have contributed the building blocks of life to Earth, Hoyle preferred viewing the cosmos as literally full of life, with planets serving as "assembly stations" where this life is allowed to evolve. Hoyle was of the opinion that interstellar clouds were made up of carbon-based bacteria, by means of which life might be seeded throughout the cosmos. Admitting that "the thought is rather fanciful," Hoyle commented that "the surface of Mars looks very much like a failed attempt at seeding life from space, a failed 'experiment' of a kind which eventually succeeded in the case of Earth."[34]

What was needed, according to Hoyle, was an essentially religious theory of life, one that "spans all the Universe," sees life as "a coherent whole" throughout the galaxy, and can accommodate the possibility of life as "intelligently guided."[35] Only the "religious instinct residing in all of us, the instinct that whispers in some remote region of our consciousness," can fathom such a view of life.[36] Thus, Hoyle advocated a living cosmos with Life as its central purpose and higher intelligence directing a grand cosmic experiment in evolution. He sometimes referred to his own theory as Cosmic Creationism.

His full theory could at times, however, become a good deal more involved and exotic than simply the idea of space aliens seeding the Earth with life. It could actually involve "our remote descendants" working their way back in time in order to fashion "carbon-based" life-forms for a remarkable purpose. Believing that their survival depended upon it, these future humans sought "an entirely new material structure to which the store of knowledge that constituted themselves might be transferred." Thus, "an intelligence . . . was led to put together, as a deliberate act of creation, a structure for carbon-based life": us.[37] We may be "hardware" developed to contain the "software that is really us." But that is not all there is to the story. These same beings, our descendants who in fact preceded us, implanted in us "the religious impulse" so that we would possess a "desire to reach to the Heavens to find our cosmic source." This is because they wanted to "build into the new representation" an awareness of where it came from. In this way they would establish "a bridge" between themselves and their creation. If our beliefs are "stripped of the many fanciful adornments with which religion has become traditionally surrounded, does it not amount to an instruction within us that, expressed rather simply, might read as follows: You are derived from something 'out there' in the sky. Seek it, and you will find much more than you expect?" "So," states Hoyle with remarkable candor, "starting from astronomy and a little physics, we have arrived at religion."[38] This also proves, he thinks, that religions placing God within the universe rather than outside of it are closer to the truth. So, "the God Brahma in modern Hinduism" as well as the gods of the Greeks and Nordic peoples may be quite close to the mark.[39]

The mistaken "trappings that are found in all religions" accrued because we "find it hard to interpret the distant voices that are guiding our development."[40] But we are getting closer to the truth as, "instead of temples and cathedrals, we now build large telescopes of all kinds."[41] This truth of higher life creating and controlling lower life is the key that unlocks the profoundest religious mysteries. "A saying that has puzzled Christians themselves, 'Many are called, but few are chosen,' ceases to be puzzling if it is interpreted in the present context. Many are the places in the Universe where life exists in its simplest microbial forms, but few support complex multicellular organisms."[42] A new mythology is required today, one that will call us constantly toward the stars to find that our true home is a distant star, and our true parents are our children.

Hoyle, himself an author of science fiction, must be considered among the most influential twentieth-century sources of the Myth of Alien Gnosis. It is remarkable how similar his views are to those of his countryman Olaf Stapledon. In his classic *Last and First Men*, Stapledon envisions a dying human race: already "on the edge of extinction, mankind is spraying countless artificial human spores into space to be carried by solar radiation to the most promising region of the galaxy." The last men "sow the universe with artificial human seed."[43] Here Genesis is revisited and rewritten through science fiction, producing a secret alien history of our origins.

L. RON HUBBARD AND SCIENTOLOGY

Perhaps the most prominent recent example of alien gnosis occurs in the work
of L. Ron Hubbard (1911-1986), founder of the highly controversial worldwide
religious movement known as Scientology. Hubbard was born in Tilden, Nebraska, and served in the U.S. Navy during World War II. Though he made
many claims about his activities that are difficult to confirm, it seems that
Hubbard was a capable sailor and participated in various expeditions to remote parts of the world. He took up the craft of writing fiction and was drawn
to science fiction in particular. Following the war, some of Hubbard's science-
fiction stories were published in pulp outlets such as *Astounding Science Fiction*, edited by his friend John W. Campbell.

An established science-fiction author by the end of the 1940s—publishing
alongside Asimov, Heinlein and Clarke in Campbell's magazine—Hubbard
was also a tireless student of psychology, Freudian psychotherapy and occult
systems. In the mid-1940s he lived for a time with the mysterious rocket scientist Jack Parsons of the Jet Propulsion Laboratory in Pasadena, California, a
dedicated student of ritual magic and disciple of the notorious occultist Aleis-
ter Crowley. By the time he met Parsons, however, Hubbard was already intimately familiar with occult practices and teaching and well acquainted with
Crowley's works.

In 1950 Hubbard published a book that set out his views on achieving complete mental health. The now famous work, *Dianetics: The Modern Science of
Mental Health,* earned a wide readership. Campbell promoted *Dianetics* in
Astounding Science Fiction and worked closely with Hubbard on the *Dianetics*
project. Hubbard was also joined in the effort to promote Dianetics by famed
Canadian science-fiction author A. E. van Vogt, who represented Hubbard's
organization in Los Angeles. Both Campbell and van Vogt eventually parted
company with the autocratic Hubbard.

Hubbard's professed goal in *Dianetics* was to provide scientific explanations for mental disorders and to offer scientifically justified solutions in his
Dianetics program. He introduced the concept of "auditing" in order to identify roadblocks to psychological health. Auditing involved reducing one's emotional reaction to reminders of painful events through repetition of the stimuli
associated with them. Once the auditing process had been successfully completed, an individual achieved a level of mental health that Hubbard dubbed

"clear." "Clears," as individuals reaching this state were called, were alleged to be able to perform all sorts of remarkable cognitive feats.

But Hubbard quickly turned Dianetics into something more closely resembling a religion, and in 1953 officially announced the founding of the Church of Scientology. A dramatic story involving a tyrant on a distant planet, nuclear weapons and invisible aliens transformed a psychological therapy technique into a religion. Indeed, Hubbard's secret account of human origins reads like a plot from a science-fiction story. According to the Hubbard narrative, 75 million years ago Earth was called Teegeeack and was part of a seventy-six-planet Galactic Confederation. Some of the planets were badly overpopulated, and so the cosmic tyrant known as Xenu sent trillions of individuals to be destroyed by nuclear explosions near volcanoes on Teegeeack. The spirits of these annihilated alien beings were all that remained, and they became clustered into groups called "thetans" or "body thetans."[44] Eventually these "body thetans" took up residence in human beings, where they cause emotional and psychological problems. Our spiritual and even physical suffering is due to the harmful effects of indwelling thetans controlling our "reactive mind," that part of us that records unpleasant life-events. Even active Scientologists who have gone through auditing still consider themselves to be timeless thetans in a body, a "temporary vessel."[45] The harmful effects thetans cause actually accumulate over a vast number of lives, for each of us is an "immortal spiritual being" whose spiritual experience "extends well beyond a single lifetime." Auditing with a device called an E-Meter can help identify and rid the effects of the body thetans within, thus restoring mental, emotional and even physical health.

This is Hubbard's hidden truth, his gnosis of the human race, typically revealed to a follower of the faith during a stage of instruction called OT III (Operating Thetan Three). The thetan narrative is the foundation of much Scientology teaching. Like so many similar stories, it involves eternal spirits already present in some other dimension or planet being embodied in human persons. And like other similar stories, knowledge of this "truth" is understood only by a few who are initiated into the particular version of gnosis. Only when this hidden alien gnosis about our true nature is recognized and acted upon can our spiritual progress take place. Hubbard believed that "the whole organized future of the planet, every man, woman and child on it, and your destiny for endless trillions of years depend on what you do here and now and in Scientology. This is deadly serious activity."[46]

ELIJAH MUHAMMAD AND THE
ALIEN GNOSIS OF RACE

Minister Louis Farrakhan, through his flamboyant speeches and large-scale events such as the Million Man March, has brought a great deal of attention to the organization known as The Nation of Islam. The Nation of Islam's foundational cosmology rests on a blend of teachings about ancient scientists, genetic experiments, distant planets and flying saucers that places it squarely in the realm of the Myth of Alien Gnosis.

Elijah Muhammad (1897-1975) cofounded the Nation of Islam with a mysterious individual named Wallace Fard, who disappeared from his home in Detroit in 1934. Elijah Muhammad taught that a scientist named Yakub created the white race through a failed experiment in genetic engineering six thousand years ago, and that these "devils" had been given the power to rule the world for a limited period of time, which was almost over. The original human race, a race of dark-skinned godlike beings, created the Earth and populated it 66 trillion years ago, and they will soon resume control of the planet.[47]

In a now-famous speech delivered in Philadelphia in 1962, Elijah Muhammad spoke of "a few events" that date back "6,000 years ago according to the word of Almighty God Allah when this world was being fashioned, the white man's world." Black people, according to Elijah Muhammad, are "members of the Tribe of Shabazz," himself a scientist who "went into what was then known as the jungle of East Asia" more than fifty thousand years ago. Shabazz "started with his family" a new civilization based on his advanced ideas "in what you call today the jungles of Africa." Shabazz had disagreed with a council of twenty-three scientists and isolated himself in order "to prove what he thought was necessary for you and I to know." This is the "knowledge [that] awakens you," Elijah Muhammad told his followers. Moreover, he emphasized that this liberating "true knowledge or science" was "kept back, hidden and it was a secret among the scientists" until an appointed time, when it should be widely revealed. Today "a new world is budding or giving birth in place of an old one."

According to Elijah Muhammad, people of African descent "have always experimented among ourselves," the experiments resulting in "the greatest and the wisest people in the universe," people fully aware of "life on other planets" where such experimentation is less common. Moreover, "the black man" existed "before the earth," a claim reminiscent of the Baha'i teaching about the eternal existence of human beings on other planets. In an updated version of polygenism, Muhammad taught that the "Black Nation of the Planet Earth" was not descended from Adam: "It is the white race that is from Adam, but not you and I." The white race is of relatively recent origin, being a mere six thousand years old. Adam "was a god himself, the father of this race of people, his name was Yakub, they called him Jacob." Thus, Elijah Muhammad apparently identified the scientist Yakub with the biblical Adam, a "very smart and wise man with a large head." This scientist, after a falling out with other scientists, took 59,999 people to "the Island in the Aegean sea, where he started grafting" the white race from them. An inferior white race was created to rule a superior black race as part of Yakub's revenge.

Before the first appearance of this invented white race—"a long, long, long, long old time before the white man was ever thought of"—black people "were ruling, not only this earth, but everything in the universe." Indeed, black people were "the makers and fashioners of the universe." This event occurred "66 trillion years ago," to which astonishing figure Elijah Muhammad adds this emphatic note: "Don't think I'm making a mistake—66 trillion years ago." At that time the planet Mars "had been serving as a moon to our Earth."

This is the hidden history of both black and white people on Earth—preexistent, godlike black people created the universe and peopled the Earth unimaginable ages ago. White people were "grafted" from the black race, and thus "they are from us." Interestingly, Elijah Muhammad argued that the theory of evolution was invented to cover this true origin story. White people have tried to "cover their birth" by claiming that they evolved "from sea life" or from "animals." Elijah Muhammad emphatically insisted that "these are facts that I defy your colleges or university professors to dispute."

The Nation of Islam's alien gnosis extends beyond the creation story as told by cofounder Elijah Muhammad. To this day the organization maintains an active interest in planetary exploration and is on record as endorsing claims that life has been discovered on Mars. Taking such discussion to be "at the cutting-edge of 'this world's' scientific knowledge," Nation of Islam finds Martian life claims to be in sync with "the divine truths in the teachings of the Honorable Elijah Muhammad."[48] Facts about life on Mars are "constantly being revealed by recent discoveries in the fields of Astronomy, Archeology, Genetics and Biology; and nowhere has this reality been more evident than in the scientific data that have come from NASA's Mars space probes in recent years."

The Nation of Islam has been especially interested in the photos taken by NASA's *Viking* and *Mars Surveyor* space probes. According to the Nation of Islam website, the probes "show what appear to be artificial, intelligently-designed structures (including a Martian sphinx-like face, massive pyramids, a city complex and underground glass tunnels) in the region of Mars known as Cydonia, and elsewhere on that planet." The statement concludes that this evidence "confirms the revelations and prophecies of the Hon. Elijah Muhammad about what the scientists of this world would find once they were allowed a peek into the heavens."

Dismissing claims that such interpretations of the photos are fantastic, Robert Muhammad writes, "The story of discovered artifacts on Mars has been circulating in scientific literature for over two decades," and "an information blanket has been imposed on this issue in the 'mainstream' media." Robert Muhammad claims that "from the moment pictures of the Cydonia region of Mars" were beamed to Earth in 1976, "some scientists in the space agency" have tried to discover the facts and "reveal them to the public, while other scientists, for reasons related to politics, religion or national security, have attempted to dismiss or cover-up this discovery." But he adds, "there is no doubt that the discovery of civilization on the Red Planet would have profound political, philosophical, and most importantly, religious implications for the scientists and theologians of this world; for it would scientifically confirm the reality and knowledge of God, as presented in the teachings of the Most Honorable Elijah Muhammad!" Elijah Muhammad "met with and was taught by God, in the person of Master Fard Muhammad, and over a period of three years was given divine revelation and prophecy from the Lord Of The Worlds." Fard is taken to have had a particular interest in Mars and its potential for life, and thus the discovery of life on the red planet would be an important proof of Nation of Islam teachings.

In a 1972 lecture series titled "Theology of Time," Elijah Muhammad provided followers with a description of life and civilization on Mars. On Mars, he also emphasized, humanity would discover the origin of the black race. "It's our Mars and our people (meaning original), so God taught me." The Prophet adds, "Our Fathers made it (Mars) with some type of intelligent beings like ourselves." The Martians "walk on two feet, and they are not White folks." Fard is said to have revealed these truths to Elijah Muhammad "in the 1930s, nearly 70 years ago." Robert Muhammad cites as support for the Martian-civilization view the work of Richard C. Hoagland, especially the book *The Monuments of Mars: A City on the Edge of Forever.* According to Robert Muhammad, Hoagland "covers in great detail the chronology, scientific analysis, and the hidden politics surrounding the discovery by this world's scientists of intelligently designed structures in the region of Mars known as Cydonia." Other proof of Martian civilization is found in mathematical codes discovered in the Martian ruins. "The description of the inhabitants of Mars given to us by the Honorable Elijah Muhammad matches precisely what scientists have found."

Elijah Muhammad taught that the Martians would be discovered to be "our people," meaning the original members of the human race. The supposed pyramidal structures on Mars resemble those found where the earliest humans resided on Earth, "in Africa, Asia, and the Americas," thus proving that they existed when the original humans ruled the Earth. Thus, "it would stand to reason that the same would be true on Mars!" Discovery of life on Mars, predicted by Elijah Muhammad, "has profound implications concerning the teacher who taught him, the god-potential in the nature of man and our true history on this planet and in the cosmos." Now, science has advanced to the point where "it could scientifically and mathematically confirm what God had shown him." Among the other experts who were cited as confirming the discovery of life on Mars is author Arthur C. Clarke. "The research and testimony of Arthur C. Clarke and numerous other scientists and scholars adds enough scientific weight and legitimacy to the assertion that signs of civilization have been discovered on the surface of Mars; and also bears witness to what the Honorable Elijah Muhammad taught about that planet for over 40 years."

A final component in the Nation of Islam's alien gnosis mythology is a persistent teaching regarding the presence of a Mother Plane, Mother Ship or Mother Wheel, a vast spacecraft that is prepared to take the faithful off the Earth and deliver them to a distant planet. In a 1996 speech, the Honorable Louis Farrakhan addressed this topic, which the organization identifies as crucial to its adherents.[49] Farrakhan explained to his listeners that "most of us, as Black people in America, have not understood the Hon. Elijah Muhammad" on several critical points. The unjust American social structure is doomed to be destroyed by God. The "mystery Babylon" spoken of in the Bible refers to present-day America.

Farrakhan asks, "What instrument is He going to use" to destroy the ancient harlot, now manifested as America? His answer is surprising. "The Honorable Elijah Muhammad told us of a giant Motherplane that is made like the universe, spheres within spheres. White people call them unidentified flying objects (UFOs)." Citing Ezekiel in the Old Testament, who "saw a wheel that looked like a cloud by day but a pillar of fire by night," Farrakhan claims this as a reference to a space wheel that "was built on the island of Nippon, which is now called Japan, by some of the original scientists." This gigantic space structure "took 15 billion dollars in gold at that time to build it. It is made of the toughest steel. America does not yet know the composition of the steel used to make an instrument like it." The wheel is actually "a circular plane," which "can stop and travel in all directions at speeds of thousands of miles per hour." Within this mother wheel are 1,500 small vehicles, each carrying "three bombs" that will be used to upset the Earth's delicate balance, which is maintained by mountain ranges.

Farrakhan reports that the Mother Wheel "is a dreadful looking thing," which white people have tried to "make . . . look like fiction, but it is based on something real." Elijah Muhammad taught that "today, that Plane is in the air, and the scientists and the astronomers of America have seen it here," though the American government denies the fact. Elijah Muhammad claimed to have "seen this Plane" and to have "sketched it many times." By his own admission he was following sketches originally created by Wallace Fard. "With my own eyes, along with my wife, and my sons, and my laborers with me and other people here in Phoenix this year, in May, stood and looked at that same Plane dotting through the sky." The Mother Plane is "an absolute Man-Made-Planet, moving at such terrific speed that you could hardly imagine it; flickering amid the stars of Heaven." The plane has been described as one half-mile square, oval in shape, capable of flying nine thousand miles per hour and orbiting the Earth at a distance of forty miles. Its many bombs contain poisonous gas that will destroy all life in "America, the Great Mystery Babylon." America will "burn 390 years and take 610 years to cool off." Farrakhan reiterated his belief in "the Wheel" during a nationwide interview with journalist Ted Koppel, and added that the apocalyptic science-fiction movie *Independence Day* was so popular with the public because many people recognized in it the truth of Nation of Islam teachings. Ironically, in this movie a black military pilot, played by Will Smith, takes the lead in saving the United States and the world from the destructive power of a vast alien spacecraft.

The Nation of Islam's secret spiritual history of the human race is inextricably bound up with notions alive in the American cultural atmosphere when Wallace Fard and Elijah Muhammad were first meeting in the 1930s to discuss revelations of a new religion for black people in America. Ancient civilizations on Mars, vast spaceships loaded with incredibly destructive weapons, advanced races creating and secretly controlling life on Earth, even spiritually advanced races held in bondage by an evil inferior race—these were common to the pages of pulp science fiction and other genres of writing. Indeed, the influence of the pulps was at its peak between 1938 and 1945. The Myth of Alien Gnosis often made its way from one literary realm to another.

ERICH VON DÄNIKEN ON PALEOCONTACT

Erich von Däniken was born in 1935 in Zofingen, Switzerland. Though he was a hotelier by profession, Däniken is best known for a series of highly controversial books that reached a peak of popularity in the late 1960s, in which he argued that extraterrestrial beings helped to shape early human intelligence, civilization and religious belief. His theories have sometimes been called "paleocontact" or "the ancient astronaut hypothesis." Däniken is also the cofounder of the Archaeology, Astronautics and SETI Research Association. Däniken has had extraordinary influence in America, Europe and other regions of the world. He has authored more than two dozen books, which have been translated into more than twenty langauges and have sold in excess of fifty million copies worldwide. His many books include *Chariots of the Gods?* (1968), *Gods from Outer Space* (1970), *In Search of Ancient Gods* (1973), *Miracles of the Gods* (1974), *Pathways to the Gods* (1981), *The Return of the Gods* (1997) and *Odyssey of the Gods: The Alien History of Ancient Greece* (2000).

Among his other ideas, Däniken believes that the course of human evolution was directed by alien intelligences, and that architectural mysteries such as Stonehenge and the Easter Island statues reflect alien influence. Moreover, certain biblical mysteries, such as the wheel of Ezekiel, are ancient references to alien contact with humans. Däniken has often been accused of misrepresenting evidence, failing to correct errors in his books, and drawing unfounded conclusions. His credibility has not been enhanced by the fact that in his background are allegations of fraud, embezzlement, forgery and tax evasion. He spent several years in a Swiss jail as a result of a conviction for tax evasion, and his forgery of allegedly ancient pottery showing aliens in UFOs was revealed on the television series *Nova*. Indeed, Däniken's importance to the propogation of an alien-based gnosis lies not so much in his questionable treatment of various peculiar evidences, as in the fact that tens of millions of readers around the world have been influenced by his strange ideas.

In *Chariots of the Gods?* Däniken's basic argument is that in prehistoric times the Earth was visited by extraterrestrial aliens who left in human culture various evidences of their visits. Moreover, these aliens also had much to do with the founding of human religious thought because humans mistook them for gods. In this way, Däniken's argument resembles that of both the Raëlian Movement and earlier arguments advanced by Churchward and others. Däniken argues that when human beings encountered the extraterrestrial visitors, they reasoned as follows: "The space travelers came from other stars; they obviously have tremendous power and the ability to perform miracles. They must be gods!" He adds details to the myth, such as that the aliens would select a particularly intelligent member of a human community, make this person a "king," and then provide him with "a radio set through which he could contact and address the 'gods' at any time." This would be "a sign of his power."[50]

Däniken argues that the basis of human social order rests on a foundation provided by the ancient astronauts. "Our astronauts would try to teach the natives the simplest forms of civilization and some moral concepts, in order to make the development of a social order possible." But alien intrusion in human affairs did not stop there, and what he adds to the account places Däniken's narrative closer to an alien gnosis myth than a simple space religion theory: "A few specially selected women would be fertilized by the astronauts. Thus a new race would arise that skipped a stage of natural evolution." This "new race," being more "advanced" than their human colleagues because of their extraterrestrial DNA, "became space experts."[51] In this reproductive interaction of the alien and the human, the divine spirit from above (the alien's own genetic material) through conception enters the physical container of the human being for the single purpose of creating a new kind of being capable of transcending the confines of Earth and ascending into Space. Däniken's ancient "space experts"—half human, half alien—have capacities and knowledge their colleagues do not, and they may enter realms closed to mere mortals. They commune with the gods.

Human religions have often been derived from ancient human veneration of the alien astronauts and their spacecraft. Thus, "the place on which the spaceship stood" was declared to be "holy ground, a place of pilgrimage, where the heroic deeds of the gods will be praised in song." Moreover, "pyramids and temples" were built on these sites, "in accordance with astronomic laws, of course."[52] In Erich von Däniken, the Myth of Alien Gnosis—secret extraterrestrial origins of the present human arrangement—grasped the attention of a generation of readers, with our past, our spirituality, and even our nature as human beings revealed to us through a free-wheeling interpretation of archaeological mysteries.

PHILIP K. DICK: SCIENCE-FICTION GNOSTIC

No author of science fiction wielded as much cultural influence from a position of greater obscurity than did California-based Philip K. Dick (1928-1984). Dick briefly studied philosophy at Berkeley but dropped out to devote himself to writing. He debuted as an author of science fiction in 1954 and published at least forty-five novels in the following twenty-five years. Dick wrote dozens of science-fiction books and an even larger number of short stories in the 1950s, 1960s and 1970s. His confident, self-effacing and witty writing captured the angst of the California drug scene of the 1960s and 1970s, relating deeply human and ironic stories of characters caught in the webs of mental illness, drug dependence, foundationless relationships and the ambiguities of consciousness, all problems with which Dick himself struggled.

Late in his life Dick fell deeper into the mental illness that had plagued him for years. In February of 1974, while recovering from minor surgery for an infected tooth, Dick reported being contacted by an alien intelligence that wanted to reveal hidden spiritual knowledge to him. He claims that he copied more than eight thousand pages of notes dictated from this source, which Dick called VALIS, an acronym for *Vast Active Living Intelligence System*. He wrote his last three novels based on this experience, including *VALIS* (1981), *The Divine Invasion* (1981), and *The Transmigration of Timothy Archer* (1982).

Though during his life he was largely unknown outside of science-fiction circles, both fame and cultural influence have come to Dick in the form of an impressive series of blockbuster movies, most produced after his death. The groundbreaking 1982 science-fiction thriller *Bladerunner*, directed by Ridley Scott and starring Harrison Ford, was based on Dick's story *Do Androids Dream of Electric Sheep?* The novelette *We Can Remember It for You Wholesale* provided the plot outline for Paul Verhoeven's 1990 movie *Total Recall*, starring Arnold Schwarzenegger. Dick's 1956 short story "The Minority Report" was brought to the theaters as the 2002 movie of the same name, starring Tom Cruise and directed by Steven Spielberg. And the recently released *A Scanner Darkly* (2006), starring Keanu Reeves, is based on a 1973 Dick story by the same title.

Why should Philip K. Dick's works of science fiction, written in response to the American social situation of the 1960s and 1970s, have proved to be so appealing and profitable in recent decades? Part of the answer to this question is found in the author's sensitive and authentic treatment of the human condition. But it is equally clear that Dick's utter preoccupation with gnostic spiritual themes, themes that have become so important to spirituality in the opening years of the twenty-first century, also help to account for his lasting popularity. And his following in Western Europe is perhaps even more devoted than is his American fan base.

Dick himself was a knowledgeable gnostic believer, and an author of deeply and explicitly gnostic fiction in which apparent realities are not real at all, ancient spiritual secrets come to light in the late twentieth century, and hidden intelligences drive the machinery of our existence. Many of his novels and short stories—some featuring vast scholarly insight into the history of Gnosticism—carried his ideas into the California drug counterculture, and from there into a broader culture that is currently being proselytized into neo-Gnosticism by products of both the mass media and the academy. In addition to Scott, Spielberg and Verhoeven, Dick is reputed to have had a major influence on the Wachowski brothers, creators of *The Matrix* and its two sequels.

Dick's quirky and partly autobiographical novel *VALIS* serves as an example of his gnostic fiction.[53] The novel's central character, Horselover Fat, is a 1970s California everyman in search of truth. Fat comes to believe, like Dick himself, that an alien intelligence called VALIS—whether mechanical or organic he does not know—has been beaming information into his brain. A spiritual force called "the plasmate" is awakened and reenters the world when the Nag Hammadi scrolls are discovered, setting in motion events that will reveal gnosis—the secret nature of our existence. Fat and his associates embark on a search for the truth about VALIS. In his spiritual questing, Fat learns that humans inhabit a spiritual prison, that VALIS is in control of human events, that a chosen few have been selected to understand this truth, and that the knowledgeable few are—through the transforming power of this gnosis—becoming gods.

Evidence of Dick's contemporary influence is discovered in the works of writers actively promoting Gnosticism, some of whom see Dick as something of a latter-day prophet. Gnostic apologist John Lamb Lash, author of *Not in His Image* (2006), comments that the gnostic revival means a turn toward the divine feminine principle known as Pistis Sophia and "the indwelling wisdom," and away from "redemptive religion." In support of this view, he cites as an authority Philip K. Dick. Gnostic insight, writes Lash, "informs his best writings, especially the VALIS Trilogy, a masterpiece permeated with genuine, first-hand, re-invented Gnosticism." Lash observes that Dick has attributed great significance to "the discovery at Nag Hammadi in December, 1945," which Dick believed reinvigorated a gnostic spirit in the world. For Lash, Dick's plasmate is Gnosis itself, "the awakening of a faculty . . . that gives insight transcending the human condition." Lash describes Dick's fictional plasmate as "a spiritual impulse charged with numinous content, a core teaching that lives and regenerates within those who learn it."[54] It is intriguing that Lash is citing as authoritative, not a scholarly work on Gnosticism, but one of Philip K. Dick's gnostic science-fiction novels.

THE DARK CITY AND THE MATRIX

The Myth of Alien Gnosis remains a powerful formula for addressing spiritual curiosity and shaping worldviews. Recently it has been a key component in a number of popular science-fiction movies and novels. Two examples help to demonstrate the popularity of the theme for modern moviegoers.

In the 1999 movie *The Dark City*, directed by Alex Proyas, a mysterious group of alien beings known only as The Strangers control life on an artificial planet, to which they have brought thousands of humans. The unidentified Visitors, who look vaguely like vampires, have constructed the artificial city in which their unsuspecting human victims live out their false lives in apparent normalcy. Each night at midnight, however, the city's residents fall asleep and have their memories altered by The Strangers, whose goal it is to discover the nature of the individual human soul that, in their evil physicality, they lack and desperately wish for. Two humans know the truth behind the appearances in the Dark City: a doctor recruited by the Strangers to assist them in their experiments, and an everyman figure named John Murdock, who possesses remarkable psychic or spiritual powers, as it turns out.

In a pivotal scene characteristic of all such gnosis-themed movies and books, an individual in possession of the truth explains the mysterious secret truth to the protagonist. Gnosis must be known by someone who has arduously searched out the truth; otherwise all is forever undiscovered deception. In *The Dark City* the doctor lets Murdoch in on the secret. Murdoch's powers and his knowledge of the desperate predicament are crucial to defeating The Strangers and liberating the residents of the Dark City. By the exertion of his divine will, Murdoch proceeds to re-create the Dark City as a light-filled, paradisiacal world. Through gnosis and spiritual power, Murdoch is transformed into a virtual god in command of a world of his own creation. So the residents of the Dark City have traded a shadowy guild of minor gods who created a false world for a single apparently benevolent minor god who has likewise created his own world. One is left to wonder whether they are any better off at the end of the movie than they were at its beginning.

A similarly gnostic theme animated the enormously popular *Matrix* movie series, the first of which was released in 1999. The three *Matrix* movies—*The Matrix*, *The Matrix Reloaded* (2003) and *Matrix Revolutions* (2003)—are perhaps the most explicitly gnostic texts among recent science-fiction films. According to *Matrix* mythology, as Steve Kellmeyer has pointed out, "we live in an illusion, creation is an evil prison in which we serve its creator, and we must be freed."[55] He adds, "Once we're acquainted with this worldview, we can see how *The Matrix* clearly unfolds as a modern retelling of the Gnostic version of salvation history."[56]

In the first installation, protagonist Neo Anderson is selected by a spiritual master named Morpheus to learn the grand secret—the gnosis—behind all apparent reality. Morpheus reveals that the entire human scene is, in fact, an elaborate, computer-generated illusion. Embodiment is a trick played on the human mind by computers, the consequence of a cosmic struggle between evil intelligences and human beings that the humans lost. Minor divinities— with names such as The Oracle, The Architect, and the Mirovingian—control events and access to knowledge, while Neo carries on a continuing struggle against a powerful demonic force, personified in the character known as Agent Smith, that tries to prevent human liberation from the Matrix.

By acquiring the gnosis that unlocks the secret of human existence, something within reach only of an elite, Neo enters a special order of latter-day ascended spiritual adepts. By technological means, major characters move freely between two planes of existence, not unlike Victorian occultists claiming access to an "astral plane" through astral projection. While inhabiting this higher plane, crucial spiritual truths are revealed that constitute a liberating gnosis.

CONCLUSION

As long as "the truth is out there," gnosis will be with us—the persistent belief in secret spiritual knowledge about the nature of human existence that, once acquired, leads to spiritual enlightenment and personal power. This idea has long cast a powerful spell on the human imagination, playing on the deep suspicion that there is something odd about our nature: our bodies apparently connect us to animals, but our souls point us toward the angels. And we, caught between the material and the spiritual, have formulated our guesses as to what play of forces could possibly have landed us in this strange position. Darwin made one famous guess (evolution); gnosis was another. In recent decades a refurbished gnosis has reemerged in the texts of science fiction, in some speculative scientific writing and in the theologies of "new" religions. This time around, however, extraterrestrials have their part to play in the cosmic drama of human existence and destiny.

Among the identifying marks of gnosis, several are especially noteworthy, each suggesting a sharp contrast with more traditional religious views. The first is the tendency in some gnostic formulations to see human beings, not as purposefully integrated material-spiritual creations, but as eternal spirits embodied in a physical casing for a time, and out of spiritual necessity. From the time of Jacob Ilive, this idea has marked modern neognostic religious narratives. Two centuries later L. Ron Hubbard appropriated the idea, placing his alien thetans in human bodies, from which they can be expelled by technological means. However the joining of spirit and matter is formulated in gnostic narratives, it is marked by either accident or utility, but not by purposeful design.

The Christian worldview presents the human being as an integrated creation, a physical inhabitant of a material universe, but also a spiritual being with an eternal destiny; humans are dust of the Earth, into which God breathed. It is not as disembodied entities that we exist eternally, nor is a disembodied state that toward which we strive. Even as resurrected beings, we will still bear the image of the Creator in physical bodies. Neither accident nor temporary fix, we were created "good" as body and spirit and will be retrieved in that same fashion for eternity.

A second gnostic marker is the notion that our lived reality is not what it appears to be, that reality is not actually real. A higher order of existence, to which the ordinary person does not have access, is where reality lies, and only knowledge of gnosis opens this realm to us. What we take to be reality is a fabrication at best, and perhaps a diabolical deception. Higher Forces are at work in crafting our experience of "reality," and nearly all of us are unaware of the nature of that crafting. Enlightenment and ascent depend on mastering the spiritual secrets. And mastering the secrets certainly requires first learning them from a master.

But the Christian worldview presents our present reality as a breathtaking and desperate fact. Our senses do not fail us, and reason seeks to make sense of a real world, not props set on a stage. If our emotions tell us that this existence is wonderful beyond belief and tragic beyond bearing, they are right on both counts. That sense and reason present a world filled with beauty and marred by death *should* set us in search of answers. But we should not settle for misanthropic secrets suggesting that we were wrong to think that consciousness reflects reality, that the world was designed to make sense, and that our lived experience really matters.

A third characteristic of some versions of the Myth of Alien Gnosis is that the alien intelligences themselves—a Council of Gods, ancient aliens buried in the sea, extraterrestrials on distant planets, mysterious Strangers from who-knows-where, residents of the impossible future or the unimaginable past—are the real managers of our lives and arbiters of our destiny. Despite our sense that we live freely and set our own course by personal choice, "some ones" or "some things" out there are the actual captains of our destiny, and our fate is in their hands. In modern renditions of gnosis, these Distant Minds often are the aliens themselves, "highly evolved" puzzle-masters who, for reasons known only to them, create us and direct us through our puny lives. They, not us and not a sovereign deity, control the unfolding of cosmic events. Given our pre-occupation with space and extraterrestrials, it is perhaps only to be expected that the alien would now be seen as the messenger of gnosis.

The Christian worldview presents a somewhat simpler and infinitely more reassuring situation. There is a Mind behind the created order of things, and it is a personal, creative and redemptive God. This God is in charge of the destiny of the cosmos he created, but he also seeks a relationship with us, a friend-ship based on an open proclamation of both his existence and his nature. Our lives are invested with infinite value by his life and image in us. And remark-ably, this God is both behind the scenes and on the scene, transcendent and imminent. The Christian doctrine of incarnation bridges the world of "them" and the world of "us" by the appearing at a moment in time of Immanuel, God with us. This ultimate self-revelation on God's part, this act of unaccountable vulnerability and incomprehensible knowing, is the final answer to gnosis, the self's dim wish for a secret that will transform ego into god.

This brings us to gnosis, itself a marker of this myth. Gnosis is the story, the account of what *really* happened, where we *really* exist, who we *really* are. Those in possession of this knowledge have a chance to escape the confines of the prison that is our lives, to ascend to a higher plane, to achieve godhood, to flee from the cataclysm to come, to leave the weaker ones behind as we fly into pleroma (Greek: *plērōma*, fullness), the realm of ultimate light. Ordinary humanity will never know this secret, but some are chosen (the reason for this choosing is seldom made clear) for this honor and this opportunity.

However, with gnosis comes the possibility of control, of power. Gnosis is, inescapably, a secret; it is information unavailable through ordinary experience, through our senses, through reason, even through intuition. It may be taught us by a Master, stumbled upon in the dark, ferreted out through diligent study and great risk, or conveyed telepathically from "them." This is the pattern of gnosis, and its appeal is undeniable. It holds out to us the allure of being in on a grand secret, of apprehending the great scheme, of glimpsing the machinery behind the scenery of our lives.

But the idea of a secret spiritual knowledge, whether revealed by aliens or someone in contact with them, leaves the power of the secret in the hands of the one or the few who control that knowledge necessary to enlightenment, indeed, to salvation. This kind of power can be, and often has been, highly dangerous. Gnosis establishes ultimate authority, authority invites control, and control encourages abuse.

The Myth of Alien Gnosis raises the question of why true spiritual knowledge of the human race, its predicament and that predicament's solution should be the possession of any group of "the few," including alien intelligences. The God of the Bible offers an alternative: entering earthly existence as a person, reaffirming the value both of Earth and of the human, his "secrets" are shared in simple stories told for the benefit of the ordinary many, and often misunderstood or ignored by the powerful few. The return to gnosis robs the world of the exquisite openness of the Christian notion of the gospel as good news.

If we ask the wrong questions, we are likely to discover the wrong answers. If our problem is that we are locked in an illusionary space-time matrix from which we need to escape, then perhaps the idea of gnosis makes sense. As a character in Philip K. Dick's novel *VALIS* puts it, "Salvation . . . is a word denoting 'Being led out of the space-time maze, where the servant has become the master.'"[57] But if salvation means redemption from a moral fall into sin, then escaping the space-time maze leaves us where we were in the first place: alienated from the God who created us. Before jettisoning one narrative involving openly proclaimed spiritual knowledge announced by a creating and redeeming God, in favor of secret gnosis possessed by extraterrestrials, it would be wise to consider what is gained and what lost in the bargain.

10

CONCLUSION

As the three of us walked back to the house, Kevin said,
"Was all that just quotations from the Bible?"
"No," I said.
"No," David agreed. "There was something new;
that part about us being our own gods, now.
That the time had come where we no longer had to believe
in any deity other than ourselves."

PHILIP K. DICK, *VALIS*

But they knew in their hearts that once science
had declared a thing possible, there was no escape
from its eventual realization.

ARTHUR C. CLARKE, *CHILDHOOD'S END*

We did not follow cleverly devised myths
when we made known to you the power and coming
of our Lord Jesus Christ, but we had been
eyewitnesses of his majesty.

2 PETER 1:16

The project of providing transcendence through science will one day be complete, according to some authorities. Myths will give way to established facts, and we will know beyond doubt what we now can only guess. World-famous physicist Stephen Hawking "seems to hope that a complete cosmological theory can be produced which will make possible 'the ultimate triumph of human reason,' namely, that 'we would know the mind of God.'"[1] We will have achieved complete knowledge and will no longer need myths to guide us. Until then, however, narratives of the type Hawking has employed will play a decisive role in how we apprehend the world in which we live.

I have been arguing that over the past three centuries some popular works of science fiction, speculative science, and the documents of certain religious movements have served as locations for developing and propagating transcendent narratives addressing ultimate questions. Because of their tendency to seek credibility from a connection to science, whether actual or fabricated, I have chosen to term these narratives "scientific mythologies." Moreover, as these myths have coalesced into a systematic explanation of our existence, nature, predicament, salvation and destiny, we are witnessing the invention of a new religious view in popular culture.

Western culture has been trained to place its trust in science. As a result of our turn toward science, other enterprises have sought to borrow credibility from the laboratory and the lecture hall, the most unexpected example being religion. Why should the supernatural and transcendent look to the natural and particular for its authority? Our long history of religious criticism and our equally long witness to the remarkable accomplishments of science perhaps suggest an answer to this question. Ultimate authority has shifted, and the shift has been toward nature and away from what claims to stand above nature. As a result, we have now entered the age of scientific religion.

There have been many calls for a new religion, a religion of the future, of space, of a new human race. We need new transcendent narratives to direct our investigations and guide our living in a cosmos increasingly at our beck and call. We need a "scientific religion," we are told. But is the phrase not an oxymoron? Has nature become enchanted again, infused with a spirit that is more than cause and effect? If so, by what mechanisms has the sacralizing of nature occurred? How did science become a source of religious insight?

Science assumed the posture of oracle of transcendent truth as an increasing number of scientists offered their opinions on how science suggests answers to larger questions, and even to the largest of all questions: What is the nature of reality itself? What is the purpose of the cosmos? Is it, perhaps, alive? What, if anything, is divine? What defines the human? Where does life come from, and where does it go? Certainly, if science can answer such questions, it can deliver to us the religion we seek. To these and related questions, members of the scientific community have increasingly presented purportedly definitive answers rather than tentative guesses. If we live in an age of scientific religion, we just as certainly have entered the era of spiritualized science.

From the very moment that science began to wax supernatural, a type of fiction developed that sought to carry the exciting possibilities of scientific religion and spiritualized science to a waiting public. In Bruno's audience at Oxford in 1583, the young Francis Godwin was already formulating in his mind a story about travel to one of the inhabited worlds that the sage had assured him were everywhere in the heavens. The great astronomer Kepler wrote not just about the science of the stars' movements, but also fiction—*Somnium*—about human movement toward the stars, with the aid of occult forces. John Wilkins helped to found the British Royal Society, but he also wrote about traveling to the moon, something he believed would one day be possible. And these writers sought to convey answers to persistent questions, not just a sense of wonder. In that process, as scientifically inspired adventure fiction drifted toward the ultimate, modern myths were being birthed. These myths in turn shaped the science that followed.

The relationship between science and the fictional narratives drawing on it has proved to be remarkably happy and durable. This was a marriage made in Space. And like most good marriages, the one between scientists and the imaginative fiction involving their ideas has been rich, complex and at times mystifying. The ever-intriguing Wernher von Braun had John W. Campbell's *Astounding Science Fiction* delivered to an address in Sweden during World War II. He was in good company: Albert Einstein was also a subscriber. Right down to the present, it is not thought unusual for a scientist to turn to the writing of science fiction, for a figure from the realm of science fiction to endorse a scientific idea, or for a famous scientist to make an appearance in a science-fiction television episode. The European Space Agency is currently soliciting ideas from science-fiction writers in order to jump start the creative process of a new generation of space exploration.[2]

Science, though it cannot speak of God as a cause, now provides our news about the cosmos we inhabit. Theology's role as a source of such information—a discipline that *does* speak of God—has been dramatically reduced. Science fiction now often interprets science's news to a waiting publice, a role once played by religious narratives. As both the source and the interpretive frame of our ideas changed, the perennial questions persisted. But the new information was lacking something of critical importance: a sense of purpose, morality or transcendence. Naturalism was never a spiritually satisfying substitute for supernaturalism. It was perhaps inevitable that at some point in the process of trading religion for science as our window on the universe, science would become religious. We thus find ourselves with new mythologies and new oracles as well. However, as science made its transformative pilgrimage from Houston to Delphi, it passed through Roswell. When science found science fiction, it found religion. Scientist Sagan, seated in his captain's char, launched out into the Cosmos in search of naturalistic wonder and discovered transcendent spirituality. "Houston, we have a prophet."

Our concern here has not been simply with the relationship between science and science fiction but also with the spiritual and religious theorizing that transpires at the intersection of the two. Increasingly science has taken on spiritual functions or weighed in on supernatural questions, and the rise of religiously oriented science fiction has only encouraged the transformation of the laboratory into a sanctuary. And yet, the rational restraint of the Judeo-Christian worldview has been eroded as the line between religious narrative and fantastic scientific agenda has blurred. Following a recent talk, a rocket engineer working for an aerospace company told me that several coworkers confided in him that one goal of their satellite research was to prove that the series of shoals and islands linking Sri Lanka to the Indian mainland—called Adam's Bridge—is actually a work of engineering as described in the epic Hindu poem the Ramayana. If they can prove that the Monkey God Lord Hanuman and a team of monkeys built the land bridge to allow Lord Rama to cross from India to Sri Lanka to save his wife, Sita, then they will have scientific confirmation for an important religious narrative. NASA satellite photos taken in 2002 have already been entered into the controversy, but they were not conclusive. We should also be aware that another panel of scientists, perhaps guided by a different narrative, went on record as saying that the shoals known as Adam's Bridge were simply a natural geological formation formed 17 million years ago.[3]

The story certainly underlines the power of narratives in our lives, for a religious account of a vast army of bridge-building monkeys under the control of a deity had captured the imaginations of these scientists in a way that the circuits and systems of their satellites could not. Spiritual narrative had trumped scientific rationality, rendering science the servant of an extraordinary tale. Facts require narratives if they are to coalesce into a coherent interpretation of our lived experience. Thus, we must exercise exceeding care in the choice of our leading narratives. Perhaps the religion Western science requires to provide it a rational framework for the future is the rationally grounded one which birthed it: Christianity.

In the introduction, I quoted science-fiction author Robert Sawyer as stating that science fiction is "the most effective tool for exploring the deepest of all questions." Whether we agree with Sawyer that science fiction is effective for addressing such questions, it is certainly the case that the genre has, in the process of addressing them, *shaped* the deep questions themselves. New "ultimate" questions confront us: Is God a highly evolved alien? Is salvation a consequence of conscious evolution? Are we becoming gods ourselves? Is truth found in the secrets of extraterrestrial involvement in our lives? Is scientific insight ultimately spiritual insight? Is there a unified field of knowledge in which the scientific eventually blurs into the spiritual?

Sawyer also opined that science fiction will "finally and at last, help humanity shuck off the last vestiges of the supernatural."[4] Science fiction's alleged capacity, not just to displace, but actually to dispose of religious explanations is noteworthy. With all the force with which science fiction is currently supplied, it remains fictional and imaginative rather than experimental or historical. In a new narrative landscape, however, there is the potential for mistaking a persuasively told story for a conclusive bit of evidence. In Arthur C. Clarke's legendary science-fiction tale *Childhood's End*, a device is brought to Earth by advanced extraterrestrials who have been placed in charge of humanity's development. The device allows Earth's residents to actually see historical events as they have transpired. The device is "a television receiver with an elaborate set of controls for determining coordinates in space and time," and linked "to a far more complex machine." This device is tuned so that people can witness "the true beginnings of all the world's great faiths." In an instant it is revealed that the foundational narratives for each of the world's great religions are false. "Within a few days all the world's multitudinous messiahs had lost their divinity. Faiths that had sustained millions for twice a thousand years vanished like morning dew." Alleged facts at the foundations of religion are reduced in an instant to fabrications, historical events to groundless assertions. Religion "could touch the minds of men no more."[5] But by suggesting that such a technology would have such an effect, Clarke has not so much made an argument as offered an opinion. It is story against story, but in the new narrative logic of the science/science fiction intersection a vivid image is more persuasive than a sound argument, a captivating narrative more compelling than historical evidence.

The Christian story is called gospel, good news of a redemptive act by the creator God in response to the crisis of creation falling under a power it was powerless to repel. The task of proclaiming and defending this gospel cannot be accomplished unless the church is aware of the challenges posed to the gospel through the products of mass culture. In the early twentieth century, the gospel faced scientific naturalism, logical positivism, Marxism and Freudianism, to name a few of the major sources of opposition to its message. Today, however, the gospel is not so much attacked as obscured by the multiplicity of similar redemptive stories. These redemptive stories often arise out of the texts we call science fiction, but also from those religious systems that have borrowed science fiction's dominant motifs. Even science today is telling redemptive tales of a cosmos moving toward a telos that we can all enjoy, and that we should help the cosmos to achieve. The good news that Christ proclaimed and enacted suddenly sounds like just another redemptive myth, not a story bearing the stamp of transcendent truth, not a narrative above all other narratives. This is the Christian church's challenge today—to reclaim its story and tell it in such a way that it stands out among all the others as authentic, as the Great Story that other stories have often sought to imitate.

At a time when many have ruled out any notion of a transcendent and timeless religious truth as irrational, it seems strange that so many should consider truth delivered by extraterrestrials or salvation through space exploration to pose rational possibilities. If aliens or deep space hold secrets to our salvation—now often defined merely as survival—they remain secrets available to the few and delivered only at their will to the rest of us. Gnosis is still gnosis, whether possessed by an ancient mystic or a modern scientist. And technologically assisted evolution toward a future humanity holds out little hope for

those who are not at the terminus point, or who cannot afford the latest enhancement technology. Those of us living during the middle of this long scientific process are doomed to live out our lives as stepping-stones to a higher
order of human being, as a necessary phase in the grand process. Our current
lives may still have meaning, but not in any ultimately meaningful way, according to the science-fictional religionists. On the other hand, Christianity
has always insisted on the ultimate worth of the existing individual, and on the
significance of one's choices.

Our new mythologies have not left us godless; they have populated the cosmos with deity upon deity, race upon race of highly advanced intelligences.
This, it often is supposed, should bring us some comfort. But exactly why it
should be considered a benefit to be under the care, observation or direction
of extraterrestrial aliens remains a mystery. Imagining a time in the not-so-
distant future when these observers finally choose to make themselves actually present on the human scene, Arthur C. Clarke envisions a sanguine scenario: "Mankind had grown to trust them, and to accept without question
the super-human altruism that kept [them] so long from their homes."[6] This
sentence—though certainly not reflecting a consensus view of intrusive extraterrestrials—amounts to a virtual article of faith in much science fiction,
speculative science and extraterrestrial religion. And yet, we do not know of
their existence, nor could we possibly know of their benevolence. Despite Steven Spielberg's great skill as a storyteller, when Richard Dreyfuss enters the
great ship at the end of *Close Encounters*, there is no assurance as to whether
he is to become a conduit of higher knowledge or an experimental rat. The idea
that abductions can be excused as necessary for the sake of extraterrestrial
science is a peculiar modern lunacy and needs to be identified as such. Alien
breeding experiments are not paths to human advancement but ancient night-
mares reasserting themselves as naive new mythologies with the imprimatur
of pseudo-science.

The future, and always the future: where we finally conquer Space and join
our alien creators we always knew were there; where through gnosis guiding
evolution, the great replacement races emerge to manage the cosmos; where
science and religion finally embrace and techno-apocalypse awakens a sleeping universe. What greater vision of the Future could we wish? And yet, such
a Future easily becomes a distraction from the present, a hope in what is to

come, when what is to come cannot provide hope unless the present also is attended to. The injustices of the present demand our attention if the Future is to be a time to be enjoyed by everyone, not just the technologically fortunate few.

C. S. Lewis recognized this temptation toward future-focus in his classic work *The Screwtape Letters*. "Our business," writes a senior devil to a junior, "is to get them away from the eternal, and from the Present." Thus, humans are to be tempted to think of the future. The future is unknown, "so that in making them think about it we make them think of unrealities." Our duty to the future—a duty principally to do justice for those who come after us—"like all duties, is in the Present." Dangerous redirection of our attention occurs when human beings are "hag-ridden by the Future—haunted by visions of an imminent heaven or hell upon Earth" and "dependent for his faith on the success or failure of schemes whose end he will not live to see."[7]

A distraction is not as dangerous as a deception, and some of the scientific mythologies we have explored belong in this latter category. The notion of a spiritually advanced race of people, a segment of the human population that has outstripped all the rest in spiritual attainment and thus earned the right to lead us into utopia, is such a deception. That one group is, through advanced genetics or the acquisition of spiritual techniques, in possession of greater spiritual insights than are their colleagues—that idea has historically proved to be very dangerous indeed. Unfortunately, science fiction has often failed to recognize this error when it was not wearing a Nazi uniform, and thus has trafficked in stories of superior races in lost lands or on distant planets, genetically altered humans with expansive spiritual capacities or insights, and the interbreeding of humans and aliens to produce a race to inhabit the promised future. When Bulwer-Lytton crafted such a vision in *The Coming Race*, he was sixty years in advance of the Nazis. Consequently his Vril-ya could without apology, though still with hubris, announce their plans to rise to the surface of the Earth and eliminate the inferior human species dwelling there. Let the reader react as one might—this was merely a matter of cold logic and the rights of the superior species.

Who can blame an honest writer for dramatizing the harsh logic of survival of the fittest and following it to the implied conclusion of a superior race, if that writer lacked the powerful moral perspective necessary to prevent such a conclusion being drawn? But such conclusions certainly are menacing at best, and potentially disastrous. This is precisely the question the scientific mythologies raise: Do they reflect a regard for people—*all* people, in *all* conditions and in *all* places—sufficient to restrain the powerful forces that science now places in our hands?

Supernaturalism—the belief in a world outside the natural world—often is rejected by the proponents of mythic narratives arising out of science fiction and speculative science. Among the problems with debunking supernaturalism and faith-views that embrace it, however, is a strong tendency to substitute something similarly transcendent for it. Unfortunately, the substitute often lacks any similarly transcendent moral view that might place restraint on strongly promoted policy or actions that seem otherwise inevitable. Richard Dawkins is among today's most outspoken opponents of supernaturalism and the faiths that incorporate it into their worldview. But in an essay titled "Darwin Triumphant," Dawkins has argued for a kind of scientific transcendence: "Darwin's achievement, like Einstein's, is universal and timeless." In answer to the "riddle" of the existence of any life at all, Dawkins adds, "The general form of Darwin's answer is not merely incidentally true of our kind of life but almost certainly true of all life, everywhere in the universe." And again, "Darwinism really matters in the universe."[8] He even wonders, "[Is there] an essential core of Darwinism" that "we might set up as a candidate for discussion as potentially beyond the reach of factual refutation?"[9] Now, if a claim is universally true and beyond the possibility of factual refutation, it comes rather close to being transcendent.

But does this transcendent core of Darwinism yield an equally transcendent moral view, and one with the weight to offset the powerful forces that confront us? Dawkins seems to have his doubts, at least at times. He quotes with disapproval a passage from H. G. Wells's *Mankind in the Making*, acknowledging that the ruthless nature of Darwinism can drive one to repugnant views. Wells writes that the "ethics" of the new world order "will be shaped primarily to favor the procreation of what is fine and efficient and beautiful in humanity—beautiful and strong bodies, clear and powerful minds." Wells continues: "The method that nature has followed" in bringing life to its present point, the method "whereby weakness was prevented from propagating weakness," is in a word "death."[10] Wells himself found nothing in his own understanding of either naturalism or Darwinism to stand against the ethic of using death as a means to a social end. His later writing in particular contains many comments about the ruthless means necessary if the coming world is to be achieved. So, what stands against such visions, such logic?

In the absence of a corresponding moral view powerful enough to constrain action, a new naturalistic transcendence is apparent in other writers trumpeting the new mythologies as well. John Gribbin and Martin Rees in their book *Cosmic Coincidences* write, "If there is no life elsewhere," then the very existence of the life-possessing planet Earth "acquires potential to spread life and consciousness through the cosmos." In this respect, "present life on Earth" may be thought of as "the beginning of a process with billions of years, and perhaps a literally infinite time span, still to run—the greening of our Galaxy and beyond by forms of life and intelligence (not necessarily all organic) seeded from Earth."[11] We certainly recognize that a mission to spread life to an entire galaxy is a transcendent, powerful and potentially dangerous notion that ought to come equipped with a suitably sound set of moral principles to guide the work. But Gribbin and Rees do not demonstrate any particular interest in such questions. Their time is spent on imagining the possibilities, leaving the task of setting limits to others, if limits are to be set.

Consider as well the arguments of Australian scientist Paul Davies, who has written about another transcendent possibility. Perhaps "each individual universe" has its own "birth, evolution, and death," but that "the collection as a whole would exist eternally."[12] Thus, the whole material system might consist of an uncreated and eternal universe that is a living and evolving entity. For Davies, another question lurks in the cosmic background. Was "the creation of our own universe . . . a natural affair," or was it perhaps "the result of deliberate manipulation." Thus, we might "imagine that a sufficiently advanced and altruistic community of beings in a mother universe might decide to create baby universes, not to provide an escape route for their own survival, but merely to perpetuate the possibility of life existing somewhere, given that their own universe is doomed."

Davies does not define *altruistic* and does not account for how this other species might have arrived at an altruistic view of things. He seems unconcerned over whether the term might mean something different to the distant aliens than it does to us. Or is the term's definition, like Dawkins's irreducible

principles of Darwinism, also universal and unarguable? For Davies, the possibility of "superbeings" who have achieved "unlimited information-processing
power" does not seem to raise any particular moral questions.[13] And this is
so even if "what we call nature is, in fact, the activity of a superbeing, or a
community of superbeings," and these superbeings are capable of "miraculous
physical and intellectual goals."[14] Such superbeinghood may even be within
the grasp of humans who, "if immortality is combined with progress," may
one day exist "in a state of perpetual novelty, always learning or doing something new and exciting."[15] Davies even suggests a theory of eternal life for our
species. Our descendents might "just move on to a younger galaxy when the
old one runs out of fuel."[16] These same descendants, like Gribbin's and Rees's
future humans, would know no limits to "their technological development."
Thus, "they would be free to spread across the universe, gaining control over
ever greater volumes of space."[17] With all of these miraculous forces in play,
Davies does not seem concerned that his speculations, powerful scientific narratives, do not in themselves provide a moral system to guide our use of the
remarkable forces at our disposal. Is there no danger in transcendent truth
and triumphant technologies lacking adequate moral vision to shape and restrain them?

In a June 2007 interview, leading genetic scientist Craig Venter announced
the creation of "synthetic life" in his laboratories. The DNA of one species of
bacterium was successfully transplanted into another bacterium, which then
divided and continued to thrive. A new species was born through strictly
technological means. Venter foresees numerous applications of the new technology, with the possibility of creating new bacteria that might produce fuels
or other needed commodities. When asked about possible "new species" scenarios involving human beings, Venter was dismissive. This was a concern of
ethicists, but not something that actual scientists were thinking about. Since
this is "the kind of speculation" that tends to "make people nervous," Venter
assured the interviewer, "I don't know of any scientists that are actually advocating it."[18] Thus are the doors closed on the larger ethical issues obviously
attending such a development.

Despite Venter's curious statement, biologist Lee M. Silver has written
about human genetic engineering, even of change from one human species
to another, in such a way that one could easily get the impression that he is

an advocate. Silver is certain that human cloning "is on the verge of happening."[19] The idea of a vastly changed human race, a product of technologically assisted evolution, is not a literary artifact of the past—it is the real science of the present. Human beings "now have the power not only to control but [also] to create new genes for themselves. Why not seize this power? Why not control what has been left to chance in the past?" Silver imagines genetic alterations to the human being that begin with simple trait selection by parents. But as technologies develop and private investment in genetic engineering provides fuel for unlimited research, even "the mind and the senses" will be within reach of genetic alteration. Alcoholism, mental illness and "antisocial behavior like extreme aggression" will be "eliminated." But that, as they say, is just the beginning. New senses might be added, as well as the capacity to perceive a wider spectrum of colors. Even "radiotelepathy" is a possibility, an idea also discussed by Dyson but ultimately harkening back to the psychics and mediums of Victorian England.[20]

Silver, usually rather cautious in his prose, ventures to the very ends of the universe in his closing chapters. New humans will launch themselves into Space (where else?) and establish colonies on distant planets. Turning from argument to science-fictional narrative, Silver writes: "In the twenty-sixth century, overcrowding on earth had reduced the quality of life so much that many GenRich [genetically rich: a new social class] parents decided to give their children special genetic gifts to help them survive on worlds that were inhospitable to the unenhanced." New species develop from the old humans; the "lung-modified, thick-skinned dark green human descendants that begin their lives on the fourth planet from the sun barely resembled the primitive Naturals still roaming the third planet Earth." Who's he calling primitive? And so it goes, until a plethora of new humans of different species have spread themselves throughout the universe, eventually resulting in "mental beings" who answer question such as "Where did the universe come from?" They arrive at the ultimate realization that they may be their own "creator."[21] Craig Venter may not consider Silver an advocate of genetic alteration of the human species, but one could certainly be excused for reading him that way.

In a 2004 essay, author Francis Fukuyama referred to "transhumanism"— the pursuit of the new humans—as the most dangerous idea currently facing technological cultures. Fukuyama writes, "As 'transhumanists' see it, humans must wrest their biological destiny from evolution's blind process of random variation and adaptation and move to the next stage as a species." The idea of enhancing human beings, even of introducing the next version of the human, may come to look "downright reasonable" when we consider the potential for technologies to alter humanity for the better. But Fukuyama fears a "frightful moral cost." Similarly, historian Dan Stone worries that eugenics is returning, but in forms that appear unobjectionable, even benevolent: choosing a child's traits before birth, selecting out through abortion infants with physical or mental handicaps. Silver, however, believes the word *eugenics* is itself the problem, not the practice of enhancement. It is one of several "anxiety producing labels" that irrationally inhibit progress.[22]

Nevertheless, according to Fukuyama, this notion of an enhanced humanity represents a dangerous juncture in Western culture indeed. He argues that "the first victim of transhumanism might be equality," with enhanced humans edging out others in a variety of ways. Certainly history suggests plenty of analogies: racism and sexism come to mind. "If we start transforming ourselves into something superior, what rights will these enhanced creatures claim, and what rights will they possess when compared to those left behind? If some move ahead, can anyone afford not to follow?" Fukuyama questions whether an adequate view of the human informs the thinking of those most intent on changing humanity into something "better."[23]

The scientific mythologies we have been considering are all matters of conjecture rather than of scientific finding. These conjectures would be of little concern if they were not potentially distracting and even misleading on some highly important questions: What is at stake? Why should we care that a powerful set of interrelated mythologies has arisen in contemporary Western culture? Why would it matter if the Judeo-Christian worldview were to be displaced by some version of these narratives? Perhaps all that we have been discussing comes down simply to a clash of worldviews: sacralized naturalism versus Christian monotheism. If so, a pragmatic argument in favor of the Judeo-Christian perspective is that it has served the Western world well, producing an open and liberal society and providing a moral foundation for acts of love and the pursuit of justice.

But this may be more than a clash of worldviews. Simply put, truth itself is at stake. If salvation is to be found in God and not in Space; if the Creator of the universe seeks us out, and we turn our hope toward another source; if our predicament is sin, and spiritual transformation in Christ rather than genetic enhancement is the pathway out—then to hope in the new myths is to deceive ourselves in rather dangerous ways.

The central question facing us is this: Are the combined forces of science and imaginative narratives of the type found in science fiction and some new religions capable of producing a reliably humane moral outlook from within a sacralized naturalistic framework, an outlook capable of withstanding any amount of commercial, political or social pressure? Lacking a moral authority higher than the pronouncements of the scientists, authors and religious inventors themselves, why should we consider that a new neo-pagan naturalism would reliably produce something morally higher than its very human sources? It seems circular to argue that, even though we are not now morally trustworthy, with scientifically guided self-improvement we will soon become so. If the human psyche, including that of the scientist, possesses a moral flaw—for which there seems to be historical evidence—then that psyche cannot out of any mechanism, no matter how grand, produce the means of its own healing. Nor are new scientific mythologies the needed answer. Such narratives, no matter how sublime, do not possess the power to lift us up and out of ourselves; they only possess the capacity to create the illusion that such a conjuring trick is possible.

Settled confidence in a false hope of one's own making is the most serious form of self-delusion. Outer space, secret histories, spiritual races, hidden realities, extraterrestrial intelligences, new humans, imagined futures, alien gnoses—these are names of such false hopes, chimeras crafted in the human imagination, objects of spiritual devotion incapable of delivering us from our predicament. In contrast to these, our newest idols, is the faith rooted in God's self-revelation, which offers the Earth as gift and home, an open history of God's interaction with the human race, a single human family, trustworthy sense experience, humans created in God's image, the future as a matter of trust in a sovereign deity, and an openly proclaimed gospel of salvation by means of divine grace. The scientific mythologies are a call to the church to proclaim anew the truths with which it has been entrusted, truths that find their source in the only authority sufficiently profound to deal with the moral challenges with which science itself will continue to confront us all.

Science fiction does not simply borrow authority from science, but as we have seen, it also shapes science in profound ways. Though science may point to God, we cannot experiment our way to God. Knowledge of the divine and of salvation must be revealed to us by God himself, who ever remains in ultimate control of knowledge as well as of power. No scientific discovery will lead us from the lab to the heavens, though it may take us to space. Nature must be explored as a gift that points us to the Giver, not as an Aladdin's lamp yielding up to the diligent inquirer unlimited powers both physical and spiritual. The biblical message is that transforming grace rather than an evolving human race is the means of discovering our spiritual destiny. Salvation is the liberating gift, not of benevolent aliens, but of a preexistent, creating and redeeming God.

NOTES

Chapter 1: Introduction

[1]Carl Jung, *Flying Saucers* (1958; reprint, London: Routledge, 2002), p. 9.

[2]Ibid., p. 17.

[3]Carl Sagan, *The Cosmic Connection* (New York: Doubleday, 1973), p. 59.

[4]Ray Kurzweil, *The Singularity Is Near: When Humans Transcend Biology* (New York: Viking, 2005), p. 374.

[5]Scott Hillis, "How to Prepare for Alien Invasion," *Reuters online*, April 25, 2007 <http://uk.reuters.com/article/oddlyEnoughNews/idUKN0934498720070425?feedType=RSS&pageNumber=1>.

[6]"Jedi Makes the Census List," *BBC News*, October 9, 2001 <http://news.bbc.co.uk/2/hi/uk_news/1589133.stm>.

[7]Thomas Hargrove and Joseph Bernt, "Y3K? Space Aliens and Androids," *Scripps Howard News Service*, 2000. For poll results, see <http://www.freedomofinfo.org/poll/roper03.html>.

[8]Sigmund Freud, *The Future of an Illusion* (1927; reprint, New York: W. W. Norton, 1989).

[9]NASA Astrobiology Institute, "Astrobiology Roadmap," Final Version, September 2003 <http://astrobiology.arc.nasa.gov/roadmap/>.

[10]Steven Dick, *Life on Other Worlds: The 20th-Century Extraterrestrial Life Debate* (Cambridge: Cambridge University Press, 1998), p. 253.

[11]Ibid., p. 253.

[12]Mark Steyn, "Francis Crick (1916-2004)," *The Atlantic Monthly*, October 2004, p. 207.

[13]Ibid.

[14]Ibid.

[15]Sagan, *Cosmic Connection*, p. 219.

[16]Ibid., pp. 241, 267.

[17]Ibid., pp. 218-19.

[18]Ibid., p. 243.

[19]Karen Olsson, "Beam Me up, Godly Being: Is Alien Abduction Real—or a Creation of Hollywood?" *Slate*, October 31, 2005 <http://www.slate.com/id/2129111/>.

[20]Bill Moyers, "Of Myth and Men," *Time*, April 26, 1999, p. 90.

[21]Steven J. Dick, "Many Worlds: Cosmotheology," *The Global Spiral: A Publication of Metanexus Institute* <http://www.metanexus.net/Magazine/ArticleDetail/tabid/68/id/2649/Default.aspx>; idem, "Extraterrestrial Life and Our World View at the Turn of the Millennium," Dibner Library Lecture, Smithsonian Institution Libraries, May 2, 2000 <http://www.sil.si.edu/sil publications/dibner-library-lectures/extraterrestrial-life/ETcopy-KR.htm>.

[22]Dick, "Many Worlds."

[23]Ibid., emphasis added.

[24]Edward Rothstein, "Sci-Fi Synergy," *New York Times*, May 24, 2005 <http://www.nytimes.com/2005/05/24/arts/design/24scif.html?_r=1&oref=slogin>.

[25]C. S. Lewis, Letter to Sister Penelope, July 9, 1939, in *Letters of C. S. Lewis* (London: Geoffrey Bles, 1966), p. 167.

[26]Thomas M. Disch, *On SF* (Ann Arbor: University of Michigan Press, 2005), p. 22.

[27]Ibid., p. 23.

[28]Robert J. Sawyer, "The Future Is Already Here," speech at the Library of Congress, November 10, 1999 <http://www.sfwriter.com/lecture1.htm>.

[29]Disch, *On SF*, p. 192.

[30]Stephanie Schwam and Jay Cocks, *The Making of 2001: A Space Odyssey* (New York: Modern Library: 2000), p. 163.

[31]Dick, "Many Worlds."

[32]Christopher Guly, "Why *The X-Files* Is Becoming our New Religion," *The Ottawa Citizen*, March 5, 2000 <http://www.cesnur.org/testi/X_Files.htm >.

[33]Northrop Frye, *Anatomy of Criticism* (Princeton N.J.: Princeton University Press, 1957), p. 64.

[34]David Samuelson, *Visions of Tomorrow: Six Journeys from Outer to Inner Space* (New York: Arno, 1975), pp. 65-66. Samuelson recognizes that science fiction is not uniform in its worldview, and that much science fiction is "dystopian." For full-length studies of this phenomenon, see Kingsley Amis, *New Maps of Hell: A Survey of Science Fiction* (London: Gollancz, 1961); Mark R. Hillegas, *The Future as Nightmare: H. G. Wells and the Anti-Utopians* (New York: Oxford University Press, 1967). Samuelson, *Visions of Tomorrow*, p. 68n.

[35]Samuelson, *Visions of Tomorrow*, p. 84.

[36]Ibid., p. 85, with emphasis added to *"adaptability."*

[37]Ibid.

[38]Robert M. Philmus, *Into the Unknown: The Evolution of Science Fiction from Francis Godwin to H. G. Wells* (Berkeley: University of California Press, 1970), p. 21.

[39]Ibid., p. 2.

Chapter 2: New Myths for a New Age

[1]Huston Smith, *Why Religion Matters* (San Francisco: HarperCollins, 2001), p. 1; quoted in Stephen Rauch, *Neil Gaiman's "The Sandman" and Joseph Campbell: In Search of the Modern Myth* (Rockville, Md.: Wildside, 2003), p. 15.

[2]James Hollis, *Tracking the Gods: The Place of Myth in Modern Life* (Toronto: Inner City Books, 1995), p. 109.

[3]Lawrence Jaffe, *Celebrating Soul: Preparing for the New Religion* (Toronto: Inner City Books, 1999), 7; quoted in Rauch, *Neil Gaimon's "The Sandman,"* p. 14.

[4]Ibid., p. 13.

[5]Smith, *Why Religion Matters*, p. 3; quoted in Rauch, *Neil Gaimon's "The Sandman,"* p. 15.

[6]Rauch, *Neil Gaimon's "The Sandman,"* p. 17.

[7]Joseph Campbell, *The Hero with a Thousand Faces* (New York: MJF Books, 1949), p. 3.

[8]Quoted in Robert Scholes, *Structural Fabulation: An Essay on Fiction of the Future* (Notre Dame, Ind.: University of Notre Dame Press, 1975), p. 20.

[9]John W. Campbell Jr., "Science-Fiction and the Opinion of the Universe," *Saturday Review*, May 12, 1956, p. 10; quoted in Scholes, *Structural Fabulation*, p. 26.

[10]Mary Midgley, *Evolution as a Religion: Strange Dreams and Stranger Fears* (London: Methuen, 1985), p. 28.

[11]Ray Kurzweil, *The Singularity Is Near: When Humans Transcend Biology* (New York: Viking: 2005), p. 4.

[12]Ibid., emphasis added.

[13]Richard Cavendish, *Mythology: An Illustrated Encyclopedia* (London: Orbis Books, 1980), pp. 8, 11.

[14]Ibid., p. 9.

[15]Ibid., p. 11.

[16]Ibid., p. 12.

[17]James Gunn, *Alternate Worlds* (Englewood Cliffs, N.J.: Prentice Hall, 1975), p. 171.

[18]Anthony Tollin, *Old Time Radio Science Fiction* (Washington, D.C.: Radio Spirits, 1995), pp. 20-21.

[19]Gunn, *Alternate Worlds,* p. 171.

[20]Mary Midgley, *Science as Salvation: A Modern Myth and Its Meaning* (New York: Routledge, 1992), p. 57.

[21]William Sims Bainbridge, "Religions for a Galactic Civilization," Nineteenth Goddard Memorial Symposium of the American Astronautical Society, March 1981, in *Science Fiction and Space Futures,* ed. Eugene M. Emme (San Diego: American Astronautical Society, 1982), pp. 187-201 <http://mysite.verizon.net/wsbainbridge/dl/relgal.htm>.

[22]Midgley, *Evolution as a Religion,* p. 31.

[23]Seraphim Rose, *Orthodoxy and the Religion of the Future* (Platina, Calif.: St. Herman of Alaska Brotherhood, 1996), p. 73.

[24]Midgley, *Science as Salvation,* p. 13.

[25]*From Here to Infinity: The Ultimate Voyage,* video (Hollywood, Calif: Don Barrett/Bob Goodman Productions, Paramount Pictures, 1994).

[26]Philip José Farmer, *To Your Scattered Bodies Go* (Boston: Gregg Press, 1980), p. vii.

[27]Peter Nicholls, editor's introduction to Farmer, *To Your Scattered Bodies Go,* p. vii.

[28]Steven Dick, *Life on Other Worlds: The Twentieth-Century Extraterrestrial Life Debate* (Cambridge: Cambridge University Press, 1998), p. 126.

[29]Nicholls, p. xiv.

[30]David Samuelson, *Visions of Tomorrow: Six Journeys from Outer to Inner Space* (New York: Arno, 1975), pp. 65-66.

[31]Ibid., p. 66n.

[32]Ibid., p. 85, emphasis added.

Chapter 3: The Myth of the Extraterrestrial

[1]Kurd Lasswitz, *Auf zwei Planeten* [*On Two Planets*] (1897), trans. Hans H. Rudner as *Two Planets* (Carbondale: Southern Illinois University Press, 1971), p. 104.

[2]Steven J. Dick, *Life on Other Worlds: The 20th-Century Extraterrestrial Life Debate* (Cambridge: Cambridge University Press, 1998), p. 125.

[3]Edmund Halley, Second paper on "The Cause of the Variation of the Magnetical Needle," in *Miscellanea Curiosa* (London: Royal Society, 1705), p. 56; quoted in Dorothea Singer, *Giordano Bruno: His Life and Thought* (New York: Schuman, 1950), p. 187.

[4]Singer, *Giordano Bruno,* p. 53.

[5]Quoted in ibid., p. 56.

[6]Ibid., p. 50.

[7]Ibid., p. 27.

[8]Ibid., p. 183.

[9]Ibid., p. 185.

[10]Paul K. Alkon, *Origins of Futuristic Fiction* (Athens: University of Georgia Press, 1987), pp. 68-84.

[11]Thomas Burnet, *The Sacred Theory of the Earth* (London: R. Norton & Walter Ketilby, 1691) <http://www.uwmc.uwc.edu/geography/burnet/burnet.htm>.

[12]Brigham Young, *Journal of Discourses*, 13:271 <http://www.sacred-texts.com/earth/ste/ste27.htm>; cf. <http://lds-mormon.com/moon.shtml>.

[13]Dick, *Life on Other Worlds*, p. 17.

[14]Walter Sullivan, *We Are Not Alone: The Search for Intelligent Life on Other Worlds* (New York: Signet Books, 1966), p. 111.

[15]Ibid., p. 154.

[16]Ibid., p. 15.

[17]Dick, *Life on Other Worlds*, p. 171.

[18]Ibid., p. 174.

[19]Ibid., p. 176.

[20]Ibid., pp. 222-23.

[21]Ibid., p. 198.

[22]Ibid., p. 216.

[23]Sullivan, *We Are Not Alone*, p. 17.

[24]Dick, *Life on Other Worlds*, p. 126.

[25]Sullivan, *We Are Not Alone*, p. 19.

[26]Ibid., p. 20.

[27]Ibid., pp. 23-24.

[28]Ibid., p. 21.

[29]Bernard de Fontenelle, *Entretiens sur la pluralité des mondes* (Paris: Blageart, 1686), trans. as *A Week's Conversation on the Plurality of Worlds*, 3rd ed. (London: A. Bettesworth & E. Curll, 1737).

[30]Ibid., p. viii.

[31]Ibid., pp. 6, 35.

[32]Ibid., p. 55.

[33]Ibid., pp. 58-60.

[34]Ibid., p. 60.

[35]Ibid., pp. 62, 64.

[36]Ibid., p. 74.

[37]Ibid., p. 108.

[38]Ibid., p. 82.

[39]Sullivan, *We Are Not Alone*, p. 34.

[40]Dick, *Life on Other Worlds*, p. 19.

[41]Ibid., p. 20.

[42]See Camille Flammarion, *La Planèt Mars et ses conditions d'habilite* (Paris: Gauthier-Villars et Fils, 1892).

[43]John Clute, *Science Fiction: The Ilustrated Encyclopedia* (New York: Dorling Kindersley, 1995), p. 109.

[44]On Tesla see Margaret Cheney, *Tesla: Man out of Time* (New York: Simon & Schuster, 2001).

[45]Dick, *Life on Other Worlds*, p. 201.

[46]Cheney, *Tesla*, p. 145.

[47]Ibid., p. 149.

[48]Ibid., p. 310.

[49]Ibid., p. 312.

[50]Ibid., p. 313.

[51]Ibid.

[52]Ibid., p. 310.

[53]Ibid., p. 301.

[54]Ibid., p. 300.

[55]Ibid., p. 302.

[56]James Gunn, *Alternate Worlds* (Englewood Cliffs, N.J.: Prentice Hall, 1975), p. 109.

[57]Frank D. Drake, *Cosmic Search*, vol. 1, no. 1 <http://www.bigear.org/vol1no1/ozma.htm>.

[58]Sullivan, *We Are Not Alone*, p. 16.

[59]Drake, *Cosmic Search*, p. 3.

[60]Quoted in H. Paul Shuch, "SETI Made Simple: What Can We Do?" paper presented at the TAPR Annual Meeting, St. Louis, March 4, 1995 <http://www.setileague.org/articles/simple.htm>.

[61]Drake, *Cosmic Search*, p. 6.

[62]Ibid., p. 6.

[63]Ibid., p. 3.

[64]Sullivan, *We Are Not Alone*, p. 16.

[65]Ibid., p. 16.

[66]See Frank Drake, "Project Ozma," *Physics Today* 14 (1960): 40-46; and Paul Horowitz and Carl Sagan, "Five Years of Project META: An All-Sky Narrow-Band Radio Search for Extraterrestrial Signals," *Astrophysical Journal* 415 (1993): 218-35, abstract <http://ntrs.nasa.gov/search.jsp?R=540676&id=4&qs=No%3D10%26N%3D4294822996>.

[67]Sullivan, *We Are Not Alone*, p. 148.

[68]Carl Sagan, *The Cosmic Connection: An Extraterrestrial Perspective* (New York: Dell, 1973), p. viii.

[69]Ibid., p. 220.

[70]Ibid., p. 222.

[71]Ibid., p. 224.

[72]Ibid., p. 241.

[73]Ibid., p. 242.

[74]Ibid., p. 258.

[75]Steven J. Dick and James E. Strick, *The Living Universe: NASA and the Development of Astrobiology* (New Brunswick, N.J.: Rutgers University Press, 2005), p. 17.

[76]Sagan, *Cosmic Connection*, pp. 243, 267.

[77]Carl Sagan, *Contact: A Novel* (New York: Simon & Schuster, 1985), p. 363.

[78]Sagan, *Cosmic Connection*, p. viii.

[79]Ibid., p. ix.

[80]Ibid., p. 101.

[81]C. Maxwell Cade, *Other Worlds Than Ours* (London: Museum Press, 1966), 183.

[82]David E. Fisher and Marshal Jon Fisher, *Strangers in the Night: A Brief History of Life on Other Worlds* (Washington, D.C.: Counterpoint, 1999), p. 194.

[83]"Actor Tom Cruise Opens up About His Beliefs in the Church of Scientology," *Der Spiegel: Online International*, April 27, 2005 <http://www.spiegel.de/international/spiegel/0,1518,353577,00.html>.

[84]Chris Hodenfield, "The Sky Is Full of Questions: Science Fiction in Steven Spielberg's Suburbia," *Rolling Stone*, January 26, 1978, pp. 33-38.

[85]Tom Paulson, "Allen Funding Sustains SETI," *Seattle Post-Intelligencer*, Friday, January 10, 2003 <http://seattlepi.nwsource.com/local/103574_cspace10.shtml>.

[86]Dick Gordon, "Is Anyone Out There?" *The Story*, National Public Radio, May 1, 2007 <http://

thestory.org/archive/the_story_240_Is_Anyone_Out_There.mp3/view>.

[87]Seraphim Rose, *Orthodoxy and the Religion of the Future* (Platina, Calif.: St. Herman of Alaska Brotherhood, 1996), p. 91.

[88]Sagan, *Cosmic Connection*, p. 42.

[89]Michael Crichton, Caltech Michelin Lecture, January 17, 2003 <http://brinnonprosperity.org/crichton2.html>.

[90]Dick, *Life on Other Worlds*, p. 116.

Chapter 4: The Myth of Space

[1]Sylvia Hui, "Hawking: Space Exploration a Necessity," *Houston Chronicle Online*, June 13, 2006 <http://www.chron.com/disp/story.mpl/space/3965730.html>. I will be capitalizing *space* on occasion when employing it in reference to mythic Space.

[2]Stephen Hawking, "To Avoid Extinction, Humans Must Colonize Space," *Yahoo! News*, November 30, 3006; quotation online <http://news.mongabay.com/2006/1130-hawking.html>.

[3]Carl Sagan, *Billions and Billions: Thoughts on Life and Death at the Brink of the Millennium* (New York: Random House, 1997), p. 226.

[4]Cyrano de Bergerac, *Voyages to the Moon and the Sun*, trans. Richard Aldington (London: Routledge, 1923); Bernard de Fontenelle, *Entretiens sur la pluralité des mondes* (Paris: Blageart, 1686), trans. as *A Week's Conversation on the Plurality of Worlds*, 3rd ed. (London: A. Bettesworth & E. Curll, 1737).

[5]Gary Zukav, *The Seat of the Soul* (New York: Simon & Schuster, 1989). On Ilive's theories, see James A. Herrick, *The Radical Rhetoric of the English Deists* (Columbia: University of South Carolina Press, 1997).

[6]Mary Midgley, *Science as Salvation: A Modern Myth and Its Meaning* (New York: Routledge, 1992), p. 26.

[7]Erik Bergaust, *First Men in Space* (New York: Putman, 1960), p. 38.

[8]Ibid., pp. 39-46.

[9]Thomas Paine, *The Age of Reason* (1795; reprint, Secaucus, N.J.: Citadel, 1974), p. 84 with its note.

[10]Ibid., p. 86.

[11]Ibid., p. 89.

[12]Ibid., p. 91.

[13]Ibid., p. 90.

[14]James Gunn, *Alternate Worlds* (Englewood Cliffs, N.J.: Prentice-Hall, 1975), p. 60.

[15]See Laurence A. Rickels, *Nazi Psychoanalysis*, vol. 3, *Psi Fi* (Minneapolis: University of Minnesota Press, 2002), pp. 122-25.

[16]Midgley, *Science as Salvation*, p. 155.

[17]NASA, "The Power of Persistence," October 21, 2006 <http://www.nasa.gov/audience/forstudents/5-8/features/F_The_Power_of_Persistence_5-8.html>.

[18]Committee members included Fred Whipple of Harvard, Cornelius Ryan of the *Collier's* staff, rocket scientists Wernher von Braun and Willy Ley, and artists Ralph Klepp, Fred Freeman, and Chesley Bonestell.

[19]*Collier's Weekly*, August 16, 1952, p. 30.

[20]*Collier's Weekly*, October 16, 1953.

[21]See, for example, *Collier's Weekly*, June 28, 1952.

[22]Bosley Crowther, "About von Braun: *I Aim at the Stars* Opens at the Forum," movie review, *New York Times*, October 20, 1960 <http://movies.nytimes.com/movie/review?_r=1&res=9E07E0D

A1E31EF3ABC4851DFB667838B679EDE&oref=slogin>.

[23] Andre Bormanis, "Loners, Renegades and Evil Geniuses," review of *Mad, Bad and Dangerous? The Scientist and the Cinema*, by Christopher Frayling [London: Reaktion Books: 2005] (December 2005), posted by Physicsworld.com <http://physicsworld.com/cws/article/indepth/23674>.

[24] The Planetary Society webpage <www.planetary.org/about>.

[25] James D. Burke, "Why We Explore: Striving Outward," posted by The Planetary Society <http://www.planetary.org/explore/why.html>.

[26] Ibid.

[27] Ibid.

[28] *Aliens of the Deep* (Disney Enterprises: 2005) <www.bvpublicity.com>.

[29] Ibid., p. 6.

[30] Ibid.

[31] Ibid.

[32] Ibid., p. 7.

[33] Quoted in Robert S. Boyd, "Been There, Done That: Despite Earlier Missions, the Moon Is Still the First Step in Exploring Space," *McClatchy Newspapers*, July 9, 2006; cf. Mike Griffin, "Our Road to Mars Goes Through the Moon," *Lunar Enterprise Daily*, December 13, 2005 <http://www.spaceagepub.com/subscribers/LDarchive/LD20051213.html>.

[34] J. Richard Gott III, *Time Travel in Einstein's Universe: The Physical Possibilities of Travel Through Time* (London: Phoenix, 2002), p. 229.

[35] Ibid., p. 231.

[36] Boyd, "Been There, Done That."

[37] Vince Belser, "Space Invader," *Wired Magazine* (November 2007): 203.

[38] Martin Rees, *Our Final Hour: A Scientist's Warning: How Terror, Error, and Environmental Disaster Threaten Humankind's Future in This Century—On Earth and Beyond* (New York: Basic Books, 2003), p. 170.

[39] Sagan, *Billions and Billions*, p. 67.

Chapter 5: The Myth of the New Humanity

[1] Arthur C. Clarke, *3001: The Final Odyssey*, ed. Shelly Shapiro (New York: Del Rey/Ballantine Books, 1999).

[2] Arthur C. Clarke, *Against the Fall of Night* (1953; reprint, Garden City, N.Y.: Doubleday, 1954), p. 150.

[3] Seraphim Rose, *Orthodoxy and the Religion of the Future* (Platina, Calif.: St. Herman of Alaska Brotherhood, 1996), p. 73.

[4] Brian Aldiss, *Trillion Year Spree* (New York: Atheneum, 1986), p. 94.

[5] Julian Huxley, "Transhumanism," in *New Bottles for New Wine* (London: Chatto & Windus, 1957), pp. 13-17.

[6] World Transhumanist Association website <http://www.transhumanism.org/index.php/WTA/index/>.

[7] The Immortality Institute <http://www.imminst.org/>.; cf. Wikipedia, "Immortality Institute" <http://en.wikipedia.org/wiki/Immortality_Institute>.

[8] Peter Sloterdijk, "The Operable Man: On the Ethical State of Gene Technology," lecture at UCLA, May 21, 2000 <http://www.petersloterdijk.net/international/texts/en_texts/en_texts_PS_operable_man.html>; quoted in Dan Stone, *Breeding Superman* (Liverpool: Liverpool University Press, 2002), p. 136.

[9] G. K. Chesterton, *Heretics* (London: Bodley Head, 1905), chap. 4; cited in Wikipedia, "G. K.

Chesterton" <http://en.wikipedia.org/wiki/G._K._Chesterton>.

[10]Mary Midgley, *Evolution as a Religion: Strange Dreams and Stranger Fears* (London: Methuen, 1985).

[11]H. G. Wells, *The World of William Clissold* (New York: George Doran, 1926), p. 83.

[12]<www.transvision2007.com>.

[13]Midgley, *Evolution as a Religion*, p. 15.

[14]For a treatment of Nietzsche's influence on Western intellectuals, see John Carey, *The Intellectuals and the Masses: Pride and Prejudice Among the Literary Intelligentsia, 1880-1939* (New York: St. Martin's Press, 1993).

[15]J. B. S. Haldane, "Eugenics and Social Reform," in *Possible Worlds and Other Papers* (New York: Harper & Brothers, 1928), p. 206: "Civilization stands in real danger from over-production of 'undermen.'"

[16]Francis Galton's books include *Hereditary Genius* (London: Macmillan, 1869), *Inquiries into the Human Faculty* (1883) and *Essays in Eugenics* (London: The Eugenics Education Society, 1909).

[17]John W. Burrow, *Evolution and Society: A Study in Victorian Social Theory* (Cambridge: Cambridge University Press, 1966), pp. 99-100.

[18]Francis Galton, "Hereditary Character and Talent," *Macmillan's Magazine*, November 1864, pp. 157-66; April 1865, pp. 318-27.

[19]Freeman Dyson, *Imagined Worlds* (Cambridge, Mass.: Harvard University Press, 1998), p. 11.

[20]John Clute, *Science Fiction: The Illustrated Encyclopedia* (New York: Dorling Kindersley, 1995), p. 114.

[21]Wells, *World of William Clissold*, p. 58.

[22]J. P. Vernier, "Evolution as a Literary Theme in H. G. Wells's Science Fiction," in *H. G. Wells and Modern Fiction*, ed. Darko Suvin and Robert M. Philmus (Lewisburg, Penn.: Bucknell University Press, 1977), p. 70.

[23]Donald A. Wollheim, introduction to H. G. Wells, *The Food of the Gods and How It Came to Earth* (1904; reprint, New York: Airmont, 1965), p. 3.

[24]Wells, *World of William Clissold*, p. 83.

[25]Wollheim, introduction to *Food of the Gods*, p. 5.

[26]Wells, *Food of the Gods*, p. 187.

[27]Ibid., p. 189.

[28]David Samuelson, *Visions of Tomorrow: Six Journeys from Outer to Inner Space* (New York: Arno, 1975), p. 14.

[29]Wells, *World of William Clissold*, p. 80.

[30]Ibid., p. 91.

[31]Ibid., p. 80.

[32]Carey, *Intellectuals and the Masses*, p. 123.

[33]H. G. Wells uses the phrase "people of The Abyss" in *Mankind in the Making* (London: Chapman and Hall, 1903), p. 110. Cited in Carey, *Intellectuals and the Masses*, p. 124.

[34]Quoted in Carey, *Intellectuals and the Masses*, pp. 124-25.

[35]Wells, *World of William Clissold*, pp. 186-87.

[36]Carey, *Intellectuals and the Masses*, p. 130.

[37]Quoted in ibid., p. 139.

[38]Ibid., pp. 140, 145.

[39]Ibid., pp. 130, 133.

[40]Vernier, "Evolution as a Literary Theme," p. 85.

[41]Samuel Moskowitz, *Explorers of the Infinite: Shapers of Science Fiction* (Westport, Conn.: Hy-

perion, 1963), p. 261.

[42]Olaf Stapledon, *Last and First Men* (1930; reprint, Los Angeles: Jeremy Tarcher, 1988), cover.

[43]See Freeman Dyson's introduction to Stapledon's *Star Maker* (1937; reprint, Middletown, Conn.: Wesleyan University Press, 2004).

[44]Ibid., p. xxi.

[45]Moskowitz, *Explorers of the Infinite*, p. 267.

[46]Stapledon, *Last and First Men*, p. xiii.

[47]Ibid.

[48]Ibid., p. xiv.

[49]Gregory Benford, foreword to ibid., p. x.

[50]Ibid., p. xiv.

[51]Ibid., p. xix.

[52]Steven J. Dick, *Life on Other Worlds: The 20th-Century Extraterrestrial Life Debate* (Cambridge: Cambridge University Press, 1998), p. 122.

[53]Franz Rottensteiner, *The Science Fiction Book: An Illustrated History* (New York: Seabury, 1975), p. 64.

[54]Moskowitz, *Explorers of the Infinite*, p. 271.

[55]Ibid., p. 274.

[56]Stapledon, *Star Maker*, p. xix.

[57]Ibid., p. xxx.

[58]Dick, *Life on Other Worlds*, p. 123.

[59]Ibid., p. 123.

[60]Stapledon, "The Splendid Race," in *An Olaf Stapledon Reader*, ed. Robert Crossley (Syracuse, N.Y.: Syracuse University Press, 1997), pp. 145-46.

[61]Ibid., p. 145.

[62]Ibid., p. 147.

[63]C. S. Lewis, "A Reply to Professor Haldane," in *Of Other Worlds*, ed. Walter Hooper (San Diego: Harcourt Brace Jovanovich, 1966), pp. 74-85, esp. p. 77.

[64]Clarke, *Against the Fall of Night*, p. 150.

[65]Ibid., p. 154.

[66]Ibid., p. 155.

[67]Roger Luckhurst, *The Invention of Telepathy, 1870-1901* (Oxford: Oxford University Press, 2002), p. 5.

[68]Ibid., p. 1.

[69]Ibid., p. 11.

[70]William Crookes, *Researches into the Phenomena of Spiritualism* (London: J. Burns, 1874); quoted in Luckhurst, *Invention of Telepathy*, p. 26; see also William Crookes, *Psychic Force and Modern Spiritualism* (London: Longmans, 1871).

[71]Luckhurst, *Invention of Telepathy*, p. 135.

[72]Ibid., p. 111.

[73]Alfred Russell Wallace, *Natural Selection and Tropical Nature* (London: Macmillan, 1890); quoted in Luckhurst, *Invention of Telepathy*, p. 86.

[74]See Raël, *The True Face of God* (Geneva: The Raëlian Foundation, 1998), pp. 37-40, 192-95, 199.

[75]Sir J. J. Thomson, *Recollections and Reflections* (London: G. Bell & Sons, 1936), p. 158; quoted in Luckhurst, *Invention of Telepathy*, p. 81.

[76]J. B. Rhine, *New Frontiers of the Mind: The Story of the Duke Experiments* (New York: Farrar & Rinehart, 1937), p. 27.

[77]Ibid., p. 28.

[78]Ibid., p. 37.

[79]Albert Einstein, preface to Upton Sinclair, *Mental Radio* (1930; reprint, Charlotesville, Va.: Hampton Roads Publishers, 2001), p. xi.

[80]Rhine, *New Frontiers of the Mind*, p. 41.

[81]Ibid., pp. 41-42.

[82]Ibid., p. 51.

[83]Ibid., p. 51.

[84]Ibid., p. 190.

[85]"Poll: Most Believe in Psychic Phenomena," *CBS News*, New York, April 28, 2002 <http://www.cbsnews.com/stories/2002/04/29/opinion/polls/main507515.shtml>.

[86]Valerie Richardson, "Scientist Takes on the Psychic," *The Washington Times*, April 23, 2007.

[87]Philip Wylie, *Gladiator* (Lincoln: University of Nebraska Press, 2004).

[88]Ibid., p. 6.

[89]Ibid., pp. 26-27.

[90]Ibid., p. 45.

[91]Ibid., p. 48.

[92]Ibid., p. 52.

[93]Ibid., p. 48.

[94]Ibid., p. 58.

[95]Ibid., p. 145.

[96]Ibid., p. 179.

[97]Ibid., p. 219.

[98]Ibid., p. 313.

[99]Ibid., p. 312.

[100]Ibid., p. 316.

[101]Ibid., p. 327.

[102]Ibid., p. 330.

[103]Stapledon, *Star Maker*, p. xxiv.

[104]Lee Carroll and Jan Tober, *The Indigo Children: The New Kids Have Arrived* (Carlsbad, Calif.: Hay House, 1999).

[105]Nancy Ann [Tappe], *Understanding Your Life Through Color: Metaphysical Concepts in Color and Aura* (Costa Mesa, Calif.: Starling, 1986).

[106]Ellae Elinwood, review of *Understanding Your Life Through Color*, by Nancy Ann Tappe, *Sentient Times*, February-March 2004 <http://www.sentienttimes.com/04/feb_mar_04/color.htm>.

[107]Ray Kurzweil, *The Singularity Is Near: When Humans Transcend Biology* (New York: Viking, 2005).

[108]Ibid., p. 387.

[109]Ray Kurzweil, "Accelerated Living," *PC Magazine*, September 2001 <http://www.kurzweilai.net/articles/art0294.html?printable=1>.

[110]Kurzweil, *Singularity*, p. 371.

[111]Ibid., p. 388.

[112]Ibid., p. 9.

[113]Ibid., p. 374.

[114]Ibid., p. 9.

[115]Ibid.

[116]Ibid., p. 389.

[117]Ibid.

[118]Ibid.

[119]Ibid., p. 390.

[120]Oscar Levy, introduction to Gobineau's *The Renaissance*, p. xxxv; quoted in Dan Stone, *Breeding Superman: Nietzsche, Race and Eugenics in Edwardian and Interwar Britain* (Liverpool: Liverpool University Press, 2002), p. 16.

[121]Publisher-posted excerpt from Francis Fukuyama, *Our Posthuman Future: Consequences of the Biotechnology Revolution* (New York: Farrar, Straus & Giroux, 2002) <http://www.fsg-books.com/fsg/ourposthumanfutureexcrpt.htm>.

[122]Midgley, *Evolution as a Religion*, p. 46.

[123]C. S. Lewis, *The Abolition of Man* (New York: Macmillan, 1947), p. 37.

[124]Ibid.

Chapter 6: The Myth of the Future

[1]John Clute, *Science Fiction: The Illustrated Encyclopedia* (London: DK Publishing, 1995), p. 124.

[2]James Gunn, *Alternate Worlds: The Illustrated History of Science Fiction* (Englewood Cliffs, N.J.: Prentice-Hall, 1975), p. 170.

[3]Science Fiction Museum and Hall of Fame brochure and map (February 2007); cf. <http://www.csulb.edu/library/subj/literature/scifi.html>.

[4]Clute, *Science Fiction*, pp. 66-67.

[5]Roger Luckhurst, *The Invention of Telepathy, 1870-1901* (Oxford: Oxford University Press, 2002), pp. 138-39.

[6]Ibid., p. 138.

[7]Ibid.

[8]Ibid., p. 202; Luckhurst is quoting novelist Arthur Machen, "Science and the Ghost Story," *Literature*, September 17, 1989, p. 251.

[9]Lockhurst, *Invention of Telepathy*, pp. 178-79.

[10]Erik Davis, *TechGnosis: Myth, Magic and Mysticism in the Age of Information* (New York: Three Rivers Press, 1999), p. 123.

[11]Luckhurst, *Invention of Telepathy*, p. 277.

[12]Arthur C. Clarke, *Childhood's End* (1953; reprint, New York: Del Rey, 1990), p. 107.

[13]Jeremy Narby and Francis Huxley, *Shamans Through Time: 500 Years on the Path to Knowledge* (New York: Jeremy Tarcher, 2001).

[14]Ray Kurzweil, *The Singularity Is Near: When Humans Transcend Biology* (New York: Viking: 2005), pp. 4-5.

[15]Ibid., p. 4.

[16]William T. Stead, "Impending Revolution" series, *Daily Paper*, January 7, 14, 18, 1904; quoted in Luckhurst, *Invention of Telepathy*, p. 138.

[17]Clute, *Science Fiction*, p. 42.

[18]Frederic Myers, *Fragments of Inner Life: An Autobiographical Sketch* (1893; reprint, London: Society for Psychical Research, 1961), quoted in Luckhurst, *Invention of Telepathy*, p. 107.

[19]Kurzweil, *Singularity Is Near*, p. 7.

[20]Gunn, *Alternate Worlds*, p. 225.

[21]Max More, "Principles of Extropy," Version 3.11, 2003, posted by Extropy Institute <http://www.extropy.org/principles.htm >.

[22]Walter Sullivan, *We Are Not Alone: The Search for Intelligent Life on Other Worlds* (New York: Signet Books, 1966), p. 34.

[23]Léon Poliakov, *The Aryan Myth* (New York: Basic Books, 1974), p. 145.

[24]Richard Cavendish, *Mythology: An Illustrated Encyclopedia* (London: Orbis, 1980), p. 9.

[25]Gunn, *Alternate Worlds*, p. 104.

[26]Mary Midgley, *Science as Salvation: A Modern Myth and Its Meaning* (New York: Routledge, 1992), p. 24.

[27]Carl Sagan, *The Cosmic Connection: An Extraterrestrial Perspective* (New York: Dell, 1973), p. 69.

[28]Isaac Asimov, *I, Robot* (1950; reprint, New York: Fawcett Crest, 1970), p. i.

[29]Clute, *Science Fiction*, p. 214.

[30]Gunn, *Alternate Worlds*, p. 147.

[31]Francis Bacon, *The New Atlantis* (1627) in *Ideal Commonwealths* (New York: P. F. Collier & Son, 1901), widely available online, as in The Internet Wiretap edition (August 1993), posted by Oregon State University <http://oregonstate.edu/instruct/phl302/texts/bacon/atlantis.html>.

[32]Louis-Sébastien Mercier, *Memoirs of the Year Two Thousand Five Hundred*, trans. W. Hooper (Philadelphia: T. Dobson, 1795).

[33]Edward S. Reed, *From Soul to Mind: The Emergence of Psychology from Erasmus Darwin to William James* (New Haven, Conn.: Yale University Press, 1997), p. 158.

[34]James Turner, *Without God, Without Creed* (Baltimore: Johns Hopkins University Press, 1985), p. 137.

[35]C. Maurice Davies, *Heterodox London: Phases of Free Thought in the Metropolis*, 2 vols. (1874; reprint, New York: A. M. Kelley, 1969), 2:254.

[36]Ibid., 2:256-57.

[37]Edward Bellamy, *Looking Backward, 2000 to 1887* (1888), e-text, posted by Project Gutenberg (August 1996) <http://www.gutenberg.org/etext/624>.

[38]David Samuelson, *Visions of Tomorrow: Six Journeys from Outer to Inner Space* (New York: Arno, 1975), p. 8.

[39]Mark R. Hillegas, afterword to Kurd Lasswitz, *Two Planets*, trans. Hans H. Rudner (German, 1897; reprint, Carbondale: Southern Illinois University Press, 1971), p. 397.

[40]Ibid., p. 397.

[41]Lasswitz, *Two Planets*, p. 16; see also pp. 26-27.

[42]Ibid., p. 59.

[43]Ibid., p. 209.

[44]Ibid., p. 36.

[45]Ibid., p. 61.

[46]Hillegas, afterword to ibid., p. 397.

[47]Lasswitz, *Two Planets*, p. 62.

[48]Kurd Lasswitz, *Bis zum Nullpunkt des Seins* [To the Zero Point of Existence] (1871), German e-text posted by Project Gutenberg <http://gutenberg.spiegel.de/?id=5&xid=1556&kapitel=1#gb_found> (no English trans.).

[49]Lasswitz, *Two Planets*, p. 381.

[50]Sullivan, *We Are Not Alone*, p. 90.

[51]J. B. S. Haldane, *Possible Worlds* (New Brunswick, N.J.: Transaction, 2002), p. vii.

[52]Freeman Dyson, *Imagined Worlds* (Cambridge, Mass.: Harvard University Press, 1997), p. 95.

[53]Mary Midgley, *Evolution as a Religion: Strange Dreams and Stranger Fears* (London: Methuen, 1985), p. 26.

[54]Haldane, *Possible Worlds*, p. 263.

[55]Ibid., p. viii.

[56]Ibid., p. 301.

[57]Ibid., p. 304.

[58]Ibid.

[59]Ibid., p. 309.

[60]Ibid., p. 310.

[61]Ibid.

[62]Ibid., p. 311.

[63]Dyson, *Imagined Worlds*, p. 158.

[64]Olaf Stapledon, *Star Maker* (1937; reprint, Middletown, Conn.: Wesleyan University Press, 2004), p. xix.

[65]Dyson, *Imagined Worlds*, p. 123.

[66]Ibid., p. 131.

[67]Ibid., p. 133.

[68]Ibid., p. 135.

[69]Ibid., p. 136.

[70]Ibid., p. 156.

[71]Ibid., p. 157.

[72]Ibid., p. 158.

[73]Ibid., p. 159.

[74]Ibid., p. 160.

[75]Ibid., p. 161.

[76]Ibid., p. 162.

[77]Ibid., p. 167.

[78]Ibid., p. 169.

[79]Martin Rees, *Our Final Hour: A Scientist's Warning: How Terror, Error, and Environmental Disaster Threaten Humankind's Future in This Century—On Earth and Beyond* (New York: Basic Books, 2003), p. 170.

[80]Ibid., p. 180.

[81]Ibid., p. 181.

[82]Ibid.

[83]Quoted in ibid., p. 182.

[84]Ibid., pp. 182-83.

[85]Frank Tipler, *The Physics of Immortality: Modern Cosmology, God, and the Resurrection of the Dead* (1994; reprint, New York: Anchor Books, 1997).

Chapter 7: The Myth of the Spiritual Race

[1]James Gunn, *Alternate Worlds* (Englewood Cliffs, N.J.: Prentice-Hall, 1975), p. 159.

[2]Trent Walters, "Who Is John W. Campbell, Jr.?" review of *Golden Age of Science Fiction,* by John W. Campbell <http://www.sfsite.com/02b/jc170.htm>.

[3]Ibid.

[4]Samuel Moskowitz, *Explorers of the Infinite: Shapers of Science Fiction* (Westport, Conn.: Hyperion, 1963).

[5]Dan Stone, *Breeding Superman* (Liverpool: Liverpool University Press, 2002), p. 66.

[6]Cited in ibid., p. 81.

[7]A. R. Orage, *Consciousness: Animal, Human, and Superhuman* (London: Theosophical Pub-

lishing Society, 1907), p. 72; quoted in Roger Luckhurst, *The Invention of Telepathy: 1870-1901* (Oxford: Oxford University Press, 2002), p. 257.

[8]On the Nobel sperm bank, see David Plotz, "The Myths of the Nobel Sperm Bank: The Truth About Who Gave Sperm, How They Used It, and Who Used It," *Slate*, February 23, 2001 <http://www.slate.com/id/101318/>.

[9]Richard Hernstein and Charles Murray, *The Bell Curve: Intelligence and Class Structure in American Life* (New York: Free Press, 1994), p. 25.

[10]Léon Poliakov, *The Aryan Myth* (New York: Basic Books, 1974), p. 38.

[11]Ibid., p. 73.

[12]Ibid., p. 169.

[13]Ibid., p. 133.

[14]Ibid., p. 186.

[15]Ibid., p. 187.

[16]Ibid., p. 188.

[17]Ibid., p. 191.

[18]Book of Mormon, 1 Nephi 16:29; see, e.g., Joseph Smith Jr., trans., *The Book of Mormon: An Account Written by the hand of Mormon, upon Plates Taken from the Plates of Nephi*, 4th ed. (Monongahela, Penn.: Church of Jesus Christ, 2001), posted by Intellectual Reserve <http://scriptures.lds.org/bm/contents>.

[19]Book of Mormon, 2 Nephi 5:21: "As they were white, and exceedingly fair and delightsome, that they might not be enticing unto my people the Lord God did cause a skin of blackness to come upon them."

[20]This idea persisted into the twentieth century. In a 1960 speech, Spencer W. Kimball, an apostle and president of the LDS (Mormon) Church, said that the Navajo Indians "are fast becoming a 'white and delightsome' people." Kimball continued, "The [Indian] children in the home place-ment program in Utah are often lighter than their brothers and sisters in the hogans on the reservation"; *Improvement Era* 63 (December 1960): 922-23.

[21]Harry L. Ropp, *Are the Mormon Scriptures Reliable?* (Downers Grove, Ill.: InterVarsity Press, 1987), pp. 39-40.

[22]Poliakov, *Aryan Myth*, p. 43; from William Blake, in "Jerusalem: The Emanation of the Great Albion" (London, 1804).

[23]Poliakov, *Aryan Myth*, p. 39.

[24]Ibid., p. 44.

[25]Ibid.

[26]Ibid.

[27]Gunn, *Alternate Worlds*, p. 61.

[28]George Edward Bulwer-Lytton, *The Coming Race* (Santa Barbara, Calif.: Woodbridge Press, 1989), p. 11.

[29]Ibid., p. 12.

[30]Ibid., pp. 14-15.

[31]George Chatterton-Hill, *Heredity and Selection in Sociology* (London: Adam & Charles Black, 1907); quoted in Stone, *Breeding Superman*, p. 63.

[32]See Mike Hawkins, *Social Darwinism in European and American Thought, 1860-1945: Nature as Model and Nature as Threat* (Cambridge: Cambridge University Press, 1997); and Gregory Claeys, "The 'Survival of the Fittest' and the Origins of Social Darwinism," *Journal of the History of Ideas* 61 (2000): 223-40.

[33]For information on Churchward and his books, see <http://www.brotherhoodoflife.com/>.

Some of Churchward's books are available online, like *The Sacred Symbols of Mu* from Sacred Texts <http://www.bibliotecapleyades.net/atlantida_mu/sacredsymbolsmu/contents.htm>.

[34]Robert Todd Carroll, "Edgar Cayce," in *Skeptic's Dictionary* <http://www.genpaku.org/skepticj/cayce.html>.

[35]Gunn, *Alternate Worlds*, pp. 105-6.

[36]John Baxter, *Science Fiction in the Cinema* (New York: A. S. Barnes, 1970), p. 79.

[37]Ibid., p. 79.

[38]Baxter (ibid., p. 84) writes that "the lost kingdom films all derived in some form from H. Rider Haggard's *She*."

[39]Ibid., p. 82.

[40]Poliakov, *Aryan Myth*, p. 22.

[41]Ibid., p. 35.

[42]Ibid., p. 98.

[43]Ibid., p. 82.

[44]Quoted in ibid., p. 78.

[45]Timothy W. Ryback, "Hitler's Forgotten Library: The Man, His Books, and His Search for God," *The Atlantic Monthly*, May 2003, pp. 76-90.

[46]Poliakov, *Aryan Myth*, p. 101.

[47]Ryback, "Hitler's Forgotten Library," p. 89.

[48]Ibid. p. 90.

[49]John Carey, *The Intellectuals and the Masses* (New York: St. Martin's Press, 1992), p. 198.

[50]Ibid., p. 199.

[51]Ibid., p. 200.

[52]Ibid.

[53]Poliakov, *Aryan Myth*, p. 104.

[54]Daniel Leonard Bernardi, *Star Trek and History: Race-ing Toward a White Future* (Rutgers, N.J.: Rutgers University Press, 1998), p. 56.

[55]David Alexander, *Star Trek Creator* (New York: Dutton Signet, 1994), p. 568.

[56]Bernardi, *Star Trek and History*, pp. 122-23.

[57]Ibid., p. 126.

[58]Ibid., p. 119.

[59]See Straczynski's cover endorsement for E. E. "Doc" Smith, *Triplanetary: A Tale of Cosmic Adventure* (1948; reprint, New York: Simon & Schuster, 2004).

[60]Bernardi, *Star Trek and History*, pp. 122-23.

[61]On the Q Continuum (July 3, 2007) <www.startrek.com/startrek/view/library/aliens/article/70700.html>.

[62]Bernardi, *Star Trek and History*, p. 125.

[63]Joseph Campbell, *The Hero with a Thousand Faces* (Princeton, N.J.: Princeton University Press, 1948), pp. 3-4.

[64]Brendan Gill, "The Faces of Joseph Campbell," *New York Review of Books* 36, no. 14 (September 28, 1989): 16-19.

[65]Bill Moyers, "Of Myth and Men," *Time*, April 26, 1999, p. 90.

[66]Steve Silberman, "Life After Death," *Wired Magazine*, May 2005, p. 141.

[67]Steven J. Dick, *Life on Other Worlds: The 20th-Century Extraterrestrial Life Debate* (Cambridge: Cambridge University Press, 1998), p. 166.

[68]Ibid., pp. 166-67. Dick quotes astronomer J. Allen Hyneck.

[69]John E. Mack, *Abduction: Human Encounters with Aliens* (New York: Scribner's Sons, 1995).

[70]Ibid., preface.

[71]Ibid., p. 3.

[72]Ibid., p. 4.

[73]Ibid., pp. 6-7.

[74]Ibid., p. 8.

[75]Ibid.

[76]Ibid., p. 9.

[77]Ibid., p. 18.

[78]Ibid., p. 17.

[79]Paul Cohn, "Belloc and Nietzsche," *New Age,* January 2, 1913; quoted in Stone, *Breeding Superman,* p. 66.

[80]Thomas Common, "The New Outlook," *Notes for Good Europeans* 1 no. 1 (1903): 1-11; quoted in Stone, *Breeding Superman,* p. 67.

[81]Stone, *Breeding Superman,* p. 67.

[82]Ibid., p. 70.

[83]Professor Lindsay, "Eugenics and the Doctrine of the Super-Man," lecture before the Eugenics Society in London, October 7, 1915; quoted in Stone, *Breeding Superman,* p. 83.

[84]Stone, *Breeding Superman,* p. 114.

[85]Thomas Common, "Defects of Popular Secularism," *Notes for Good Europeans* 1, no. 2 (1903-1904): 47-48; quoted in Stone, *Breeding Superman,* p. 67.

[86]The phrase is from the Nietzsche editor Alexander Tille (1866-1912); quoted in Stone, *Breeding Superman,* p. 68.

Chapter 8: The Myth of Space Religion

[1]For a detailed discussion of UFO cults and related topics, see James R. Lewis, *The Gods Have Landed: New Religions from Other Worlds* (Albany: State University of New York Press, 1995).

[2]Robert A. Heinlein, *Stranger in a Strange Land* (1961; reprint, New York: Ace, 1987), p. 308.

[3]William Derham, *Astro-Theology, or, a Demonstration of the Being and Attributes of God, from a Survey of the Heavens* (London: W. Innys, 1715).

[4]See A. D. Atkinson, "William Derham, F.R.S. (1657-1735)," *Annals of Science* 8 (1952): 368-92.

[5]Derham, *Astro-Theology,* pp. 33-34.

[6]Ibid., p. 1.

[7]Ibid., p. 218.

[8]Emanuel Swedenborg, *The Worlds in Space* (1758; reprint, London: The Swedenborg Society, 1997), p. 1.

[9]Ibid., p. 113.

[10]Ibid., p. 93.

[11]Ibid., p. 25.

[12]Ibid., p. 14.

[13]J. N. Loughborough, *The Great Second Advent Movement: Its Rise and Progress* (Nashville: Southern Publishing, 1905), p. 180 <http://www.ellenwhitedefend.com/DOWNLOADS/The%20 Great%20Second%20Advent%20Movement.pdf>; idem (reprint, New York: Arno, 1972), p. 260.

[14]Mrs. Truesdale letter, January 27, 1891 <http://www.biblebelievers.com/SDA/SDA2.html>; also D. M. Canright, "Her False Vision About the Planets," in *The Life of Ellen White* <http:// www.ellenwhite.org/canright/can20.htm>; Canright cites *Early Writings of Ellen G. White,* p. 32 <http://www.nisbett.com/reference/ew/default.htm>.

[15]John Jacob Astor, *A Journey in Other Worlds* (New York: D. Appleton, 1894).

[16]Ibid., p. 294.

[17]Ibid.

[18]Ibid., p. 374.

[19]Ibid., p. 377.

[20]Ibid., pp. 379-80.

[21]Ibid., p. 316.

[22]Ibid., p. 318.

[23]Ibid., p. 320.

[24]Duane K. Troxel, "Intelligent Life in the Universe and Exotheology in Christianity and the Baha'i Writings" <http://bahai-library.com/unpubl.articles/extraterrestrials.html>.

[25]Troxel (ibid.) cites, among other passages in Baha'i literature, statements in *The Kitab-i-Aqdas*, p. 56 <http://www.sacred-texts.com/bhi/aqdas.htm>.

[26]Troxel ("Intelligent Life") cites *Sayings and Quotations* (SAQ), p. 197.

[27]Troxel ("Intelligent Life") cites *Gleanings* (GL), p. 150.

[28]Troxel ("Intelligent Life") cites a letter written on behalf of Shoghi Effendi, February 9, 1937, *Lights of Guidance*, p. 478.

[29]Troxel ("Intelligent Life") cites *Tablets of Bahá'u'lláh*, p. 188.

[30]Troxel ("Intelligent Life") cites *Light of Divine Guidance*, 2:82.

[31]Troxel ("Intelligent Life") cites *Lights*, #1374.

[32]Troxel ("Intelligent Life") cites *Gleanings* (GL), p. 163.

[33]Troxel ("Intelligent Life") cites *World Order of Bahá'u'lláh*, p. 132; *Citadel of Faith*, p. 5.

[34]Troxel ("Intelligent Life") cites a letter written on behalf of Shoghi Effendi to an individual believer, December 24, 1941; *Lights*, #1555. The Baha'i faith accepts some of the major teachings of Ellen G. White.

[35]Whitley Strieber, *Communion: A True Story* (New York: Avon Books, 1987), p. 76.

[36]Ibid., p. 50.

[37]Ibid., p. 117.

[38]Ibid., p. 122.

[39]Ibid.

[40]Ibid., p. 227.

[41]See the website Clonaid: Pioneers in Human Cloning <http://www.clonaid.com/news.php>.

[42]Raël, *The True Face of God* (Geneva: The Raëlian Foundation, 1998), pp. 17, 20.

[43]Ibid., p. 21.

[44]Ibid., pp. 23, 25, 28.

[45]Ibid., p. 200.

[46]Ibid., p. 189.

[47]Ibid., p. 192.

[48]Ibid., p. 176.

[49]Ibid., pp. 196-97.

[50]Ibid., p. 198.

Chapter 9: The Myth of Alien Gnosis

[1]John Lamb Lash, *Not in His Image: Gnostic Vision, Sacred Ecology, and the Future of Belief* (White River Junction, Vt.: Chelsea Green, 2006), p. 289. For a review of Lash's book, see Jonathan Kirsch, "The New Gnosticism," *Los Angeles Times*, December 3, 2006 <http://chelseagreen.com/2006/items/notinhisimage/Reviews>.

[2]Lash, *Not in His Image*, p. 288.

³Ibid., p. 284.

⁴Ibid., p. 295.

⁵Freeman Dyson, *Imagined Worlds* (Cambridge, Mass.: Harvard University Press, 1997), p. xiii.

⁶Martin Rees, "Living in a Multiverse," in *In the Far Future Universe*, ed. G. F. R. Ellis (West Conshohocken, Penn.: Templeton Foundation Press, 2002), pp. 65-88.

⁷Dyson, *Imagined Worlds*, p. xiii.

⁸Ibid., p. xiv.

⁹*U.S. News and World Report*, April 7, 1997, p. 28.

¹⁰Ibid., p. 30.

¹¹Jacob Ilive, *The Layman's Vindication of the Christian Religion, in Two Parts* (London: J. Ilive, 1730), p. 4.

¹²Ibid., p. 7.

¹³Jacob Ilive, *The Oration Spoke at Trinity-Hall in Aldersgate-Street: On Monday, Jan. 9, 1738, Before the Gentlemen of the Grand Inquest of the Ward of Aldersgate: In Answer to Dr. Felton's Two Discourses on the Resurrection of the Same Body* (London: J. Wilford, 1738), pp. 22-23.

¹⁴Jacob Ilive, *The Oration Spoke at Joyners Hall in Thames Street: On Monday, Sept. 24, 1733, Pursuant to the Will of Mrs. Jane Ilive, Who Departed This Life Aug. 29, 1733, aetat. 63, . . . by Her Son and Executor* (London: T. Cooper, 1733), p. 59.

¹⁵Joseph Smith, "Sermon on Plurality of Gods" (1844), in *History of the Church*, 7 vols. plus index (Salt Lake City: Deseret Book Co., 1991), 6:473-79 <http://www.freerepublic.com/focus/religion/660660/posts>.

¹⁶Joseph Smith, "King Follett Discourse" (1844) <http://thriceholy.net/Texts/Follett.html>.

¹⁷See Robert M. Price, *H. P. Lovecraft and the Cthulhu Mythos* (Mercer Island, Wash.: Starmont House, 1990); and Steven J. Mariconda, *On the Emergence of "Cthulhu" and Other Observations* (West Warwich, R.I.: Necronomicon, 1995).

¹⁸H. P. Lovecraft, *Miscellaneous Writings* (Sauk City, Wis.: Arkham House, 1995), p. 113; quoted in H. P. Lovecraft, *The Call of Cthulhu and Other Stories*, ed. S. T. Joshi (New York: Penguin Books, 1999), p. xv.

¹⁹H. P. Lovecraft, *Selected Letters*, 5 vols. (Sauk City, Wis.: Arkham House, 1965-1976), 3:314; quoted in Lovecraft, *Call of Cthulhu*, p. xvi, with original emphasis.

²⁰Lovecraft, *Call of Cthulhu*, p. 393.

²¹Ibid., p. 385.

²²Ibid., p. 155.

²³Ibid., pp. 154-55.

²⁴Joshi, editor's introduction to ibid., p. xvii.

²⁵Ibid., p. 164.

²⁶George Hunt Williamson, *Other Tongues, Other Flesh* (Amherst, Wis.: Amherst Press, 1953), from Sacred Texts website <http://www.sacred-texts.com/ufo/otof/index.htm>.

²⁷Ibid., "The Great Influx," book 1, chap. 1.

²⁸Ibid., "The Migrants," book 3, chap. 1.

²⁹Walter Sullivan, *We Are Not Alone: The Search for Intelligent Life on Other Worlds* (New York: Signet Books, 1966), p. 89.

³⁰An interview with Fred Hoyle, July 5, 1996 <http://www.panspermia.org/hoylintv.htm>.

³¹Fred Hoyle, *The Intelligent Universe* (New York: Holt, Rinehart & Winston, 1984), p. 9.

³²Ibid., p. 48.

³³Ibid., p. 49.

³⁴Ibid., p. 107.

[35]Ibid., pp. 110, 141, 160.

[36]Ibid., p. 161.

[37]Ibid., p. 226.

[38]Ibid., pp. 235-36.

[39]Ibid., p. 236.

[40]Ibid., p. 239.

[41]Ibid., p. 245.

[42]Ibid., p. 251.

[43]James Gunn, *Alternate Worlds* (Englewood Cliffs, N.J.: Prentice-Hall, 1975), p. 144.

[44]See Jon Atack's widely cited study titled *A Piece of Blue Sky: Scientology, Dianetics, and L. Ron Hubbard Exposed* (New York: Carol Pub. Group / A Lyle Stuart Book, 1990) <http://www.cs.cmu.edu/~dst/Library/Shelf/atack/contents.htm>. For another oft-cited study of Hubbard and Scientology, see Russell Miller, *Bare-Faced Messiah: The True Story of L. Ron Hubbard* (New York: Henry Holt, 1987) <http://www.cs.cmu.edu/~dst/Library/Shelf/miller/>.

[45]Janet Reitman, "Inside Scientology," *Rolling Stone*, March 9, 2006, pp. 55-67.

[46]L. Ron Hubbard, "Keeping Scientology Working" (February 7, 1965) <http://carolineletkeman.org/sp/index.php?option=com_content&task=view&id=168&Itemid=201>; quoted in Reitman, "Inside Scientology," p. 57.

[47]The following excerpts are from The Honorable Elijah Muhammad, "Christianity vs. Islam," transcribed from an audiotape (Philadelphia, November 7, 1962) <http://www.muhammadspeaks.com/ChristianityvsIslam.html>.

[48]The following excerpts are from Robert Muhammad, "Is There Human Life on Mars?" in *The Final Call: On-Line Edition* (May 22, 2001) <http://www.finalcall.com/national/mars05-22-2001a.htm>.

[49]Honorable Louis Farrakhan, "The Divine Destruction of America: Can She Avert It?" speech delivered at Mosque Maryam, Chicago, June 9, 1996 <http://www.finalcall.com/MLFspeaks/destruction.html>.

[50]Erich von Däniken, *Chariots of the Gods? Unsolved Mysteries of the Past*, trans. Michael Heron (New York: Bantam Books, 1968), pp. 10-11.

[51]Ibid., p. 11.

[52]Ibid., p. 12.

[53]Philip K. Dick, *VALIS* (1981; reprint, New York: Vintage Books, 1991).

[54]"Approaching Gnosticism: Through the Eye of the Heart" <http://www.metahistory.org/ApproachingGnosticism.php>.

[55]Steve Kellmeyer, "The New Gnostic Gospel: An Ancient, Secret Heresy Lurks Inside the Movie 'The Matrix,'" *Envoy* 4, no. 5 (2000): 34-39, esp. p. 39, posted by Catholic Education Resource Center <http://www.catholiceducation.org/articles/arts/al0097.html>.

[56]Ibid., p. 37.

[57]Dick, *VALIS*, p. 188.

Chapter 10: Conclusion

[1]Mary Midgley, *Science as Salvation: A Modern Myth and Its Meaning* (New York: Routledge, 1992), p. 89; the Stephen Hawking quote is from *A Brief History of Time* (New York: Bantam, 1988), p. 175, chap. 12, posted by Scribd <http://www.scribd.com/doc/3511/Stephen-Hawking-A-Brief-History-of-Time>.

[2]Barry James, "European Space Agency Boldly Goes to Sci-Fi Fans for New Ideas," *International Herald Tribune*, May 19, 2000 <http://www.itsf.org/press/iht.html>.

[3]For a description of this fascinating controversy, see Ruth Gledhill and Jeremy Page, "Can the Monkey God Save Rama's Underwater Bridge?" *The Times Online*, March 27, 2007 <http://www.timesonline.co.uk/tol/news/world/asia/article1572638.ece>.

[4]Robert J. Sawyer, "The Future Is Already Here," speech at the Library of Congress, November 10, 1999 <http://www.sfwriter.com/lecture1.htm>.

[5]Arthur C. Clarke, *Childhood's End* (1953; reprint, New York: Del Rey, 1990), p. 67.

[6]Ibid., p. 68.

[7]C. S. Lewis, *The Screwtape Letters* (1942; reprint, San Francisco: HarperSanFrancisco, 2001), letter 15.

[8]Richard Dawkins, *A Devil's Chaplain: Reflections on Hope, Lies, Science, and Love* (Boston: Houghton Mifflin, 2003), p. 79.

[9]Ibid., p. 81.

[10]H. G. Wells, *Mankind in the Making* (London: Chapman & Hall, 1903); quoted in Dawkins, *A Devil's Chaplain*, p. 10.

[11]Johns Gribbin and Martin Rees, *Cosmic Coincidences* (New York: Bantam Books, 1989), p. 291.

[12]Paul Davies, *The Last Three Minutes* (New York: Basic Books, 1994), p. 138.

[13]Ibid., p. 142.

[14]Ibid., p. 153.

[15]Ibid., p. 154.

[16]Ibid., p. 149.

[17]Ibid., p. 153.

[18]Neal Conan, "Are We One Step Closer to Artificial Life?" *Talk of the Nation*, National Public Radio, June 29, 2007 <http://216.35.221.77/templates/story/story.php?storyId=11606644>.

[19]Lee M. Silver, *Remaking Eden: Cloning and Beyond in a Brave New World* (New York: Avon Books, 1997), p. 108.

[20]Ibid., pp. 237-38.

[21]Ibid., pp. 240-50.

[22]Ibid., p. 217.

[23]Francis Fukuyama, "The World's Most Dangerous Ideas: Transhumanism," *Foreign Policy* 10, no. 3 (September-October 2004) [September 1, 2004] <http://www.mywire.com/pubs/Foreign Policy/2004/09/01/564801?page=4>.

Index

A for Andromeda, 66, 227
abductees, 185-88
Abductees: Human Encounters
   with Aliens, 186
Abdu'l-Baha, 205
The Abolition of Man, 127
The Abyss, 38, 93, 94
Adam and Eve, 220, 233
Adam's Bridge, 250-51
The Advance into Space, 81
Aetherius Society, 194-95
Africa, 175, 217, 232, 235
Against the Fall of Night, 97,
   112, 130
Age of Reason, 79
Age of Revelation, 210
Ahura Mazda, 183
Aldrin, Buzz, 92
Alexander the Great, 52
Alien, 16, 23
Aliens, 38, 93
Aliens of the Deep, 38, 93-94
Allah, 232
Allan and the Ice Gods, 175
Allen, Paul, 70
Allen Quartermaine, 174
Allen telescope array, 70
Also Sprach Zarathustra, 98
Amazing Stories, 138-39
America, 236, 237
American Revolution, 79
Ames Brothers, 84
Anakin Skywalker, 184
Anaximander, 52
Anaximenes, 52
Anderson, Paol, 131
angels, 47, 218
Anglo-Israelism, 168
Anglo-Saxons, 167
Angrest, Matest, 67
anima, 174
anti-Semitism, 164
Apocalypse, 158
Applewhite, Marshall, 24
Archaeology, Astronautics and
   SETI Research Association,
   237
Arctic, 175
Arisians, 181
Aristarchus of Samos, 52
Around the World in Eighty
   Days, 169
Arrhenius, Svante, 226
Arroway, Ellie, 70, 192
Aryan myth, 163, 176-79, 189
Aryans, 160, 166, 170, 176, 177,
   178

Ascended Masters, 194
Asia, 165, 210, 232, 235
Asimov, Isaac, 30, 65, 111, 130,
   131, 138, 160, 230
Astor, John Jacob, 57, 58, 201-4,
   209
Astounding Science Fiction, 160,
   230, 249
astral plane, 243
astrobiology, 51, 93, 94
astronauts, ancient, 238
Astronomy and Cosmology, 227
Astronomy Populaire, 56
Astro-Theology, 197
"At the Mountain of Madness,"
   222
Atlantic Monthly, 80
Atlantis, 172, 173
Atlas Shrugged, 183
auditing, 230-31
Australia, 14
Ayesha, 174
Baal, 196
Babylon 5, 40, 115, 162, 181, 196
Back to Methuselah, 100
Bacon, Francis, 136, 139-42, 151
Bacon, Roger, 142
Baha'I, 204-6, 211
Baha'u'llah, 204-5
Bainbridge, William Sims, 35
balloon flight, 54
Banneker, Benjamin, 197
Barrett, Sir William, 117
Bates, Harry, 15
Bates, Joseph, 200
Battlestar Galactica, 40, 168-69,
   196
Baxter, Stephen, 131
BBC, 14, 75, 227
Bear, Greg, 121
Bell, Alexander Graham, 114,
   132
The Bell Curve, 162
Bellamy, Edward, 144-45
Benford, Gregory, 109
Benoit, Pierre, 175
Bensalem, 141
Beresford, J. D., 101, 121, 122
Bergaust, Eric, 74
Bernal, John Desmond, 82, 83,
   92, 110
Bernardi, Daniel, 179-82
Bible, 191, 218, 219, 246
Big Bang theory, 226
Bigelow, Robert T., 95-96
Billions and Billions, 63
Biogenesis, 217

biological universe, 21
The Black Cloud, 25, 28, 227
Bladerunner, 136, 240
Blake, William, 167
Blavatsky, Madame H. P., 116,
   171, 172, 173, 194, 223, 224
Boan, Bob, 14
body thetans, 231
Bonestell, Chesley, 84, 85, 88
Book of Mormon, 166
Bormanis, Andre, 87
Bostram, Nick, 99
Boyle Lectures, 197
Bradbury, Ray, 33, 87, 92
Brahman, 229
Breeding Superman, 159
The Brick Moon, 80, 82, 145
British census, 14
British Israelites, 168
British Labor Party, 105
British Planetary Society, 82
Bruno, Giordano, 42, 45, 46,
   198, 249
Buck Rogers, 83, 182
Buddhism, 59, 165
Bulwer-Lytton, George Edward,
   30, 58, 115, 160, 162, 169-71,
   172, 173, 175, 183, 223, 254
Burke, James D., 90-91
Burnet, Thomas, 46, 47
Burroughs, Edgar Rice, 30, 34,
   61, 66, 115, 175, 176
Burrow, John W., 103
Bush, George W., 75
Butler, Samuel, 169
Byrne, David, 92
Cal Tech, 7
"The Call of Cthulu," 222-24
Cambridge University, 82
Cambridge University Press,
   21, 226
Cameron, James, 16, 38, 93-94
Campbell, John W., 13, 24, 30,
   83, 117-18, 138, 160, 230, 249
Campbell, Joseph, 29, 31, 39,
   182-83, 185
Canada, 14
canals on Mars, 60
Čapek, Karel, 138
Captain Adamus, 168
Captain Nemo, 216
Carey, John, 107-8, 178, 179
Carroll, Lee, 122
Carter, Jimmy, 50
Carter, John, 66
Catholic Church, 53
Catholicism, 205-6